P9-DMX-552

WITHDRAWN

BY LAURIE R. KING

MARY RUSSELL

STUYVESANT & GREY

KATE MARTINELLI

AND

Riviera Gold

Riviera Gold

A NOVEL OF SUSPENSE FEATURING
MARY RUSSELL AND SHERLOCK HOLMES

Laurie R. King

BANTAM BOOKS

NEW YORK

Riviera Gold is a work of fiction. Names, characters, places, and incidents are the products of the author's imagination or are used fictitiously. Any resemblance to actual events, locales, or persons, living or dead, is entirely coincidental.

Copyright © 2020 by Laurie R. King

All rights reserved.

Published in the United States by Bantam Books, an imprint of Random House, a division of Penguin Random House LLC, New York.

Bantam Books and the House colophon are registered trademarks of Penguin Random House LLC.

LIBRARY OF CONGRESS CATALOGING-IN-PUBLICATION DATA
Names: King, Laurie R., author.
Title: Riviera gold: a novel of suspense featuring Mary Russell and
Sherlock Holmes / Laurie R. King.
Description: First edition. | New York: Bantam Books, [2020] |
Series: Marie Russell and Sherlock Holmes; 16
Identifiers: LCCN 2020001853 (print) | LCCN 2020001854 (ebook) |
ISBN 9780525620839 (hardcover; acid-free paper) | ISBN 9780525620846 (ebook)
Subjects: LCSH: Russell, Mary (Fictitious character), 1900—-Fiction. | Holmes,
Sherlock—Fiction. | GSAFD: Biographical fiction. | Mystery fiction.
Classification: LCC PS3561.I4813 R58 2020 (print) | LCC PS3561.I4813 (ebook) |
DDC 813/.54—dc23
LC record available at https://lccn.loc.gov/2020001853
LC ebook record available at https://lccn.loc.gov/2020001854

Printed in the United States of America on acid-free paper

randomhousebooks.com

2 4 6 8 9 7 5 3 1

First Edition

Book design by Caroline Cunningham

To all the grey-haired ladies out there,

filled with wisdom and mischief.

And yes—to some of the men.

Riviera Gold

PROLOGUE

Why had I never considered the possibility that an arms dealer might wield actual arms?

I'd probably assumed that a man who dealt in deadly munitions was only dangerous in the abstract and large-scale—like a battle-field commander incapable of euthanising the family pet.

No: *naturally* a person like this would have a gun to hand. And no ordinary old weapon, but the sleekest, most modern of automatic pistols. Not that the model made any difference at this range, not when it was pointed directly at my heart.

A child could not miss.

A moment of cold silence washed over me, followed by an absurd tumble of questions. Would it hurt? Yes, it was bound to hurt—but would my mind register the pain, or even the muzzle flash, before flickering out? Did the man have any idea who I was? Could he know that pulling the trigger would bring down the wrath of the British government? Did he have any clue that the young woman before him was wife and partner to none other than Sherlock Holmes? Was he really prepared to ruin this spectacular carpet?

—and then I wrenched my thoughts away from idiocy and my eyes off the mesmerising black circle, looking past it into the old monster's dead eyes.

I cleared my throat. "I wonder if we might have a little talk? Preferably before you shoot me."

CHAPTER ONE

Clara Hudson: a conversation

The warm air smelled of honey.

The air outside had been sharp with the usual London stinks of horse dung and coal-smoke and rain, making the Duke's townhouse a welcoming refuge. Granted, by the end of the night the pleasure would be reversed, with exhausted, footsore dancers stumbling away from the smell of sweat and the stifling miasma of women's perfumes and men's hair-oil. But for now, drifting from portico to cloak-room, hallway to the ballroom itself, all was promise and sparkle and the sweet aroma of beeswax candles.

Clarissa, whose escort was bent in some confusion over her dance-card, caught the apricot colour of silk in a slice of mirror and took a half-step forward to admire the dress. It was new and expensive—very *à la mode,* the result of many hours of poring over sketches with the dressmaker. The fashion for a long, well-corseted torso suited her, and the lightly bustled train at the back emphasised a woman's front in a way that would have been judged indecent just a few years ago. The nakedness of her shoulders, front and back, was both innocent and tantalising, and the curve of her hips would, she had learned, tempt a dance partner's hands into a drift downward as the evening progressed and the golden candles began to gutter and wink out, one by one.

She reminded herself to be wary of men who had shed their gloves—and not only because of the stains their palms left on silk.

Her thoughts were interrupted by a figure in black, coming towards her in the looking glass. She turned, pleased that here was one acquaintance who might turn into a friend—an actual friend, rather than a useful name or camouflage. (It helped that she was married, and therefore out of the competition.) "Dear thing, I was wondering if you'd come. Though how you manage to look so festive and delicious in black, I cannot know."

The two exchanged near-kisses, and the newcomer shook her head in appreciation of Clarissa's apricot silk. "Speaking of delicious! Oh, I do look forward to getting out of mourning and being permitted to dance again."

"When you do, the rest of us will have to work twice as hard to be noticed."

"That is not something you need to worry about, my dear Miss Hudson. So what mischief have you got up to, since I saw you last?"

"Mischief? Me?"

The two laughed, and then Clara's gentleman claimed his dance, and they were away.

The two young women met up again over supper, when Clarissa's favoured partner and the other woman's rather boring husband parked them in seats, presented them with full glasses, then went off to load plates with tempting morsels.

Clarissa tried to cool her face with a fan the same colour as her dress. "A night this warm, I'm a bit envious of your getting to sit at the sidelines. My face must be horrid and red."

"Just nicely pink. I'm impressed that you haven't yet lost bits of your train to some careless set of shoes."

"I was stepped on twice, but neither time fatally."

"Trains are not the most practical things for the dance floor. So tell me, before the men come back, is there anyone you're hoping for an introduction to?"

Clarissa Hudson eyed her possible, would-be friend, wondering just how much the woman knew, or had guessed. A married acquaintance could be an asset, since the rules binding women's behaviour were relaxed the moment a ring went on. She'd even seen some of them smoking! But this one, married or not, was both new to London and an amateur in the sport of playing men. It was hard to judge how far her amusement would go before it turned suddenly to shock—or disdain. Either could be fatal to someone in Clarissa's position.

Still, even the most innocent of girls would be forgiven a degree of curiosity towards the opposite sex. After all, wasn't that what the Season was for? And she was twenty years old: at the height of her powers when it came to feminine games. "I don't suppose you know that tall gentleman with the striking eyes, speaking with the Earl of Shrewsbury?" The man was older than they, perhaps thirty, and impeccably clothed from his gleaming blond head to his polished black shoes. There was an air of vitality about him that promised, at the very least, an interesting conversation.

Plus, everything about him spoke of money.

"You mean Zedzed? We haven't been formally introduced, but from what I hear, I'm not sure he's someone you need to know."

"Whyever not? And surely that's not his actual name?"

"No, it's from all the *zed*s in his name—he's Russian, or was it Greek?"

"How exotic. But why mustn't I meet him?"

"He has some rather dubious antecedents. An embezzlement trial, among other things, a few years ago."

"He couldn't be too bad of an egg, not if the Duchess invited him."

It was the sort of remark a naïve young thing would make—but then, naïve was the rôle Clarissa Hudson was playing these days. Her friend-to-be gave a little shrug.

"If you think so. I'm pretty sure my husband knows the Earl— I'll have him bring the two men over for an introduction. Once he's finished deciding whether I want salmon mayonnaise or chicken."

While the woman in mourning craned her head in hopes of catching her husband's eye, Clara gazed over her fan at the Earl and his companion. Mr "Zedzed" was really quite good-looking. She was not in the least surprised when he felt her scrutiny and turned those intense, pale eyes on her. But she was surprised at her own reaction.

A shiver ran down her spine.

Other girls would interpret this as a shiver of delight. Other girls would raise their fans and turn to a nearby friend and giggle, taking that physical reaction as the first sign of love.

Clarissa Hudson knew better. Oh, she was well practiced at teasing behind a fan, at pretending innocence, at making use of the cloud of nearby girls to tantalise a male—but she also knew that the intensity of that return gaze was a danger sign. Turn away. Easier quarry lay elsewhere.

She sat, pinned by those pale and speculative eyes. The stuffy air closed in around her, cloying and heavy, until she forced her hand to reach out for the other woman's arm, to tell her not to bother asking for that introduction . . .

Too late.

After that night, Clara Hudson was never quite as fond of the odour of honey.

MAY TO JULY, 1925

Venice
and the
Riviera

CHAPTER TWO

V enice had been . . . unexpected.

Not that it didn't meet my every anticipation. Venice proved every bit as colourful and warm and entertaining as one might wish, taking my memories of past times and piling on a myriad of piquant experiences that would continue to amuse, on into my old age. Venice had been Cole Porter and moonlit adventures, an island of mad women and a community of sun-maddened expatriates. The place had awakened in me a bizarre gusto for cabaret dances, harmless flirtations, and lethargy—all of which I would have sworn impossible mere weeks earlier.

Of course, the serene city on the lagoon was also, in this modern era of 1925, Mussolini's Blackshirts and age-old corruption— threats that we had brought with us—and a startling revenge that Holmes and I could never have shaped on our own.

As I say: unexpected.

Had it not been for the Honourable Terrence Shields-McClintock, a new and almost instantaneous friend, I expect I would have stepped away from the society of Lido sun-worshippers without a thought, grateful to escape back into my normal world.

(Not that my normal world existed any more. Nothing awaited me in my Sussex home but solitude and the hum of beehives in the orchard. Holmes was off on some unlikely task—yes, that is *The* Holmes, Sherlock Holmes, my teacher-turned-partner-then-husband—while our housekeeper, Mrs Hudson, the very heart of the home, was . . . Oh, Mrs Hudson. Beloved and comforting presence, gone away, perhaps forever.)

As we lounged on the Venice Lido one day in early July, the Hon Terry had interrupted these sad and pointless thoughts. "You need to come sailing with us. Truly."

I adjusted my sun-hat against the rays. "Terry, I've spent the past two weeks in a series of increasingly odd watery excursions, from gondolas to speed-boats—"

"Stolen speed-boats."

"—*borrowed* speed-boats to—God help me—skis on top of water. If I don't go back to the mainland soon, what form of transport might be next? Saddling a gargantuan sea-horse? Donning artificial gills? In any event, why would anyone revert to an outmoded form of transport that takes weeks to arrive at a place one can reach by train in a day?"

"Because you'll never get the chance again, not on a sweet boat like the *Stella Maris*."

"I'll probably never get the chance to enjoy frostbite on Everest or being eaten alive by dingoes in the outback, either. Yet somehow I manage to live with the knowledge."

"She's a stunning piece of work, is the *Stella*. Far too good for her owner."

"Who is going as well." I'd met the man. Digby Bertram Wellington-Johnes ("Call me DB—all the gels do!") was such a stage version of English Colonel, from hearty laugh to veined nose to long-out-of-date slang, that I kept waiting for him to give himself away by a wink. The most interesting thing about him was why on earth he'd decided to buy a sailboat rather than a country house with a hunt nearby. A story he'd started twice in my presence and had never got to the end of.

"Oh, he's not a bad sort. A smidge dull, granted."

"A smidge? The man makes a dishrag seem exciting."

"Well, yes. But there'll be great food. And you do like the others, and the Italian coastline is just smashing, and there's loads of interestin' ports along the way."

"Terry, I get seasick."

"So we'll put you up at the prow. Or you can work the rigging, that'll take your stomach's mind off things."

"Crews never let guests do any of the actual work."

"This crew does—I know the Captain, he's happy to shout orders at anyone."

"Really?" Hard, mindless labour did sound more appealing than watching waves go past. (Or listening to an empty house creak and settle.)

"I posalutely guarantee it. And when we get there, you'll be just shockingly fit and brown, so burstin' with human kindness that you could lose it all in Monte and just smile as the croupier hauls away all your lovely lolly. That's the voice of experience, don't you know?"

One key word in the deluge reached out and tugged at my ear. "Did you say Monte? As in Monte Carlo?"

"Didn't I say? We're headed for the Riviera."

"You didn't, no."

"Well, we are—or DB is, at any rate. And yes, it's the very same Monte. Den of iniquity, the principality of pauperdom, city of suicides. Then again, it's also where Diaghilev's Ballets Russes has set up. And the Princess Charlotte's a charming girl."

"Who?"

"Heir to the throne? She and her husband run the place while her father the Prince is off in France. They've got the bit in their teeth, going to bring Monaco into the modern age."

"You don't say."

For a man whose intellectual achievements consisted of memorised poetry, the Hon Terry could be remarkably perceptive when it came to people. Something in my response betrayed my weakening, and he was on it in a flash. "Aha—Monte Carlo, so Mrs Russell has a secret vice! Do we have to keep you from the tables?"

"I doubt it. I've never seen the appeal in setting fire to a lot of banknotes. No, it's that I have a ... friend, who may be living there."

"Oh jolly good! Any friend of yours is bound to be a ripping gal. She is a gal?"

"She was once."

"So it's settled. Yes? You'll come a-sailin' with us?"

He might have been a spaniel begging for a thrown stick. Still, I had to admit it was tempting. As he'd said, how often does one meet the opportunity to circumnavigate Italy on a spectacularly lovely sailing yacht? The dullness of our stage-colonel host would be counteracted by the surprisingly amiable company of the Hon Terry and his friends. And if the weather turned, if the company palled, if seasickness, rich food, or the steady diet of lotos gave me indigestion, there would be any number of ports along the way that would provide an escape home.

"Oh, all—"

He did not let me finish, merely shouted in glee and threw his arms around me, so impetuous a gesture that it brought with it a flash of my long-dead brother.

And so I had said good-bye to my husband and set off on the *Stella Maris* with the Hon Terry and friends; twenty-two days of education in the subtle interactions of canvas and rope, tide chart and compass. I spent my days learning the language of wind in the sails and water in the seas, while scrambling to carry out orders. I spent my nights shovelling down huge servings of delicious food, then falling into my bunk to sleep like the dead. My hands blistered and went hard, my skin burned and went brown, while I learned about pulling in partnership, the proper way to throw my weight around, and just how deadly a gust of wind could be. When we were under sail, I was never entirely free of seasickness, but I did find that when I was busy enough, or exhausted enough, I could ignore it.

One night when we were halfway up the Tyrrhenian, with Sicily behind us and the outline of Sardinia yet to appear, it came to me that I had been quietly learning other lessons as well, from this man with no more intellect than a retriever. The Hon Terry was teaching me about friendship.

I had no family, other than the one I had made through Holmes. My few friends were from University, since I'd somehow never found the time to create more. But on board the *Stella Maris*, distracted by aching muscles and thirst and hunger, the bursts of shared laughter and effortless camaraderie opened my heart.

In turn, I found I was ever more impatient for the end of the voyage—or rather, for the person I hoped to find there.

It was ten years since the cool, War-time morning in 1915 when I stumbled across Mr Sherlock Holmes on the Sussex Downs. Ten years since the afternoon I'd met the woman who would become my surrogate grandmother. Mrs Hudson called herself a housekeeper, but from that first day, she was so much more.

In all the decade that had followed, all those long years when I came to know her worn hands, ageing face, and greying hair better than I knew my own, I never suspected that the heart beating under those old-lady dresses and old-fashioned aprons might belong elsewhere. Never suspected that she had been anything but a landlady-turned-housekeeper—until the past May, when a case brought to light a colourful, even shocking history. The history of a woman named, not Clara Hudson, but Clarissa. A history that came to claim her, and drove *my* Mrs Hudson from her home.

The thought of losing her had been more than I could bear. I pleaded to know where she was going, how she would get along, what she would possibly do without us. Her reply was less an answer than a vague observation—but as a straw, I would continue to grasp it until it crumbled.

It had been night. The motorcar that would take her away had been idling at the front door, and Mrs Hudson had paused in the act of pulling a pair of travelling gloves over those work-rough hands to consider my question. When she'd looked up, she had not looked at me, who loved her, nor at Sherlock Holmes, who had lived with her for more years than I had been alive. She had not even run her eyes over the doorway that she had polished, swept, and walked through for the past twenty years. Instead, straight of spine and with no sign of hesitation, she had lifted her head to gaze resolutely out into the darkness.

"Do you know," she'd said thoughtfully, "I've always been fond of Monte Carlo."

CHAPTER THREE

Twenty-two days after making our way out of the Venice lagoon, the *Stella Maris* was sailing, not alongside a coastline, but towards one. I was every bit as trim and brown as Terry had promised. Also, perpetually hungry, always thirsty, and profoundly tired of an endlessly moving deck beneath my feet.

Tired, too, of some of my fellow passengers—not Terry's friends, but those of our host, DB. As a group, their humour was heavy-handed, their conversation patronising, and they proudly demonstrated their wit by using quotes that were either stale, or inapt, or simply wrong.

Such as DB's proclamation now, as we drew near the Riviera coast: *"And in the afternoon they came to a land where it was always afternoon."*

Terry and I winced, as if we'd heard an ill-tuned piano. I waited for Terry to continue the quote—with words Tennyson had actually written.

"'All round the coast the languid air did swoon, breathing like one that hath a weary dream,'" he dutifully supplied.

"Wrong time of the month for a full-faced moon, though," I

noted. This, too, was part of the ritual, the two of us joining forces in the subtle mocking of ignorance.

It was probably a good thing we planned to disembark soon, before our mockery grew shameless. I gave DB a smile that I hoped looked friendly rather than apologetic, and went below to shove the last things into my valise. Terry followed, standing with his shoulder propped against the doorway.

"So, have you thought about stopping with us for a bit?" he asked.

I pushed my unruly hair out of my eyes, wondering where I had put my scissors. "Terry, you must be truly sick of me."

"Mary Russell, I don't know what I'll do when you leave! Who else understands my jokes?"

I put on a puzzled expression. "Terry, have you been making jokes?"

"Har har."

"Your friends laugh. More than I do, really."

"Patrice laughs when he knows it's supposed to be a joke, and Luca laughs because he doesn't want to admit he missed it in English. Oh, do come along, just for a couple of days. It'll be a new experience to talk to people without watching their heads bobble with the waves."

"Oh, I couldn't. The people you're staying with will be plenty crowded with the four of you."

"No, we're at an hotel."

"Really? What kind of Riviera establishment is open in mid-summer?"

"Most of 'em do close—this one did, until a couple years ago. But the more guests they can pull in, the better the chance they'll keep it open next year."

"Why on earth would they want to?"

I got to my knees to check under the bunk for stray pens and wayward stockings, half-listening as Terry prattled about a note that caught up with him in our last port, from a friend extolling the virtues of summer holidays on the Cap d'Antibes. It seemed that the hotel there, which for its thirty-some-year history had indeed sensibly closed its shutters for the summer season, was recently talked into staying open by a handful of mad Americans with deep pockets and a perverse affection for broiling under the sun. They paid well, but considering the hotel's plenitude of rooms, it would help, as Terry said, to round up a few more paying guests.

So: extend my leisure holiday, or return to empty Sussex?

First, the obvious question. "Who else is coming?"

"Luca, Patrice, and Solange," he said promptly. His sailing friends—but none of DB's abrasive guests. Luca was a pleasant young man Terry had taken up with in Venice. Patrice was a friend from Terry's university days, and Solange, his wife. The five of us had contrived to give the slip to the *Stella*'s other passengers in nearly every port we'd visited.

I laughed. "Then yes, I'd love to join you in a half-deserted, baking-hot, off-season hotel. Though just for a day or two. I do have a life to return to."

"Books," he said dismissively. "Rot your brain."

Terry knew nothing about my other life—the real one, with Sherlock Holmes. In Venice, people had known my husband as "Mr Russell," amateur violinist, in a bohemian sort of marriage to a much younger and somewhat idiosyncratic bluestocking. Which were not difficult rôles to play, since we were both precisely (if not exclusively) that.

One night on the *Stella Maris,* under the spell of moon and friendship and more than a little alcohol, I had come near to blurting out the truth. Solange had been reading a detective story, and the others began proposing alternative solutions to the mystery. The name Holmes was on the very tip of my tongue—until Terry said something jolly that made me actually picture him in an investigation: stepping in the foot-prints, pocketing a vital clue, and refusing to believe that one of his friends could do anything so dashed unsporting as commit murder.

At that, I remembered the threat of endless prying discussions about the mythic, near-fictional character Sherlock Holmes, and firmly shut my mouth.

But despite the mild effort of keeping up the act, spending a day or two on the French coast was not a bad idea. If nothing else, it being a land of Phoenicians, Greeks, Romans, and Ligurians meant that it would provide any number of aqueducts, amphitheatres, rural museums, and quaint villages for me to visit. It would give my muscles time to recuperate, and give me a chance to let Holmes know where I was. And yes, to see what I could do about locating Mrs Hudson in the nearby principality of Monaco.

Of course, it was always possible that the straw I was so eagerly grasping at was a complete delusion. That the word "fond" had been not a hint, but a vague reflection, or even a deliberate ruse. That our housekeeper with the racy history had in the end gone to another place altogether.

The *Stella Maris* was headed to Cannes, a few miles along the coast, but the captain put in first to the more workaday harbour at Antibes, to take on fresh provisions for lunch. This was convenient for us—doubly so, because enough fishing boats were out at sea that we were given a berth at the docks rather than having to be tendered ashore. As usual, the boards underfoot seemed to sway more than the boat had, so I paused to make a nonchalant survey of the view while my equilibrium ceased its spinning and grabbing at nonexistent walls.

The view was worth admiring. To the south, a piece of rocky land extended out into the appropriately azure water. Along the eastern horizon lay the long line of the Alpes Maritimes, while north of the harbour stood the high, stark walls of a castle. The town itself was a typical Mediterranean jumble of red-tiled roofs, smelling of dust and fish.

Terry paused beside me to study the rocky promontory south of town. "That might be the Cap d'Antibes."

"Didn't you say there was a beach?"

"P'raps it's on the other side." He turned his sun-glasses at the waterfront road. "You see anything that looks like a hotel car?"

The hotel car proved to be two ancient taxis with five good tyres and a pair of unbroken head-lamps between them. Those who were staying on the *Stella Maris* thought this was hilarious, but the affection between DB and Terry, a bit strained during recent days, returned as we took our leave. They waved us off, we waved them good sailing, and we piled into the taxis as the drivers, cigarettes hanging from their lips, tossed the last bags and valises in on top of our sweating bodies, strapped Terry's new and peculiar-looking skis onto the roof, and ground their motors into gear.

We stopped three times along the way: the first time to let Luca out to be sick (the previous night had been a raucous one on board); the second time while a small boy herded some goats across the road; and the third time for what remained in Luca's stomach.

The promontory we had seen from the harbour was indeed the Cap, although the larger part of it was hidden from view. The Hôtel du Cap proved to be on its far side, set in a cultivated pine forest overlooking the Mediterranean. A palm-lined entrance drive led to an establishment both large and grand—more luxurious than I had expected.

During the winter, I had no doubt that its halls would ring with the accents of those escaping the cold of the European north and the American east. Now, in the sweltering heat of midsummer, the voices inside the doors were a mere echo of its high-season glory. Luca, for one, welcomed the relatively cool silence, and was quickly ushered away to our rooms, as were our bags. The skis did cause the porter momentary puzzlement—not only were they strangely wide, but July was not the usual time for hotel guests to take a jaunt up into the Alps. However, any luxury hotel is accustomed to the peculiarities of guests, so the man merely checked that Terry did not wish to keep the skis in his room, and took them away.

When the lobby was empty again, Terry suggested we take a look at the sea. The four of us wandered through the grounds to the centre of the summer merrymaking, and looked down.

"Good heavens," I said.

The hotel was on top of a cliff, but it had embraced its rocky setting—and got around its lack of a beach—by gouging a large swimming bath into the cliff itself. Above the pool stretched a brilliant white pavilion with arches and shades, stairs leading down to the open sea below. Halfway along the stairs lay the pool and its terrace, the geometric edges making for an odd contrast with the organic stone, although the people below—be they splashing, drinking, or lounging on pool-side chaises, fully exposed to the beating sun or sheltering under the striped umbrellas—seemed untroubled by the unnatural symmetry. For those who wanted actually to swim, diving-boards thrust out into the open sea, where floating platforms were decorated with lounging figures.

The hotel was where Edwardian formality lay. Outside, it was all Twenties.

Solange declared her intention to don her bathing costume and join them. Patrice amiably agreed to accompany his wife (they were newly wed, so he tended to be amiable about most of her demands). To my surprise, Terry was less enthusiastic, merely telling his friends that he'd see them in the bar later.

When they had trotted off to chivvy the maids into digging their costumes from the trunks, he turned to me. "Fancy a walk?"

"Absolutely. Though I may need a hat."

I had lost five hats on the way from Venice, since the wind on board a ship will pluck off all but the most robustly anchored headgear. Here it was not only dead calm, but uncomfortably hot, without a breath stirring the leaves.

"You might want a towel, too," he said. "In case we find that beach."

So I fetched my surviving hat, and a towel. Also a large silk Venetian scarf under which I could shelter, a flask of water to stave off dehydration, and—need I say it?—a book.

CHAPTER FOUR

The Cap d'Antibes may once have been a place of thistles and desolation, but at some point in the past century this wilderness had been claimed by the rich. As a result, villas had sprouted, tropical gardens were coaxed into existence, and narrow lanes were lined with the gates of winter homes. The afternoon was quiet, the sun baking our shoulders until we dropped down onto the northern slope, and even then, the path Terry and I described wove back and forth to take advantage of any overhanging trees.

Fortunately, there was little traffic.

In the end, we came to a beach, a pale-gold crescent of sand between a low stone wall and the blue waters of a little bay. Where the right-hand point of the crescent faded into trees, some skiffs were tied. Closer to hand was a café—but it was shut for the season.

"Perhaps," I suggested as we sidled into a patch of shade, "three in the afternoon is no time to linger under the Riviera sun."

There was one person in sight: a man dressed in baggy linen trousers, a striped French jersey, and cloth espadrilles. His head was bound with what looked like a large bandage, although I thought it was probably a way to keep the sun off his scalp.

He was wielding a rake, shifting washed-up sea-weed towards the far end of the beach.

Not that the solitary labourer was the only evidence of life. Further along the sand—the nice, well-raked sand—were indications that people had not only been here, but planned to return: a festive blue-striped changing-tent, half a dozen leaning beach umbrellas, some sand-covered bamboo mats, a picnic basket. A pile of inner-tubes, water-wings, the bloated shape of a blow-up rubber horse, half a dozen buckets and some small shovels testified to a family. Either that, or the raking gentleman planned to top his pristine surface with a sand-castle.

Terry studied the signs of civilisation, then ran his eyes along the rest of the beach. All the way down to the groundskeeper, the sand was clear. After his bent figure, a strip of sea-weed had been left by the receding tide. I made a small wager with myself as to what Terry would do . . .

And won.

"Let's get you settled," he said, "and I'll have a word with that chap. He might know when people will show up again. And anyway, seems a bit rude to take advantage of his work without giving him a tip."

"Terry," I said, "you are a very nice man." It was hard to see beneath the dark lenses and hat-brim, but I could tell he was blushing.

I spread my towel on a bit of the sand, arranged the scarf as a personal tent, took a swallow of already-warm water, and opened my book. Tiny waves lapped. Seagulls bickered. I watched the pantomime drama unfold down the way.

Terry had set off under the assumption that the man in the head-cloth was a groundskeeper, hired to clear the sand each day. I noted that this work would be less Sisyphean here on the placid Mediterranean than on an English beach, where a day's tides may rise and fall twenty feet.

The man with the rake turned at Terry's approach. Terry stopped to ask a question about the missing family, one hand sketching a gesture towards the tent and mats. The stranger replied. There was an exchange of some kind, then Terry's posture went straight as he registered surprise. A moment later, the two men were shaking hands, and the other fellow leaned on his rake handle while Terry assumed his familiar happy-retriever stance.

So: not a hired groundskeeper, but an off-season resident of one of the villas. Most probably the one that Terry had been told to look up, by a mutual friend.

It was a cycle I had witnessed at least a dozen times since meeting the Hon Terry, the easy shift from stranger to chum through shared interests, friends, boarding school, or some distant blood relationship.

I took another swallow of water and turned a page. From time to time, I glanced at my companions. The man with the rake resumed his labours, Terry keeping him entertained with talk. The band of sea-wrack grew shorter, the conversation more animated. When the two men turned to come back up the now-spotless beach, they walked as brothers.

I tucked in my book-mark and stood to meet my inadvertent host. Terry trotted forward in his eagerness.

"Mary, this is the very chap I was ordered to hunt down here! Ain't that a sign it was meant to be? Gerald, this is Mrs Mary Russell, a friend from Venice. Mary, meet Gerald Murphy, an artist and a gentleman."

I knew him for an American even before he spoke, from the way he pulled the brief head-cover from his thinning hair and extended his hand.

"Russell? And you've been in Venice—say, I think I know your husband. Doesn't he play the violin?"

"That he does," I said in surprise. Not many people in the world thought of Sherlock Holmes as a musician.

"Then I met him last month at Cole's place—Cole Porter?"

"Oh, of course! Very pleased to meet you, Mr Murphy."

"Please, call me Gerald. Your husband and Cole spent days putting together music for a 'do' at Cole's palazzo. And Terry here says he crashed that party, but what with half the people in masks and drink flowing like the canal outside, I have no clue if we actually met. Sara and I were still pretty high when we left Venice the next morning," he added with a laugh.

My relief at this close call made my greeting effusive. "Oh yes, that was *quite* a night! And thank you for sharing this lovely patch of sand with us. Though I'm afraid the next tide will bring your labours to naught."

"It's not our beach, we just camp out here. As for the sea-weed, raking's a kind of meditation. The first clear-up of the season is a job, but after that it's like shaving, or cleaning your brushes after a session. The world is fresh and clean, water meeting sand, a blank canvas ready for life."

Murphy was a likeable sort, friendly and confident without feeling in the least pushy. His smile was easy, his accent was Boston modified by an Ivy League education—Yale?—and some years in Paris.

"You're an artist, then?"

"I paint a little."

I found myself smiling back at him as I gestured at the empty mats behind me. "It looks as if your colleagues on the canvas of life have abandoned you, at present."

"The children rest in the afternoon. Some of the grown-ups, too, for that matter. They'll all be back when the sun is lower. In the meantime, can I offer you two some shade and a drink? Warm, I'm afraid, but better than sea water."

Terry and I gathered our things and followed our host to his empty encampment, where we sheltered gratefully beneath the striped umbrellas and accepted, with a degree less enthusiasm, beakers of tepid sherry from a half-empty bottle he took from the picnic basket.

The drink was just as disgusting as one might imagine, although

Terry manfully slugged his down. Murphy seemed not to notice the temperature, but sipped his as he embarked on the required circuit of small-talk that served to identify one's place in the world and how—not if—the two of us might be related. And indeed, eventually (though not that day) he and I did discover that we were distant and much-removed cousins, linked by various people who infested America's tightly knit Society from Boston to Philadelphia.

That afternoon, however, I mostly sat and counted the waves while the two men performed the ritual, exclaiming at a series of links and overlaps in their worlds. They then moved to interests, seeking out common ground. Terry—who compensated for his sickly childhood with an adult passion for adventure and speed— told the dubious American about our adventures in water-skiing, how he and I had introduced the sport to the Lido set, using a pair of standard Alpine skis, and how he was looking forward to trying out the wider blades he'd had made in Venice. Murphy, intrigued, said he had a friend with a speed-boat who might like to learn.

It then being Murphy's turn, he proceeded to tell his two politely uncomprehending English guests about the growing enthusiasm of artists and writers for the South of France during the summer. We nodded, mopping the sweat from our faces, and drank some water.

At last, the two men settled on their common interest in fast machinery, burbling happily along about speed-boats and the requirements for pulling skis, racing cars and the recently reintroduced Monte Carlo Rally, and sea-planes and the thrill of the Schneider Trophy, scheduled for another run in October.

Thinking that I ought to contribute in some minor way to the exchange, I asked about said trophy—and then had to do nothing but nod and make noises for a good twenty minutes, as the two told me all about this race for sea-planes that had begun up the coast in Monaco before the War, only to be won and taken away to Italy, followed by Britain, and now the United States.

"Hmm," I said. "Really?" "Imagine that!" An aeroplane flew over, too high to see if it had pontoons. The tide continued to recede, the line of shadow from the hill behind us crept across the sand—and eventually, we heard voices.

Murphy's face lit up and he scrambled to his feet.

"Here we are," he declared, as a caravan of people spilled out onto the sand, separating into two directions as they did so. Half a dozen small, noisy individuals with sun-bleached hair raced directly down to the water, trailed by a young girl in daringly short trousers and an older woman wearing a rich blue dress and wide-brimmed hat. The others came towards us—apart from one slim young man wearing clothes ill-suited to an afternoon on the sand. This one called something at the back of the two nannies, lifted his hat in our direction, and turned to leave.

The glimpse offered by that brief salute was of a striking, even beautiful young man. His features were as perfect as a Hellenistic sculpture, with olive skin, curly hair, and startling green eyes that seemed to glow from within. I wanted him to join us—a sentiment that Gerald Murphy clearly shared.

Gerald cupped his hands to call across the intervening sand. "Niko—come and meet some new friends!"

But the figure merely sketched an apologetic gesture to the world at large, as an indication that his presence was required elsewhere, then tipped his hat again with a graceful bow and walked away.

Gerald chuckled. "He never joins us on the beach. I don't know if he doesn't like sand, or just doesn't want to spoil his shoes. 'Course, he might be busy—some people do actually earn a living."

"Who was that?" I asked.

"Greek guy named Niko Cassavetes. He's a friend of—well, everyone, I suppose. Really nice, incredibly helpful to newcomers along the coast. He even managed to put together a fireworks display for us Yanks—but of course, the moon was so bright on the Fourth, he talked us into waiting till Bastille Day. Really impressed the locals—I think the whole population of Antibes was lined up at the harbour that night. Except for some of you Brits. Anyway, you're sure to meet Niko, sooner or later."

The others had continued down the beach in an attitude of triumphal procession, many of them carrying some kind of basket or crate. At their lead was a woman of quiet dignity, wearing a long dress of such timeless fabric and design it might almost be called folkloric.

"I thought for a minute Niko might actually join us," Gerald told her, relieving her of a fabric-draped straw basket.

"He said he had an appointment, but he also has a new pair of shiny shoes, which may have been more to the point. Hello," she said, aiming a welcome at Terry and me.

"This is my wife, Sara," Murphy told us. "Sara, this is Mrs Russell and Terry McClintock. Terry's the fellow Didi was talking about—remember her cousin, the Honourable? Turns out they were at that bash Cole and Linda put on last month in Venice, the 'Come as your Hero' one, though we're pretty sure we didn't meet. Oh, but Mrs Russell's husband was Cole's partner, the guy with the violin!"

"Oh, yes!" Sara exclaimed. "Cole *loved* that. Great to meet you at last, Mrs Russell."

"And I should thank you, for allowing us to share in your shade."

"She was polite over the warm wine I handed her," Murphy told his wife. "But she'll be glad for a cold one to replace it."

Sara then held out her hand to Terry. "A pleasure to meet you, er, Sir Terry?"

"Oh f'reavens sake, I'm no more honourable than the next man. Call me Terry."

Sara Murphy was a natural beauty with a direct, compelling gaze and a tawny mop of hair, as inviting as the warm sea waters. "And Mrs Russell—welcome to our gipsy camp."

A man would fall in love with this woman, I thought, and fling himself at her feet. I was not unaware of the impulse, myself. "Call me Mary," I urged, and was rewarded by a smile like a blessing.

Baskets were opened, drinks poured, fruit and biscuits distributed, gay toasts made to friends old and new. The people around us were, if not as stunning as the elusive Niko, nonetheless an extraordinarily handsome group, golden with the sun and eager to absorb Terry and me into their midst. Most were American, and most were a good ten years younger than Gerald and Sara.

Rapid-fire introductions were made, to Rafe and Zelda and John and Olga and a couple of others whose names flew past me, comprising a novelist, a dancer, two artists, an actress filming in Nice, and her lover collected along the way. Sand was shaken from straw mats and travelling rugs, seats were taken, drinks poured—for a couple of the newcomers, conspicuously not their first of the day, or even their fifth. The actress had her male escort cover her with coconut oil, then pushed down the straps of her bathing costume so as not to have unsightly pale lines, and arranged herself on a mat to bake. Down the beach, the two nannies folded the children's discarded garments into neat piles and stood chatting, backs to the adults and eyes on what seemed like a large number of small splashing bodies.

Sara was explaining to Terry and me how they came to be here—and yes, the Murphys were indeed those mad Americans who had coaxed the Hôtel du Cap into remaining open during the quiet months, two years earlier.

"Paris is so *awful* in the summer, don't you think? But Antibes—this place is just Paradise. All we have to do is talk our friends into coming down to visit, which hasn't proved too hard—the Train Bleu is such a treat—leave Paris at dinner and have lunch in Antibes. And now that Gerald and I have our own house—we've just finished the renovations, praise be!—we can even offer people a place to stay, or work. You'll come to dinner tonight, both of you."

"That's a lovely offer, Mrs Murphy—" Terry started.

"Sara. None of us are formal here."

"A smashing offer, but I promised my friends that I'd join them for dinner, back at the hotel."

"Bring them along! We adore new people, and there's plenty of food. Unless they're horrible and boring, that is." Her smile let us know that she refused to believe either of us could have anything to do with such a creature as a boring human being.

"No, all three of them could charm the monocle off Joe Chamberlain. Couldn't they, Mary?"

I nodded. "Having spent the past weeks living in one another's pockets, I cannot say I was ever bored." Shocked, perhaps, and often baffled, but not bored.

That led to a question of how Terry and I came to appear on the beach together, which led to the *Stella Maris,* then back to Venice and the Porters and another set of mutual friends and distant cousins. As before, I was happy to let Terry take the lead with this recitation, since my own history, unless tightly edited, would inevitably lead to those same Sherlock Holmes discussions I had thus far managed to avoid. The conversation followed the track of water-skiing, then motorcars, and splintered into two or three separate groups.

Three of the gathering—Zelda, Olga, and the lover—were talking about dancing, although the desultory pattern of their talk suggested that the two women were tired of each other. The actress and Terry debated recent films. Two of the men argued about art—a sculptor who was not dressed for the beach and clearly found sand in his shoes irritating, and a young painter who rarely got to finish a sentence. Sara lay paging through a tattered copy of Mrs Beeton and making notes. She and her husband participated in all three discussions, tossing in the odd remark and directing things away from troubled waters.

I allowed Murphy—Gerald—to fill my glass again, and ate a biscuit as I watched the antics of the six happy children.

Sara Murphy noticed the direction of my eyes. "Do you have children, Mary?"

"My husband has a grown son and a granddaughter we see whenever we're in Paris." I blinked in surprise. It was not a reply I usually gave, even to friends, since it invariably led to the further question of whether I wanted children, and why I did not have them, neither of which were easy to answer.

Fortunately, either Sara was more sensitive than most, or she had learned that it is better to let a person walk through a conversational door than try and drag them through it. "How sensible of you—a ready-made family without the teething and toilet-training."

I laughed, and she went back to her *Household Management*. My gaze wandered down again to the splashing figures, without whom the little cove would have seemed strangely empty.

What would it have been like to have had a childhood of bare limbs and sun-warmed sand, I wondered? My own memories were of scratchy woollen bathing costumes, compulsory parasols, and being dragged off to shelter the moment the sun grew high. Unlike those golden bodies, flailing and chattering and pausing to examine some bit of aquatic wildlife. Paradise, indeed . . . and I would not think about the fact that the Biblical inhabitants of Eden soon met a snake.

One of the smaller children, young enough to be uncertain on her feet, sat down hard in the water and began to wail. The nannies took this as a signal to gather the three youngest charges, retrieve the piled garments, and make their way to the adult gathering and the snacks that lay at hand. Near the mats, the children split up— a boy of about five with sun-bleached hair to Sara, a girl slightly younger claiming Zelda, while the other child, of uncertain sex, stayed with the young woman in the short trousers.

Small hands were brushed off and filled with biscuits, small hats untied and removed, then all three round little bodies were plunked down inside the striped tent where the slim young nanny took out a picture book. The older woman, tasked with keeping her eye on the remaining children, settled onto a beach chair facing the water. Gerald took her a glass of wine and shifted one of the umbrellas so she was out of the sun. She murmured a thanks, and took a deep swallow from the glass before working its base into the sand.

The groups had shifted: sculptor and actress now discussed a film, Sara was chatting with Olga about a recipe, Zelda was flirting with Terry. Gerald and I talked about sailboats for a minute, then he turned to the stray lover to ask about Cannes, leaving me free to think my thoughts. After a minute, I tried settling down into the travelling rug, wriggling my shoulder blades to create a comfortable hollow in the sand. My legs were in the sun, but the umbrella shaded me from the waist up. I found that if I rested my glass on my stomach, I could take a sip by merely raising my head.

I was, in short, indulging that unexpected taste for lethargy.

The older nanny's dress, I thought drowsily, was quite a pretty colour—the blue of the deeper waters off the coast. I wondered what its neck-line looked like. (She had her back to me.) Something about her was vaguely familiar. The set of her shoulders. Perhaps I'd seen her earlier, among the chairs at the hotel's pool?

As if she'd heard the thought, the woman seemed to take a deep breath. Her manicured fingers rose to untie and pull off the sun-hat, revealing the back of an attractive haircut, unabashedly grey but fashionably modern. She took another sip of wine, returned the glass to the sand, and braced her hands on the arms of her chair. I thought she was going to walk down and speak with the older children. Instead, her shoulders turned as she swivelled in her chair. Her face came into view.

And my glass flew into the air.

Mrs Hudson.

CHAPTER FIVE

Mrs Hudson: a conversation

The lady of the house opened the door herself, and swept onto the sun-washed street to embrace her long-awaited guest. "Clarissa Hudson, oh my darling thing! I *never* thought this day would arrive—come in, you must be exhausted. Mathilde, dear, have the driver carry her things in, then we'll take tea in the garden. We've put you in your usual room, Clarissa, the one with the harbour view. Oh, it's *so* good to see you. When I got your cable last week I danced for joy—positively skipped across the carpet, didn't I, Mathilde? Though on the telephone you did sound just a touch down. My, what a delightful frock, it does marvellous things for your eyes. Paris, yes?"

"Where else? Ah, *bonjour, Mathilde, ça va?* You're looking well."

"*Merci, Madame.*"

"Come in, Clarissa, she'll take care of it. It's lovely in the garden at this hour—the last roses are still blooming. But perhaps you'd like to freshen up first?"

"I'm fine, thanks."

"Are you? Really?"

"I think I will be. Though you're right—when you reached me in

Paris, I was at something of a low point. I was actually thinking about going back and facing the music. But you convinced me that old and grey though I am, it may not yet be time to fade away. So I came."

"And I am so pleased. I hope the train was not too distressing?"

"It was perfectly comfortable. I'm glad you suggested the Train Bleu—not only convenient, but filled with the most entertaining people."

"Americans, yes? Quite mad, all of them, but they can be charming. Here, take this chair, the view will soothe your spirits."

"My spirits are already much soothed by being here."

"How long have we been anticipating this day?"

"Do you know, I think we talked about living in Monaco the very first winter I knew you. Forty-nine years ago."

"Forty-nine? Impossible! I refuse to believe it was longer ago than last summer."

"Says the white-haired lady."

"And you, Clarissa—you had your hair cut off!"

"I'm not used to it yet, I keep reaching up to adjust my pins. I haven't had short hair since I was a child."

"It's terribly *chic*. That's from Paris, too?"

"I had to convince the *coiffeur* that I wanted the same cut as the young woman beside me. He tried to talk me into a Marcel wave, and couldn't believe I wanted it bobbed."

"It's just as well you didn't ask for an Eton crop, he'd have fainted dead away."

"No doubt. As it was, he charged me a ridiculous amount. In fact, I went through a great deal of money in Paris, altogether."

"New hair, new frock—a totally new you."

"I even replaced all my undergarments."

"A solid investment. There's nothing like new lingerie to boost a woman's self-esteem. And you're here now, so your room, my kitchen, Mathilde's car—my clothes, even, should any of them fit you—are yours for as long as you like."

"Thank you, dear, but I mustn't abuse your hospitality. I'd like to set up on my own, as soon as possible."

"I've been asking around, as you suggested on the telephone—though what you said was very mysterious."

"One doesn't like to go into detail with the Exchange listening in."

"I know—it's so bad here in little Monaco, no sooner do you hang up the earpiece than the doorbell rings with someone who's heard the news."

"I figured that would be the case. And I'll go into details later, when you and I are quite alone."

"We're alone here. There's only Mathilde, and she's well accustomed to secrets."

"There's no hurry, merely something I wanted you to think about, in case you have a friend who knows something about money. Not a banker, necessarily, but someone who—"

"Ah, tea! Mathilde, I see you managed to get some of those adorable little macarons from Madame Renault—clever girl."

"My, look at that spectacular tea-tray. Mathilde, you are an artist. How did you guess that I haven't had a decent cup of English tea since I left Sussex eight days ago?"

"Thank you, Mathilde, we'll pour, you go on and hang up Clarissa's things before they are crushed beyond salvation. Clara, dear, is anything locked? Do you want to give her the keys?"

"Oh, there's just the one little valise that's locked, never mind that, it's mostly papers and a book. Nothing that needs hanging. Thank you, Mathilde."

"Here, I'll be mother—I hope you don't mind India tea. What were we talking about? Oh, yes, bankers. I may have just the man."

"Another time. Let me just enjoy sitting still and being with you."

"Indeed, plenty of time to talk business when you've had a rest. But you're not needing to arrange a loan, are you? You did say you had a *little* money, yes?"

"I have plenty to get me started, thanks. Just not enough to keep me going—not in Monaco."

"It is an expensive sort of place."

"There's a rather intriguing possibility that I want to talk to you about—or I suppose, four of them. But that's terribly complicated and we both need to have our wits about us when I explain."

"Sounds exciting—but yes. Take some days to catch your breath. I have set up a few appointments and introductions. People you might find useful—a few of those charming Americans, and a local boy who is not only highly decorative, but terribly useful. He's new since your last visit. You'll just adore him."

"I knew I could count on you."

"Now, do take one of those pretty little macarons. They're absolutely to die for."

CHAPTER SIX

It was fortunate I hadn't drunk more than a glass of the Murphys' wine. As it was, I staggered to my feet in astonishment—but had enough of my wits about me to spot the warning in Mrs Hudson's eyes and the sharp little shake of her head. My exclamation made it no further than my front teeth, and though I swayed with reaction, I managed to stop myself from leaping across the bamboo mats to throw my arms around her.

But the others were staring at me in astonishment. Seconds passed before realisation flooded in and I looked down at my sodden front. "Bite," I managed to choke out. "Or sting—something. Not sure—anyway sorry. Um. Maybe a refill?"

Gerald laughed as he reached for the bottle. "A body sure does feel the booze fast in hot weather," he remarked, retrieving my glass and filling it again.

Talk resumed. Mrs Hudson ate a biscuit. Sara went back into one of the picnic bags and came out with a basket of luscious purple grapes, passing them around. I drank my wine and surreptitiously studied the woman in the blue dress.

Had it not been for that warning shake of the head, I might

have wondered if this was Mrs Hudson's well-groomed twin sister, but no: behind the plucked and darkened eyebrows and the touch of colour on her lips, it was her profile, her lifted chin, the straight line of her back and the age spot beneath her left ear—all were precisely what I had last seen driving away from our home at the end of May.

I reminded myself that, in May, she had been in disguise—brown of hair and unsuitable of dress. And at various times over the years, Mrs Hudson had helped Holmes by playing rôles such as housekeeper for a German spy, or shop-attendant in a blackmail case. But the truth was, Mrs Hudson—*my* Mrs Hudson—had been in a kind of disguise all the years I knew her. She had carried out the rôle of landlady on Baker Street, and later that of Sussex housekeeper, not as a natural thing, but as a necessary act of contrition.

I will admit that in the weeks since that revelation, my acceptance of it was merely intellectual. My heart had no idea what to do with it.

Could today's appearance be another disguise? If so, why? Had she come here deliberately, leaving a track of crumbs for me to follow? Or—an even more appalling thought—was this a collaboration with Holmes? Was my own husband and partner deceiving me? Was there some case too sensitive to trust me with? Or perhaps I should say, too top-secret?

Even taking into account my distaste for any task performed in the service of Mycroft Holmes—my spymaster brother-in-law, a man of enormous power and troubling ethics—I could not imagine Holmes accepting a case that required lying to my face.

But if this was not another disguise, did that mean I was now looking at the real Mrs Hudson? She'd lost a stone, gained a sense of fashion, and submitted to a great deal of pampering in order to become this attractively groomed woman who sat on the beach and drank wine with wealthy expatriates. Was she the Murphy children's governess? The parents were treating her more like a guest than an employee. Perhaps that was something Americans did now—at least, these Americans. But surely that blue frock was too simple and well cut to be cheap, that grey hair too expensively styled?

My interest was not as well hidden as I'd thought. Sara Murphy noticed the way my gaze kept creeping over to the woman in the chair, and she made a little noise of irritation. "Oh, sorry—I forgot to introduce you two. Mary, this is our saviour, Miss Hudson. She's such a love—our nanny had to be away for a few days and dear Miss H volunteered to step into the breach and keep us from madness. Miss H, our new friend Mrs Russell."

I stretched my arm across a couple of supine bodies to take the hand of my all-but-grandmother, looking into her eyes and seeing nothing there but polite acknowledgment. We shook. Her skin felt considerably softer than mine, after my three weeks spent hauling ropes.

"Pleased to meet you, Mrs Russell. Have you been here long?"

Very well: two could play this game. I settled back onto my knees. "We just arrived. My friend Terry and I hitched a ride on the sailing yacht of a friend of his, and I've barely got my land legs back under me."

"Welcome to the Côte d'Azur."

"Thank you. And you, Miss Hudson—have you lived here long?" My voice was innocent, though she must have seen both curiosity and amusement in my eyes.

"Not very long, no, although I've visited on and off over much of my life. I decided to retire here. Well, I say retire . . ."

She glanced across at Sara Murphy, who laughed aloud. "Miss Hudson here is no more retired than . . . well, she's less retired than any of *us* are, that's for sure."

"What is it that you do?" I asked.

"For lack of a better term, I call it consulting."

I couldn't stifle a cough of laughter—but then cleared my throat to make it sound like a simple cough. Sherlock Holmes billed himself as a consulting detective. "About what do you 'consult,' Miss Hudson?"

"Whatever is required, Mrs Russell. For example, do you know Monte Carlo?"

"I've not yet been there, although an old friend seemed to have some considerable affection for the place." She was good. Her face betrayed no sign that she might know who this old friend was. "I'm aware that Monte Carlo is the part of Monaco where Grand-papa goes to lose the family estate and White Russians hide out from the Bolsheviks."

"And there is the problem in a nutshell," she responded. "The Casino was once magnificent and world-famous, the gardens are still lovely, the harbour is first-rate, but as you say, the place has gone out of fashion. The Crown Prince, and especially his daughter the Princess Charlotte, realise this, and wish to expand its potential audience beyond the roulette wheels and card tables."

"And you understand this sort of . . . consulting?"

"I understand it very well, Mrs Russell."

At this last, rather emphatic statement, Sara Murphy picked up the odd flavour to the exchange. Not that she could begin to understand the thread of tension, but she instinctively moved to deflate it. "The Casino's trying to develop a plan for the future," she explained to me. "As a way of dusting off the cobwebs and moving a little more into the Jazz Age. One of the things Miss Hudson was considering is: how can the Casino and baths appeal to people more like, well, Gerald and me? People who want to have a good time, but don't care to spend all day indoors, or to leave our families behind. It was a happy coincidence that, as I said, our nanny was called away for a few days just when Miss Hudson needed some children to experiment on."

"Happy timing, indeed."

"Oh, it really has been! She comes up with the most extraordinary means of combining entertainment with education. Patrick's a bit young, but Baoth and Honoria have adored the past week.

The lives of starfishes, how the moon links to tides, invisible ink—all sorts of things that keep them happy and busy."

"Quite the little Baker Street Irregulars," I said drily.

"Funny you should say that," Sara said. "She had all three of them tracking us through Juan-les-Pins the other day. We'd look up and there they'd be, peeping around a corner."

"How very amusing. Miss Hudson, you and I must talk about your little project."

"I look forward to it," she replied.

And with that, just before she turned away, there was a brief flash of herself, an all but imperceptible lowering of one eyelid. Then she pulled a pair of tinted sun-glasses over her made-up eyes and disappeared into the obscurity of a woman of sixty-nine years.

After a time, the young nanny, who seemed to be attached to the other three children, walked down to the shore to retrieve those still in the water. They ignored her for a time, then realised their own hunger and pounded out of the water and across the sand to demand food, drink, and adult attention.

The abrupt influx caused the dozen adults to pull in, shift their interests, and settle into a new configuration. Sara and Gerald, who had been on separate mats, now came together with the children. Terry watched the tableau with his usual good humour. The others looked on with something close to bemusement, as if wondering why an adult would actively choose the company of small children. Only one betrayed open exasperation: the young man not dressed for the beach, whom Gerald had introduced as "Rafe, a brilliant sculptor." Rafe had been talking about his work, and made little effort to hide his irritation. He stood, brushing sand off his trousers, and said he had to get back to the studio.

If he was hoping for us to beg him to reconsider, it did not happen. Indeed, our hosts were oblivious. Instead of turning their offspring over to the nannies, they had given themselves wholeheartedly to a discussion of the walking patterns of crabs, showing neither embarrassed impatience nor exaggerated solemnity. It was clear that both parents considered their three children at least as interesting as any of the adults within earshot.

I looked at Sara's bent head, at Gerald's intent focus, and felt my heart twist.

I might have been watching my own mother and father, when I was young and filled with innocent enthusiasms.

The sun went lower, the party dispersed. To my surprise, Sara's mention of dinner turned out to be not a vague and future suggestion, but a firm and definite invitation: tonight, at the Murphys' villa, with the absent Luca, Patrice, and Solange. And informal, not evening wear. Terry and I accepted, with thanks—Terry because he was always eager for a party, and I because it would give me a chance to drag Mrs Hudson aside and find out what was going on.

Back at the hotel, I inflicted my sweat-soaked, wine-stained, sand-caked person on the desk personnel long enough to write out a handful of brief telegrams, addressed to places that Holmes might see, such as *The Times, The Telegraph,* and *Le Figaro.* I then retreated to my room for refreshment both internal (many glasses of cool water) and immersive (a bath that was pleasingly tepid but fragrant with bath-side unguents). When I was no longer an offence to humanity, I phoned down to the desk in hopes of an emergency hair-dresser—and such was the hotel that they had one available, instantly. She did not even blink (well, at least she did not run down the hall screaming) at the state of the head that confronted her: frazzled by sun, desiccated by salt, and untouched by scissors for longer than I could remember. When she was finished, I looked in the glass and dug out a hefty tip, every *centime* of which she had earned.

I felt somewhat less like a piece of leather by the time I met up in the bar with the others. When the sun was near the horizon, we climbed into the tram that plied up and down from the centre of Antibes, and rattled along the ridge.

There was no trouble finding Villa America from the tram stop: just follow the noise. Shiny cars lay parked along the verge, and the gate stood open, welcoming us into a garden with lanterns hanging from the trees and music coming from the gramophone. Voices rose in a score of conversations, as what seemed like half the current population of Cap d'Antibes gathered on the Murphys' harlequin-tiled terrace, to drink and laugh and occasionally dance to the music.

Unfortunately, Mrs Hudson was not one of them.

"Oh, too bad," I told Sara Murphy, hoping my disappointment was not too obvious. "I'd hoped to have a talk with her. She's not staying with you, then?"

"Heavens no, she has a place in Monte. She leaves early—she doesn't like to drive along the cliff road after dark."

That was the second time in one day I found myself gawping in stupefaction. Mrs Hudson in couture I could manage. Mrs Hudson in lip-stick, with a bob in place of her tidy bun? Perhaps. But Mrs Hudson—at the wheel of a car?

Mrs Hudson?

CHAPTER SEVEN

That thunderbolt took some getting over, but after a couple of gin fizzes—maybe three—I had managed to lock the image of my aged housekeeper motoring the cliffs of the Côte d'Azur into the portion of my brain devoted to honest politicians, winged pigs, and other unlikely but remote possibilities awaiting verification.

The gathering at Villa America grew into a well-behaved riot. Thirty or so sleek individuals stood around shouting at each other over the music, glasses in hand. Few stopped to admire the glorious sunset framed by palms and cypresses, merely shifting over to stand beneath the lamps hanging from the branches of a well-kept and remarkably mature garden, with the occasional scent of mimosa pushing aside the women's perfumes. The actress had brought some friends, Zelda had brought a writer husband, and Terry had spotted some old chums, and was introducing them to Solange and Patrick.

However, a dinner it was not. There was food of a sort, in the form of hastily improvised canapés laden on trays, which were instantly reduced to crumbs. But there was plenty of alcohol, from cold wine to the cocktails that Gerald was energetically shaking up at a table to one side.

As on the beach that afternoon, most of the guests were Americans, either regular visitors to France or semi-permanent Paris residents. No one else I spoke with had a home in Antibes. Several were staying here at Villa America, which had a number of smaller dwellings scattered around its sizeable grounds.

One of the few non-Americans was Rafe Ainsley, the handsome, petulant sculptor from the beach. He seemed to feel that genius raised a man above the need for tidy dress and good manners, and wore an air of superiority in place of jacket and tie. His accent laid dubious claim to the working-class, although as the night went on, clipped Eton-and-Baliol tones began to surface, and one began to notice that his unironed shirt and unkempt trousers had been custom-fitted, his scuffed shoes were new and similarly bespoke, and his wrist-watch was a model that I had myself once purchased as a hefty bribe. Driven by perverse curiosity, I edged into the conversation around him.

It proved to be less an exchange of views than a series of pronouncements: about Art, and Integrity, and Movement, and a series of other capitalised nouns. Chief among them was Surrealism. Surrealism was the only pure form of Artistic Vision. Everything else was an imitation of life, a corruption of vision, the shallow play of Sunday-afternoon watercolourists.

Rafe Ainsley (not, please note, Ralph) was English. Rafe Ainsley was an artist in a world of mere aesthetes, fakes, and fools. When someone asked where he sold, he scoffed at the idea of commercialism, announced that he had Patrons Who Understood What He Was Doing, then shrugged and admitted that his work was in galleries, although he found it painful to see it there.

Rafe Ainsley worked in bronze, which he declared the only true medium for art, ageless and incorruptible. Rafe Ainsley had much to say in favour of Art As Craft, and went on for some time about the shallowness of painters who could not mix pigments or sculptors who did not know how to apply a finish. Rafe Ainsley was somewhat taken aback when I agreed with both these points—and astonished when I knew the names he was flashing around. Brancusi and Léger, Epstein and Gaudier-Brzeska, the Primitivists and Vorticists—all brought his grudging approval. Picasso? I asked. A genius, he declared. Duchamp? A shrug. Damian Adler, Alice Wright? Damian he knew, and respected (a good thing, since Surrealist Damian Adler was Holmes' son and thus, peculiar as it seemed, my very own stepson) but he turned up his nose at the woman's name. A judgment, I suspected, less connected to her art than to her sex. He had much to say in favour of the Benin bronzes and African influence in Cubist art and the manifesto of anti-art and . . .

I could tell that I puzzled him. My hands were nearly as rough as his, and my skin far browner, but my silk dress—new from Venice and, unlike his attire, freshly ironed by the hotel—looked as expensive as it had been, while my accent and attitude declared my status. We argued over Cubism and Neoplasticism and a few other -isms, which I had been reading up on ever since meeting that unlikely stepson, Sherlock Holmes' only child from a long-ago liaison.

Rafe Ainsley was not a man to welcome contrary opinions. Generally, and particularly at someone else's party, I tend to excuse myself from the bluster, but every so often I enjoy a nice, vigorous exchange of views. Those around us coalesced into sides, cheering on whichever of us made a good point, branching off into side arguments of their own. Ainsley ploughed on, interrupting my statements, sweeping away my preferences, acknowledging none of my assessments, waiting for me to fold beneath the masculine authority of his views. All the women and quite a few of the men were soon calling out my points, while his face went increasingly red and he cast around for the polite equivalent of shoving an opponent in a bar.

But I should have known that this was the sort of man for whom

"No" from a woman meant "Ask me again." His face cleared when he found his ultimate weapon. His pugnacious shoulders went back and he glanced at his fellow men to summon their attention.

"Mrs Russell, you are a magnificent Amazon! You must pose for me. A full-length sculpture—as Academia," he declared. Then he added, "Nude, I think, but for your spectacles. And a book."

My solemnity faltered, picturing Holmes' face, but Ainsley did not notice. Self-important men rarely do. He informed me that I would come visit his summer studio (one of the Murphy guest houses) but while I was trying to construct a response other than open laughter or overt hostility, we were interrupted by a voice at my elbow.

"Rafe, sweetie, leave the poor girl alone, not everybody thinks you're God incarnate. And anyway, I think some more of your friends have arrived."

Sara Murphy looked pointedly towards the house, where five people had come to a halt just outside the French doors.

Ainsley thrust his empty glass at her and set off across the crowded terrace, jostling elbows here and there. To my fascination, the sculptor became a different person as he crossed the tiles. His slump disappeared, his chin came down, the angle of his head and way he moved his hands changed, from brash and dismissive to polite and attentive. Startlingly close to deferential.

Not friends, I thought. These were people he wanted something from.

They looked like Russians—of the White persuasion, not Bolsheviks. Those languid hands and imperious noses could only belong to aristocrats, while the out-of-date dresses and the sheen on the men's evening suits betrayed their current tight finances. In one of our stops along the Italian coast, I'd picked up a pre-War Riviera guide-book, which reminded me that Monaco had been a favourite playing ground of the Czar's closest friends and family. These were five Russians who had got away with their lives in 1917, but had left their fortunes behind.

Except one: a tall, slim figure in his late fifties with pale skin, hooded eyes, and a narrow silver streak in hair that was otherwise a uniform black. He wore a beard, a facial decoration so intricate and sharp-edged it might have been ink, and, unlike the others, he knew his hosts well enough to have worn informal light-grey linen rather than proper evening wear. The suit was new and spotless, his shoes, polished to a twinkle. The heavy, old-fashioned watch-chain across his marginally darker grey waistcoat was the rich, red colour of high-carat gold.

He allowed Rafe to shake his hand, then turned to Sara, who had followed behind the sculptor. The Russian's smile became more genuine as he bowed over her hand, thanked her, and made the introductions that Rafe hadn't bothered with. Sara greeted each one, received gracious finger-shakes from each, and stood back to encourage them to move out onto the terrace.

She watched Rafe lead them in the direction of Gerald Murphy, while I tried to decipher the expression on her face. Sad, but also affectionate. Sara knew the bearded Russian, though perhaps not well. She liked him. Then her gaze extended outward to the rest of the gathering—easy, calm, self-contained, yet attentive to the least detail. Like a mother cat near her kittens, content that they were entertaining themselves, yet ready to intervene if need be.

Sara noticed me and smiled, so I moved over to where she stood.

"Thank you for inviting Terry and me. You have a lovely home."

"Aren't we lucky? I sit out there for hours, drinking in the view."

I obediently turned to appreciate it. The house, near to the ridge of Cap d'Antibes, looked over the wooded peninsula to the sea beyond. The lights of Cannes glittered along the coast, with smaller twinkles scattered here and there, including out at sea where a ship was heading towards Italy. At this hour, the garden was little more than odours and shadows, but even at night one could tell that a lot of work had gone into it. I commented on it to Sara.

"Yes, that's what made us fall in love with the place—the previous owner travelled all over and had a passion for exotic trees. All we had to do was tidy around the corners. Next time you're here during the day, I'll show you around."

"I'd like that."

The gramophone record came to an end. Sara glanced down at Rafe's discarded glass in her hand, gave a wry shake of the head, and went back inside.

I stood looking at the magical scene of happy people illuminated by lamp-light. I was sure there were any number of them I would enjoy talking with, but as I finished my drink, I noticed a tray heaped with empty glasses. Adding my own, I picked up the tray and went after Sara. As I neared the doors, I glanced up to see a row of small faces in an upper window. I wagged my fingers in a greeting. They ducked below the sill, although the gleam of their sun-bleached heads betrayed them.

I managed to back my way through the doors without dropping any glasses, tracing the sound of running water to the kitchen. There I found a generous room with modern fittings and a variety of art: that on the walls ranged from professional to a child's drawing of a horse; that on the shelves included a similar mix of adult sculptures and peculiar figures made from glued-together stones, shells, snippets of wire, and kitchen ware. This was a room for the family, not for servants, although the surfaces were at present a chaos of biscuit tins, dirty pans, used cocktail shakers, crumb-covered trays, and piled dishes. And as I suspected, no house-maid in sight.

"I brought in some things," I said. "I'll wash, you dry?"

"No, no," she protested. "You mustn't." But I was already edging her aside and laying glasses into the soap-filled pan. "Oh, Mary, you should go—well, if you don't mind . . . ?"

"My cooking skills extend to opening tins, but I'm a dab hand at dishes."

We got through the washing in minutes, chatting happily about art and the music playing outside—sent by friends in America, in regular shipments. The horse was by her daughter, Honoria. The cobbled-together figures, which she called "readymades," were in fact the work of adults.

"Art that is anti-art. Like Duchamp, you know?"

I studied the tin-funnel-turned-cocktail-glass with an olive made from a glass eye, the cocktail-shaker-turned-woman with stone features, dishrag dress, and wire hair, and the hair-brush made out of a porridge-paddle and nails. I supposed I should be grateful that the Murphy kitchen gallery of readymades did not include a Duchampian pissoir.

When the glasses were sparkling again, she loaded the trays for another round on the terrace, and indicated the packets on the work-table. "We've run out of the makings for cheese toast, but if you'd like to put those on some plates, we can take them out, too. Don't bother making them pretty—just dump and carry."

"I can do that." So I did, pouring things into bowls and flinging them out to the ravening guests. Half an hour later, the pantry was bare, the uproar from without rising, and I had donned an apron to start a second batch of glasses.

She studied her shelves. "I'll need to shop tomorrow, that's for sure." And then she added something under her breath that sounded like, *If the bank will cover our cheque.*

"I take it rather more guests showed up than you expected?"

She shook her head, by way of agreement—then with a little cry of triumph came out with a half-empty bottle of cooking wine. Without asking, she found two glasses and splashed some in. "You must think we live in a loony bin, but this is definitely not the usual evening at Villa America. A friend invited friends, and didn't think to mention it."

"Oh dear." I accepted the drink, which to my surprise was actually a good wine, only slightly flat. "It can be irritating when house-guests grant themselves a family's rights and none of the responsibilities."

Sara, after a large swallow, reached for a clean dish-towel. "Rafe means well, but like a lot of artists, he thinks the world revolves around him."

"I don't suppose he'll toss something into the kitty for expenses, either."

"Oh, it's all right—if no actual food appears, they'll all set off shortly, I imagine for Juan-les-Pins. The Count often ends up there."

"Count . . . ?"

"Vasilev. The one with the beard. Eve-something Vasilev."

"Yevgeny?" It was a common given name in Russia. "The same as our 'Eugene.'"

"Really? Sounds ever so much more glamorous, doesn't it? But yes, that sounds right. The Czar's banker. Terribly nice man. How incredibly awful it must be, to have lost everyone and everything. The Bolsheviks shot his wife and son, took his house, killed most of his friends. The only reason he's alive is that he was off in America putting his daughter into some special kind of hospital. Her lungs, was it? Someone told me he was a personal friend of the Czar—they grew up together, and he was godfather to one of the girls. Can you imagine? Your entire world, lined up and shot. For God's sake don't mention Lenin or Stalin or any of those to him—he gets frantic at some of the headlines."

"The papers say that some of the royal children could still be alive."

"You think so? I don't." She shuddered, and took another large swig from her glass, so I hastened to offer distraction.

"Well, the Count seems to have made a new life for himself here. Not that it removes memories, but he looks to be prospering. Is his daughter still alive?"

"Far as I know. In one of the Western states—Nevada or Colorado or something. The Count is forever going there, to see her. Though Rafe said he's going to move there permanently, before long. The Count, I mean."

"Well, he certainly makes for a decorative addition to a gathering," I said. "Have you known him long?"

"Oh, you know how it is in a place like this, you come across pretty much everyone at some point. Although it's true, the Count doesn't tend to mix with the likes of us."

"Because you're too bohemian?"

"We're too American. Common, I guess."

"Yet he wants to live in the States."

"Funny, I know. I think he's just trying to get out of Europe before the next trouble starts up. And I suppose he'll choose his neighbours carefully in America, to avoid the likes of us." She grinned.

The thought of Sara and Gerald Murphy being judged "common" was a bit absurd. Yes, she'd made that comment about money, and they were making do without a maid tonight, and yes, many of the things around me—from Sara's dress and the simple furniture to the earthenware plates, cheap glasses, and stainless-steel cocktail shaker in the sink—looked like purchases from the local market. So without a doubt they watched their expenditures. On the other hand, they did live in a beautiful house in the South of France, with no sign of gainful employment, and the shelves had plenty of Venetian wine-glasses, eggshell porcelain, and monogrammed silver cocktail shakers to go around.

However, I knew what she meant by "common." Money or not, there were many corners of Society where I—a Jewish, half-American woman—was not welcome.

"Your own three children seem more than happy to be living in a foreign land. I saw them looking down from the window upstairs."

She brightened instantly. "Poor things, they're used to music and talk at night but I expect this is a bit too much to ignore. Mademoiselle Geron got back this afternoon—that's our nanny. Our proper nanny."

"Rather than the improper Miss Hudson," I murmured.

She laughed in delight. "It's true, every child should have an improper nanny. However, Mademoiselle Geron is definitely better for everyday things. Such as putting them to bed, once the racket on the terrace begins to die down."

"I can remember staring down at parties through the stair-rails myself, as a child."

"Well, we're out of food, and the drink'll be gone soon, so we can all go to bed. In the meantime, I should get back to my guests."

"Even the uninvited ones."

"Especially those."

"Bed is sounding good, I will admit. It's been a long few weeks."

"You must tell me all about it. A three-week sailing trip sounds like pure ambrosia—Gerald and his friend Vladimir are plotting a boat for us. Vlad's some kind of a cousin of Count Vasilev, I think, though he also helps Gerald with paints and canvases and all sorts of things other than designing a boat. Anyway, if we don't talk again tonight, shall I see you at La Garoupe, tomorrow?"

"Is that the name of your little cove? I'd like that."

I watched Sara move into the crowd, touching an elbow here, kissing a cheek there. She looked like no one else on the terrace—hair casually gathered, little makeup, wearing one of her signature long flowing cotton dresses rather than anything fashionably above-the-knee and down-the-back. All the other women looked very young. And when she ended up at her husband's side, their arms linked in a manner that made them both seem more complete.

I could join them. But that would mean another drink thrust into my hand, and I was feeling the effects not only of alcohol, but, as I had told Sara, of three sun-baked weeks and the unrelenting company of others. It would also mean joining Rafe Ainsley and the Russians, and although I was interested in the man with the inked-on beard, the thought of more sparring with the sculptor was exhausting.

The two men did make for a striking contrast: the one, sturdy, brown, slightly pugnacious, and deliberately untidy; the other, thin, pale by comparison, beautifully mannered, and fastidious about his person. Yet they seemed to know each other well.

A burst of familiar laughter drew my attention: Terry and Luca, standing under one of the hanging lamps with two beautiful young men who had to be dancers and might have been twins. I walked over to join them, listening for a moment to their earnest discussion of the Côte d'Azur's potential as a venue for water-skiing, before I laid a hand on Terry's arm and spoke into his ear.

"Terry, I'm about to fall asleep on my feet, but when you leave, will you thank Gerald for me? I've said good-bye to Sara, but he's in the midst of a conversation I don't want to interrupt."

"Mary, you can't go now—things are just getting started! Here—meet Misha and Vitya, they're with the Ballets Russes, in Monaco. Do you know it? Diaghilev's lot? They were just telling me about some of the productions they've done in Paris. Diaghilev talked Gerald and Pablo Picasso into painting the backdrops. One of them had Sara helping Coco Chanel with the costumes."

"Sounds amazing. Lovely to meet you, but I'm going back now. Bit of a headache," I lied. Before he could make a gallant offer to accompany me, I added, "Don't worry, I have a torch."

He beamed at me, somewhat owl-eyed, then turned the beam at his new friends. "Mary here is such a good little Scout, always prepared."

"Have fun, Terry. See you tomorrow."

I tucked in my elbows and, after a last discreet wave at the small, blond heads—down to two now, I saw—I threaded my way to the house and the door and the lane beyond.

The tumult fell behind, making my head ring with the sudden change. I reached into my pocket for the pen-light, then decided that the moon, though young, might be sufficient once my eyes had adjusted to the dark.

I tried to remember when I had last been alone. Weeks? Not since leaving Sussex, at any rate.

I stood for a time, waiting for the sense of relief to settle in, but oddly, it did not. I had craved solitude, time and again, but now that I had it, I felt oddly . . . alone. Aware of a faint and inexplicable thread of melancholy. One that had permeated the entire evening.

Melancholy? Where did that thought come from? Not from Sara and Gerald, surely—they were the most contented people I had met in a long time. And not from having missed out on seeing Mrs Hudson—that evoked a far more complicated emotion. This came from . . . ah. The Russians. Five men and women who had stepped onto the terrace, shadowed by tragedy and ending.

Poor things. Who would have thought it, ten years ago?

The sea-mist had gone, the night was warm, and there was sufficient brightness to show the faint gleam of tram-tracks that led to the hotel. I went slowly off, pressing up against trees or into gateways the few times a car approached. From time to time I would pass a house with lights and voices and gramophone music, but for most of the way, the only illumination was from the sky, the only song, that of nightingales. The Riviera might not be the Tropics proper, but its climate seemed to encourage the planting of exotic plants: the air smelled of frangipani and orange blossom, with the faint astringent odour of olive trees that took me back to Palestine. I was tempted to climb a wall into one of the dark and silent gardens, to stretch out on some neglected lawn or dusty bench and watch the fireflies, but I did not. I followed the tram-lines and came eventually to the hotel, whose corridors echoed from the impact of my heels.

Up in my room, I left the windows open and climbed inside the folds of mosquito netting, that I might listen to the distant pulse of sea against cliffs. We could hear such a thing at home in Sussex, if the night was still and the waves high.

Where was Holmes, anyway? I missed him, after nearly a month apart. That must be why I was feeling so unaccountably sad—I was in need of his acerbic presence, the bracing opposite of romantic melancholy.

I turned to bury my head into my pillow. Maybe tomorrow, I thought sleepily, Terry and I could teach the Murphys how to water-ski.

CHAPTER EIGHT

Mrs Hudson: a conversation

"Clarissa, you shouldn't have brought those naughty pastries—I want to gobble them all."

"I couldn't resist, when I saw them in Madame Renault's window—they reminded me of that time in the Ritz."

"I claim one of the pink ones."

"Have them both."

"How did the meeting go?"

"Your banker friend is an interesting fellow."

"But you've met Yevgeny before, haven't you?"

"Once or twice, though I don't think we've exchanged more than half a dozen words until today. How do you know him?"

"I must have met him, oh, thirty years ago? Yes, the year before Hugo and I married. He was very young, but terribly handsome. He used to come here with the Romanovs every winter, and bring his family. His adorable wife, who was the size of a doll, would invite me to tea so their children could practice English. Two sons and a daughter. He was so proud of his family. And he doted on the girl. Now she's the only one left."

"Her lungs are bad, I heard."

"Lungs? No, it's her nerves. She was always a delicate thing, enormous dark eyes, pale hair. The most charming pianist. When the Bolsheviks came . . . you know. They were men, in a mob, and they were angry. They killed the boys and the mother outright, but when Yevgeny got there, the daughter . . . well, she was still alive."

"Oh dear God."

"But Clarissa, you mustn't let him know that you've heard this. I heard it from Zedzed—the Count himself never tells people any of it. If the girl comes up in conversation, he says that she was away when her mother died, in a hospital in America. In fact, she only went afterwards."

"How terrible."

"I gather the poor child didn't speak a word for years. The only thing that helped was getting her as far away from Russia as possible, and giving her as few reminders as could be arranged. He even managed to find a sanitorium that has only women doctors and nurses—for a long time, she couldn't bear the sight of men, even her own father. He says she's tolerating him more easily now."

"That does explain some things about the man."

"He is a bit of a puzzle. But he does have beautiful manners, and he could be very useful to you."

"So I imagine. He has friends in all sorts of places. Although some of them, to be perfectly honest, I had hoped I was finished with."

"You're talking about Zedzed."

"Oh, that nickname."

"I think he liked how amiable it made him sound. But seriously, Clarissa, once he learns you're here, he'll want to see you. And you can't possibly refuse him."

"I will be seventy years old next May. One would think that a woman my age might have outlived her past."

"Clarissa—"

"You're right, dear. I'm merely grumbling."

"You did know he was here before you got on the train in Paris. And you know that if he's in Monaco, it's impossible to avoid him."

"I said I would see him."

"Of course, he is married now."

"He was married before. Several times."

"This one is different. I've come to know her fairly well, and find her a much sweeter person than one would expect. And he, to all appearances, remains quite besotted with her, even after all these years."

"Well, he's bought her an entire principality as a wedding gift. That shows some affection."

"Clarissa, you must take care not to—"

"Yes, yes, I'm being catty. I shall watch my tongue and treat Zedzed as an old friend. But that doesn't mean I'll go out of my way to see him."

"I know. Still, the occasional snake in the garden seems to be the cost—"

"—of doing business."

"—of living here, I was going to say. Like hurricanes in the Bahamas or earthquakes in California. When in Monaco, we do as the Monégasques. Oh, but speaking of doing business, I have something for you, Clarissa—two somethings. First, I found this the other day in one of my photo albums."

"Good heavens, look at us. Look at your waist! Mine was never that tiny."

"Mine wasn't either, I couldn't breathe."

"What year is this? 'Ninety-two, maybe?"

"It must have been, because it was taken on board the *White Ladye,* and I stopped using her in 'ninety-three. This would have been February or March? During the Season, at any rate—and certainly one of the years your Mr Holmes was thought to be dead."

"In Tibet, of all unlikely places. Still, it let me spend an entire year away from Baker Street."

"Oh, but can you make out that necklace you're wearing?"

"It's—isn't that the one?—"

"The very same! And that brings me to the second thing: *le voilà*—it just arrived this morning."

"Oh, your agent found a buyer! And my, what an impressive stack of notes. You must take half."

"Absolutely not. I'm more than comfortable here, my husband is generous. And after all, I was the one who had the pleasure of wearing the thing, all these years. Since you didn't want your Mr Holmes to come across it in your sock drawer."

"Wouldn't *that* have been awkward! I'd forgot how handsome those diamonds were."

"You shouldn't have had me sell it. We'd have figured out something."

"Good heavens, no. Diamonds are meant to draw attention to a smooth young neck, not to wrinkles and age spots. So bless you, my dear old friend, these funds will get me started nicely. And blessings on that sweet young man who gave it to me. He'd never have imagined what would become of his gift."

"Would you have married the boy, Clarissa? If his father hadn't been such a prude?"

"Probably not. I don't think he really cared for women all that much."

"He cared for you—clearly."

"The necklace was by way of a parting gift. And I think a last gesture of rebellion against his family before he went off to marry the sweet young neighbour they'd chosen for him. He died fighting the Boers, did you know that? Such a nice boy. Such a lot of nice boys, who died too young."

"We'll raise a glass of bubbly in his memory, when you have a sitting room of your own."

"I may have found one—Count Vasilev's green-eyed young Greek boy wants to introduce me to his landlady. She has a small house to let, which looks nice from the outside."

"I hope it works out. Do you think you will miss England?"

"Yes. And no. I'll miss the people. Mary and Mr Holmes are the closest I have to family now—except for you, naturally. But I shan't miss the winters."

"Do you wonder how they are getting on without you there in Sussex?"

"Oh, I imagine by now Mary's hired one of the women from the village. Neither she nor Mr Holmes care much about the state of the floors, but they will draw the line at eating Mary's burnt offerings. The girl never did master the oven."

CHAPTER NINE

The next morning, I woke luxuriously late, well after dawn. I stretched hard, enjoying the whisper of the Hôtel du Cap's crisp linen—on a boat, nothing is dry, from bedsheets to biscuits. Through the windows came the rhythmic sweep of a gardener's rake on gravel. I rang down for a tray, had a bath, drank my coffee and ate my croissants while wrapped in the hotel's towelling robe, with nothing more to do than watch sailboats and merchant steamers ply back and forth, out on the azure sea.

In an hour, I was jittering with a mix of caffeine and boredom. Dear God, how could people bear to take holidays?

I dug out my nice, new, least-skimpy-available bathing costume and pulled on a linen dress, adding hat, sandals, and my bright Venice bag with a few things for the beach. I could hear sounds from the direction of the cliff-side swimming pool, but when I came out of the hotel, I turned the other way, to retrace the route to the cove that Terry and I had taken the previous afternoon.

The beach was magnificent in the relative cool of morning. There was even a second group of visitors, down at the far end. Up at this

end, the umbrellas were straight and the blankets pristine, awaiting the late-rising artists and dancers. Sara was all alone, lying
prone under a wide hat, a long pearl necklace descending along her
brown spine. A young nanny—the returned Mademoiselle Geron,
no doubt—was watching over the three Murphy children in the
shallow waves. In the distance, a figure swam across the open end
of La Garoupe bay.

I arranged my towel at a distance, so as not to intrude on Sara's
nap. I took a swallow of mineral water, laid my book on the towel,
and went back to the bag for my sun-glasses, which I hadn't worn
since leaving the *Stella Maris*. The cord I'd tied around the ear-
pieces, insurance against losing them overboard, had gone stiff
with salt. I'd only just succeeded in loosening one of the recalci-
trant knots when I heard my name.

It was Sara, urging me to join my camp to hers.

I took my things across the sand to where she lay. "I thought
after last night, you might like to sleep."

"I was dozing, a little. Though I've found that mothers never
seem to sleep very hard."

"You have nice children." They were in fact nice—not only well
mannered, but friendly and unspoilt.

"They're turning out a lot more interesting than I'd expected."

I laughed at the surprise in her voice. She smiled, and rested her
chin on her forearm again.

Sara Murphy was a very beautiful woman, even with no trace of
makeup. Her face was focused, alive, and uniquely her. The Russians at the party had been, in their own bloodless fashion, flirting
with her.

"I hope Terry managed to convey my thanks to Gerald last
night, before he went off to sleep under a bush?" I was amused to
hear my voice tightening into its American accents.

"He probably did. Again, I apologise for the riot. We'll plan
another dinner, a proper one. Though p'raps not tonight."

I returned her grin, said that no apology was required, and resumed my attempt at freeing my dark glasses. She watched me picking away.

"I wore these on the boat," I explained. "They saved me from going blind, but three weeks of salt air turns twine to steel."

"There's sure to be a knife or some scissors in that basket."

I went to look, and found both silver grape-scissors and a sheathed fruit-knife with a blade sharp enough for brine-cured twine. I exchanged my regular spectacles for the dark ones, and the world instantly became a more comfortable place.

"That's better."

She turned onto her back, fiddling with her hat until it provided shade without covering her eyes completely. The long pearls were now gathered down her front side. "I know you met Cole and Linda when you were in Venice, but did you manage to spend any time with them?"

"The Porters? Yes, they invited Ho—" Oh dear: what was "Mr Russell's" first name? "They invited *Sheldon* and me for dinner, at that amazing palazzo they have on the Grand Canal."

"Ca' Rezzonico. Spectacular, isn't it? And you were at the Hero party there, too, I think Gerald said? On the Saturday?"

"Briefly." Just long enough to kidnap a would-be gate-crasher.

"I hope you enjoyed it?"

"The word 'memorable' comes to mind."

Sara had a magnificent, deep laugh. "What about your husband—Sheldon, you said? Is he with you?"

"Not at the moment. He had people to see in Roumania, though he might join me later."

"What does Sheldon do, other than play the violin?"

"Pretty much whatever he feels like," I said, which was only the truth. "When Terry offered me a place on his friend's sailing yacht—I met Terry in Venice, on the Lido—I thought sailing around Italy sounded more interesting than rattling around on a series of trains into the mountains of Roumania. So here I am."

"Linda asked us back to Venice at the end of summer, but I think we'll stay here. The children are happy, and the summers there can be a bore. It's hot, it smells—and *so* many tourists this year."

"Even with the growing threats from Mussolini's people."

"Dreadful man, isn't he? I hope they get rid of him soon. But yes, Venice is just too popular for its own good. That's one of the reasons we bought a house on the Côte d'Azur rather than on the beaten path. The crowds here can be bad in winter, but we've kept a small place in Paris, to escape to. This time of year the only people are those we invite ourselves."

"Doesn't it get awfully hot, by the end of August?"

"No worse than Paris—and there's always a breeze in the evening. We've sort of got into the rhythm of afternoon siestas and late nights. Like summer holidays when I was a child: no responsibilities and loads of hours to play and swim and turn brown."

"I had a couple of summers like that," I mused. "My father owned a cabin on a lake, out in California."

"So you know what I mean. Oh, it won't last forever—it's too perfect. The children will grow up, people will move on, there'll be something tedious like money or illness or squabbles among friends. They're even saying there will be another War, before too long. But that just means that these years with nothing but family, friends, and sun, the beach and the garden and the sea—they're just so precious. And all the sweeter for knowing they'll pass."

Even without the threat of a second War, I did not think that the Cap d'Antibes would remain an idyllic retreat—not when one thought of the crowds spilling across Venice. But why ruin this nice woman's simple pleasure with a suggestion that her Riviera could become another Lido watering hole? "Yes, Venice was great fun, but one doesn't hear many nightingales there."

"Oh, aren't they just the loveliest? I often sit in the moonlight, listening to them."

I chuckled, picturing the doyenne of Lido parties, Elsa Maxwell, trying to invent a game based on nightingales. Sara turned her head, looking a question at me.

"I was just thinking about the Lido crowd, and a friend of Terry's whose great passion is inventing party games for adults."

"Elsa Maxwell."

"You know her?" This really was a small world, down among the pleasure-seekers.

"Who doesn't? Thank God the woman hasn't got her claws into the Riviera. Don't get me wrong—I adore Elsa, even though I frankly loathe big parties, and she's the sort of hanger-on I usually find appalling. But the woman's so utterly unapologetic about what she is, a person can't help but love her."

"I know just what you mean. One knows full well that she has a thousand 'intimate friends,' but still, it feels such an honour to be considered one of them."

"I don't suppose you happened to be around when Elsa and Cole and Linda all came face-to-face?"

"Oh yes, I certainly was."

"Aha—sounds like a story there! Tell all."

All was precisely what I had no intention of telling, since it would involve political back-stabbing, international relations, something perilously near to blackmail, and the true identity of "Sheldon Russell"—but I could tell *some,* and tack decorations on it. So I did.

Even in its sanitised version, the story of how we dragooned Cole Porter into an act of mild, but highly satisfactory revenge not only entertained his friend Sara, but definitely placed me on the side of the angels in her eyes.

With that tale, I became family.

Still, affectionate though Sara Murphy was, she was also a born mother, fiercely protective of those close to her. Any wrong step—any perceived betrayal of her trust, once given—would be instant cause for dismissal from the inner circle. That lovely smile would go polite, invitations would cease to flow, and information would be shut off at the source.

Thus, I let a good half-hour of lazing and chatter go by before I casually worked the conversation around to Mrs Hudson. Or, as she was here, Miss.

"Tell me, Sara, other than lying about in the sun, what should I try to do while I'm on the Riviera? Antibes looked like a nice place to spend a morning. What about Cannes? Or maybe Monte Carlo—is it worth a visit?"

"We tend to pop over to Juan-les-Pins instead. Just nearby, nice places for dinner, good bands for dancing—you must come along."

"But not Monte Carlo?"

"I'm not keen on casinos, but if that's what you're looking for, the one at Juan-les-Pins is loads more fun. To my mind, the nicest thing about Monaco is all the gardens. And the children enjoyed the aquarium, when we took them. Still, people seem to like the place."

"Your friend Miss Hudson, for one."

"Well, she's old enough to remember it as a wild and naughty place. Which it may have been once, back in the days when ladies wore crinolines."

"You sounded more enthusiastic yesterday, when you were talking about her consulting for the Princess."

"I didn't want to be rude to her face. If she can find a way to make a few francs out of the crooks who run the country, I wish her the best."

"Are there crooks?"

"Oh, I s'pose any city has crooks. But some of those in Monte Carlo . . . not sure I'd want to eat with them at the next table." Her voice had gone surprisingly cold.

"The Casino does attract all sorts, I suppose," I mused, trailing bait in the water. She did not take it, but merely pressed her lips together, so I let it go for the time being. "And I'll admit the idea of a tiny principality that's carved a niche in the world of high finance has piqued my curiosity. I may wander over, just to see what the fuss is about. Do you suppose I could talk Miss Hudson into showing me around?"

"I'm sure she'd be happy to. I'll scribble her a note and let her know you're interested—I don't know when she'll be back on the Cap." So saying, she twisted around to retrieve the note-book that I had seen her writing in from time to time, and added *Write Miss H* as a reminder to herself.

"Thank you," I said, although I'd have preferred a telephone number. Then, before she could think about my continued interest in a grey-haired child-minder, I continued with a question about her Russian guests the night before. That led us into Bolshevik revolutions and the fragility of inherited money and how she'd heard that among the Casino's greeters were a Duke, a Grand Duke, and a Prince who'd spent their pre-War years merrily losing their family fortunes.

· "Actually, they're sort of sad," she commented. "I mean, it's nice of the Casino to hire the old relics so they don't starve, but having them propped up in the corners doesn't exactly stir up a gay old time among the customers."

"Well, some of the Russians must have got away with their purses intact. Count Vasilev certainly doesn't appear to be count-ing his every ruble and kopek."

"He does live nicely. He has a fabulous villa in Monte Carlo, and he's commissioned a whole series of bronzes from Rafe. And he has this gigantic sailing yacht for parties—although come to think of it, that might belong to a friend. We had a perfect day on board earlier in the summer, and I'm afraid Gerald now finds our own little *Picaflor* small beans by comparison. That was when Gerald started talking to our friend Vladimir—Vladimir Orloff, he's the Count's cousin, did I mention?—who trained as a boat designer before the War, and ended up painting sets for the Ballets Russes, then came to work for Gerald stretching canvases and things and tutoring the children, who adore him—anyway, Vlad's promised to build us a proper schooner."

I took a moment to sort out the free-ranging thoughts and the Russian shipbuilder from the Russian Count. I could understand

Count Vasilev's wanting to live in Monaco, and being a patron of the arts was a customary hobby for the aristocracy, but sailing? "I have to say, the Count doesn't look much like a sailor."

"Oh, I'd say it's more or less required for his class, wouldn't you? Those gleaming white naval uniforms all the Russians seem to be photographed in? Though in his case, it's sitting with guests on a shaded deck while the scenery goes by. Come to think of it, that day Gerald and I went out with him may be when we met Miss Hudson."

"On a sailing yacht, how fine." I kicked myself—if I'd been aware that Mrs Hudson knew the Count before she met the Murphys, I'd have cornered him at the party. "So if Rafe is doing a series of pieces, does that mean Count Vasilev will be a regular around Villa America?"

"I don't think so—they're not portrait busts, so far as I know."

"Pity," I said. "I'd like to see that interesting beard of his rendered in bronze."

She flashed me a look of such impish mischief, she might have been her daughter's age. "Oh, isn't it fabulous? How long do you suppose he spends on the thing every morning? I find myself staring to see if it's plucked or shaved."

"Quite a contrast with Mr Ainsley."

She laughed. "In all ways."

"What about Rafe? Is he an old friend?"

"No. He is one of the Paris crowd, but we only met him this past winter. We were supposed to have someone else in the guest house, but the poor man developed lung problems and had to go to Switzerland. When Rafe heard, he sort of invited himself as a replacement. It's fine—and anyway, he's leaving soon, going to spend a few months in the States. Rafe's great fun. If he's not too drunk. And he is talented, in a masculine sort of way."

Masculine meaning rough, I thought. "He told me he's working while he's here. And it sounded as if he casts his own bronzes. Don't tell me you have a foundry on the grounds?"

"Good Lord, no—he sculpts here, but found a place in Antibes to do the actual pouring, where they let him help. Though you're right, Gerald was thinking about setting one up in an out-building, until Rafe invited us all for what he called a demonstration pour. We made the mistake of thinking of it as a party, and about a dozen of us went—but oh my goodness. I had this pretty silk dress that I planned to wear for Easter and it was spoiled completely. But I guess Rafe likes doing them, and they are interesting, no doubt about that. He has another one coming up soon. Tuesday, I think?"

"I'm surprised he has the patience for demonstrations to *hoi polloi*," I remarked. "He seems a bit dismissive of people who aren't artists."

"He can be a little abrupt, can't he? And secretive—he goes off to the foundry at all hours, won't show even Gerald what he's done until he's all finished. But he likes to lecture, as you'll have noticed, and he does enjoy the manly showmanship, stripping down to his under-vest—which, I was amused to see, the other workers don't do. He had a pour one scorching day in June, just before Gerald and I set off for Venice, and most of the group left early to go find a drink. The only ones who stuck it out were me and Gerald and a couple of the Russians, who seemed bizarrely fascinated. Though I'm not sure if the fascination was in the process of pouring molten bronze into a mould, or watching the muscles of the young man doing it."

We thought it over, and agreed that there was no accounting for the tastes of the aristocratic mind.

CHAPTER TEN

The sun climbed in the sky. Sara and I talked and the children played. Others came wandering in to take up positions on mats and join in what appeared a morning ritual of sherry-and-sweet-biscuits. Mrs Hudson was not among them. Gerald had come back from his swim and helped the children into a canoe to paddle about. I decided to go for a swim, using the Murphys' striped tent to change. I wrapped myself in a concealing towel before I emerged, and paused to ask Gerald's advice about local hazards. Sharks, jellyfish, jagged rocks? Speed-boats? But he assured me that the little Baie de la Garoupe was friendly and unafflicted, so I thanked him and continued down to where the tiny waves broke, tossing my towel and spectacles onto dry ground before wading in.

The water passed over my skin like silk, not as warm as the Venice lagoon but far cleaner. Up and down I swam, back and forth, blissfully thoughtless. By the time I returned to the beach, the encampment's population had grown. I recognised Terry and Luca even without my glasses, but when it came to the others, I was glad I had left my possessions down the beach a way. I may have grown less sensitive over the years about my various scars, but I still find the questions intrusive.

It being near to midday now, Sara and Mademoiselle Geron took the children off for lunch and a rest. Gerald began to gather the adults, drawing us into his orbit with a promise of a grown-up lunch under the lime tree on Villa America's terrace. We climbed the slope through the odour of hot leaves and the drone of cicadas, but when we came to the main road, I turned to follow the tram-tracks while the others continued on. I had gone some distance before Terry noticed and called a protest at my back.

I turned to give him a reassuring wave and called, "I have some things to do, Terry. Have fun, I'll see you tomorrow."

At the hotel, I scrubbed my salt-permeated body, ate a hearty lunch, and stretched out under the mosquito net for a couple of hours.

When the sun was lower in the sky, I dressed carefully, tucking a compact, lipstick, and necklace into my handbag, and set off in the hotel car for Monte Carlo.

The road narrowed after Nice, then rose, becoming a cliff-top track so precarious that I was tempted to leap out and walk the rest of the way. I'd thought it would be simpler to motor than take the train to Monaco, but I would re-think that for the return trip.

When we crossed into Monte Carlo, my finger-nails stopped digging into my palms and I started anticipating a drink.

But first, I wanted an overview of this place that had claimed Mrs Hudson's heart. I told the driver to leave me off not at the Casino, but on the boulevard along the harbour-front. He glanced back at what I was wearing, which did not look suitable for a sail-ing cruise, then gave one of those eloquent French shrugs and con-tinued without further comment through the old town to the waterfront.

The ancient harbour of Port Hercule was the reason for Mona-co's existence, but it was no longer the realm of fishermen and smugglers. These boats gleamed with polish and fresh paint. Some were low and sleek and built for speed, their bodies too stream-lined for bunks and galleys. Others were intended for comfort, including one or two vessels so large they could have housed an English village. Grandest of all was the *Bella Ragazza,* some seventy metres of yacht so magnificent it would have been the envy of King George himself. I instantly coveted its lines.

Yes: even I, a person for whom sailing was a mixed gift, felt a stir of acquisitive lust at the glossy teak and polished brass before me. Didn't I need a beautiful boat, really? True, sailing made my stomach heave, and even a placid outing left me aware that the sea was an unforgiving place of infinite danger—but just look at the loveliness of those lines, listen to the cheerful jangle of the rigging . . .

I caught my thoughts and deliberately turned my back on the water, to survey the Principality itself. To my left, at the top of a steep peninsula dotted with scrub and trees, was Monaco-Ville, the country's oldest section. The palace was there, and around it, according to the guide-book, the primary offices of government. Locals called it The Rock, a blunt spit of land some two hundred feet high at its ridge. The Prince must have a spectacular view.

To my right lay the newer quarter of Monte Carlo, on another rocky plateau above the sea. According to the map, the Casino and opera house were at the top of the wide promenade rising from the harbour. Behind Monte Carlo, one could see the trailing end of the Maritime Alps.

Between these two high sections of Monaco was the district called La Condamine. *Con-* and *dominium*—"shared ownership"— referred to ground worked by the cliff-dwellers perched on both sides. Not that much agriculture went on in La Condamine these days. So far as I could see, the main crop of Monaco today was harvested from the wallets of visitors. However, the area did appear to be a place of gardens, with palms and other trees around a pleasing mosaic of villas in many sizes and styles, set into the rising slopes.

Behind it all lay the high, thinly-wooded ridge line of France. A single sniper up there could cover the entire Principality.

But what an odd thought. Why would France want to lay siege to Monaco? If this place did not exist, this social pressure-valve of casinos and opera houses, this shelter for riches and place to avoid taxation, its neighbours would have had to invent it.

I strolled along the seafront, the harbour to my right. Following the promenade would take me from boats and gardens to a land of hotels and expensive entertainments, musical or financial. Flowers rioted along the path. Cars putted busily down and slowly up. The air smelt of salt water and jasmine, although I could see none of it growing in these cliff-side public gardens. Birds sang, a train puffed across the bridge joining the plateaus, palms whispered in the breeze, the music of sailboat rigging came from below. A Siren song, I thought, luring the unwary onto the cliffs.

Though to be fair, with France and Italy crowding in, the options open to such a tiny country were limited. And like any watering place, Monaco required a lovely and compelling face in order to keep a roof over the heads of its actual residents.

Halfway up the promenade, I paused to look over the harbour and town. The Rock across from me, the harbour below, its breakwater sheltering the gleaming hulls. There was even, moored among the sea-craft, an exotic cousin to their polished hulls: one of the sea-going biplanes that so thrilled Terry, lightly perched on its pontoons, brilliant white.

What was it about this place that appealed to Mrs Hudson? For twenty years, her rooms had looked onto a small, but private bit of garden—her quiet retreat, where a housekeeper might sit undisturbed on a pleasant afternoon. On the times I'd been invited in, I found nothing special about it, no elaborate design or exotic plants. Still, it was a place of tranquillity, and moreover, a place that was hers.

For a person whose entire life, as I learned this spring, had been rooted in danger and upheaval, I was beginning to see the appeal of a tranquil retirement.

The turmoil in Mrs Hudson's life began when she was still in the womb. In 1855, when Victoria sat on the throne and war raged in the Crimea, her father fled England to avoid prosecution for his crimes, leaving behind a pregnant young wife.

In that same year, a merchant banker named Jack Prendergast was arrested for embezzling a quarter million pounds from his clients. He was convicted, sentenced to transportation, and taken in chains onto the *Gloria Scott*, a ship bound for Australia.

One of the sailors on that ship was James Hudson.

Once away from England, off the coast of Africa, Prendergast bribed the crew to mutiny. But the mutiny went wrong and the ship sank. Prendergast died with his confederates. A mere handful of survivors got away. One of them was James Hudson.

From then on, Hudson lived as a confidence man, joined by his clever daughter, Clarissa. From the time she was eleven years old, the two fleeced the gullible from Sydney to London—until, at the age of twenty-one, she fell in love. Hudson lost his meal ticket, and in desperation, turned to blackmail.

That was when the situation came to the attention of a curious young undergraduate by the name of Sherlock Holmes. The case of Hudson's blackmail was the first in Holmes' long and illustrious career. It brought him to Mrs Hudson, to Dr Watson, and to the world.

But he never found Prendergast's stolen money.

£250,000 was a mythic sum in the 1850s. Impossible to believe a fortune that huge might simply be swallowed by the waves—particularly once it came to light that Prendergast had bragged to his shipmates about having the balance of the money "right between my finger and thumb."

It was assumed that Prendergast meant it was being held by one of his onboard confederates. But surely not in the cumbersome form of coin or bullion? Even the ship's captain would have found it difficult to conceal that much gold on the small, crowded *Gloria Scott*.

Only much later did Holmes discover that Jack Prendergast, in his final days before the police net closed around him, had been to see a man named Bishop, a ruler in London's criminal underworld. Bishop's son, who later inherited the family business, had not been privy to the transaction, but he remained convinced that the old man had helped Prendergast convert his stolen fortune into something small and portable. Something that might indeed be held between finger and thumb.

But what? A deed? A banker's cheque? A diamond to rival the Koh-i-Noor?

And what had happened to it? Did it go down amidst the wreckage of the *Gloria Scott*? Or had one of the survivors found it, and spent it all on house and home and respectability?

No one knew—and yet the belief in Prendergast's fortune lived on. Just this past winter, seventy years after the *Gloria Scott* sank, James Hudson's grandson learned of the mystery, and another generation succumbed to the spell of missing treasure.

A fortune held between finger and thumb. It could not possibly still exist—not after a mutiny, a shipwreck, and a lifetime in the shadows.

Could it?

It was as much a mystery as Mrs Hudson herself, who in her youth had perfected the techniques of teasing money out of rich men, then left that life behind to become first landlady, then housekeeper. A placid chatelaine, an excellent maker of strawberry jam and hot scones.

Perhaps that piquant contrast was the key. She had been content as a Sussex housekeeper not despite, but *because* of an illicit youth amongst the bright lights. Just as now, she was content in Monaco, because this showy haunt of the rich and powerful was also a place of small, intimate gardens revealed only by a glimpse of leaves and a scent of flowers on the air.

I had never before considered Mrs Hudson as a complex person. That was Holmes' job, and to a lesser degree, mine. But the more I learned about this elderly woman—who she in fact was, rather than who she seemed to be—the more intriguing I found her. And the stronger my determination grew that she should be given a chance to succeed.

During all this reflection, my feet had continued carrying me along, up to the broad terrace before the Opera House. The Casino, I knew, was around its back. However, a little further on, according to the map, was a police station (on a street blessed by a grotto, or so the name Spélugues suggested). A police station where I, a wealthy visitor in a district catering to money, could enquire about a friend recently moved to Monaco, and expect some degree of assistance.

First, however, I wanted that drink, as much for thirst now as a wish for alcohol. After a brief pause to admire a yacht approaching the harbour, sails out for the afternoon breeze, and behind it a business-like steamer heading for some Italian port, I turned on my heels to follow the path into the beating heart of Monte Carlo.

With the sun going low, the outdoor tables of the café that overlooked the park and Casino were crowded with drinkers—some, I supposed, anticipating a night around the tables, others lamenting a disastrous afternoon. Normally, an unaccompanied young woman would be looked at askance in a restaurant filled with expensive people, but since neither my dress nor my attitude resembled those of a *femme de nuit,* I thought my chances of being seated and served were fairly good.

In the end, asserting my propriety was not necessary.

When I had scattered my telegrams on the wind the previous afternoon, I knew that sooner or later, one would find its target. Twenty-four hours was too early for the notice to appear in any newspaper agony pages—and yet, I felt less surprise than a sense of inevitability as I saw an arm go up at the back of the café terrace. An arm attached to a tall, thin man in his sixties with a narrow moustache and glossy dark hair, dressed in a perfect evening suit, his long legs extended, ankles crossed to show the gloss on his shoes. Pearl shirt-studs, diamond cuff-links, a diamond sparkling from the little finger of his right hand.

And, I saw as I closed in on his table, a gleam in his grey eyes.

I bent down to kiss his cheek, and allowed the waiter to seat me in the chair across from him.

"Hello, Holmes. What took you so long?"

CHAPTER ELEVEN

Mrs Hudson: a conversation

Clara Hudson smiled at the tiny bubbles of champagne rising up in the glass, then lifted it, first to her newly furnished morning room, and then to her oldest friend. "Here's to homes, and friends, and to growing old in Monaco."

"I'll drink to the first two, but you and I aren't going to grow old. *Salut!* Ah, the first swallow of champagne is always the best. And seriously, Clarissa, I hope you'll be happy in this little place, for a time at any rate. But I am going to keep my ears out for a flat closer to me, since I'm not sure I'll manage that climb more than once a week, even with Mathilde to push me along."

"I don't know. Oh yes, I would love to be next door to you, but even if I had the money, it might be more sensible to remain here, an invisible old woman in a dull corner of the city. And your pretty Greek friend with the green eyes is a very convenient neighbour."

"Ah, one is never too old to admire a handsome face."

"True. Although, dear thing, I shouldn't trust the boy *too* far, if I were you. It wouldn't do to lay temptation too close to him."

"Clarissa, I learned *that* lesson almost as early as you did. Still, you have sufficient funds for the time being?"

"I do. And I've decided, about the . . . *other thing* that you and I talked about."

"The four *'papers'* that we mustn't let anyone see or even mention out loud, except when we can see a hundred feet in every direction and the only ears belong to insects."

"You think I'm being overly cautious?"

"Of course not, you're being very sensible, I'm just not accustomed to talking in code about *the papers* and *the things*."

"Well, thank you for indulging what Mary would probably call my paranoia. At any rate, I think I'll go ahead with our banker friend. For one of the four, at any rate."

"Are you sure? I do know others in the financial world, if you prefer someone a little more established."

"It would terrify me to put it into the hands of an actual banker. I have no idea who he'd have to report it to. And my rheumatism would not be happy, ending my days in a prison cell."

"Don't be absurd, it's just a piece of paper!"

"True. And if this one goes nowhere, you and I can think about who to turn to for the next."

"Where are the others? You told me Niko might have a safe place?"

"He has a place, one that ruined a perfectly good pair of shoes, but I do not wish to leave them there for long. Sooner or later he'll stumble across them. But I do have an idea of where to move them. Should I tell you, when I decide? It would be a pity to lose track of them if I were to get run down by an omnibus."

"You may whisper it in my ear any time."

"I'll do that."

"Oh, it is rather exciting, isn't it? *Such* a lot of money."

"Do you know, I can barely think of it in those terms. Too many uncertainties."

"Not counting on our Count, eh?"

"My doubt lies in the . . . *paper* itself. As for him, well, I have to trust someone. Better the scoundrel I know than one who takes me by surprise."

"Yevgeny is no scoundrel!"

"Of course not, dear heart—I'm sure he's honourable among friends. But he does have some questionable acquaintances."

"This is Monaco—who *doesn't* have questionable acquaintances?"

"Some more intimate than others. Well, we shall see how it plays out. If the *thing* is worthless, lesson learned. And if someone along the way helps himself to it—well, that's a different lesson learned. At least I haven't been silly enough to put all four eggs in the same basket."

"I've always wondered what that meant. Doesn't one *want* to collect all one's eggs at the same time?"

"Dear heart, your social class is showing. If you'd ever had to train a clumsy young house-maid in ill-fitting shoes, you'd know why you don't want her to risk all the day's eggs at once."

"It is so odd to think of you in those terms, Clarissa."

"Sussex was indeed another world."

"Oh, I *hope* this goes smoothly! Though if you change your mind about him, I'll happily write to one of my friends in Paris, or America. And *I* wouldn't take a commission on it, you can be sure of that."

"No, you've done quite enough. You welcomed me here, you got me started, you showed me a direction. Without you, I'd be standing with my nose pressed to the Casino windows. And I'd like to be finished with this transaction soon, before Mr Holmes shows up."

"You really think he will?"

"I have no doubt. Any week now, I'll turn around and *poof*! There will be Mr Holmes, dressed as a street-sweeper or a preacher or a riverboat gambler. And once he's found me, if I haven't got this ... *thing* swept out of the way of that inquisitive nose, I'll need to wait until his attention moves on. Which could be years."

"Even if you're an invisible old lady?"

The two old women laughed, and Clarissa filled their glasses again.

"It's true that Mr Holmes is more likely to underestimate a woman than a man, but only marginally. He hasn't trusted me since 1880."

"What you're doing is not criminal!"

"Isn't it?"

"Well, any crime involved was committed long ago, by someone else entirely."

"I'm not sure Mr Holmes would see it that way."

"Clarissa Hudson, I do not know how you managed to put up with that man."

"What choice did I have? I was a criminal! I stole money from men—"

"Your father did that."

"I helped. And though I was a child when I started, by the end I was a willing participant. If it hadn't been for Mr Holmes, I'd have ended up in prison for sure. And I say he didn't trust me, but that's absurd. Twice now he has not reported what would have led to a charge of murder. Twice! Don't you doubt that both those episodes lie heavy on his mind. And now, as an old woman you'd think would have learned her lesson, back I go, flirting with the hangman."

"Clarissa, no, you mustn't say that! Don't even think it. None of this has been your doing."

"I have killed—"

"Stop!"

"Dear thing, there is blood on my hands. I owe my very life to Mr Holmes. Just because the life he gave me was closely restricted does not change that it was a gift."

"Gift? Pah! I'm going to put away the champagne, it's making you weepy."

"It *was* a gift. And remember, in the end, he did let me leave

England. Who could blame him if he decided to check on me, to be certain that his trust was not misplaced? Though when he does show up, what will he find? Clarissa Hudson, surrounded by people like Zedzed the arms dealer and Niko Cassavetes with the shady antecedents. There's not a lot I can do about that, but I can at least make sure that the . . . *things* are well out of sight."

"You're far too forgiving, Clarissa. Forty-odd years of having that man looking over your shoulder. And not even the benefits of marriage."

"Benefits? Could you imagine being *married* to the man? Mary Russell is a brave young woman. And it was forty-*four* years—well, minus his absences."

"Ah, those absences. Such mischief we all got up to, when you had the freedom to roam."

"We did have fun, didn't we?"

"Oh, Clarissa, even if we only get up to old woman mischief, it's going to be so *good* to have you back!"

CHAPTER TWELVE

Materialising out of nowhere was a traditional part of the Sherlock Holmes mystique. However, I knew his methods all too well, and it did not take long to put the pieces together. My telegrams had not summoned him into a mad aeroplane dash from out of a distant Roumanian mountain. Nor had his spymaster brother been keeping tabs on me. Holmes had not noted the distinctive soil on a passing shoe and matched it with the hair from a Gibraltar ape and a flower known only in Monaco . . .

None of those things had been required—because he was already here. I'd told him three weeks ago in Venice roughly where the *Stella Maris* was going, and approximately how long it would take. He knew back in May that his long-time housekeeper was thinking of heading to Monte Carlo. It was no great leap to know that I would, finding myself on the Riviera, seek her out. All he had to do was wait in a place near the well-beaten path. Although that did leave the question of *why*.

But I started with his cuff-links.

"Really, Holmes—diamonds?"

He raised one wrist to give the garish object an approving look. "Hideous, aren't they?"

"The suit is nice, though. Italian?"

"I had it made as I passed through Rome."

One did not "pass through" Rome on the way from Roumania to Monaco, or even from Venice, but I ignored the blatant red herring. "I see you decided to keep the moustache."

"I did shave it, upon leaving Venice, but I let it grow again before I came here. It seemed to go with the diamonds." His fingers came up to smooth the narrow line on his upper lip.

"A most precise decoration," I said. "Though not as carefully engineered as one I saw last night near Antibes."

"Ah: you have met Count Vasilev."

God, the man's omniscience could be irritating. I gave up and went for straight interrogation.

"How long have you been here, Holmes?"

"Only a day or so."

"How many?"

"Two," he admitted. "And a half."

"Have you found Mrs Hudson?"

"I have seen her."

"But you don't know where she's living?" I was surprised—after two days, I'd have thought Holmes would not only have located her house, but her maid, her hair-dresser, and her bank-manager as well. Perhaps things worked differently in Monaco. And perhaps asking at the local police station wouldn't have led me to her, after all.

"Not yet. Either she has been remarkably inconspicuous, or the Monégasques I have spoken with have been singularly close-mouthed. She is definitely here—I have seen her three times, although each time she has been going somewhere other than home. And before you ask—no, we have not spoken. I do not believe she has spotted me."

"You're *spying* on her?"

"I would not put it that way, precisely."

"How would you put it?"

"I am attempting to confirm that the agreement I reached with her, long ago, still stands."

That agreement had amounted to a sort of lifetime parole: she could remain in England, but only under his roof, living a life of obedience and morality.

"You honestly don't trust her?"

"Should I?"

"Holmes, this is Mrs Hudson!"

"A woman linked to the deaths of two men. A person who was once Clarissa Hudson, a gifted swindler and natural-born confidence trickster, who spent her most lucrative years working the casinos of Europe. Who only gave up that life when I narrowed her choice to leaving England, or remaining under my eye in Baker Street. Who 'coincidentally' chose to retire to a place heavily populated by those sheltering fortunes both legal and otherwise."

"Holmes, neither of the deaths was murder, and her ... swindling was a lifetime ago. As a young woman. Under her father's influence."

"A father who left behind a huge question mark at his death. A question of some quarter million pounds."

"Oh, Holmes, we're not back in *that* pipe-dream, are we?"

"The Prendergast case has never been closed to my satisfaction."

A glass of wine had appeared before me. The air took on the odour of Holmes' cigarettes. I sat, unseeing. Or rather, I sat seeing two paths open before me.

In May, I had learned that my beloved Mrs Hudson possessed a History that was scandalous, adventurous, and criminal.

Mrs Hudson, who had looked across her kitchen at a truculent fifteen-year-old girl—a girl who set out one morning from her dead mother's house, dressed in her dead father's jacket and her dead brother's cap—and perceived not the ink-stains of education and the accents of an upbringing, as Sherlock Holmes had seen, but the clear signs of pain and hunger and emptiness.

Everything I assumed about Mrs Hudson—everything I *knew*—had been tipped on its head this past May. I had killed a human being myself, during that same time, and yet my thoughts dwelled less on my act than on what I had learned about her. That indicates how deeply the revelations had shaken me.

I wasn't even given time to absorb the news before she was gone, fleeing from the law (yet another impossibility to wrap my head around). Soon after, Holmes and I were caught up in the search for a missing woman, the case that had taken us to Venice. All of which meant that my time on board the *Stella Maris* had been my first opportunity to merely sit, out on the deck in the dead of night, and contemplate the moon's, and my own, reflections.

It seems a touch absurd to say that I had grown up during that summer. At the age of twenty-five, most women have long entered into adult responsibilities. But the orphaned and the displaced often cling to the remnants of childhood, and during those deck-top meditations, I realised that such had been the case with me.

I resented Mrs Hudson's lies, the false face she had deceived me with. And I resented Holmes, for keeping it from me, his wife and partner. As if I had any right to require a full confession from her—from either of them—for a thing that happened long before I was born. But I was very young when I lost my family. The loss of Mrs Hudson felt like a second abandonment.

That summer, as I began to step back from childish resentments, I also began to see that young Clarissa Hudson did what she did in order to survive. Would I not have done the same, had I been raised by criminals? She had changed when she needed to, and she had kept her dignity even at the harshest of accusations. Including accusations from one who loved her, yet felt betrayed by surprise.

I realised, during those silent nights on the *Stella Maris,* that what I wanted most was not to tell her that I forgave her. What I wanted was for her to forgive me, for having judged her.

And now here was my husband suggesting I was wrong.

No.

"No," I said. My eyes came at last into focus. His cigarette was nearly burned down, his glass empty. Mine appeared untouched, so I reached out and took a swallow, grimacing at its temperature, before I met his even gaze. "You're wrong. She was little more than a child when she started, with a sister to support and a career criminal for a father, and she did what she had to. She is no longer that person. Whatever brought her to Monte Carlo, it was not to rob the rich."

He smiled, as he crushed out his cigarette. And it was a true smile, not a patronising expression—I knew those well enough, God knows. "I hope," he said, "that you are right. In the meantime, shall we carry on with this performance of our own?"

"Sorry, what performance is that?"

"The one you are dressed for."

"I dressed for the Casino, in case I needed to go in."

"Exactly. A place I have seen Mrs Hudson enter twice."

"She's not in there now, is she?" I was alarmed at the idea of appearing to be tracking her down.

"Not that I have seen."

"I don't know, Holmes. Can't we just go have dinner instead?"

"Afterwards. It may not prove necessary, to provide ourselves with the masks of English fools, but you will find the Casino an interesting experience. Although—I don't suppose you brought your passport?"

"I always have my passport when there's a chance of meeting up with you, Holmes. One never knows when we'll be bolting for the nearest border."

"I trust that bolting will not be on the agenda for this evening." He returned his slim cigarette case to an inner pocket. "But since you have your papers, my good wife, and since it will not only permit us to establish ourselves here, but grant you a view of what keeps Monaco afloat, I propose that we spend the evening in the Monte Carlo Casino."

I opened my pocket-book to retrieve the emeralds I had brought, just in case, and bent so Holmes could fasten them around my neck. I then stood, slipping my arm through his.

"Proposal accepted, husband mine. Let us go and lose some money."

CHAPTER THIRTEEN

Holmes and I crossed the paving stones to the Casino de Monte-Carlo, that nineteenth-century enthusiasm of Beaux-Arts balustrades and statuary, cornices and draperies, friezes and sashes and all the decorative flourishes under the heavens. Its portico was ornate, its light fixtures as intricate as its doorways and leaded windows and—in short, this was a façade that, were it rendered in icing-sugar, would have made the perfect Society wedding-cake.

It was not huge, as these sorts of places go, merely an impressive gem in a delicate setting. The height of its entrance stairway was nicely judged: raised enough from the pavement to separate its fortunate guests from the hurly-burly of the streets, yet low enough not to intimidate—or to challenge the unfit. The cost of our clothing earned us the doorman's bow—or so I thought, until I realised that it was Holmes he was saluting. A coin disappeared into the man's palm, and he greeted Holmes with an accented "Welcome back, sir" as he drew open the door with a gesture worthy of royalty and ushered us into an expanse whose very air smelled expensive.

"Russian?" I asked Holmes when we were inside.

"A baron, who broke the bank here back in 1910."

"Before the bank broke him," I commented. No doubt one of the "relics" Sara had mentioned, given small pensions by an appreciative Casino.

"Seven out of ten Russian names on the Casino files in 1914 died of violence," he pointed out. "Give me your passport, I'll register you with the Commissariat."

He walked across the elegant foyer to the discreet window, a husband vouching for his wife. This made me think of Mrs Hudson, and it dawned on me that I hadn't told Holmes anything about my days in Antibes. He didn't know that I'd met her on the beach, that I knew about her interests here, that she looked well and happy.

Unless . . . ?

No, I'd have spotted him lurking in the distance. Which meant that I knew something he did not. And since it is on such minor pleasures that marriages are made, I was smiling when I moved to join him at the Commissariat's window.

Would-be guests of the Casino were required to fill out a sort of membership card. Holmes had done his earlier, which simplified my own. While he exchanged a sheaf of banknotes for the gambling counters used on the tables—no mere *jetons*, but *plaques* that started at 100 francs—I moved into the entry to study this temple to the gambling arts.

The low foyer opened into an atrium like a jewel-box, two storeys high. Marble columns supported balustraded galleries under an ornately worked glass ceiling, its light making the room feel larger than it was. The last hour of daylight hid the shabbiness of chipped paint and worn carpeting, and brought a warm gleam to the gilt that overlaid the wall garlands, the ceiling cartouches, the pillar capitals, and any other surface that had held still long enough to be garnished. Art Nouveau piled atop Belle Époque, leaving no surface without ornamentation.

It ought to have been dizzying, if not actually qualm-inducing, but for some reason, it was not. Perhaps I was merely distracted? But when we had finished with the attendant's card and set off into the sequence of rooms that made up the Casino, I found myself gawking like a farm-girl come to Times Square.

It was not what I'd expected. According to my tattered, pre-War guide—at any rate, reading deep between its lines—the Casino had been founded by a glib hustler who talked his way into the good graces of Monaco's royal family, and was hired to pattern a casino on the lucrative one in Bad Hamburg. However, I'd been to Bad Hamburg, and this was an entirely different exercise in design. Despite its formality, and perhaps because of its air of smoke-stained dilapidation, it felt oddly intimate, less a business than a private club or home (though a home designed by Inigo Jones and furnished by a century of colonial pillage). The opulence here was on a human scale, the chairs around its gaming tables designed for comfort, in colours that soothed rather than stimulated. The whole seemed designed to confirm one's taste and sense of "belonging." A place to settle the moneyed classes into long sessions at the tables, leaving behind the crass worries of daily life, international politics, and looming bankruptcy—and, to ease the nouveau-riche class into feeling they were moneyed. A quite brilliant piece of architectural psychology.

"Russell, stop gawping like a child at a shop window," Holmes murmured.

I suppose my pleasure was a bit blatant, so I tucked away my expression, replacing it with a sort of languid and approving curiosity.

I had little taste for gambling—money, that is, though one might say that my entire life has been a wager against chance—and few substantial skills when it came to cards. Of course, a woman may always act as a decorative accessory on a male arm, but unless I wished to hover at a distance while Holmes had all the fun, I needed to stick to games that demanded no more skill than laying gaming tokens onto the table.

So the roulette wheels it was. As with everything else under the Casino roof, the machines were perfect: gleaming mahogany, a polished bronze spindle at its centre, and an ivory ball that hopped crisply along the numbers until it chose one to nestle into. Simple, hypnotic, and—when combined with the Casino's discreet and free-flowing alcohol—potentially devastating to one's bank account.

Several of our table-mates had note-books in which they built or adapted their systems, jealously guarding their pages from nearby eyes. I, on the other hand, spent my first hour losing enough to see an undergraduate comfortably through Oxford, dismissing every loss and laughing happily at every win. Holmes came out slightly ahead of me, but at my next wager, with my last worn *jeton* before me on the table, I won. Then won again, and again after that. Seeing my pile grow before me, I experienced the first pang of the gambler's hunger. I did my best to lose it all, but by the end of the evening—we had planned on dinner at 9:00—I had nearly four times the counters I started with.

Weirdly fascinating. Utterly compulsive.

On one level, I was aware of being sucked in by the spin and drop—a seduction that had begun the moment I walked up the Casino steps—but that made it no less real. If anything, the challenge of resisting made the act that much more irresistible. The money didn't matter: the spurt of triumph at winning did. The entire world narrowed down to a small ivory ball and the blur of black and red, slowing to receive it.

At 9:30, Holmes finally laid a hand on my arm and more or less dragged me away. On the steps outside the Casino, the clean air was like a slap on the face. I may have even swayed a little. Some time later, I realised that Holmes' fingers were still wrapped around my upper arm.

"Well," I said. "That was . . . interesting."

"Is it not?"

"How much did I win?"

He told me—or I think he did. The sum meant nothing, although I could have recited precisely how often I had won, and with which numbers. As the flush faded from my skin, I noticed people walking past, the street-lamps in the little garden before me, the good clean odour of salt air. I pulled my wrap up around my shoulders, and shivered in the warm air.

"*Stop up your men's ears with wax, that none of them may hear,*" I murmured.

"Pardon?"

"Holmes, please don't ask me to do that again."

"Why not? You won handily."

"Exactly. I feel as if I'd washed down a pound of chocolate drops with a bottle of champagne."

He laughed. "You're hungry. Come."

"Where are you staying?" I hadn't thought to ask before, though I'd assumed it was in the hotel adjacent to the Casino. But when we had crossed the Casino forecourt, he led me past the Hôtel de Paris and down a side street to another, equally grand Belle Époque façade that bore the name Hôtel Hermitage. Being dressed already meant that we could go directly to its restaurant—one of its restaurants, I suspected—and fortify the inner woman.

My heart sank a bit when the wine steward came bustling over and greeted Holmes as a long-lost brother, a sign of impending lengthy discussion and negotiation. Fortunately, Holmes noticed my face five minutes into the recitation of virtues, and said that we'd have that, and the lady was ready to order.

We gave our orders, ate some bread, and I then returned to the topic that had bothered me since I'd taken that breath of fresh air. "Holmes, do not let me become a casino addict."

He raised an eyebrow. "Do you currently find yourself craving a return to the roulette wheel?"

"God, no."

"Then I do not think you need to worry. More wine?"

I was not convinced. Still, Holmes did have enough experience with addictive habits to recognise any such tendency in his wife. "If you say so. And no, I won't have any more, thanks. Though if I'm to face a taxi drive back along the coast, maybe I should drink myself unconscious."

The hovering wine steward nearly dropped the cobwebbed, dust-encrusted bottle he had exhumed from the depths. He could not have looked much more shocked had I expressed an interest in being served his bouncing baby son for my dinner. When he had refreshed our glasses, he placed the wine back into its nest, moving it a little further out of my reach before he wandered off, bereft.

Holmes waited until he was out of earshot before saying mildly, "As you like. Although when I checked in, I did mention that my wife might be joining me." Nothing about him suggested that it mattered one way or the other to him—nothing but the quiet humour in the back of his eyes that traced a feather-light finger all the way down my spine.

I cleared my throat. "Well. I should hate to disappoint the management."

"No doubt the hotel could find you a toothbrush. Along with any sort of clothing you might desire, from chain mail to chador."

"True. Money may not buy happiness, but a good hotel can smooth out any bumps in the road."

I did not fool him one whit. But then, neither did I believe his apparent lack of interest in my preference. A plate appeared. I took up my fork and knife. "Why choose the Hermitage?"

"It is a hotel that respects the privacy of its guests. Also, I deemed it marginally less likely that I would walk down a hallway and encounter someone who knew me."

I glanced around at the elaborate walls, the sparkling crystal and gilt overhead, the rich detail in the polished column. "Why? It seems a very nice place."

"It is. Merely not the first choice for an English visitor."

"Because of its Russian name?"

"Because of its Russian guests—historically, at any rate. Before 1917, the Hermitage was a favourite with the Romanovs and their friends. And you will have noticed the voices, even now."

I nodded as if I had been paying attention to the accents from the adjoining tables. "Would this be where the Russians I met last night are staying?"

"Your friend Vasilev himself has taken a house here, but the others, certainly. Including those who come to Monaco to do business with Basil Zaharoff."

I dropped my fork. "Zaharoff? The munitions dealer?"

"Basil Zaharoff—or more correctly, Vasileios Zacharias Zaharoff. Known as Sir Basil, although he has no more right to that title than any other he's claimed, including Count and Prince. 'Man of Mystery,' 'Merchant of Death,' 'The Richest Man in Europe.' His intimates, of whom there are a surprising number, call him Zedzed."

"Dear God, what is that man doing here?"

"He has wintered in Monte Carlo since the Casino was young, back in the 1880s. I understand that he and his new wife are here as often as they are in Paris."

"That can't be good for Monaco's reputation. Couldn't the country . . . I don't know. Disinvite him?" Basil Zaharoff was a Greek-born Russian who had become an agent for the Nordenfelt Guns company in the 1870s and built what was rumoured to be the third or fourth greatest personal fortune in the world. He was single-handedly responsible for some of the worst atrocities of the past half-century. Indeed, he had entered the vocabulary of wickedness with the eponymous *Système Zaharoff*, which functions thus: A political dispute is found that links emotional loyalties with economic competition. Hints and rumours are dropped on both sides, stirring the passions. Politicians are bribed and newspapers bought outright—again, on both sides of the dispute—to stoke the fears and resentments into open hatred and panic. Baseless rumours and accusations fly, wild campaigns on both sides escalate, riots take place, and finally war breaks out. At which point, both sides turn to Zaharoff to buy their competing armaments. The man was said to move the leaders of the world's nations around like his personal chess pieces—and if Sara Murphy knew he lived in Monaco, that would explain her preference for Juan-les-Pins.

"They can't disinvite him, no, although they do seem to expect him to keep up a respectable front while he's here. Zaharoff is now the primary owner of the Société des Bains de Mer, which owns half the businesses in Monaco. Including the Casino."

Revelations like this made me uncomfortably aware of how naïve I was, when it came to the world's dark currents. "Holmes, I know that small places like Monaco have to survive somehow, but—Zaharoff? It must feel like having a poisonous snake under the settee."

"They would tell you that compromises are necessary."

The conversation was coming perilously close to our arguments over the dirty deeds his brother Mycroft considered a necessary part of preserving Britain from its enemies. I wasn't about to resume that disagreement here and now. "Well, at least we didn't give him any of our money at the tables this evening." I reached for my cutlery, then hesitated. "Holmes, please tell me he doesn't own the Hermitage, too?"

"Oddly enough, no. Not yet, at any rate." My appetite had become less enthusiastic, but I took up my fork and knife, comforted by the minor reassurance that eating here would not contribute to a man who made his living through warmongering, blackmail, and wholesale battlefield slaughter.

"So, a Greek arms dealer essentially owns Monaco."

"The man owns companies, land, and politicians all over Europe."

"Have you had dealings with him?"

"Not directly, although we have met. Twice. The second time, I failed to notice his outstretched hand."

"Then let us hope he doesn't walk in before we've finished our dinner."

"The man is old, and I believe his colleagues go to him, when there is business to discuss."

"Good to hear." Refusing a man's proffered hand would have been a duelling offence, not so long ago. And so far as I knew, the man was only a decade or so older than Holmes: there could be plenty of venom left in the creature.

I pushed away all disquieting thoughts and addressed myself to my plate of excellent veal. When I had laid down my fork, the plate levitated off in one direction as my salad circled in from the other: Monaco's sleight of hand was not confined to its casino. However, with my hollow innards no longer taking up the major part of my attention, I could now turn to other matters.

"Holmes, do you honestly suspect Mrs Hudson of being up to no good?"

"No," he said.

The monosyllable was not quite as definitive as I might have liked. "No . . . but?"

He made a face. "Russell, I have known the woman since I was nineteen. Our years together began and ended with deaths—two deaths for which Clarissa Hudson was peripherally responsible. 'Peripherally,'" he repeated sharply. I subsided. "For four and a half decades, she lived under my roof and walked a path that *I* set for her. This spring, had you asked me, I'd have agreed that she had changed. And yet the moment her past came back to her, she stepped up to meet it with precisely the kind of behaviour that characterised her youthful criminal history."

"Holmes, I think you're being"—I caught back the word *paranoid*—"overly suspicious. But I know better than to try and talk you out of it, so I'll merely ask, what do you propose to do? Skulk around and see who she's meeting with? Because I can tell you, among her acquaintances are the most harmless Americans one can imagine."

I paused, waiting for him to reveal that he knew all the details of my two days on French soil, but miraculously enough, it appeared that he had not been watching from the nearby trees or an anchored fishing boat. So I described for him the American colony of artists, writers, and hangers-on I had found in Antibes—and, the unexpected appearance of our Mrs Hudson.

"She is providing entertainment for a group of *children?*" One eyebrow went up at this dubious picture.

"So? How much of her life did she spend organising the Irregulars? To say nothing of an endless series of ill-trained scullery maids. If there were such a degree as Children's Psychology, Mrs Hudson would be given a DPhil without having to sit an exam. Who better to figure out a means of enticing rich young parents to spend their time and money here in the Principality?"

"Rather like your friend Miss Maxwell is doing in Venice."

"Exactly. But that does not answer my question of what you intend to do. You've been here for three days. Have you caught any faint scent of wrongdoing in her vicinity?"

His hand shifted the silver cigarette case an inch or two along the table. "I have not."

"During which time I imagine you've used all the tricks in your basket, from disguising yourself as a street-corner layabout to drinking in pubs with any person you've seen her come into contact with."

"Not all of my 'tricks.'"

"Just most of them. Holmes, I know this will be a radical proposal, but maybe you and I should just go and talk with her? In any event, she's seen me now. She's sure to assume you're here, too."

He nodded, less in agreement than an agreement to think about it. He held his table napkin to his moustache and laid it down definitively beside his plate. When his eyes met mine, I realised—vaguely, in an unoccupied corner of my mind—what it was that drove people to gamble.

"Are you finished?" he asked.

"Yes," I said. "Oh, most certainly yes."

CHAPTER FOURTEEN

I n the morning, faced by an empty wardrobe, I phoned down to
the front desk. As Holmes had suggested, the Hermitage was
an establishment well accustomed to the varied needs of wealthy
guests. The neat French lady's maid who appeared at our door five
minutes later noted down my measurements and my requests—
not too short, not too extreme, and conservative about the chest
and shoulders—with neither shake of the head nor moue of distaste. Twenty minutes later, I was picking through an assortment
of remarkably fashionable garments that more or less fit me. Ten
minutes after that, Holmes and I set off for a pre-breakfast stroll
along the yacht-sprinkled Port Hercule.

There seemed to be more masts than the previous afternoon.
Was this week-end traffic, or did yacht owners prefer beds to
bunks, and spend only their daylight hours out at sea? Perhaps
they had all spent Friday night in the Casino? In any event, the
occasional waft of coffee and bacon showed that the residents were
rising. The sea-plane was still there, its wind screen shaded against
the Mediterranean sun. Closer in, two grease-stained men discussed an engine whose parts were spread across an impressively

large area. Out nearer the breakwater, two sailors walked up the ladders at the top of the *Bella Ragazza* and vanished into the deck house.

"Do you suppose that big yacht belongs to the Prince?" I wondered.

He shook his head. "The last Prince was an ardent marine explorer, but not the present one. That ship does resemble the *Hirondelle,* but it is far too new."

We had reached the far end of the harbour, where the breakwater stretched out to protect all these rich-men's playthings. A bench there invited contemplation, so we sat.

"One can hope the *Bella Ragazza* isn't owned by some competing member of the royalty. It would be rather hard to avoid seeing, from half the windows in the Palace."

In fact, Monaco's royal family was probably relatively secure, being among Europe's oldest. Its coat of arms commemorated the 1297 seizure of power, when a nobleman of the Grimaldi house led a group of disguised soldiers, swords hidden beneath Franciscan robes, through the gates of the mountain-top castle. That particular Grimaldi was tossed out a few years later, and a cousin-turned-stepson (the royalty of Europe is ever complex) became the head of the Grimaldi line—although actual ownership of Monaco was not established for some 120 years, when one of the three princes who took turns with the crown (cf.: complex) simply purchased the country outright. Even then, tussles continued.

Monaco had no resources other than its setting—once strategic, now merely scenic. Most of its princes chose to live in Paris. Two external bits of agricultural land had been lost in the mid-nineteenth century, leaving behind a Prince, a church, a mouldering palace, and a few hundred Monégasque fishermen and olive farmers.

The House of Grimaldi clung to its Rock through determination, trickery, open battle, financial shrewdness, and—most intriguing—its willingness to let a woman take over whenever the line lacked sons, or had a ruler behind bars or distracted by the lights of Paris.

Strong and imaginative women had been the saving of the Principality. In the last century, the ineffectual and impoverished Prince Florestan, a man much taken with the theatre, married an actress named Maria Caroline Gibert de Lametz—then promptly hurried back to Paris. Princess Caroline, on the other hand, took one look at the bald, rocky Principality at the foot of the Palace, and decided it would make a fine personal stage.

She sent a man to the German spas for a report on what made for a successful watering place. Next, she had Florestan legalise gambling in Monaco—a country surrounded by lands where cards, dice, and the wheel were forbidden. She found a willing partner in François Blanc—scam artist, double-dealer, and showman extraordinaire. They set up the wholesome-sounding Société des Bains de Mer—or more grandly, Société Anonyme des Bains de Mer et du Cercle des Étrangers du Monaco: SBM for short—and tucked the Casino in behind it. The years that followed saw a sequence of elaborate and thinly-propped swindles that nearly collapsed any number of times, and yet, against all rational expectations, the SBM and its Casino—along with the baths that gave it all a face of healthy respectability—not only survived, but thrived.

Ten years after Caroline's death, another woman took up the challenge, this time an American named Alice. The prince she married was interested, not in theatre, but in oceanography, so while he was off at sea, she brought in culture, from opera companies to Serge Diaghilev's Ballets Russes. Caroline and Alice between them dragged their adopted country out of penury and into the modern era, providing an object lesson in how big an edifice could be built atop the shakiest of foundations. Walking back along the harbour towards our somewhat delayed morning eggs, I told Holmes what I had read about Monaco, particularly the striking role of women in this unlikely place.

He nodded. "One does wonder what the world would look like if all its countries were given over to the women to run for a time."

"Good heavens, Holmes—we'll make a feminist of you yet."

"A person need not wear a label to see the sense in a thing."

Sherlock Holmes was often accused of misogyny, but I'd found his scorn equally divided between the sexes. If anything, my Victorian-era husband tended to regard women as having the greater (if more often thwarted) potential.

"Have you come across the current Princess?" I asked.

"Charlotte? I have not met her, although one tends to see her here and there."

"Do you know anything about her? Some people at the Murphys' party made her sound like another Princess Caroline. It got me to wondering what she was like."

"She is the heir presumptive—the Prince's actual daughter, though born out of wedlock and later officially adopted during the War. France insisted on it," he explained, "since the next in line was a German." (As I said: complicated.) "The Prince mostly leaves Monaco to her—and her husband, although he seems a bit of a ne'er do well. The two of them are particularly interested in the arts, and wish to establish Monaco as a cultural centre. A sort of Paris on the Riviera, as it were."

"Caroline brought the Casino, and Alice the Ballets Russes— and if Princess Charlotte has a vision for Monaco that reaches beyond the gambling rooms, that could be good news for Mrs Hudson. I don't imagine her savings will take her far without some kind of a second career."

"Mrs Hudson has many hidden talents," he said, which I decided to take as an agreement.

All in all, I was feeling more sanguine about our landlady's future in this unlikely place. Perhaps on our way through the Hermitage's Eiffel-glass lobby, I would pause to chat with the desk man, about how to locate an old friend. He might be of more willing help to a young woman than he had been to a grey-haired foreign gentleman. In any event, given the size of Monaco, how many elderly Englishwomen named Hudson could there be?

"And not only the Ballets Russes," I remembered, "but racing events as well. Terry and Gerald Murphy were talking about a Rally that takes place in the winter season. Also something about sea-planes. Or was it flying boats? Is there a difference?"

"Flying boats are winged boats, landing on their bellies. Sea-planes are aeroplanes with pontoons—such as that one."

The object in question had shifted slightly and was now catching the sun, its white paint polished to brilliance.

"Handsome thing," I commented. So long as one was not required to ride on it.

After a moment, I let my shoulder lean slightly, to press into his. "I've missed you, Holmes."

He glanced down at me, surprised. I smiled. "Though you'd have murdered someone if you'd come sailing with us. Where have you been, these past weeks?"

"I told you, I went to Roumania."

"Ah, I thought that might be some kind of whimsy. What's in Roumania?"

"Yet another interesting woman," he said. "One with an intriguing problem."

"Should I be jealous?"

"You should be interested. It isn't every day one encounters a problem to do with vampires."

I drew back, and had opened my mouth to demand an explanation, when we were interrupted by a familiar voice.

"Why, if it isn't Sailor Mary—and heavens me, her husband! Well met, the both of you."

The Hon Terry leapt up from the bench he'd been sitting on and came to shake Holmes' hand, with enthusiasm and the name Russell that Holmes used in Venice. He then more or less dragged us over to the seat for introductions. "You both know Luca, I think—

and this is Johnny Perez, a friend of Patrice's, lives here in Monaco, if you can believe it. Johnny, this is Mary Russell and her husband. Mary came with me on the *Stella Maris*. Mr Russell is a musician. Johnny lives here, at the Sun Palace—and did you see that 'plane down on the water, the white one? That's his! He gives people rides and sprinkles adverts over the beaches on Nice and Cannes. Isn't that a marvellous way to make a living? Here, sit down, do."

"No, Terry, we're headed back to our breakfast. But what are you doing over here? I thought you were staying on the Cap?"

"Johnny showed up last night, invited us to go up with him— one at a time, naturally, the thing's a two-seater. So we popped up on the first train."

"You were certainly up early!"

"We never actually made it to bed. Patrice is coming along in a bit, to see a man about a boat. Might have a chance at skiing, later in the week."

I laughed. "Terry, I've had enough of skis for one summer, thanks. You have a fun day, gentlemen."

"Oh, Mary, I say—did you hear about that jolly nanny person of Sara and Gerald's?"

"The girl? Mademoiselle Geron, I think Sara called—"

"No, the older one. Miss Hudson."

Silent fingers closed over the sea-front. I made a sort of creaking noise, since I couldn't seem to shape actual words, but fortunately he took that as a request to continue.

"Seems she's been arrested." I felt Holmes go rigid.

"Arrested?"

"I know, butter wouldn't melt, wouldn't you have said? But seems the old cat has some life in her, 'cause they found a fancy man at her feet and a gun in her hand."

"Mur . . ." I could not pronounce the word.

"Murder, right. I say, Mary, are you feeling quite well? You've gone a decidedly odd shade. Maybe you—"

I sat down, hard.

CHAPTER FIFTEEN

"Do you want to remain 'Mr Sheldon Russell,'" I asked Holmes, "or is it time to throw your true name about?"

The horse taxi—Monaco did have a few, so as to save visitors from arriving at a hilltop destination winded and sopping—had clopped its way up The Rock to the Medieval buildings that were the oldest section of the Principality. We very nearly got out and pushed the creature up some of the steeper bits.

"Let us see how far we get without it," he replied.

I nodded in agreement, and launched up the ornate staircase of the Palais de Justice.

The desk man at the Hermitage had given us little more information about this purported murder than Terry had, in the form of a French newspaper with a brief paragraph to say that an elderly English woman, who had recently come to the Principality, had been arrested for shooting a young Frenchman in her Monte Carlo apartment.

Some rapid questioning and telephone calls had modified the report: she was not a tourist, but a resident; her dwelling was not an apartment but a house—and not in Monte Carlo, but in the upper reaches of La Condamine. And the dead man may not have been French.

Mere quibbles, all of those, against the hard fact that he had been found, dead, on her floor.

A bare ten minutes after climbing the ornate Palais de Justice stairway, we came down again, armed with a note and a feeling of anti-climax. Not only had we not been required to conjure up authority with the mighty name of Sherlock Holmes, no one even objected to our questions. Indeed, the Monégasque equivalent of a desk sergeant had gone so far as to sketch a crude map to the gaol on the back of our visitor's permission note.

I'd been surprised to find that Monaco had a gaol, rather than just a locked room at the back of the police station. The sergeant did admit that it was used mostly for prisoners on remand. Once found guilty, they were shipped off to France to serve out their terms.

Despite the map, it took some time to locate the prison entrance. We'd been told it lay between a pleasure garden and the grand Oceanographic Museum, but we were quartering the park in search of something resembling a gate when a flustered young man in a bizarre costume burst out from a hole in the wall. His lower half wore every-day tweed, but his torso sported a confection of scarlet, white, and gold, tailored for a larger man, that looked like a costume from a regimental museum. His arms were wrapped around a combination of file-folders and a hat with an elderly ostrich-feather plume.

We watched this vision scurry by. I said to Holmes, "It's a little early in the day for a fancy-dress party. Was that Alice's white rabbit, or an official in court uniform?"

"If so, there should have been a sword as well. Where the devil did he come from?"

We tracked the door down. The man who answered our ring gave the clear impression that he had hastily put on his coat and snugged up his necktie.

"*Oui?*" he snapped impatiently.

Holmes addressed him in flawless Parisian French, telling him that we wished to see a prisoner, and holding out the note the desk sergeant had given us.

The guard didn't bother looking at it, although he did draw himself up a bit and replied with a trace more deference. However, what he said was that the lady would not see us.

Holmes told him to ask her.

The guard replied that she hadn't been willing to see the English Monsieur from the vice-consulate just now, so why should she want to see us?

She may care to see her friends the "Russells" instead, Holmes told him firmly.

The man threw up his hands and slammed the door. I glanced at Holmes. "Was that a gesture of 'Oh for pity's sake, go away I'm eating my lunch,' or was it 'Oh if you insist, I'll go ask her then come back and tell you no'?"

"Let us assume the latter," he replied. While we waited to find out, we located a shaded seat. He lit a cigarette. I watched the boats heading towards the harbour. Just as my patience was about to run out, the door opened.

The guard looked considerably tidier and much chastened. When he ushered us into the interview room, I could see the cause: he would not meet Mrs Hudson's eyes. Her expression was one I had seen her turn on a careless house-maid.

The guard silently closed the door.

Mrs Hudson—that bobbed hair!—was standing behind the chair on the prisoner's side of an ancient wooden table. "Hello, Mr Holmes. I hadn't expected to see you quite this soon. And Mary, I should have said the other day how well you're looking. You've gone very brown."

"You too," I said. "But—oh, hello, Mrs Hudson! I was so happy to see you!" Impulsively, I circled the table and threw my arms around her. She gingerly returned the embrace, giving my shoulder a reassuring pat as she pulled away.

"You shouldn't have come here—a dreary place on a lovely day. I hope you've been enjoying the Murphy family? Such delightful people. Do sit down."

I could only stand and gape. She was talking as if this bald and unsavoury cell was her sitting room and we were visitors collecting jumble for the church sale. This was taking English phlegm to an extreme.

Fortunately, Holmes knew how to sweep aside nuance. "You know why we're here."

"I trust you did not imagine I killed that poor boy."

She was addressing Holmes, but I was the one to reply. "Of course not! But what on earth happened?"

She merely waited, calmly meeting the eyes of her long-time employer.

Who did not issue any blanket reassurance as to his own faith in her innocence. He pulled out a rickety chair and sat down. I took the one beside him. When she was also seated, he barked out a command.

"Tell us what you know."

"Why?"

Holmes bounced off that placid monosyllable as if it were a glass wall across a pathway. I imagine my face wore the same startled expression. An old woman in a stone cell—surely she'd be abjectly grateful for any friendly face, any faint promise of help?

Apparently not.

We both sat back, literally, to study the person across the table from us. The dress she wore showed no sign of having been slept in. Her new hair style was similarly neat, her nail varnish intact, her lips tinted with the same lipstick I'd seen on the beach the other day—though her face, bare of makeup, betrayed every one of her near-seventy years.

Nonetheless, she also looked as indomitable, and unflappable, as ever.

"What do you mean, 'why'? Holmes demanded. "Are you perhaps *enjoying* this time behind bars?"

"Prison appears to be my fate, either here or in England. I imagine the food here is better than Holloway. And my cell does have a magnificent view. They seem to have put me in an office, rather than in the usual bowels of the place."

The two of them locked gazes across the splintered table-top, glowering on one side and seemingly indifferent on the other. I was just thinking that I wanted the trick to her composure when I felt Holmes shift—and before he could rise and stalk out, I blurted the first thing that came to mind.

"Doesn't the boy's death deserve an investigation?"

Only then did it come to me that her phrase—"that poor boy"—had been more than an impersonal category. She knew the victim, and felt some affection, or responsibility, or both, for his welfare. She'd inadvertently handed me the way to prise her open.

Her impervious look took on a tinge of remonstration—*et tu, Brute?*—but I did not retract the question. Holmes remained seated. After a moment, she sighed.

"You're right, Mary. I am of limited good inside this place, and the lad deserves better. But first, what are you two doing here? Mary, I understand—you and your friend passing through on a sailing yacht from Venice—but you, Mr Holmes? You don't appear to have spent the past weeks under the sun going a fashionable brown, but this only happened yesterday. Or did you come here because your brother reported that I was seeing the wrong sorts of people?"

"Were you?"

"Oh for heaven's sake, Monaco is the size of Hyde Park with half the population of Eastbourne. A person can't help coming into contact with everyone from trash-man to prince, merely walking down the street."

Her reply was the merest fraction too pat, her face a little too smooth: there was a lie there somewhere. But then, why not? Our very presence here intruded on her privacy. I could not blame her for resisting where she could.

Besides which, I had to ask: "Is she right, Holmes? Have you had Mycroft spying on her?"

"I have not."

I was going to press him—just because Holmes did not ask his spymaster brother to watch her didn't mean Mycroft wasn't doing just that—but he cut me off.

"Mrs Hudson, kindly proceed, as succinctly as possible. Visiting times may be lim—"

The door behind us clattered open. We turned to see the guard negotiate the doorway bearing the French version of a tea-tray, with three cups, a small coffee pot, and a jug of heated milk. But I noticed the colour of the liquid coming from the spout, then the absence of aroma, and a wary sip confirmed my suspicions: not good French coffee, but an attempt at tea, using old leaves, under-boiled water, and a pot that had not been scrubbed after it last bore coffee.

Mrs Hudson, proud wielder of teapots and baking trays, looked askance at the offering. So much for her claims of the prison's superior kitchen.

"They may need some time to learn the subtleties of English tea," she admitted, and apologetically nudged the hot milk in my direction.

All three of us added a lot of sugar and milk, stirred hopefully, and took sips. Then all three of us set our cups back on the tray.

Still, the interruption did indicate both that Mrs Hudson would not suffer from neglect while she was here, and that our visit would not be cut short by her gaoler's petty authority.

Mrs Hudson cleared her throat, then resumed.

CHAPTER SIXTEEN

"I have been coming to Monte Carlo since 1877," Mrs Hudson said. "It was the Christmas season, I was twenty-one, and the place was magical.

"As both of you know, my father and I . . . lived by means that were not entirely above board. And I will admit, our weeks here were lucrative. However, that was the only time he and I came, since the following year I was busy elsewhere, and then I had a child and . . . well, you know the story after that.

"I have come back several times over the years, but each of those was an actual holiday, with my only transgressions the small sins any person would indulge in around a Casino table. I may have presented myself as someone other than a housekeeper. As I may have permitted you to think I was visiting family in Australia, or my friend Ivy, when in fact I was here. With other friends.

"I enjoy Monaco, and not just for the Casino. After so many English winters, I relish the warmth and the gardens, to say nothing of the setting—why, even those who live in cliff-side hovels may have a millionaire's view. And I find the community here invigorating: the excitement of risking all seems to permeate the very air, even for those who never set foot inside the Casino itself.

"When I came here in May, I was not looking for a holiday, but a home. I used some of my savings to buy clothing as I passed through Paris, so that I didn't step down from the train looking like a housekeeper. My friend here introduced me to her friends, one of whom had a small house I liked and could afford. I established myself at the local bank, with an eye to building my claim to a year's residency, after which any income—including the pension you so kindly arranged for me—would be free of taxation.

"Still, Monaco is not an easy place to live on a limited budget. I knew I would need a source of income. Nothing," she said firmly, "against the law. This place has learned a great deal about catching criminals since the 1870s. If I wanted to live here, I needed to stay absolutely above the board."

She cast an oddly demure look down at her hands. "Nonetheless, even legitimacy can open some interesting doors. And being a tiny place, Monaco brings one into some interesting circles. Occasionally those provide opportunities for a future."

Holmes was radiating impatience. She picked up the pace. "I met Niko through my old friend. Whose name, before you ask, I will not give you. She doesn't need you at her door asking impertinent—"

"Wait," I interrupted. "You said Niko?"

"Yes, Niko Cassavetes."

"You mean—wasn't he that beautiful young man who came to the beach the other day? Oh dear. Is that who died?"

"You didn't know?"

That animated Hellenistic sculpture with the green eyes. "No. We only heard the vaguest of news this morning, and the newspaper thought he was French. Then at the police station, we thought it simpler to stick to the main point. Which was finding you."

"I see. Yes, his name is—his name was Niko Cassavetes, and

although he didn't look particularly Greek, with those eyes, I did hear him talking to one of Gerald Murphy's friends about the fighting in Thessaloniki."

Wait—had this "boy" been a child soldier? The figure on the beach could have been too far away to reveal his age. "How old was he?"

"In his early thirties, I should say. Small, though, and with delicate features. I suppose one thought of him as younger."

I revised my picture of "that poor boy" up a decade or two, and nodded for her to continue.

"He's a—he *was*—a handsome lad. And clever. A good ear for languages, which was more or less how he made a living. As I understand it, he turned up in Monaco three or four years ago, a sailor left ashore after an injury. He scraped a living doing odd jobs until the expatriate community discovered his knack for tongues. Greek, and naturally French, but also Russian, Italian, something that might have been Turkish, and a bit of German. His English was basic but clear, with a charming accent. He could drive a motorcar, and had lovely manners. Word got around, and people hired him as a valet, a secretary, a local guide—anything, really—especially during the busy winter season.

"He was not, let me be clear, a gigolo. Some assumed he was, and I imagine he could have done quite well for himself, had he decided to branch out." Before I could decide how I felt about Mrs Hudson talking so easily about male escorts, she went on. "And so far as I know, he was no confidence-trickster. He was . . . not overly concerned about legality, and no doubt he accepted gifts of cash or nice clothing, but I never heard of him actively stealing anything."

"He was a pet," Holmes said.

"A useful one. He knew everyone—I met him my first week here. And Niko was the reason I was on the Murphys' beach the other day.

"As you know, between the heat and the mosquitos, summer is not an attractive time on the Riviera. Most winter residents close up their houses in May, which leaves year-round workers with sparse income. However, in recent years, a number of hotels and cafés along the coast have seen a trickle of visitors, particularly Americans, who find an appeal in baking themselves to a crisp on sweltering beaches. And, when the sun goes down, in drinking and making mischief. This year, the trend has become startlingly obvious—and these people are not here because they can't afford the Riviera in winter.

"Niko first encountered the Murphys and their . . . 'set' I suppose one would call it, two years ago. No doubt he found their taste in off-season holidays a boon to his bank account. And they were happy to pay for his assistance in all sorts of things, from finding a house to hiring a boat to tracking down a favourite kind of sketching pad. If one wants Bastille Day fireworks or a metal foundry for an artist's bronze sculptures, Niko is your man. Although I cannot imagine the heat of a foundry in August."

"That sculptor would be Rafe Ainsley?"

"None other." *Was that a faint air of disapproval?*

"Bit of an upstart," I commented.

"I understand that he is a respected artist of the modern sort."

"There was a Russian count talking to him at the Murphys' party the other night. Sara said he has commissioned some pieces. They were an odd pair, but thick as thieves."

"Count Vasilev." *Or was it distaste?*

"If you dislike these men, why consort with them?" Holmes said.

"Because they are people who pay generously for help in smoothing their time here, whether by locating a yacht or entertaining children. A kind of smoothing, I might note, that I spent much of my life doing for you."

I felt like cheering at this sign of tart resistance—and I must have betrayed some small reaction, because she shot me a quick glance before returning to Holmes. "At any rate, Niko introduced me to the Murphys in early June, as they were preparing to leave for Venice. We had a most interesting conversation on their lovely terrace, and two weeks later, I had the basis for a proposal to the Société des Bains de Mer—you know who they are?"

"We do."

"The SBM have begun to worry about the decreasing popularity of Monte Carlo with the younger generation. The Casino has always strived for an air of dignity and exclusivity, and the Jazz Age threatens to leave it behind. After I met the Murphys and their friends—people who struck me as representative of the modern age—I came up with some ideas on how that might be avoided. How the SBM might regain a sense of wholesomeness and fresh air while preserving the piquant fun."

"Ideas for whom?"

"The directors of the SBM in general, and the Princess Charlotte in particular."

This caught Holmes' attention. "You have met her?"

"I did point out the intimacy of the community here, did I not? Yes, we were introduced by a friend."

"The same nameless one?"

The grey head nodded. "They agreed to my shaping a more detailed proposal, which could lead to a contractual agreement. Until . . . this." Her gaze swept the dingy room, ending up on the milk-scummed liquid in the cups before her.

"And young Monsieur Cassavetes. How did he come to die in your front room?"

She winced. "Poor Niko. And poor Madame Crovetti, who will be faced with scrubbing the floor-boards. That's my landlady. Although I fear that after this, she will have my things taken down to the street. At the least, I shall need to write her a substantial cheque."

"Mrs Hudson," Holmes warned.

"I don't *know* how Niko came to die in my house. I was not at home. I was there earlier—I even saw him, briefly, when he knocked on the door—but I had an engagement so I told him I would see him in the morning."

"What time was this?"

"Three, half-past, maybe? Around then. He spotted me coming home and wanted to talk, but I needed to bathe and dress so I told him it would have to be in the morning." She gave us a sad smile. "One more regret to add to a life."

"How did he happen to see you coming home? Was he waiting for you?"

"Not necessarily. Niko lived next door to me."

"I see. Was Madame Crovetti his landlady, as well?"

"That was how I met her. My friend here introduced me to Niko, who told me that his landlady was looking for someone quiet to rent a small house."

"And you left for your . . . appointment when?"

"A few minutes after four."

"What time did you return home?"

"After eleven. I hadn't planned on staying out for dinner, but my friend urged me, and it being informal and in a private home, what I was wearing did not matter. We dined, the others left, I had a last drink, and walked home. When I turned on the light . . . there he was."

"Who is your solicitor?"

"My—oh. Well, let us see if I'm still here tomorrow. Perhaps I shan't need one."

Holmes did not grace that with a reply. "And the policeman who is assigned your case. Do you know his name?"

"The man I spoke with last night was named Jourdain. A grim sort of individual, but he seemed thorough."

The little window in the door behind us slid back on its tracks, as it had done twice before. This time, Mrs Hudson gave a small wave of the hand. "I believe my gaolers may be attempting to deliver luncheon."

"Well, we mustn't delay that," Holmes snapped. I realised abruptly that I was exhausted. Holmes, too, seemed to be fraying a bit. And yet, the prisoner—a sixty-nine-year-old woman who had discovered a dead friend, been arrested, spent the night in prison, and been interrogated first by the police and then by Sherlock Holmes—sat as straight-backed and self-possessed as ever.

Holmes shoved back his chair, which cracked but did not completely fall to pieces. "We will either return or send a message, when we have news."

She rose, too. "I would appreciate that. Niko really was a lovely young man. I . . . I hope I am out of here in time for his funeral." For the first time that morning, she showed signs of distress.

"I shouldn't count on it," Holmes said flatly, and turned to the door.

I stopped to give Mrs Hudson another quick hug, then hurried after him, not catching up until he was across the public gardens.

"Holmes, you didn't have to be so brutal. You can tell she's mourning her friend."

"Even if she was the one to shoot him?"

"You don't believe that." When he did not answer, I grabbed his sleeve and forced him to stop. "You cannot believe Mrs Hudson killed that young man."

He raised his head to study the blue horizon, then at last let out a breath. "I do not see why she would. But I have been blind to that woman in the past. I will not trust my instincts now. Nor yours."

I could see there was little point in argument. Even less point in asking if we planned on investigating. "Where do you suggest we begin?"

"The police," he said. "I need to see how much of a mess they've made of it so far."

CHAPTER SEVENTEEN

We retraced our steps to the Palais de Justice, and then to the local police station down in the town, but at neither of them did we find Inspector Jourdain. However, we did locate the foot-patrol officer who had been first on the scene: a squat, swarthy man in his fifties with suspiciously black hair beneath his cap. His French had a faint Italian accent, which I would learn was that of the native Monégasque.

To my surprise, he did not hesitate to tell us where Mrs Hudson lived, and seemed willing to answer our questions, so long as we let him continue his patrol of the narrow streets. With Holmes beside him and me on their heels, he confirmed that the young man, having been found on the floor of Madame Hudson's house, had been shot in the chest.

"Was the gun found?"

"It was not."

"Who notified the police?"

"The lady herself, from her landlady's telephone."

"What time would that have been?"

"Well before midnight. Eleven twenty, perhaps?"

"Who was in the house when you got there?"

"Just the English lady. Some of the neighbours stood outside, but she had not let them in, not even Madame Crovetti, who owns the houses. Indeed, she only permitted me inside enough to see the body, and then demanded that I stay back until *l'inspecteur* arrived. A most decisive lady, Madame 'Udson." I thought that "Madame" here was less an indication of married status than it was the honorific for a lady too old to be addressed as Miss.

"You know her, then?"

"I know everyone in my area. She came in June. We have spoken from time to time."

"What was she wearing that night?"

"Wearing? Her clothes, Monsieur. A dress. Blue perhaps, or green? Flowers along the . . ." His fingers sketched the line of his collarbone.

"Were there bloodstains on the dress?"

"No, Monsieur. Except—yes, along the bottom."

"The hem?"

"There, yes. It had rubbed upon her, you know. Stockings." He was embarrassed at having to refer to a woman's legs.

"She was not wearing that dress when we saw her, just now."

"No, Monsieur. We permitted her to take a valise."

How civilised. And potentially foolish.

"What about the blood in the house?"

"*Oof*—there was a lot!"

"Splattered, or in a pool?"

The sideways look he gave Holmes was his first sign of puzzlement. His reply was slow in coming. "There was a pool of it, Monsieur. Around his chest where he lay."

"What kind of floor? Carpet? Wood? Tile?"

"Boards. Well polished."

"How dry were the edges of the pool?"

At that, our informant stopped dead, to look back and forth

between us. "Monsieur, Madame: what is your interest in this matter?"

I spoke up first. "The lady is a friend. If it happens that the victim was shot long before she arrived home, and if it happens that we can determine that she was elsewhere, your *inspecteur* should know, before the true killer slips out of Monaco."

"*L'inspecteur* is a good man."

"We are not questioning that. And if the blood was very fresh, or if someone heard the gunshot *after* she returned home, we will stand away." A lie, but this fellow wouldn't know that. He also wouldn't know that all this talk about pools of blood was making me distinctly queasy. It was not all that many weeks since I'd dragged a man from a pool of blood myself.

"What colour was it?" Holmes asked.

"The blood? It was red."

"So dark red it seemed black, or turning to scarlet?"

"It was clearly red—though Monsieur, the light in the room, it was not bright."

"I understand."

"But half an hour later, when I helped to turn him over, the pool's edges were going dry."

Holmes stared at him, as if a dog had fetched back a treatise on spheroid objects instead of a ball. "Good man!" he said after a moment. "How dry?"

"Only the edges."

"But visibly so? Noticeable from standing distance, that is, rather than kneeling on the floor?"

"Monsieur, *I* noticed it. Once the covers were taken from the lamps so we could see, that is. But then, I was in the War. I spent many hours watching blood dry."

I was impressed. Not every copper would be so observant, or would understand why this lunatic series of questions mattered. Not all of us had co-authored a monograph on the drying times of blood under various conditions and on a variety of surfaces.

"Were photographs taken?"

"Some."

"And your Inspector Jourdain: did he notice the edges as well?"

He gave that French noncommittal dip of the head. "*L'inspecteur* has excellent eyes, Monsieur."

We could but hope.

By now we were standing before one of those clusters of dwellings that are found on the outskirts of any wealthy neighbourhood, a place where the better servants live. In Monaco, those would probably be croupiers, shop-keepers, and low-level bureaucrats, while the actual sons and daughters of toil rode the train in from France every morning. Even the wealthiest of towns had odd and uncomfortable corners where, until some enterprising soul decided to flatten their homes for a block of luxury flats, the middle working-class citizens would stay quietly, stubbornly on.

In other words, in no way hovels. The residents might spend their days at work rather than at play, but they were not the people who scrubbed toilets or gutted fish.

Our constabulary guide had stopped on the road before just such a backwater. It was up at the edges of La Condamine, a diminutive cul-de-sac among the sort of cliffs that had made Monaco both impregnable and largely unbuildable over the centuries. The lane was essentially a wide spot some fifty yards deep. The brief terrace of three conjoined buildings seemed to press against the cliff at the back. The first unit, nearest the actual road, looked like a warehouse converted to flats—two storeys tall, but its windows were all in the lower half, and a large, bricked-in rectangle surrounded the present small doorway.

The house at the far end was an actual house, with windows on both storeys.

Jammed in between the two was a smaller dwelling that had been scrubbed, painted, and tidied to within an inch of its life. Large earthenware pots on either side of its steps held bright flowers pinched into matching cascades of colour. The shutters were closed tight. The door had been fitted with a small brass viewing grille at Mrs Hudson's height, over which a note was tacked: *Entrée interdite.* The card bore the insignia of the Monaco police.

"Mrs Hudson won't be pleased with that hole in her fresh paint," I said, in English.

"Assuming she comes home to see it," my pessimistic husband pointed out, before continuing in French. "Is it permitted to enter?"

"*Désolé,* but *l'inspecteur* will need to approve that."

"But of course. Is there any more that you can tell us about our lady friend?"

"Only that she always seemed friendly and of good cheer. I hope—Monsieur, Madame—that you are correct and that your friend is set free soon."

We thanked him, shook his hand, and strolled off down the busy adjoining road . . . then two minutes later reversed our steps to the innermost dwelling, whose front-room curtains had twitched while we were on the lane outside.

We knocked. After a pause to establish that she had definitely not been watching us out of her window, the door came open.

She was a small, dark, bright-eyed woman of around fifty, with strong hands and a straight back. A shop-keeper, I thought—if not the shop's owner. And one of the better establishments, to go by her neatness and pride.

"Madame . . . Crovetti?" Holmes began in French, with the air of a person who might at any moment bend down to kiss her hand.

"Yes?"

"We are friends of the lady who lives in the house next door. Your tenant, I believe?"

"Yes."

"You are aware that the lady has been arrested?"

"Yes."

"I hope you do not imagine that she could have done such a thing." He managed to sound remarkably sincere.

She was not impressed. One shoulder came up, then dropped: a shrug.

Before Holmes could launch into a false protest of Mrs Hudson's angelic person, I slid my own question in.

"The police haven't let you in yet, have they? To clean."

The flash of her dark eyes showed I'd hit the true problem. "The boards, they shall need to be sanded and finished afresh. Very expensive."

"If Madame Hudson doesn't pay for it, I will."

Her expression turned thoughtful. After a bit, she gave a small nod. "As tenants go, she has been most respectable. Until this."

"It was not fair to you—or to her," I said.

A definite softening.

"Did you know the young man who died?"

She raised her eyes to study the lane outside, then with a sigh drew open the door. "Come."

CHAPTER EIGHTEEN

I t being well into the afternoon, Madame Crovetti gave us wine rather than coffee. After a brief hesitation, she brought over a bowl of almonds with an old silver nutcracker sticking out of the top, and we launched into an amiable if untidy conversation.

The reply to Holmes' question was yes, she knew Niko Cassavetes. He'd been a friend of her son, and for nearly two years had been letting a room in the warehouse building at the end of her little terrace block. She was sad to hear of his death.

"What was he like?" I asked.

"Very beautiful."

"I agree—but as a person?"

Her expression was fond and the phrase she used would, I thought, translate into "plausible rogue"—a likeable sort, but with some shady associates.

"So," Holmes suggested, his attention, to all appearances, on the almond he'd placed between the nutcracker's jaws, "you may not have been completely surprised at the manner of his death."

"The manner? Yes—and yet not entirely, no. But the place? I knew Madame 'Udson was using him for a few tasks, but so do we

all. Niko has been the odd-job man hereabouts, for some time."
Her phrase was *homme à tout faire*—but not, it transpired, for jobs
related to leaking pipes or uneven doors. "I thought it would be to
do with driving, or an introduction to some of his friends in the
artistic community. But that she would have to do with *guns*." Her
distaste was strong, as it had not been at the idea of minor criminality. Interesting.

"How did Madame Hudson come to hire rooms from you?"

"Niko learned that an English lady was searching for a house,
and gave her my telephone number. I was happy enough to have
her. It is too quiet here, without neighbours."

"But didn't you say that Niko lived here, down at the end?"

"Yes, and my son as well. But Matteo is away, for a time, and
Niko is—Niko *was*—a young man with a busy life, often keeping
him away at night. It is a comfort to have another person nearby,
in the evenings."

I could well believe that: the nearest street-lamp was on the
main road, and walking down the cul-de-sac in the dark would be
eerie. "Madame, do you know where Madame Hudson was yesterday afternoon?"

"I would think she was where she goes every Friday afternoon."

"Where is that?"

She primly shook her head. "I know only that on Fridays, she is
generally away. I do not know what time she goes or returns—I am
at the shop until last thing at night. Perhaps you should ask her?"

"Alas, we have not been able to reach the inspector in charge of
her release." A true statement, if meaningless.

"There is little more I can say. Other than the lady does have
friends—friends from before she came here."

We both looked up from our smashed almonds. Seeing our interest, Madame went coy.

"I should not speak. She is a private woman, I think."

"She is also an old woman, locked in a cold cell. While the blood hardens on your floor-boards and the killer of Niko Cassavetes walks free."

To do her credit, the third point seemed nearly of equal weight to the second. She pursed her lips and took a turn with the nutcracker, dropping a perfect almond into a bowl. "The dress she wore, when she came to my door late at night to telephone the police."

"The red one?"

"I have not seen her in a red dress," she said—hardly surprising, since I had invented the garment as a mere prompt. "It was her *eau de Nil* frock, with a spray of embroidered *violettes* along the neck. She bought it from me, and it is a favourite to her, for functions of the afternoon."

"As opposed to evening cocktail parties or dinners?"

"Ladies' gatherings," she specified.

It was hard to picture Mrs Hudson in an afternoon salon, chatting about hair styles and Paris fashion and . . . whatever it was groups of women gossiped about.

"Were these perhaps English ladies?"

"How would I know?" she said tartly, handing the nutcracker over to Holmes. "A *dame* would not invite the likes of me to her home."

Something about the way she said the word caught my ear. Did she simply mean a grand lady?

Holmes had heard it, too. "By '*dame*,' you mean . . . ?"

"A lady of the bath."

She'd lost me. An attendant at the thermal baths was an unlikely hostess for a ladies' salon. The phrase sounded like one of those chivalric positions handed down from Tudor days—though were there female members of the Order of the Bath? I opened my mouth to ask for clarification, only to be distracted by the expression on Holmes' face.

"A lady of the bath? Good Lord." He seemed to be having a

brainstorm, or heart attack, his features contorted by a paroxysm of . . . humour?

"Madame," he said, "is it possible that you know where this Lady makes her residence?"

"Somewhere above Sainte-Dévote."

He dropped the silver nutcracker and reached across the table to take our hostess's hand. "Madame, we must be gone, I hope to see you very soon, in the company of Madame Hudson herself."

With that, he was out the door.

I grabbed Madame Crovetti's hand for a hasty shake.

"And you, Madame," she began. "If you require any clothing suitable to your visit in Monaco, you could do no better than my shop in town. Just up from the Casino, on the Boulevard du Nord."

The last was called at my back as I scrambled to follow Holmes. He'd been forced to wait for a motor to go past, so I did not quite need to break into a run.

"Holmes, what on earth was that about? Who is—are you laughing?"

He was—or at least, brimming over with amusement and surprise, as if Madame C. had given him a taste of past joys. "Madame de la Bathe," he said, as if repeating the punch-line of a joke.

"Yes, I heard what she said. Who is Mrs Bath?"

"Not Mrs: *Lady*. Lady de Bathe."

"Very well, but—wait. Lady de Bathe? Wasn't that . . . ?"

He all but rubbed his hands with pleasure. "Yes. None other than the Jersey Lily herself: Lillie Langtry."

CHAPTER NINETEEN

Mrs Hudson: a conversation

THREE WEEKS EARLIER

"Clarissa, what beautiful earrings!"

"I know."

"You don't sound very happy about that. Where did you get them?"

"A present from Zedzed."

"Oh."

"I made the mistake of admiring them in his hearing."

"Well, they're lovely—and they'll look perfect with that Poiret dress."

"Lillie, I couldn't possibly wear them."

"You couldn't possibly *not*, considering where they came from."

"I could tell him I've developed a skin sensitivity. Or that I'm saving them for some special occasion."

"If Zedzed thinks you have rejected his gift, he will take it personally. He could make your life here very difficult."

"I could say his wife wouldn't approve?"

"Doña Maria would not object."

"How could she have married the man? Do you think she hasn't noticed how, I don't know—empty he is? Sometimes, watching him when he's looking elsewhere, I find myself wondering how many people he's killed."

"Clara, don't!"

"Oh, Lillie, you're right. Sorry. It's just—I hate the notion of being forced to leave this place over a mere pair of earrings."

"'O what a tangled web we weave, when first we practise to deceive.' Shakespeare has a *bon mot* for every situation, doesn't he?"

"He does, but that isn't Shakespeare."

"Isn't it?"

"I made the same mistake one time, talking with Dr Watson, and Mr Holmes set me straight. It's from Sir Walter Scott, one of those interminable poems of his—a poem about a woman named Clara, come to think of it. She loves a man, another man wants her, there's a forged letter and a duel and a battlefield. Terribly rousing."

"I do hope the villain of the piece isn't named Basil."

"No. Nor have I got bricked in behind the wall of a convent, which is what happens to her. Though if I disappear, that's where you could start searching."

"Clara, you must be seen wearing these."

"I know. But . . . hmm. Perhaps *I* don't have to keep them."

"I certainly don't think you should sell them."

"I don't mean that—I mean, what if they weren't actually, strictly speaking, mine? Here, put that one back into the box, and let's pretend there's a ribbon around it. And so: 'Lillie, my dearest friend, I missed your birthday this year. Would you please accept these by way of a belated gift? And I am sure my affection will overcome any unfortunate antecedents the earrings might once have had.'"

"Clarissa, you cannot simply *give* them to me."

"I just did. So now I can say, 'Oh, Lillie—what lovely earrings! They would go perfectly with that Poiret dress I bought in Paris. Might I possibly borrow them, for a few days?'"

"Would that make you feel better?"

"It would make me feel as though I shared a secret with my closest friend."

"Then by all means, you may borrow 'my' earrings for as long as you like. As I borrowed your diamond necklace for all those years."

"Thank you."

"Tangled webs, indeed. Who would have imagined, all those years ago, that when you and I were this age, we'd be faced with a problem whose foundation we were then laying down?"

"Neither of us could have imagined being old. And back then, Zedzed was just another clever, handsome businessman who knew all the right people."

"Back then, he was the same shiny brute, but we were too simple to know the difference."

CHAPTER TWENTY

L illie Langtry was one of those "professional beauties" of the Victorian era who were essentially famous for being famous—or perhaps infamous. Nowadays pretty girls shot to prominence through the cinemas, but professional beauties were a phenomenon of Holmes' youth, a series of lovely young women of good station who made a minor splash during their first Season, then during their second worked their way up through the balls and dinner parties that mattered, capturing the eyes of Society's fashionable painters, finally to explode into the public imagination through the thrilling new technology of the photographic camera. They would become necessary ornaments at every dinner party and social event, their lovely faces appearing in popular journals, shop windows, and even on the walls of private homes (Mrs Langtry's portrait, rumour had it, had spent time on the bedroom wall of the young Prince Leopold until Victoria spotted it).

Of the professional beauties, Lillie Langtry was undisputed queen. Painted by Millais and Burne-Jones, sketched for postcards, awash with invitations, friends with everyone from Oscar Wilde to William Gladstone, she had branched out (beauty itself being no guarantee of income) into acting, soap-endorsing, horse-racing, and a series of more-or-less discreet liaisons with earls, impresarios, potentates, and princes—most famously, the Prince who became Edward VIII. She'd lived in California for a time, raising horses, and married an American, gaining U.S. citizenship. Judge Roy Bean named a saloon for her. During her career, she had filled theatres acting in everything from vaudeville to *Macbeth*.

After which, apparently, she had married an English baronet and then retired—in amicable separation from her husband—to Monte Carlo.

I learned this from Holmes' infatuated musings as we wandered towards the town. He shook his head in fond memory. "I first saw her on the Haymarket stage, when Watson dragged me off to *She Stoops to Conquer*. Our first winter on Baker Street, as I recall. An extraordinary presence."

I tried to picture him and Dr Watson as silk-hatted young men-about-town, roaring in laughter at the comedy of manners that finds a high-born woman plotting to capture the affections of a man who prefers girls from the lower classes.

No: my imagination would not stretch that far.

"They say she was very beautiful."

To my surprise, he had to think about it. "I'm not sure she was. Oh, certainly Mrs Langtry was well put together, but the appeal was not a surface effect. She was ... forthright. When she looked at an audience—or I suppose at a painter or a camera lens—there was neither ambiguity nor hesitation. She was fully there, and one felt oddly privileged."

I studied my husband, wondering if the sun was getting to him.

"A flight of fancy, I know," he admitted. "And yet it is a perennial question as to why some individuals capture the imagination—the public's heart, one might say—while others with what appears equal qualities and intelligence do not. It may indeed have something to do with the latter," he mused. "Mrs Langtry had an exceptional mind, quick and supple, if largely untrained. I also found it little short of extraordinary how few enemies she made over the years."

"It sounds as if you knew her. Other than from a seat in the audience."

"We have met two or three times, though I was not using my own name. She even hired me briefly, back in the Nineties. A minor investigation to do with one of the trainers at her racing stables."

English Society being a small village, there were few important people of the past two generations that Holmes hadn't encountered at some point.

"Well, it looks as if you'll have another chance to meet."

To my surprise, considering how close-mouthed the residents had been when it came to finding Mrs Hudson, it did not prove difficult to narrow down the location of one of the Principality's more famous residents. Indeed, I realised later, we might have stood on a random street-corner and asked the first half-dozen passers-by. Instead, we went about it rather more deliberately, choosing the sorts of shops that might cater to the great lady: first a stationer's, then an upscale greengrocer's, and finally a milliner so discreet the window had only a dramatically placed dusting of feathers atop an expanse of black velvet.

The delicate gent in this shop agreed that he knew her, protested that he couldn't possibly reveal where she lived, admitted that everyone from the street-sweeper on up knew anyway, and when we regretfully made to take our leave, seized the opportunity to participate in the adventure, however small it might be, by revealing the stairway on which the Langtry house could be found.

We thanked him, promised we would never reveal his collaboration, and extricated ourselves before he could talk himself into closing up shop to accompany us.

Theoretically, a visitor could stroll from one end of Monaco to the other in an hour, and circumnavigate it in a morning. In practice, that only applied to goats.

The postage-stamp nation compensated for its brief outline by piling on as many additional square metres as it possibly could, via cliffs, chasms, tunnels, bridges, and the odd underground wine cellar. Its rapid development over the past half-century had begun with narrow viaducts thrown across ravines to tie together the various rocky plateaus, first for trains and then for other wheels. Any pedestrian who tried to give these a miss needed stout knees and good wind. I could see why Mrs Hudson had shed a stone.

This particular vertical thoroughfare had its feet in religion, with a church occupying the bottom of a deep gorge that separated the districts of Monte Carlo and La Condamine. The church of Monaco's patron saint, Sainte-Dévote, stood tempting God's patience with the billion tonnes of rock that towered on either side. A minor tremor would bury the church to its bell-tower—which was perhaps the point: that each day of its continuing existence proved the congregation's excellent relationship with The Divine. However, as Holmes and I walked by the church's façade, I could not help reflecting that St Devota—who came to Monaco posthumously when a dove guided the storm-wracked ship carrying her bones to safe harbour—had earned her martyrdom by stoning.

The Escalier Sainte-Dévote was precisely as advertised: a stairway which had been hacked into, and bolted on to, the side of a cliff. In the lower reaches, the cliff's face was not quite vertical, although some of the sections above our heads could have satisfied a plumb bob. Over the centuries, determined plants had driven roots into invisible footholds. The semi-tropical equivalent of buddleia and wallflowers clung to every crack, with spiny cactuses and spear-tipped agaves threatening a careless step. Where larger hollows permitted actual soil to accumulate, trees had been nurtured, so that our climb up a hillside baking under the late afternoon sun would be briefly overshadowed by palms, citrus, or an occasional olive.

We paused, regularly, in these scant patches of shade so as to admire a flower, or a bird, or the view. The stairs went on. My throat grew parched. Even Holmes was beginning to look a bit worn by the time we reached the landing that our helpful shop-keeper had told us to look for.

There, in the inadequate shade of a lemon tree, we paused to admire the antics of some birds, spending an inordinately long time debating whether they were house sparrows or the Eurasian variety, with Holmes suggesting the rock sparrow, even though it does not resemble the others in the least. When we had finished the discussion—voting unanimously for the common sparrow—the steam had ceased to rise off our heads, and our legs were able to consider forward motion.

We found the door, we worked the knocker, we straightened our clothes and hair. The woman who answered was slim, French, forty, and clearly well accustomed to acting as a gate-keeper for Mrs Langtry. Naturally, she refused us entry until we had firmly in-sisted that her employer would wish to speak with us, and that we were friends of Mrs Clara Hudson.

She nodded, making her disbelief clear, and closed the door in our faces. A few minutes later, her footsteps returned, the door came open again, and we were ushered through the villa and into the garden.

Where, in no time at all and in no uncertain terms, our case was knocked from our hands.

CHAPTER TWENTY-ONE

———————————————————

Lillie Langtry might be in her seventies, but she clearly saw no reason to permit age to slow her down, or even to deserve an acknowledgment. Her celebrated auburn hair was perhaps not quite the colour nature had intended, and her famous violet eyes had dulled to merely blue, but she had not ceded an inch of her height or a shade of her assurance.

She held out her hand like a queen. Holmes responded in kind, by giving her fingers the kiss he had merely sketched to the landlady earlier. I squelched the impulse to curtsy, and gave her hand a firm shake.

But she paid me little mind. Instead, she was studying my husband as if he were a box of chocolates. "I know you, don't I?"

"We met many years ago, Lady de Bathe. A small matter of a missing letter."

"You may as well call me Mrs Langtry, everyone does. A letter . . . ? Ah! You're the Pinkerton agent."

I could feel his wince, but it did not show on his face. "Something along those lines."

"What brings you here, Mr . . . Russell, you said? Another black-mailer?"

"A death. A young man found shot, in the house of one of your acquaintances."

Her imperial flirtation went a touch cool. "You mean young Niko?"

"I do."

"I have nothing to say about the boy, save that he was a nice lad, and hard working."

"So I have been told, but it is your other friend who concerns me at present. The one in whose front room he was found."

"Clarissa? What do you want with her?"

I thought it was time to interrupt, before Holmes gave her the unvarnished truth. "We want to help. She's an old friend, and we're hoping to give the police some evidence as to her innocence."

"Oh, you needn't worry about that," Mrs Langtry said. "It's taken care of."

"I beg your pardon?"

"Clarissa Hudson does not require your assistance. I've told the Inspector to let her out. He says it will probably not happen until tomorrow, which is irritating. Still, she should be here in time for dinner—I've told Mathilde to arrange something a bit festive, to take the taste of prison out of her mouth."

Now, even at my relatively young age, I had spent enough time among the rich and powerful to be familiar with their blithe assumption of authority. Why I was shocked to find it here, ordering around police inspectors, I was not sure—but I was.

Fortunately, Holmes managed to keep a firmer grasp on the essentials. "Was she with you when the murder occurred?"

"Certainly," she replied, then kicked the foundations out from under the statement by continuing, "What time was that, exactly?"

Exactly was an impossibility. Even *approximately* would require a close study of the police photographs, a visit to the scene, an estimate of the volume of blood spilled, the surface beneath the body, and the humidity and temperature of the room—followed by a lot of calculations on paper.

None of which slowed Holmes down. "Early evening," he said. "Around sunset."

"Then she was here. She hadn't planned on it, since my afternoon salons end at six o'clock. However, I had dinner guests coming at seven, and the wife of one of them rang to say she was unwell, so I asked Clarissa to stay on in her place. It was to be informal, the men in day suits, and since she would not have to go home to dress, she agreed to join us. Mathilde produced a very nice piece of fish *en papillote,* and I served some of my own wine. Did you know I have a vineyard? In California? Well, to call it 'mine' is something of an exaggeration, but I did get it started. They tell me the future of wine lies in California."

Holmes stepped deftly around the distraction. "Who were your guests?"

"I'm not sure I should tell you. Should I? I suppose it's hardly a secret—they drove in openly through the streets. It was Sir Basil and Count Vasilev. They are old . . . friends."

Did I imagine that brief pause before the word friends?

"Sir Basil. Do you mean Basil Zaharoff, the arms dealer?"

"Yes. And if I may be frank with you, he was the reason I asked Clarissa to remain here for dinner. It was Sir Basil's wife who'd sent her apologies, a woman whose company I thoroughly enjoy. With Doña Maria absent, I thought the two gentlemen might find the situation . . . inappropriate. And in any event, having the two of them and the two of us made the evening feel more balanced."

She was an actress, but not a great one. One could feel that she had in fact felt the need for support, rather than a mere balance of the sexes. "So, Sir Basil is a friend of yours?" I asked.

"No." The reply had come too quickly, and she knew it. She gave an uncomfortable laugh. "Well, one would have to call him an old acquaintance. Clarissa and I met Zedzed in, oh, it must have been

1877 or so. In London, it was, at a ball. I doubt you ever saw her like that," she said to me, "but Clarissa was stunning. So alive! The men positively flocked around her."

Mrs Hudson? A glittering, attractive Mrs Hudson, clothed in silk at a formal ball. Clarissa Hudson and . . . *Zedzed*? A jarring diminutive, for a man into whose hands the nations of Europe would bleed. Clarissa and *Sir Basil* had known each other. When they were young, and attractive, and flirtatious. It was all beginning to feel like the day a child realises that her parents—her *parents*—had once . . . (had more than once . . .)

My appalled musings were shattered by Mrs Langtry's delighted laugh. "Yes, dear thing, your Mrs Hudson cut quite a swathe through the blades of Europe."

"And now she's here," Holmes broke in sharply, "still cutting a swathe through the ranks of the wealthy and the criminal."

"Wealthy, perhaps, but criminal? Oh, yes, one does come across all sorts of individuals in Monaco. People come here for many reasons. One doesn't tend to ask about their pasts."

"Basil Zaharoff has a past that is difficult to overlook," Holmes pointed out, his voice icy.

She sighed down at her hands. "He is a clever man, and can be utterly charming when he chooses. He was a familiar presence in the circles I once moved in—a regular at Sarah Bernhardt's table—but he is not a person I generally invite into my home. My original invitation was to Count Vasilev, since Clarissa is rather hoping that he will support a project she has put before Princess Charlotte. But the Count then asked if he might invite Sir Basil and his wife. I agreed. Clarissa said she would leave before they all arrived, and speak with the count another time, but then Doña Maria bowed out, and I asked my friend to keep me company. And she did."

"How do you know Count Vasilev?" I asked her.

"I've known Yevgeny for years. He used to spend the winter seasons here, when the Romanovs all came down from St Petersburg. And of course, he has lived here since the Revolution. He can't very well return to Russia, since he was not only a personal friend of Nicholas, but he was the Czar's banker as well. Although truth to tell, I don't know if that was literally the case. I will say, Yevgeny seems to be one of the few White Russians who had the foresight to put money into European banks, before the War."

"I met him the other night, at a party on the Cap d'Antibes. He's an art collector."

"This would be at Villa America? Yes, the Count collects many things, but I understand that modern art has caught his eye."

"It sounds as though you know the Murphys, too?"

"I have met them, naturally. Not that I would regard myself as a part of their 'circle.' My interests lie more in theatre and dance."

"Diaghilev rather than Picasso?"

"Yes—but, oh, the Spaniard's sets for *Parade* during the War were intriguing, and his drop curtain for *Le Train Bleu* sent shivers up my spine. He's married to a dancer, you know."

"I've met her, though I didn't realise who she was until—"

Holmes shouldered back into the conversation. "Was anyone else here, last night?"

"Just the four of us. And Mathilde, naturally."

"That is your housekeeper?"

"My companion."

That explained the woman's somewhat possessive attitude at the door.

"And what time did the dinner end?"

"The men left early, just after ten o'clock. Clarissa stayed for perhaps half an hour—we both needed a good, stiff drink—then set off for home. On foot, though Mathilde offered to ring for a car.

"And that," she said, "was what I told Inspector Jourdain. Now, I have an evening planned and need to dress. But perhaps you'd like to ring here tomorrow, in the afternoon? We shall see if Clarissa is feeling up to visitors."

She rose, gracious but imperious, forcing us to our feet as well. She held out her hand, then waited expectantly for us to turn and follow the black-clad Mathilde from the room.

We had little choice but to do so. Through the house, out of the door, onto the street. The door was closed before we had turned around on the pavement.

The street looked remarkably normal. Not at all as it should to a person who had just been swept outside like débris from beneath a carpet.

"Well," I said. The Jersey Lily had been a revelation. I might never look upon wrinkled skin in quite the same way. "Why do I get the feeling that she knew who you were?"

Holmes replied by drawing his cigarette case from its pocket.

An elderly man in work-stained clothing rode slowly past, his bicycle chain clicking. Once that excitement was over, I glanced at my husband, who was squinting through smoke as he meditated on a glimpse of distant mountains at the end of the street. Shadows were climbing up their flanks as the sun went low. The morning seemed a long time ago.

"If we're not needed here," I said, "we could return to my room on the Cap d'Antibes. Or if we are staying on, I should ask them to send my things."

No response.

"I suppose the Hon Terry could bring them, if he's coming back. So, are we staying on, or leaving?" Nothing. "Should I have the Murphys build a camp-fire on the beach with my suitcases? Hello, Holmes?"

His eyes withdrew from the far horizon. "Sorry?"

"Are we accepting dismissal?"

He looked at the Langtry house, and chuckled.

"What a refreshing and salutary experience, to be shown the door so very firmly."

"Are. We. Leaving. Monaco?"

"Don't be preposterous."

Of course not. Sherlock Holmes, taking orders from two old women?

"That's a relief. So, what do we want to poke into first? The bank? Her house?" But with the last word came a stark image. My heart sank. "Oh, Holmes. The blood. If Mrs Hudson is let out on bail, we can't let her return home to that. The man was her friend. Bad enough she . . ."

I found it hard to finish the thought. *Bad enough she had to scrub her own son's blood from the floor-boards in Sussex* . . . "Do you think the police would allow us to have it cleaned?"

"I require a telephone."

Retracing our steps down the cliff-side *escalier* left us nearly as weak-kneed as climbing them had. At the bottom, we made for the nearest café and settled in with a large bottle of mineral water and two large glasses of wine.

Neither of us spoke, although the sound of furious thought was almost audible.

After a while, Holmes rose to search out a telephone. With this call, he was marginally more successful than he had been, although not entirely so.

"Jourdain will see me," he said, resuming his chair, "but not until tomorrow morning, after church. And he confirmed that, short of other evidence to the contrary, Mrs Hudson will probably be released in the afternoon—but into Mrs Langtry's custody."

"Did you ask—"

"He has no objection to the house being cleaned. He regards their photographs as sufficient evidence."

Which was nonsense, but who were we to argue?

"If we are here for the night, then, would you like to go help me scrub a floor?"

"No. Tonight, Russell, we shall return to the Casino."

CHAPTER TWENTY-TWO

Mrs Hudson: a conversation

TEN DAYS EARLIER

"Well, Lillie, the deed is done."

"Which one, dear heart?"

"The one involving the *paper*. He's taken it off to Paris to hand it to his gentleman there."

"Oh, how exciting! Aren't you excited?"

"More relieved, I think. Like when I would have the house to myself for two full days and I could give it a proper tidy, top to bottom. As soon as that *thing* is really gone, there will be no evidence that Clara Hudson is anything but a law-abiding old woman, retired to a small Mediterranean country for its pleasantly warm climate."

"Oh, Clarissa, you always could make me laugh. The thought of you as a law-abiding old woman."

"I am. Or will be. I hope that when Mr Holmes shows up, I can give him a face of bland virtue."

"Or you could ask Niko to drive him off with a stick."

"No. I'm actually looking forward to seeing him, once the Count has finished and my hands are clean."

"Why did you never put a dose of arsenic in the man's curry, anyway?"

"He was always a sort of challenge, I suppose. Do you remember, Lillie, how freeing it felt, at the end of the day, to take off one's corset? When one could take a proper breath for the first time in hours?"

"Oh yes! Sheer heaven."

"And yet, once you'd drawn that first delicious deep breath, there came this creeping sense of uncertainty. A sort of . . . floppiness about the spine and torso, as if one's organs were about to spill out onto one's knees."

"Who can forget? When fashion finally changed and I gave up whalebone for good, I used to get the most dreadful backaches. A corset kept one upright for hours, with no effort at all. Without it, a chair had no more support than a three-legged stool."

"And walking about felt as wobbly as a rubber balloon filled with water! And the next day, when the ties pulled in and snugness returned, it was hard to breathe, but it was also familiar and safe. Well, it was a little like that, living under the authority of Mr Holmes. I had fewer choices and decisions. And honestly, Lillie, since most of the choices I'd made didn't turn out that well, it was something of a relief to have fewer of them to make."

"How do you suppose Mr Holmes would like being compared to a set of stays?"

"Hah! It's been many a year since I've seen the man blush, but that might do it."

CHAPTER TWENTY-THREE

A t the thought of returning to the Casino, a place that had sucked my will down to a dry nubbin, I dug in my heels, but Holmes insisted. Eventually I gave in, though not to take any active part. "I'll sit with the other female companions and watch, Holmes, but I won't put my money down on that damnable wheel again."

"Perfect. Far easier for you to keep an eye on the room if you're not being mesmerised by the spin."

We returned to the Hermitage and put on our evening wear, with me clipping on the jewelled decorations that were a modern woman's substitute for hair long enough to pin up. We ate first, Holmes allowing the sommelier to talk him into a bottle of wine older than I was, then strolled arm in arm along the lamp-lit pavements to the Casino de Monte Carlo.

The place came alive at night. During the day, the Casino was a building that worked too hard to impress, but with the velvet sky overhead and the spill of chandelier light down the steps, with the sweep of silken gowns and sparkle of jewels, any shabbiness vanished and its fairy-land grace and intimacy came to the fore.

I still had no intention of falling under its spell. Instead, I settled in among the accompanying wives and friends. The women studied my cursory hair-do and bluestocking spectacles, trying to weigh such gaucheries against the undeniable expense of my dress and the brilliance of my emeralds. Apparently, I passed muster, because when I gave the most blatantly pampered of them a polite smile, she graciously inclined her head. All around me, feathers settled with this sign of acceptance, and the women turned their attention to the tables again.

I, however, studied the room in a way I had not done before. The real gambling, those high-stakes games that saw racing stables and country estates change ownership in a night, took place in the *salles privés* upstairs, a sort of gentlemen's club well removed from the rattle of ivory balls and the squeaks of excited ladies. For the people down at this more public level, the mere sensation of exclusivity was quite enough.

Slowly, I began to notice patterns. The nervous gestures of the addicts, the taut faces of those whose luck was gone, the widened shoulders of men who felt the Fates shining upon them and knew they could do no wrong. The careful note-taking of those who believed that the odds favoured not the house, but the one with a System. The dedicated drinking of a man who would be slinking home in disgrace—if he went home at all.

And then I saw, across the room, what I realised Holmes had been waiting for: Lillie Langtry, on the arm of a tall, distinguished man some fifteen years her junior. A man with a white streak in his hair, a precisely trimmed beard, and a beautifully fitted evening suit.

Holmes saw them a moment later. He went still, tracking their progress across the floor, making note of their every movement. Lady de Bathe's arm was lightly looped through that of Count Vasilev, long ebony gloves setting off the brilliance of diamonds around her wrist. Her head was inclined towards his, to hear something he was saying, although her gaze remained outwards to the room. Interested, but not intimate.

Then I saw her change, in some subtle but undeniable way. Her pace hesitated, her posture straightened, her glove pulled back until only the fingertips were making contact with the Count's forearm. Then he, too, noticed whatever had caught her eye, and stopped. Mrs Langtry's arm fell away as she took a small step to the side.

The Count's reaction to the person coming at them, who was still out of view to me, was less ambiguous. He smiled. At the same time, his head and shoulders went slightly back, turning him from a man displaying a handsome woman on his arm to a subaltern facing a friendly but vastly superior officer.

When the person appeared, I heard Holmes make a sound. This was a man of Mrs Langtry's age, a rotund figure with brilliant white hair, moustaches, and goatee. He stopped before the two. Lillie Langtry put out her hand. He grasped her fingers and made a brief bow over them, then turned to the Count, shook his hand, then gave a regal nod. She stepped back so he could proceed without having to change his course in the slightest. They watched him move off, then turned, to continue their way, disappearing from view.

I was not surprised when Holmes finished his hand and gathered up his *plaques*. But I was taken aback when, instead of following the Jersey Lily and her companion, he steered me towards the exit.

We paused to cash in his *plaques* and *jetons,* enough to buy him several bottles of that stupendously expensive wine. I wondered if he had cheated, made a note to ask him how, and then we were outside in the balmy night air.

"Who was that man?"

"None other than Basil Zaharoff."

"Good Lord."

"Indeed."

It felt a bit like hearing that a casual passer-by had been Vlad the Impaler. Hardly surprising I had not known Basil Zaharoff by sight—his photograph appeared in the newspapers even less than his name did, and the name was mostly spoken in whispers and in back rooms.

I followed Holmes down the Casino steps and around to the coast-side promenade. At the railings, Holmes dug his tobacco out of his inner pocket. When the stimulant was burning, he squinted across the breakwater below.

"Lady de Bathe moves in some troubling circles," he remarked.

"Well, as Mrs Hudson pointed out, it is a small city."

A glance with a cocked eyebrow put me in my place, but I persisted. "I know, and I most certainly wouldn't want Basil Zaharoff kissing *my* hand. However, I get the impression that anyone of stature who spends more than a brief time in Monaco has to choose between shaking a distasteful hand and making a deliberate, and possibly dangerous, social offence. Am I wrong?"

"The woman showed no sign of distaste."

"That wasn't what I saw."

"She smiled at the man. She initiated a handshake. She was still smiling when she and Count Vasilev walked away."

Slowly, I shook my head. "Holmes, I think you're wrong. Oh, I'd agree that the Count respects Mr Zaharoff, and would like to ingratiate himself rather more thoroughly, but Mrs Langtry's immediate impulse on seeing Zaharoff was to stop dead. She did not, quite, though her hand had come nearly free from the Count's arm before she realised it, and moved to stay with him. And yes, her face was polite throughout, but she'd braced her shoulders, to fight the impulse to flee. And the moment Zaharoff shifted, intending to continue walking, she made haste to step away, so as not to come into any further contact with him."

"I saw nothing of the sort."

I thought about mentioning the other thing I had noticed, but I could not swear to it. The Count had obscured my view, but I'd seen the beginning of a motion my own hand recognised: Mrs Langtry had given a quick and unconscious swipe of her right palm down the side of her gown.

The retort was on the tip of my tongue—*Holmes, you see but you do not observe*—but I stifled it, and turned, to put my back against the railing. "Holmes, I am among the least vulnerable of women, physically or financially. Yet even I understand a woman's retreat from confrontation. How we use polite masks as covert resistance."

Even to our husbands.

"Lillie Langtry is no stray chicken surrounded by foxes," he protested.

"My dear man, *every* woman has felt herself surrounded by foxes at one time or another. If not by wolves."

It was an uncomfortable confession, coming from a modern woman who proclaims her autonomous state. However, though he be a man, Holmes was nonetheless a fair one. My admission gave him something to meditate upon, while we walked along the terrace gardens and back to our rooms at the Hermitage.

CHAPTER TWENTY-FOUR

"How long do you suppose it takes to clean a floor, Holmes?" I asked him the next morning.

"It never seemed to take Mrs Hudson long," he replied. But then, if she'd worked all day on her knees, would he have noticed?

"I imagine it will take me most of the morning."

"You should arrange with Madame Crovetti to have it cleaned."

"If Mrs Hudson weren't being freed this afternoon, I might. But this being Sunday, I think the only way to be sure it gets done is to do it myself."

"I could help," he said, as reluctant as I'd ever heard him. "When I have spoken with the elusive Inspector Jourdain."

"I'll clean. You go talk to him."

"Leave a message for me here, if you wish me to join you."

We drained our coffee cups and went our separate ways.

Again I climbed, up roads so steep that they might as well have been stairways. When the house at the cliff base came into view, I began to consider how best to get inside. Also, to catch my breath and peel my sodden clothing away from my skin, wishing the evening breeze would start up early.

No luck.

However, my ill fortune in climatic issues was repaid by ease of access: Madame Crovetti was standing on Mrs Hudson's front steps, emptying a watering can into the pots on either side of the door. Her clothing suggested she was just home from church.

"*Bonjour,* Madame," I greeted her. She returned the greeting, and asked if I had found the Lady of the Bath. I said I had, told her that Mrs Hudson was to be released, agreed with her that this was most excellent news—and then sadly pointed out that the floors would be a shock to that good lady.

"However, Madame, it seems that the police have no objection to my cleaning up. So as to save her the distress."

"Truly?"

"Absolutely. *L'inspecteur* himself gave us permission. I don't suppose you have such a thing as a key?"

At the question, she reached into her pocket and took out a ring bristling with keys, fitting one into the latch. I thanked her and slipped around her, bracing myself against what I was going to find inside.

A hallway led down the centre of the house, with two pairs of doors. Of the nearer pair, the one on the right was open, its mate on the left closed, while the two at the end of the hallway were both slightly ajar. Shutters had kept the house cool in comparison to the street outside, but the first thing I did was go through the open right-hand doorway to throw open the windows and shutters: the body had not lain in the house long enough to putrefy, but the air smelled of decay.

It had not happened in this space, a sort of morning-room retreat for the lady of the house, rather than for visitors—especially any visitors requiring the services of "Miss Hudson," the fixer and smoother-of-ways. I stood in the wash of sunlight, studying the view—a surprisingly generous stretch of the Mediterranean, considering the cliffs all around, through the gap at the end and above the low buildings beyond.

I had never known Mrs Hudson with a home of her own. For more than two decades, her quarters had been a portion of Holmes' Sussex villa. Before that, 221b Baker Street was a house she had owned outright, but it, too, came to her through Holmes.

What would it mean to a person, to go from those Sussex rooms to this? From closed-in and subordinate, living in rooms entered through a kitchen and whose view was a small, enclosed garden, to a place with doors she could lock when she wished, walls that kept others out, and a view that stretched over the endless sea?

Had there been a single morning since she moved here in June that she had not flung open her shutters with joy?

The house was hers, of that I had no doubt. Spotless, spare, and with none of a Victorian's fuss and formality. I looked over the room, enjoying its colours, and though she'd left Sussex in a hurry, with the barest of possessions, I saw a number of familiar objects. A favourite shawl, tossed over the back of the settee for cool evenings. An ancient, hand-made child's dolly, grey with love and even limper than I remembered, slumped atop a book-shelf. And on the wall nearby . . .

It was a small watercolour of the Beachy Head cliffs on a stormy day: a sweep of green hillside, the sharp white chalk bluffs, and a tumultuous sky over seething waves. I'd bought it in Eastbourne a month after I'd first met her, when I'd learned that the next day was her birthday. And though it had been a hasty purchase, of a local landmark so widely depicted as to be cliché and cheap enough for my limited purse, I realised as I studied the piece that it was actually fairly well done. I could understand why she had found a corner in her suitcase for it.

Not that I had noticed it missing from her rooms in Sussex. I had not even spotted the frame she must have left behind rather than risk a valise full of broken glass. The frame it wore now was much nicer—and, I noticed, the room itself suited it beautifully, with shades of that same green in the cushions, echoes of the grey-and-white sky in the tiny, subtle print of the wallpaper . . .

The cushions were new, the paint fresh, the wallpaper, too. Those echoes were no happy accident: they were deliberate.

I was amused, and touched, as I thought about that birthday, and about her other birthdays, and about meeting her in the first place and all the hours we'd spent together, and only slowly became aware that I was standing there trying to work up my courage. The air itself was less troubling, but I could not remain in this innocent room. I took a steadying breath and walked back into the hallway, only then noticing the red-brown smudges on the floor. I took care to step around them, and reached for the door-knob leading to the other front room, the one suitable for guests and potential clients.

The smell that spilt out would have been alarming even if I didn't know what it was. The dark stain, halfway between door and window, was an obscenity scrawled on polished floor-boards. Some of the droplets had been completely dry when the police arrived, though the careless boot-tracks leading down the hallway from the centre of the main pool showed that the deeper portions had only been half set.

I picked my way cautiously through the dim room to the window and shutters, shoving both open as far as they would go. With the sunlight spilling in, I could see that the bullet had stopped Niko's heart not instantly, but after a few seconds. Small droplets spattered the painted wall, and the colourful throw-rug near the desk was beyond salvage. However, the cleaning itself wouldn't take me more than a few hours.

But before I could start, there was another, even more unsavoury task: I had to search Mrs Hudson's possessions.

I did not imagine this would take long, either, since she'd only been here a few weeks, and—apart from whatever clothes she had bought in Paris—her possessions had fit into two valises. And indeed, her bedroom at the top of a narrow stairway held a fairly sparse collection. Mostly new clothing, a few pieces expensive enough for the Casino or dinner parties. The garments she'd brought from Sussex were dull in comparison, and resided at the back of the wardrobe. A pair of shoes that had been her good footwear had been downgraded to garden work, with traces of greyish mud around the soles. Looking from them to the trim pumps on the other side of the wardrobe, I couldn't blame her for making a clean start of things.

Drawers I pulled out, to feel the sides for hidden envelopes, and the photographs on her dressing table I slid out from their frames—though I was perfunctory in these gestures, since Mrs Hudson knew all the places an intruder would look at first. Then I went more deeply: tapping the wardrobe for hollow spaces; climbing up to inspect the toilet cistern; examining all the edges of the mattress for places where the stitching had been opened, then re-stitched. All the while I felt intrusive and ashamed, but I knew that if I did not do this search, Holmes would.

I worked with great precision and scrupulous attention to detail, taking forever to get the bed re-made in exactly her manner.

In the end, I came away with only two things of interest.

The first was when I pulled open a drawer and was faced with an exaltation of silk and lace, in a rainbow of colours. It took a moment to translate the contents into clothing, and a longer moment before my mind accepted that if this was Mrs Hudson's bedroom, then these were very probably hers.

I'd seen Mrs Hudson's sturdy undergarments on washing day, glimpsed when the wind revealed their discreet inner positions on the line, but those were garments best described as practical. Nothing like this frothy celebration of beauty. Chemises and camisoles, two short corsets and at least a dozen surprisingly non-voluminous knickers, an actual brassiere—in brilliant green . . . I stared, unwilling to lay a hand on such intimate things. I'd always thought of Mrs Hudson as womanly, but these were . . . feminine.

Though why should I be shocked? Even old women liked pretty

things. Why would they not secretly enjoy luxurious garments that were hidden from view?

Assuming these were intended to remain hidden from view: Mrs Hudson was not much older than Holmes—just because she'd never had a gentleman friend while I knew her didn't mean . . .

I slammed the drawer shut, my mind as unable to follow that thought as my hands were unable to reach into the silk. But then, Mrs Hudson of all people would know not to hide anything of value in her underwear drawer. That was the first place even a rank amateur burglar would look.

The other intriguing item I found was sitting openly on the back corner of her dressing table: a small jeweller's box containing a pair of stunning gold earrings, with dark red garnets around ovals of intense purple amethyst. They were old, their edges burnished by wear, and the colours of the stones, a touch garish by day, would be magnificent under candlelight.

I replaced the box precisely where I'd found it, then continued to the rest of the room. The search did not take long. No loose floor-boards, no hidden stashes of high-denomination banknotes, nothing to indicate that the woman living here was anything but a grey-haired lady with a colourful past and an unexpected taste in undergarments.

No sins that I could see.

The other room under the eaves contained her two valises and a larger suitcase so new the sides were unscuffed. I found nothing in the cases, nor in the rest of the storage room, so I went back down the narrow stairway and crossed the hallway to the final door, the one to the kitchen. And here at last I found Mrs Hudson—or at least, the Mrs Hudson I had known. The pans were twins of those she'd used daily, the plates were similar to her every-day ware, the arrangement of utensils and the scrubbed surfaces spoke of her presence.

I searched this room even more closely than I had the bedroom, bending down to poke into every crevice, stretching to see atop every shelf, sifting through every stoppered container. I found nothing but painted wood, newly laid shelf-paper, and dried goods.

I was relieved—both at finding no sins, and at the reassurance that some parts of her Sussex life had come with her.

I located her store of rags and cleaning equipment—behind the scullery door, where she'd kept them in Sussex—and pulled them out, along with the less pristine of the two aprons and the pair of rubber gloves used for the truly dirty jobs. I filled the bucket with soapy water, and carried it and the rags to the sitting room.

I had got as far as laying sodden rags over the black puddle when I heard the front door open. I scrambled up to cut her off.

"Oh, Mrs Hudson! I'm *so* sorry, I'd hoped to have this finished by the time they let you—ah. *Bonjour,* Madame Crovetti."

The landlady, too, was dressed for a dirty job, carrying a bucket and mop of her own. The two of us set to work, with me tackling the really unpleasant portion while she concentrated on the lesser stains on the wall—in silence at first, until I asked her a harmless question about her shop and she seized with relief on the distraction of chatter.

With care, that kind of conversation can reveal a great deal, and the good lady was so fixed on any topic other than what lay under her scrubbing rag that she did not notice how often the circuitous talk returned to touch on details of her tenant's life.

The previous afternoon, the landlady had said that Mrs Hudson came to her through Niko Cassavetes, who was a friend of her son, Matteo. A son who was "away for a time." Where, and for what reason, were not forthcoming, although as we worked and chatted, I came to suspect that he was either serving time or evading arrest. Whatever the reason, it caused her embarrassment rather than fear or shame, and made her shift the talk sideways, rather than go silent altogether.

"It's nice that you stayed in touch with your son's friend, Niko," I commented. "I imagine boyhood friendships here last forever."

"No, Niko was not from here," she said. "He came to Monaco

perhaps three years ago." That agreed with what Mrs Hudson had told us.

"But you met him through your son?"

"They came across each other somewhere, as boys do."

"From what they were saying in Antibes, Niko didn't have a set job, but did work for all sorts of people? That must have made things difficult, during the off-season."

"Niko always seemed to find something. He was a nice boy, good manners, though to be honest, subject to minor temptations."

"The sort of man one would trust with one's daughter but not with one's change-purse?"

She smiled sadly. "I had to tell him that if he was more than two months behind on his rent, he might come back to a changed lock."

I turned from my disgusting task of wringing out blood-stained rags. "How long had he been your tenant?"

"Two years, next door." She pointed her chin towards the adjoining converted warehouse. "That is my son's house. He asked if Niko could use the back rooms, which are dark and not very nice. But they fixed them up a little, and for a young man who spent most of his days out and around, they were comfortable enough. In truth, the past six months, I've been glad to have a man living nearby. I suppose I should let Niko's rooms out. Though it will be awkward, until Matteo returns to approve."

I made some vague noise of sympathy and took the bucket of filthy water to throw out the back door—but oddly, I found the door not just locked, but permanently shut with a dozen large screws. Or rather, so it appeared. Closer examination showed that most of those screws had been sawn off and their heads reinserted, leaving only two holding the door in place.

I could certainly understand—no cautious person would sleep comfortably in a house with no exit out the back. The permanent closure must have been done before Mrs Hudson moved in—and she, being a person both sensible and cautious, had preserved the look of the blockade without the actual thing. There was even a screwdriver perched atop the door jamb, for the remaining two fastenings.

Well, if she didn't want Madame Crovetti to know that she'd done this, I wouldn't point it out. Instead, I lifted the bucket into the scullery sink, whose porcelain was old and chipped but, like anything of Mrs Hudson's, clean enough to eat from. The sluice water tipped, dumped . . . and the revolting colour of blood and waste filled my world. A colour somewhere between brick and chocolate, dotted with cooling suds, swirling and draining and leaving behind a lot of small pieces . . .

My gorge rose, and I added the contents of my stomach to the pitted sink. I slapped the faucet handle as wide open as it would go and tore the oppressive rubber from my hands, then set about rinsing and scrubbing and rinsing again. At some point I was aware of someone behind me, but she said nothing. A few minutes later, I heard the front door close.

Eventually, I shut the water off. I used Mrs Hudson's clean dishtowel to dry my face and glasses. Deliberately, I arranged the cloth on its rail, pulled the gloves back on, and wrung the clean, wet rags out into the sink again and again and again until they gave off nothing but clear water.

I filled the bucket with fresh water, and returned to the task at hand.

Had Mrs Hudson been sickened by her similar task, back in May? The stains she had feared were my blood, but had in fact been even worse . . .

I wrenched my thoughts away from that memory and set about scouring every tiny trace of brown from the cracks between the boards. Countless buckets later, the harsh afternoon sun glaring across the room, the stain was gone. Madame Crovetti's walls were damp but spotless. The blood-soaked carpet had vanished, and the air smelled of Jeyes Fluid, sunshine, and the lemon I had squeezed into the final bucket—a thing I had known Mrs Hudson to do.

I sat back on my heels to pull off the gloves for a last time. During this final rinse, the landlady had returned, empty-handed. She stood in the doorway now.

"How does it look?" I asked her.

"The boards will show the effects of water. Once they are dry, I will have them polished."

I nodded. While she set about closing all the windows and shutters, I polished clean the bucket and sink, gathering the scrub-brush and rags for the dust-bin. When everything was as near to perfect as I could make it, the two of us stood to look at the purified room, shoulder to shoulder in a job adequately done.

"The portion of your son's house that Monsieur Cassavetes was letting," I said. "Would it be available? For a short time, while your son is away?"

"For you?" The note of near-scandal in her voice warned me that the rooms were unsuitable for a young woman, even one with hands resembling untanned leather, who had spent the day scrubbing a floor on her knees.

"For an acquaintance. He is doing some work here and was thinking of taking rooms rather than having to ride the train in every day from Nice."

I could see her weighing the potential income against the idea that letting the rooms without her son's approval was an admission that he was not returning soon. "Perhaps," she said. "If your friend is respectable."

"Oh, terribly. Perhaps I might look at them?"

"Now?"

"If you have time. I shall be seeing him tonight."

She reached for her heavy ring of keys, and locked one door before walking along the narrow pavement to open the next.

CHAPTER TWENTY-FIVE

My brother died when he was young, so I have never lived with an adolescent boy or a male undergraduate, but I instinctively recognised the signs. Mismatched furniture, inadequate lighting, sparse kitchenware, and despite Madame Crovetti's efforts, the musty odour of unwashed clothing.

The surfaces were tidy and all the corners clean, but short of hauling the furniture out for the rag-and-bone man, there was not much she could do about the smell of dirty socks.

She muttered something about "boys" as she led me rapidly through the rooms, but I pretended not to hear, or to notice the pinkness of her neck. The place was something of a maze, its conversion from storage to living quarters having been less planned than piecemeal. At the back of it stood a solid door set into a wall that was little more than wallpaper over rough boards, the paper puckered over every crack and seam—although the door itself had been varnished recently, its hinges and knob polished. The lock yielded to one of her keys. She let me step in first.

The quarters of the Greek boy did not smell of old socks. They smelled of spices and lemons. The furniture was inexpensive but chosen with care. There was a Turkish carpet on the floor, small but of high quality, and a pair of thick, colourful tapestries—bed covers, really, but nice ones—covering the wall behind the settee, edge to edge and ceiling to floor. The rooms had no kitchen, but a kettle stood on a single gas ring, and two shelves above a small deal table held various pans, cooking implements, and jars with everything from rice to pickled lemons to dried oregano. Basic, but a vast improvement on what lay in the actual kitchen next door.

The bedroom was an oddly shaped space that I realised must be jammed in beneath the cliff-face. Its back wall was angled, not as sharply as a dormer roof but enough that the eyes did not try to see it as straight. A row of hooks acted as Niko's wardrobe, holding everything from a warm dressing gown to an evening suit in a garment bag. The shoes tucked into the angled space behind the garments ran a similar gamut, from gleaming patent leather to worn but polished brogues to a pair of colourful satin bedroom slippers. At the end, looking oddly English, stood a pair of rubber Wellingtons, new but for a tidal mark of dried grey soil around the foot. These, unlike the other footwear, rested on a sheet of newspaper.

I spotted something on the back wall of the impromptu wardrobe, but I did not want her to see my nosiness. Instead, I coughed, then stepped away from the wall and eyed the room as if measuring it for my fictitious, would-be tenant. "Does Niko have any family?"

"I know of none, but my son may. Why do you ask?"

"I was just wondering what one does with things left behind by a tenant. I suppose you have to wait for the police to tell you?"

I'd heard of landladies swooping down to sell a tenant's possessions before they were in the ground, but to Madame Crovetti's credit, the thought of profit had clearly not occurred to her.

Until I introduced it. She admitted she did not know.

"Well, don't hurry to clear Niko's things, once the police give you permission," I told her. "My friend might be interested in the fittings as well." I coughed again, patted my chest, and said, "I seem to have picked up an irritation. Would you be so kind as to bring me a drink of water? Or, I could get it, if you don't mind?" I gave another cough.

Had her son's part of the house been up to this room's standards, she might have made me get my own glass of water, but at the thought of me in the kitchen . . .

"Just a moment," she said, and went to find a glass that would not offend. By the time she returned, I was back in the sitting area, smoothing my rumpled hair. I thanked her profusely, drank the water down, and handed her back the glass.

"That's much better, thank you. Can I let you know tomorrow, about whether my friend would be interested? Or possibly the next day?"

I followed her through Matteo's rooms to the street, where I thanked her again, made note of her telephone number, then walked down to the road while she returned to her own house at the cul-de-sac's end.

Once out of her sight, I turned to study the warehouse-turned-living quarters. The cliff-face was indeed pressed up against the back of it, but the two neighbouring houses appeared to stand free of the rock itself. And Mrs Hudson's scullery door, the one some-one had fastened shut, must lead somewhere.

I turned away with that lightness of heart that came with dis-covering a fact before Holmes found it, and made my way through the town to the Monte Carlo district, and the Hôtel Hermitage.

Presenting my damp and grubby person to the desk, again I re-quested their assistance in the matter of appropriate dress. Again the French maid appeared, followed by several reasonable approx-imations of my requested "dark trousers and simple shirt, suitable for gardening" and "women's simple short-sleeved frock." I gave her another generous tip.

Feeling doubly virtuous, as a cleaner of floors and a purchaser of clothing, I rewarded myself with a hot bath, a cup of tepid liquid resembling tea, and—as there was no sign of Holmes—a nap.

Holmes came in an hour or so later, shirt and hair rumpled, tie missing, jacket slung over his shoulder, smelling of beer—and displaying that familiar air of smugness that meant he'd moved a case forward. Fortunately, I could say the same.

But first, I rang down for tea—this time being very specific: English, as opposed to Russian; Indian, not smoked; plain, not sweetened; brewed fresh in a pot with boiling water rather than tapped from a steaming samovar; and in cups instead of glasses.

When I finally hung up the telephone after this lengthy negotiation, Holmes' features had taken on a trace of amusement.

"What?" I demanded. "You don't think I'll get it?"

"Revolutions have happened, I agree."

"If we're staying here long, I may need to assemble the makings for proper tea. You suppose I can find one of those electric kettles we got Mrs Hudson?"

"In London, perhaps."

I grumbled, and went to wash the sleep out of my face. When I came out, I found him on the balcony with a laden tray of tea. Tea that didn't smell of smoke, or of stale coffee. Tea that came with china cups. There was even a plate of crustless sandwiches, and another of iced biscuits.

The day improved, on all fronts.

CHAPTER TWENTY-SIX

Mrs Hudson: a conversation

"Lillie, bless your deep bath-tub and your copious geyser. I feel like a new thing. And tea! You'd have died at the prison's idea of 'tea.' It tasted of unwashed coffee pots."

"What a dreadful experience, my dear. I shall have a word with Princess Charlotte, when next I see her."

"You'll do nothing of the sort—they were very polite, and poor Inspector Jourdain had no choice but to arrest me. And anyway, he's let me walk free, thanks to you. For now."

"What do you mean, 'for now'? You can't imagine he'll arrest you again?"

"Lillie, the boy was found dead on my floor."

"But you were *here* all afternoon. And surely there's—I don't know—fingerprints and things they can test."

"I hope they are satisfied with those."

"They will be. And when you've finished your tea, Mathilde is chilling a bottle of champagne, to make you forget the taste of prison. Another biscuit?"

"I shouldn't. Oh, maybe one."

"Your Mr Holmes was here, and his delightful young wife. They're both calling themselves 'Russell' at the moment."

"One can hardly blame him for not using his name."

"But honestly, can they imagine I don't know who they are?"

"Why should they? Until last week, they had no idea you and I were even acquainted, much less friends."

"More fools they. Do you know, I'd forgot that he'd worked for me briefly, back in the Nineties. Heaven knows what name he was using then. I'm afraid I called him a Pinkerton agent, when he reminded me."

"That was cruel of you."

"He did rather bristle. But the man is even more terrifying than I remembered. On the other hand, Mary is perfectly delightful. I cannot believe the dear child got down and scrubbed your floor herself."

"I hope that's all she did."

"What do you—oh. I didn't think. But I suppose she would feel obliged to snoop. Should I have put them off?"

"I'm very glad you didn't try—there would be nothing more guaranteed to have them turn the entire street upside-down."

"Not Mary, surely?"

"She has been an apt pupil. Although she has recently been learning not to agree with everything her teacher tells her."

"A difficult lesson for one so young. Not that she'll remain that way long, married to him."

"She'll be grey by thirty. Were you and I ever that innocent?"

"How old is she, in fact?"

"She turned twenty-five in January."

"When I was her age, I'd been married for five years, the Millais portrait was hanging in the Royal Academy, and I'd just started with the Prince."

"At twenty-five, I was signing the deed to the Baker Street house."

"Would you want to be that age again?"

"My bones would, but the rest of me? I don't think so. I've been outrageous, and I've been responsible—and when I turned grey, I became invisible. It's a relief, not being young. And in any case, you and I have outlived most of the gay young boys and girls we knew."

"The only thing I miss about being young is the clothes. Though I'm afraid your Mary doesn't care much for clothing."

"She's always been far too serious-minded for that. Even before she arrived on our door."

"Well, I am sorry he showed up before you and the Count had concluded your . . . transaction."

"Can't be helped. And perhaps poor Niko's death will distract him from me. He's not convinced of my innocence, but he does seem willing to believe that I didn't shoot the boy."

"Do you have any idea who did?"

"A man who found him an inconvenience. A man who could shoot ten boys and not dirty his hands."

"Zedzed? No! Why would he want to kill Niko?"

"Because Niko stole something from him? Because Niko looked at him the wrong way? Because *I* looked at him the wrong way and Niko was my friend? Who knows? But who else could it have been?"

"He was with us."

"I don't mean he pulled the trigger himself. Zedzed wouldn't need to."

"What are you going to do?"

"I don't know. I suppose eventually, if no one does anything, I'll have to talk to Mr Holmes about it. But not yet. I need to let matters lie, just until the *paper* is dealt with."

"Niko liked you, Clarissa. I think he would be happy if his death served to distract Mr Holmes from your business."

"He'd have been happy if he could have made a profit from it."

"You would have been generous, Clarissa. You always have been."

"Have I? It's nice to think that."

"Oh Clara, what long and interesting lives we've led."

"Lives that promise to grow no less interesting in the future, thanks to you."

"No—my thanks to you! And now that your teacup is empty, we're going to open that champagne and drink to a lost friend, and to the lucrative partnership he would have adored being part of."

CHAPTER TWENTY-SEVEN

Holmes and I sat beside the ravaged tea-tray with our heels propped on the low table, saucers balanced on our stomachs, faces comfortably shaded from the lowering sun. The sandwich plate held only the less-identifiable creations. The biscuits were gone.

"Holmes, I take it that Inspector Jourdain was helpful?"

"Not more than he could help. The Inspector does not appear to welcome the assistance of amateurs. Particularly on a Sunday."

"Didn't you tell him who you were?"

"I decided that he would be even less enthusiastic over the meddling of foreign experts."

"That will make matters difficult."

"To be fair, the man does show signs of competence. And once he'd asserted his clear and undisputed authority over the investigation, he agreed to meet with me tomorrow—in a park, lest one of his superiors takes note—to show me the police photographs. He does not appear to be dismissing the investigation merely because Niko Cassavetes was a foreigner with dubious connections."

"What sorts of connections?"

"Jourdain would provide no details, but he did betray an attitude towards Madame Crovetti and her son Matteo that made me suspect it lay there."

"Madame Crovetti is a criminal? What does she do, sell fake fashion out of her shop?"

"As I say, he gave no details."

"And yet you've clearly filled in some of the gaps, from the way you came swanning in stinking of beer. A pub, right? Hence, working class rather than where the bureaucrats linger."

He stretched out his legs, looking very satisfied with himself. "We were told that Niko Cassavetes arrived in Monaco three years ago following an accident aboard a boat. We knew his manners were good, his skills more those of a personal servant than a deck hand, and he was pleasing in appearance. So yes, I went into the Monaco equivalent of a pub, near enough to the harbour for convenience, yet far enough away to be no attraction to the tourist.

"I presented myself as the chief steward on a large steam yacht due to tour the Mediterranean in the winter, scouting out local assistance. In particular, I required a man accustomed to sailing, with good manners, who spoke several languages and could drive a motorcar, and who was familiar with Riviera society. And, preferably, pleasant-looking."

"Did any names other than his come up?"

"Surprisingly, yes. One of them was Matteo Crovetti, interestingly enough—although it was agreed that the final requirement disqualified him, unless my employer was willing to overlook the scars of smallpox on his face, and by and large it was agreed that he probably did not drive."

"Well, most of the people here speak several languages, and Madame Crovetti would have taught her son manners. Is he a sailor?"

Ah—I'd hit the key to his self-satisfied air. He milked it by draining his cup and leaning forward to return it to the tray, then sat back again, fingers laced over his shirt-front.

"The Crovetti family are smugglers."

"What? You mean her shop *is* a front?"

"Madame Crovetti, by all appearances, is nothing more than a respectable seller of expensive frocks. However, she married into a well-known family of Monégasque smugglers. All I spoke with agreed that this was in the past, that smuggling as an industry has been all but killed off. Even Crovetti senior, before he ran away with Madame Crovetti's best shop model, had reformed, and had started a business building and hiring out luxury yachts to the winter residents. He is rumoured to be doing that same thing now in the Caribbean. But when I asked if young Matteo might be available for hire, there was a certain degree of uncomfortable laughter, and I was urged to try one of the other names on offer."

"That confirms the impression we had from Madame Crovetti, that there was something embarrassing about her son's absence."

"It would also explain why Inspector Jourdain suspects that Niko Cassavetes was supplying more than artists' sketch-books and American fireworks displays. However, I was more interested in Jourdain's fervent insistence that, once I have satisfied myself with the photos, I have nothing further to do with the matter."

"So why show them to you at all?"

"I may have given him the impression that I mistrusted the skills of the Monaco police department when it came to investigations. Also, that if I was convinced that they did know their jobs, I would be satisfied with providing legal defence to the lady accused of the young man's murder, and promptly withdraw my nose from their business."

"His is a common enough attitude, when it comes to the meddling of professional amateurs like you."

"True. Except that the degree of urgency points to some deeper concern. As if he has been ordered to distract me from the shark in the waters."

I looked at him over my cup. "Are we talking about Basil Zaharoff? Or does Monaco have a whole collection of world-rank criminals?"

"He's not the only scoundrel here, though he is the biggest."

The shadow from The Rock was creeping across the harbour, taking the bright gleam from yachts, skiffs, and the white seaplane. "Holmes, I do understand the compromises people make when it comes to money, but in a place this small, where the Prince can stand at his window over there and survey the entire populace? I'd have thought there would be a bit more . . . distaste. If for no reason other than snobbery."

"Neutrality has its ethical costs. Being unable to choose a side and take a stand may be good for business, but hard on the self-esteem."

"And I suppose that this Prince does spend his time outside the country, like all the others," I mused. "However, surely that can't be all you came up with? You've been gone all day."

"Being rebuffed by the police took less than an hour, and drinking establishments tend not to fill until the afternoon. In between, I had time to hire a car and be outside of the prison when Mrs Hudson came out."

"Who picked her up?"

"A driver—who took her directly to the house of Lillie Langtry. And in the next two hours, the only person to go in and out was the companion, Mathilde, who was gone for forty minutes and returned with a string bag of vegetables and a small box from the local patisserie."

"So they don't plan on holding a large party tonight."

"If they do, the guests have little appetite for cake."

"Good. So if they're busy eating pastry, perhaps I could offer you a spot of housebreaking?"

That cheered him right up. First, I reviewed my day, skipping over the cleaning and that disturbing lingerie to focus on Mrs Hudson's furnishings, the contents of her wardrobe, and finally, the gold-and-garnet earrings.

"The fact that she did not wear them in Sussex does not mean those are new," he noted.

"Although the box they are in is. And I'm fairly certain that she hasn't had them for long."

"Why?"

This was somewhat embarrassing, having so recently protested Holmes' lack of faith in our housekeeper. "You remember how I told you that some years ago, on a visit home from University, I had a poke through Mrs Hudson's things?"

"Where you found a derringer, and her son's birth certificate."

"That's right. She did have some nice pieces in her jewellery box, but these earrings were not among them. And the placement on her dressing table, by themselves, rather than in her little jewellery box, would suggest that they are recent acquisitions."

"Perhaps she bought them in Paris, to go with the clothing she purchased."

"They weren't the kind of things she'd have bought herself."

"Too expensive?"

"Too . . . unnecessary." Did I know her taste, I wondered? I hardly knew her any more—but I felt that the Mrs Hudson I knew, in any of her guises, would prefer solid beauty to showiness. "The evening dresses she bought in Paris are on the edge of ostentatious. Still appropriate for an older woman, yet aiming to make an impression. If she'd bought a pair of earrings to go with them, she'd have chosen something more extravagant."

"So, a personal gift?"

"I'd say so."

"I see. And are the earrings related to your proposal of house-breaking?"

"Only indirectly. She also had a pair of old shoes with a kind of grey mud on the soles."

"I do not yet know Monaco well enough to identify its soils."

"Perhaps I can help. After we'd finished cleaning, I talked Madame Crovetti into taking me next door, into that converted warehouse. Her son Matteo lives there, or does when he's in the country. Two years ago he let his back rooms to Niko Cassavetes. Who has a pair of Wellingtons with a similar grey soil on them."

"Aha." The sound was praise indeed.

"And you know that massively expensive bottle of wine we drank the other night?"

"The Château de—"

I cut into his loving recitation of its pedigree. "That one, yes. The one with the grey sort of dust on it."

He raised an eyebrow. "The same?"

"Certainly very similar to the naked eye."

"Any idea where?" Because clearly I did.

"I might have."

"Hence, the housebreaking."

"But not until Madame Crovetti has gone to bed."

"We have time for dinner, then."

"Though perhaps not another entire bottle of expensive wine."

"My friend the sommelier will be disappointed."

He was. But it did mean that we were both stone-cold sober when we slipped away from the Hermitage, dressed in dark clothing and with various tools in our pockets. We kept to the lesser streets, and found no lights on in Madame Crovetti's trio of buildings. The nearest street-lamp was far enough away to make picking the lock more a matter of touch than sight. Once inside the musty space, I switched on my electric torch, leaving my hand loosely across the lens in case our keen-eyed police constable happened by.

I let the muffled beam play over the furniture, then checked the other rooms as well, but the only creatures I saw had multiple legs. We did find a back door—one that was not fastened shut. It opened onto a narrow delivery lane behind the other two houses, but we explored no further, lest Madame Crovetti be lying awake.

I led Holmes back through Matteo Crovetti's rooms to the crude dividing wall with the well-kept door, where I paused to run my light over the creased wallpaper.

"This divider is more recent than the building. It looks to me as if they decided to chop a storage shed or workshop into two sides with a rough wooden wall, then at some point, covered over the cracks with flowered paper. You can see how well that works." I opened the door, running the unshielded beam over the room behind, but it, too, was empty. Once the door was closed, I switched on the electrical lamp near the settee and reached behind it to pull aside the bedcover-tapestries. As I'd anticipated, they were there to block draughts around a set of wide delivery doors. "This would have been the access for carts and such, making deliveries around the back of the Crovetti house." The doors had been sealed shut, although twenty minutes with screw-driver would free them.

I let the tapestry fall, and took Holmes to the bedroom with the sloping back wall. In Niko's makeshift wardrobe, I lifted some garments off their hooks to reveal the wall behind. "Does that look like a door to you?" I asked.

It did not, in fact, resemble a door. It would have looked like a bodged-together wall over a raw cliff-face—except for the greyish soil, ground into the floor-boards.

I held the torch while Holmes dropped to his knees in front of the suspicious patch of wall. His sensitive fingers ran up and down the roughly painted surface, concentrating on an area that looked marginally more grimy . . .

It clicked.

I expected a cubby-hole, a place to store small, but valuable possessions. I watched Holmes lean inside the cleverly disguised doorway—then he rose and stepped through it.

CHAPTER TWENTY-EIGHT

"Good lord—an actual smugglers' cave?" My voice echoed, suggesting size. The light from Holmes' torch bounced over pale, lumpy walls, from somewhere beyond a turn in the passageway. I climbed through the narrow door, avoiding the crate of beer just inside the entrance, and followed the boards laid across the damp floor—inadequately, as one foot sank into a chalky puddle, giving me a shoe to match those of Niko and Mrs Hudson. The space was tight, the ceiling pressed down, but if Holmes had gone before . . .

Once past the turn, the walls fell away. I straightened, and my jaw dropped.

The room was immense, our torches barely adequate to illuminate the stalactites dribbling down above our heads. Holmes turned his beam onto the nearby walls, but I kept mine pointed upwards, staring into the mesmerising fingers. A drip echoed from some distant puddle. I was dimly aware of a metallic rattle, then the scrape of a match, and a warm light filled the cave. Shadows leapt, then went still, as Holmes hung a paraffin lamp from its hook near the entrance.

The cavern became marginally less immense. Towards its walls, many of the descending calcium fingers had been broken away, either deliberately or at the passage of some load. On the floor, stalagmites had been hacked off to clear the ground for the smugglers' goods. Vestigial steps had been carved into a rise at the back, some thirty feet away, beyond which our beams suggested further rooms.

Another drip sounded.

At last, we pulled our attention away from our surroundings and on to the reason for our presence here: the contents of this smuggler's cave.

On either side of the central pathway, crude tables and cruder hunks of wood served to keep valuables from the damp floor. Some of the boards on the ground were former tables, long since collapsed, while others looked like crates that had been emptied and smashed flat. I had seen smugglers' caves before—Sussex has a long history of contraband goods and the efficient plundering of wrecked ships—and while this cave was certainly large enough to funnel illicit rum into half of France, it did not appear to have ever been used to the full.

But it had been used recently. Shipping crates narrow enough to clear the entrance waited on either side. The rough tables close to the door had little dust on the tops, and some of the footprints in the wet patches had not had time to lose their definition.

Holmes went to examine the boxes to the left, leaving me those on the right. Without a pry-bar, I could not see into all of them, but only one had a snug lid, and most of the things bore an air of abandonment. A case of cigarettes so ancient and damp, even a desperate old lag would look askance. Six bolts of once-spectacular Indian silk fabric, mouldering to destruction under a waxed-cloth tarpaulin. Five identical gramophones with inlaid wood cases that would have brought a tidy sum—before the Great War, and before dampness had frozen the works and sprung the veneer. Two cases of perfume bottles with peeling labels. Mother-of pearl buttons, ivory-handled boot-hooks, Deco-styled hairpins that had long lost their gleam.

"A lot of old tat over here," I told him. "No sign of drugs, just some cigarettes that have fallen to pieces. If Madame Crovetti's son was smuggling, he was either very bad at it, or someone has cleared out the good stuff."

His reply was a thump and a screech of nails. I turned to find him prising up the top of a wooden case some thirty inches wide, using an iron bar so large he could not possibly have brought it in his pocket. Laying the top aside, he plunged his hands into tangles of excelsior. The aroma of fresh wood was startlingly crisp and alive in this place.

I went to look over his shoulder. "That box hasn't been sitting here since 1910," I said. The others on his side were also of a more recent vintage than those I'd been poking through.

Beneath the packing material were half a dozen identical leather jewellery boxes. He opened one, and held it up to show me a beautiful silver filigree-and-carnelian necklace with matching earrings, barely tarnished. He put it aside. The next box held another set, equally stunning, but made of pale gold with blue Turkish chalcedony. The next three were silver, each a different personality, each with unique stones, some clear and faceted, others opaque. The last was the most beautiful yet, rose gold with a spray of faceted gemstones that seemed to dance in different colours.

"That's a striking piece."

"A stone called diaspore," Holmes commented. "Mined in Turkey. Its colour changes with the light."

He shut the box to excavate the second layer. Smaller boxes, of the same manufacture, containing bracelets with faceted stones.

He thrust the pry-bar under a second lid. This crate held the equivalent decorations for men: sets of shirt-studs and cuff-links in one layer, intricately engraved cigarette cases in the next, some with gems inset, each in its own fitted leather case. Two other boxes held similar bits of expensive beauty, from hair bandeaux and hat decorations to cigar-cutters and key fobs.

There were two cases that did not match those with the jewellery. One was larger, and filled with Cuban cigars. The other held dozens of vicious-looking knives that had nothing to do with food preparation.

When we had finished, we packed it all away, straightening the nails and tapping them into place. At the end, we stood back, thinking.

"Those are all things with a heavy luxury tax."

"And knives of the sort forbidden in Italy," he pointed out.

"Maybe those were on their way out of the country? But the necklaces and money clips look like the expensive souvenirs sold by shops near the Casino."

"Shops such as Madame Crovetti's?"

"Perhaps I should drop by and have a look."

"Interesting that there is no sign of cocaine," he mused. "That seems to be the smugglers' favourite at present."

"Matteo Crovetti has been gone for six months," I said. "So these boxes have to be Niko's work. He's definitely been in here—that delicate foot-print is from his boot. But that doesn't explain Mrs Hudson's presence. A stranger, dropping straight into a smuggling ring within weeks of her arrival? I suppose the chalk on her shoes could have come from elsewhere. There must be other caves in Monaco? Oh good heavens," I exclaimed. "The police station on Spélugues Street. I thought it meant a grotto with a saint—but it meant cave. Right?"

"I understand that portions of Monaco resemble a petrified sponge, with everything from purpose-built wine cellars to a vast natural complex rumoured to be underneath the Jardin Exotique. But demanding a different source for the grey mud requires us to accept the possibility of coincidence—"

"Which God forbid," I muttered.

"—and it is, you will admit, more probable that matching stains on the shoes of two immediate neighbours would come from the same place. Beyond that, I would require the use of a microscope."

"Mrs Hudson as the partner of a smuggler? That doesn't exactly match her known history." Unless our landlady had spent the past twenty years as a secret member of the age-old fraternity of Sussex smugglers? Clara Hudson: the Moriarty of the Sussex Downs. A pirate in disguise . . .

I shook my head, wondering if the oxygen was thin in the cave, then noticed the motion extending down my shoulders. "It's cold in here, Holmes. Can we move back into the building?"

But his eyes travelled across the cavern to the primitive stairway. "You go back. I'd like to see what lies beyond."

So naturally I went with him, and naturally I slipped on the greasy rock—twice—and scraped my already abused hands. I didn't know if he was looking for a murdered Matteo Crovetti or the crated-up Crown of St Edward, but all we found were indications that this had once been a busy smuggling operation, mostly suspended now.

In the third, last, and smallest cavern, a natural stone seat had clearly found use throughout the ages. The centuries of litter around its base included a peculiarly shaped stalagmite that, on closer examination, proved to be a bottle placed there so long ago, the drips of stone had entirely enveloped the glass beneath.

"No cocaine, no dead bodies. Not even any paste tiaras," I said to Holmes.

"Plenty of nooks and crannies," he noted.

"Do you want to search all of them?" I asked. "If so, we'll need more paraffin for the lamp."

To my relief, he turned back to the steps so we might slither our way through the smugglers' cavern to the entrance, and the warmth beyond.

CHAPTER TWENTY-NINE

It was three a.m., and I was wrapped in one of Niko's bedcovers. My shivers were starting to recede, thanks in part to a glass of the dead man's brandy in my hand. Holmes had one, too, and was making use of an ash-tray he'd found in the room next door—where his quick search had also given us a spare key, a suspicious absence of financial records, and a casual assortment of smuggled alcohol and tobacco. Though no indication of drugs.

"Is she in danger, Holmes?"

"Mrs Hudson? No." He then spoilt the reassurance by adding, "At any rate, not immediately."

"A man was killed in her home."

"Yes, a man—not her. I believe the intention of laying a body literally at her door was to have her arrested. Although I cannot yet see if the arrest served merely to remove her from the playing field for a time, or was meant as a threat."

"People don't generally commit murder as a threat."

"Some people do. And this was no random victim. Whatever the point of using Mrs Hudson's sitting room may have been, someone wanted to be rid of Niko Cassavetes. That young man is the centre of this, somehow. A Greek sailor, come to Monaco some three years ago, hires himself out as an *homme à tout faire*, letting rooms from a family with a history of smuggling, who provide him a place to stash goods. He meets an English housekeeper with a criminal history, who's in need of an income, and arranges for her to take rooms with that same smuggling family."

"But Holmes, we've already agreed that the Riviera is a small village, especially in the off-season. Wouldn't it be more extraordinary if a 'fixer' and a free-lancing housekeeper *didn't* know each other?"

"To find Russian nobility joined with artistic Americans is not so preordained. That appears to be Niko's doing."

"But to what purpose? And what about Lillie Langtry? She must be Mrs Hudson's nameless friend, who introduced her to Niko in the first place."

"But not to Basil Zaharoff. The three of them seem to be old . . . acquaintances."

"Well, I suppose I could return to Antibes and see what Sara and Gerald can tell me about Niko. Do you wish to join me?"

"I need to speak with Count Vasilev."

"I'd bet Mrs Langtry would be happy to help you there. She seemed very taken with your moustache."

Fortunately, he did not grace the remark with a reply, merely ground out his cigarette in the ash-tray, then took it and the glass back to Matteo Crovetti's side of the quarters. I returned the borrowed wrap to the bed and followed, carrying the key that he had found.

"Will anyone notice if this key is missing?" I asked.

"Will it matter if they do?" So I used it to lock the door as we left, and dropped it into a pocket to return.

It was nearly four in the morning as we walked the silent lanes, our voices little more than murmurs. "I can take the train to Antibes tomorrow—later today, I mean—but I'd like to hear what

Inspector Jourdain has to say. Do you think he'd mind my joining you?"

"No more than he minds speaking to me in the first place. But yes, you go back afterwards. I shall keep the room here at the Hermitage. Our business in Monaco is far from over."

Parting already? I pushed down my disappointment. "I also want to see Mrs Hudson before I leave. I'll ring Mrs Langtry first, to make sure she's there."

"No doubt the hotel exchange can connect you. Is there any reason for me to come?"

There was every reason for him to stay away, but I did not think it would ease matters to put it so bluntly. "No, I just wanted a chat without the guard listening in. Just to say hello. We can both go see her in a day or so."

To my relief, he agreed, and I cheerfully tucked my arm through his as we walked through the pre-dawn city. At the Hermitage, our late entrance caused less distress than the dust on our clothing. Clearly, guests of the Hôtel Hermitage were expected to dress properly for all late-night excursions.

At a more reasonable hour, quite a long time after dawn, we rose and broke our fast with coffee and rolls. Inspector Jourdain was expecting us—or half of us, at any rate—in the park at ten. Though perhaps he would not appreciate a female person wearing evening dress, chalk-smeared trousers, or a frock that had been worn for scrubbing a floor. I sighed and rang down a third time to see if my French lady's maid could summon yet more garments out of the air.

Unfortunately, she was unavailable. And her replacement, though armed with my measurements, was also armed with a peculiar sense of taste.

I had no time to protest, or even look too closely at the frock, I merely threw it on and bolted out of the door.

As we might have guessed, Jourdain kept us waiting. As we sat on the designated bench in a quiet corner of a dull park, I took my first look at what I was wearing. It had been chosen by someone with an Edwardian sense of taste. Either that, or a malicious sense of humour.

"I look like a chintz armchair," I said.

Holmes glanced at the girly frock, and turned away—but not before I saw the brief quirk of his lips.

I plucked at the stiff sprig of lace on my inadequate bust, and sighed. "I suppose it could have been worse."

"Yes?"

"At least the flowers aren't too pink."

"As a disguise, Russell, it is effectively misleading."

"I hope I can make it to my room in the Cap before the Hon Terry spots me."

"Mrs Hudson will be entertained," he commented.

Inspector Jourdain was not, but then I didn't imagine that sour face would find much in his world to amuse him. He was no more approving of Holmes' trim suit than of my fashion atrocity, or indeed, my very presence.

"Who is this?" he demanded.

"My partner, Miss Russell."

"That was not what we agreed."

"Did you bring the files?"

"I cannot show you official police files."

"Why not? I don't need your interview notes, merely the photographs and anything of interest which your coroner may have found. He has done his autopsy, I trust?"

"Saturday morning."

"I don't expect he's written up his report yet, but no doubt he at least gave you a verbal one?"

Jourdain hesitated—but if he hadn't meant to show us what he had, why agree to meet?

With a show of irritation, he snatched an envelope from his inner pocket and slapped it down on the bench beside Holmes.

Though when Holmes pulled out its contents fully within my view, the policeman drew breath as if to protest.

I found him staring at me with a look of outrage. Perhaps Holmes had been right: the dress disguised me, making me into a person who would faint at the photograph of a dead man. I gave the poor fellow an encouraging smile, and turned to the photos. The policeman lit a furious cigarette and began to pace up and down.

There were, as I had feared, only a handful of photos. The first, taken in situ, showed Niko Cassavetes, head resting on the little carpet Madame Crovetti had discarded, the rest of him surrounded by the black pool that I had spent the previous day removing. I found myself rubbing my fingertips as if his blood remained beneath my finger-nails, even though I'd worn gloves. He lay between the wall and a settee, face up but turned slightly onto his left side, left arm sprawled across the floor, wrist up, his right arm draped over his chest. He was wearing casual duck trousers and shirt-sleeves, the shirt either white or some pale colour, its sleeves rolled halfway up his forearms. The photograph was not completely clear, but he appeared to have a single bullet hole directly over his heart.

Holmes thumbed through the other pictures, looking for an autopsy photograph of the victim's back, and failed to find one. "Did the bullet go all the way through?"

"No," I said. Jourdain's pacing stopped. "I cleaned the room. There was no bullet hole in the wall or furniture behind him."

The man's eyes narrowed at this contradiction between my appearance and my words, but he nodded. "She's right. The coroner dug it out of him."

"The calibre?" Holmes asked in a patient voice.

"Nine millimetre." The policeman then added, reluctantly, "Possibly the Browning Long."

"Used by half of northern Europe's police and military for the past twenty years," Holmes remarked.

"I have a Browning myself."

If the bullet had passed all the way through Niko's chest, more blood would have pooled beneath him. It had not, but as I thought earlier, the stain was too wide for death to have been instantaneous. The heart had beat a few times before stopping, sending the blood welling up over his chest but not hard enough to spray the room with blood.

Holmes dug out his pocket magnifying-glass and bent over the earliest photograph, showing the body as the police had first seen it. "What did your analysts make of the blood-drying time?" he asked.

Jourdain's lack of a response was in itself the answer: either no one had noticed, or Monaco had no such analysts. Probably both. I braced myself for a barrage of science and superiority that would leave both men with hackles raised, but to my surprise, Holmes drew a deep breath, held it, let it out—then merely mused aloud as he continued to scrutinise the dry, unsmeared drops and the trampled edges of the blood pool. "Those drops—hard surface, warm day, even in this humidity they would dry in less than an hour. The pool, of course, is another matter. There is some interesting work being done on the relative drying times of blood, taking into account temperature, humidity, surfaces, and so on. I could send that to you, if you like. However, that constable who was first on the scene might have noticed how dry it was when he arrived. Since, as you know, a standing pool of blood takes two or three hours to turn from very dark to brighter red, and another two or three hours for the edges of the pool to begin showing a dry rim. He may have had a chance to notice its state before the rest of your colleagues came in and ... disturbed the scene."

I waited for him to drive the point home—that a bright red pool that was only beginning to go dry at the edges suggested a shooting time of six o'clock at the earliest, while Mrs Hudson had been gone by four and did not return until after eleven. But again, discretion surfaced, and Holmes merely folded away his glass, dropping the subject of drying times entirely to turn his attention to the actual subject of the photograph. The dead man lay calm, lips together, his eyelids nearly shut over those extraordinary eyes. His hair looked even lighter than it had on the beach that day.

"More Pathan than Mediterranean Greek," Holmes commented.

"Is that where those eyes came from? I did wonder."

The hair on Niko's forearms was similarly light—at the least, on his right arm, where the rolled-up sleeve lay well down from his elbow. At the shirt's edge, the skin had a dark stain that did not appear to be a spatter of blood. A tattoo? The shape resembled a mermaid's tail. His left arm lay stretched out across those boards that I had scrubbed: palm up, fingers curled, shirt pulled back to the fold of his elbow. Studying the musculature, one could see other signs—along with the tattoo—that despite his delicate build and good manners, this young man had been no bookish office worker. Holmes had described him as more personal servant than deck hand, but that arm had been accustomed to physical labour: the fingers were small but powerful, knuckles heavy, his palm crossed by minor scars. Even in its slack state, the veins and tendons of his wrist stood out, as my own had begun to do after three weeks of working sails.

I saw no tattoo stains on his left arm, though the image was clear enough to count each sun-bleached hair along the upper side of it. Though . . . I raised the photograph, squinting at the details. Halfway up the forearm, a patch of hair seemed to be missing. I sorted through the other photographs, but though they included one showing his nude chest—graced by another tattoo—none included the full length of Niko's left arm.

Holmes passed the last photograph to me. This one came out of order, and showed Niko's chest. He was lying on Mrs Hudson's floor, but had been turned onto his back. On his left side, the shirt was saturated with blood, but the right side and shoulder were largely untouched. I could see none of the small black specks that resulted when a gun went off close to fabric.

"The shooter was not close," Holmes said to the policeman.

"Probably ten feet or so away."

"Just inside the doorway, then," I noted.

"Most likely."

"Why didn't anyone hear the gunshot?" Holmes asked.

Jourdain reached out to sift through the photographs, stopping at the earliest in the sequence, showing Niko on the floor. His brown-stained finger tapped the back of the settee, where a sort of travelling rug had been tossed. A rug that hadn't been there when I saw the room, and yet I had overlooked it in the photograph. "There were burn marks on that thing. Like might have happened if it was wrapped around a gun."

"Would that muffle a gunshot?" I asked in surprise.

"Some. Perhaps enough to make it sound like a backfiring engine. We get a lot of those here, with all the hills."

But with that unseemly burst of cooperation, Jourdain withdrew. The rest of his answers were terse and uninformative, and in a few minutes, he snatched back the photographs and shoved them into his pocket.

"I hope that satisfies you that we can manage this without outside help. Now, please, go away and allow me to do my work."

He stalked off, the latest in a long line of policemen who disapproved of Sherlock Holmes and his techniques.

CHAPTER THIRTY

Holmes, inevitably, lit a cigarette. But I had got to my feet, perhaps in protest, and found myself walking in the general direction that Inspector Jourdain had gone. I stared down at the pavement, deep in thought, and somehow avoided being run down by motors or trams. Some time later, I became aware that Holmes had spoken. "I'm sorry, Holmes—what was that?"

"I asked if you were intending to lunch?"

I found I had blindly migrated into a patch of shade—namely, a small café with so many umbrellas, its terrace might have been roofed. "It's early, but why not?"

We ordered something, and eventually I said to Holmes, "Do you think Niko might have had a tattoo done?"

His eyebrow quirked at me, questioning my statement of the obvious. "The mark beneath the sleeve on his right arm? What would that have been, if not a tattoo?"

"I mean the left arm. That swathe of hair missing from his upper forearm. Though the photo only showed the edges of it. Don't they usually shave off any hair before doing a tattoo?"

He slowly transferred his napkin from table to lap, eyes focused far away.

"You didn't see it?" He shook his head. "Ah. Never mind. It was probably just a mark on the photograph."

"Not necessarily. Although I'm not sure what a newly installed tattoo might tell us."

"I suppose nothing." But I didn't think it was just a mark on the print or a fluke of shadow. And if that was the case, then I had noticed something the eyes of Sherlock Holmes hadn't caught. Triumphs are sweet—even those that mean nothing.

But Holmes was not willing to dismiss it, even as a sign of his failure. "Did the skin look discoloured? Tattoos leave the skin around them irritated and red for a time."

My turn to look into the distance and think, then shake my head. "I can't be sure. But any redness would have been minor—or further around the arm."

"Excellent work, Russell. It could help us narrow down the man's movements during his final days."

"Really? I mean, how?"

"There can't be that many tattoo parlours in Monaco."

"Are we going to hunt down tattoo parlours?" Meaning, was *I* going to.

"I rather doubt Jourdain will do so."

"Well," I said, "at least the search area is limited."

"True. Which is why I shall remain in Monaco and follow that scent, while you return to Antibes and see what the Murphy set has to tell you."

"Really? You don't want me to hunt down tattoos?"

"Hmm. I suppose in this modern and emancipated era, a young lady might be given entry into such places, but—"

"No, that's quite all right. You take the tattoos, I'll take the artists. Shall we meet up at the Hôtel du Cap?"

"As soon as I am free."

We ate a perfectly decent lunch, then went our separate ways.

I went back to the Hermitage, in part to sort out clothing for the laundry so I did not have to keep buying things, and in part to telephone to Mrs Hudson.

The former I managed without mishap, although I was sorely tempted to exchange the peculiar flowered dress I was wearing for yesterday's wrinkled garments. The phone call was less successful.

I did reach her, at the home of Lillie Langtry, and I did manage to express my happiness that she had been granted release. But I did not succeed in convincing her to see me.

"Oh, Mary, dear, I'd love to see you, but today will be so filled with lawyers and such like, I shall be terribly distracted. Perhaps tomorrow, or even the next day? Everything should have settled nicely by then."

Either that, I thought, or Jourdain will have you back in gaol. "Shall I ring at this same number, tomorrow morning?"

"They did tell me to remain with Lillie, although I hate to make demands on a friend's hospitality. Yes, try here first. If you don't reach me, I may be back in my own house. Do you have Madame Crovetti's telephone number? She will bring me a message, if you catch her before half-nine."

"I have that number, yes. And, Mrs Hudson? I—we—she and I, that is—cleaned your place. You don't need to worry about going home."

"Oh, I know dear, I've spoken with her. Very kind of you, though I'd have managed."

"I have no doubt of it. But you, well, you've cleaned up so many of our messes over the years, Holmes' and mine, that I was . . . well. I am grateful."

Particularly for that last mess, the blood I had spilled, drying on the floor.

"I know, child. But thank you. I shall see you in a day or two. Give my greetings to Mr Holmes."

And the connection went dead.

I'm not sure how long I sat, gazing at the expensive boats in the harbour—the white sea-plane was missing, I noticed, and the enormous *Bella Ragazza* was having its decks scrubbed—before my meditation was broken by a gentle rap on the door, which came open just as I reached for the handle. The cleaning lady retreated immediately, amidst a storm of apologies in French with a Monégasque accent.

"No, come in," I told her. "I was just leaving." And to illustrate the fact, I fetched my hat and took a last, despairing, glance at the mirror.

She apologised again for disturbing me, explaining that the desk had seen my husband leave but had failed to notice I was not with him and . . .

"Absolutely no problem," I reassured her, and to prove it, went out of the door, amused at this minor breakdown of the great hotel's communications system. Like a village, where information and mis-information alike spread with ease.

My feet slowed, and stopped. A village. Where everyone knew Lillie Langtry. Might that apply to all of Monaco's prominent residents? Because sooner or later, either Holmes or I would need to speak with the shark in these waters. The one that Inspector Jourdain was so fervently trying to keep us from.

The one who had known Mrs Hudson since she was a coy young grifter.

I was curious, though I had no wish to come into personal contact with the man. Perhaps a chance meeting, in public, with many witnesses to hand . . .

It might help to know where the man lived. Not that a hotel that valued the privacy of its clients would permit its desk clerk to hand over an address, but perhaps if I asked a less obvious source of information . . .

I walked back to the room and stuck my head inside, catching the cleaning woman as she gathered up the ash-trays and waste-baskets. "Sorry, may I ask—do you know Sir Basil Zaharoff? Who he is, I mean?"

"But of course, Madame."

"Is it possible you know where I can find his offices, or perhaps his home?"

"Oh, Madame, I am sorry, I do not."

"That's fine, I'll ask—"

"But I know where his rooms in the hotel are."

"He has rooms here?"

"As an office, yes? For when he is doing business, you know?"

"I see."

"Shall I take you?"

"Heavens no, I wouldn't dream of interrupting your work. But, perhaps the room number . . . ?"

To my astonishment, she was so flustered—either by her own gaffe at intruding upon me or by the unheard-of respect shown her *work* by a guest (or perhaps by the disarming floral print I wore) that she recited it. Taking care to show nothing on my face but vague appreciation, I nodded and closed the door on her dawning expression of horror—her realisation that she might have put a foot wrong.

At the end of the hallway, I heard the door come open, so I took the downward stairs, to set the poor woman's mind at rest. I paused on the landing for a count of ten before turning around, going all the way to the top floor.

Zaharoff's office suite was at the end of the hallway. It seemed to be cleaning time here as well, since the door was standing open and I could hear voices from within. I rapped at the door, then stepped inside to ask the cleaners if they knew when his secretary might be—

No cleaners. And not an office, really, but a luxurious suite of rooms, so high over the harbour that it was on a level with the Palace itself. This room was dominated by an enormous walnut desk and decorative touches that had to be personal—a sumptuous carpet on the floor, an Ottoman scimitar on the wall, a Fabergé egg on the desk.

And behind the desk, not a secretary, but the rotund, elderly man I'd glimpsed in the Casino on Saturday night: pale eyes, white moustache, pointed goatee. The Merchant of Death himself, Europe's Man of Mystery, the richest monster in Europe, ran a piercing gaze over my person from hat to shoes. Unfortunately, my frock had no effect, because he reached down into the desk and came up with a gun.

Why had I not considered the possibility that an arms dealer might wield an actual weapon?

CHAPTER THIRTY-ONE

S herlock Holmes hoped his wife was having a productive cup of tea with their former housekeeper. The day had just begun, and he was already regretting his choice of rooting out all the wielders of ink and needles.

He had expected that the modern little moustache he wore at present would be a problem, when it came to slouching into tattoo parlours and asking about the wares. Still, if that had been a tattoo on the police photograph, and he'd missed it, he had ground to make up. Slouching into any shop-front that resembled a tattoo parlour was the only way to make amends.

The first surprise was how many there were, in a place like Monaco.

But that was nothing to his astonishment at seeing the customers. A tattoo was no longer a thing for the decoration of navvies and stevedores, applied in a dim hole-in-the-wall that stank of whiskey and sweat. The last parlour he had walked into had been brightly lit, with ferns in the window and a gramophone record chortling away, with the person in the chair a woman, younger than Russell, having dark lines added to her eyebrows. Or more precisely, having lines added to where her eyebrows would've been had she not plucked them out.

None of the tattooists, however, betrayed any recognition when he asked about a handsome young man with brilliant green eyes.

Interest, yes. Recognition, no.

He could only trust that Russell was having more luck than he.

CHAPTER THIRTY-TWO

I'd walked into the hotel room expecting an office, with secretary and appointment books. Beyond that, I suppose I had blithely assumed that any businessman who dealt in deadly munitions was only dangerous when it came to his wares on a battlefield. But of *course* a person like this would have a gun to hand—and not one of his flawed, liable-to-fail designs, but the sleekest, most modern of automatic pistols.

Pointed at me. Directly at me. So close, a child could not miss—and why should a man with so much blood on his hands even hesitate? He couldn't know who I was—could have no idea that pulling the trigger would summon the wrath of not only Sherlock Holmes but British Intelligence as well, and though yes, it would be nice to have a bullet to match with the one taken from Niko Cassavetes, I'd rather it not be me who had to bleed onto that beautiful carpet beneath my—

Oh, for God's sake, Russell, *do* something.

I cleared my throat and forced myself to look away from the gun, meeting his intense blue eyes and trying to piece together a smile. "I wonder if we might have a little talk? Preferably before you shoot me."

A man's voice came from the adjoining room, speaking Russian. Zaharoff said something in reply, and the man entered, moving fast. He was big and scarred and heavily muscled, a man I knew was a bodyguard even before I saw the gun inside his coat, but Zaharoff waved him off before he could tackle me to the ground. The old man made an irritated gesture at the open door behind me and snapped out a command. Flushing, the bodyguard stalked past me into the hallway. I did not hear the door close.

"Sir Basil Zaharoff?" I asked, although the honorific rather stuck in my throat.

"Who are you?" His English was only lightly accented.

"My name is Mary Russell. I'm a friend of Clara Hudson."

"Who?"

"Clara—Clarissa Hudson? You had dinner with her, the other night? At the house of Lillie Langtry?" Why did all my statements insist on coming out as questions?

"Yes. Pleasant woman." He made it sound like a category: old man; young girl; pleasant woman; loathsome, double-dealing, big-amistic seller of second-rate guns—again, I wrenched my thoughts back into line.

"Indeed, she said it was a good evening. However, I'm not sure if you know that there was an . . . accident at her home, that same evening. A young man died?"

The terrifying eyes gleamed at me like something out of the woods at dusk—and then, as abruptly as a switch being flipped, they changed. The skin beside the eyes crinkled, the moustache twitched, the old man's posture slumped, sweeping away all traces of menace. I was looking across the desk at a genial grandfather. Who now glanced down at the gun in his hand and put it cautiously away, sliding the drawer shut as if to keep the weapon from leaping out.

"I'm sorry, I don't know why you alarmed me," he said. "Most ill-mannered of me. My dear, what can I do for you?"

The transformation was breath-taking—and I speak as a person whose husband can adopt new personas at the drop of a hat. "I, er, yes, I apologise for intruding. I just, the cl—" I caught myself before I could reveal the source of betrayal, and changed it to: "a clerk I talked to recently mentioned that you had a suite of rooms in this hotel, and I figured they'd be on the top floor, so I thought I'd come and see if I could make an appointment. Or something."

He thought for a moment, then put on a good-natured smile. "Well, you seem to have found me. I'm very glad I didn't accidentally shoot you. Although I imagine Feodor took the bullets out, he generally does. Feodor is my secretary."

The presence of his "secretary" behind me made the skin of my back constrict, but I made an effort and did not turn around.

I did not think that gun was empty. I did not imagine any servant of this man would dare to disable his weapon.

Still, two could don a mask of charm. And I did have the frock and spectacles going for me. "I quite understand, these are hazardous times." I dredged up another smile. "I wouldn't think of bothering you, were it not for Miss Hudson's troubles. The police actually imagined that she was responsible. That she *shot* him. Can you believe it?"

"Young lady, I can't see that this is anything to do with me."

Friendly or not, it was interesting that his first reaction was denial. Or perhaps that was merely habit. "It isn't, I suppose. But the police want to know where she was when he died. So I thought I might just clear things up by asking you: she was at Mrs Langtry's until you and Count Vasilev left, wasn't she?"

"Miss Russell—is it Miss?"

"Mrs, in fact."

"Mrs Russell, I have no idea how long Clarissa stayed, after the Count and I left. She and Lillie are old friends, and the ladies do like to gossip. However, shouldn't the police be asking these questions?" His dismissive tone suggested how very unlikely a police interview of Basil Zaharoff would be.

"They should be, yes. But I believe they're rather afraid of you, sir."

For the first time, the old man looked at *me* rather than at the problem I might represent, studying me with as much attention as I'd ever seen Holmes give a problem. At the end of the examination, he startled me for the third time in as many minutes. He smiled.

This smile was genuine. Warm, amused, and personal. He dropped into the chair behind the desk, and gestured me towards the unoccupied one. I obeyed, perching on the very edge of the seat.

"A police inspector is afraid, and yet a young woman is not?" I had not mentioned Jourdain's rank, but then, a man like this would know everything that went on in the Principality. He might even know the true identities of Mr and Mrs Sheldon Russell.

I chose my words with care. "I think you are a businessman. I think you have spent your life balancing profit against risk, and that you tend not to act rashly. I think you would not choose to . . . act against a young English woman who comes to you with questions. I think you would find it simpler to give her answers, and not threats."

He sat back, threading his fingers together over his paunch, eyes sparkling. "Ask."

"Thank you. As I said, Miss Hudson is a friend. I need to know how much trouble she's in, before I can continue with my travel plans." Which was nonsense, but I wore a face—and a dress—for innocence.

"I, too, regard Clarissa Hudson as a friend," said the old monster. "I have known her since we were young and carefree, although I have only seen her a handful of times since she arrived in Monaco, some weeks ago."

"I think you also knew the man? Niko Cassavetes?"

His Father Christmas veneer went thin for an instant, then returned full strength. But not from surprise. Anger? "Is that who died? The Cassavetes boy?"

"You knew him?"

"I knew of him. I may even have come across him, once or twice. He did some small jobs for one of my friends, nothing too demanding. Mostly filling in for others."

Smokescreens require large quantities of smoke: the longer the explanation—such as this one—the greater the deceit.

"Jobs on boats?" To actually use the word "smuggling" might be pushing my luck.

"So I understand."

"Could I talk to this friend of yours who employed him?"

"How would that help Miss Hudson?"

"Certain . . . elements of Niko's life appear to be less than legal," I said. "If he had an argument with some criminal associate, it could remove Miss Hudson from suspicion."

The old eyebrows rose. "Are you suggesting that my friend knowingly employed a criminal? Or perhaps you suggest that I killed the boy myself?"

The edge in his voice made my organs cramp. "Sir, I doubt there's a man in Monaco less likely to shoot Niko Cassavetes dead than you." With his own hand, that is.

"I am relieved you think so," he said, the jolly old elf. "Now, young lady, amusing as this has been, I have a busy day."

I forced a last question out of my tight throat. "Niko did some work for you, too, didn't he? He seemed to work for pretty much everyone in Monaco, at one time or another."

"This and that. But not in a while, and nothing illegal." He made a show of getting laboriously to his feet. "Do I need to have Feodor show you the door?"

Hearing his name, the hired brute looked inside. For a moment, I was tempted to see whether his muscles, or my skills would win out—but that would involve a lot of smashed furniture and yet another set of clothing, so I thanked the monster politely and with a final glance out at the spectacular view this man all but owned—harbour, Palace, town, and the Mediterranean beyond—I straightened my shoulders and took my flowered artificial silk out of the luxurious suite, down the stairs, and out of the hotel itself.

I managed not to break into a run, or even turn to see who was following me, all the way to the train station at the foot of the Casino.

But I can't say I took an easy breath until the train doors rattled shut. When the cars jerked into motion at last, I eased my head back against the rest and waited for my racing heart to slow.

CHAPTER THIRTY-THREE

The Riviera train line had one other stop inside Monaco, but once the rails left the Principality, they were allowed to emerge above ground and become scenic, travelling at the coastline as far as Nice, then meandering in and out.

I did not notice much of the glorious view. My mind was working harder than the engine that pulled us.

Basil Zaharoff. A man in his late seventies, Greek-born, but Russian-named, due to his family's period of Russian exile. He learned his early lessons in criminality with the Istanbul fire service, setting houses aflame that they might be saved and treasures "recovered"—for payment. A lifetime in crime, bigamous marriages to wealthy women, sales of disastrously inadequate military hardware to both sides of conflicts—conflicts he had helped to create—coupled with industrial sabotage, let him compile a truly stupefying fortune during the Great War. He made friends in high places, and took care to purchase respectability with huge donations to worthy causes. His deft manipulation of newspapers, banks, and elections helped ensure an Allied victory, leading to high honours in France, England, and Greece—though whether those were meant to reward his service, or to ensure his silence, was a matter of debate. He had recently married his long-time lover, one of the richest women in Spain, a woman who had used her position to further his business interests. And then he had bought himself a principality, for the comfort of his later years.

Those eyes of his, switching so instantly from deadly to congenial. I felt as if I'd just tip-toed through a nest of scorpions.

What was Zaharoff's link to Niko Cassavetes? The richest man in Europe and a young *homme à tout faire* made for unlikely colleagues, and even less likely friends. Oh, I could well imagine that Zaharoff had his busy hands in the smuggling trade, but any direct tie between the two would be like a friendship between King Edward and an apprentice gardener.

Yet I'd have sworn that Zaharoff had reacted to the dead man's name. That he not only knew who Niko was, but knew that his death could be a problem.

His uneasiness had lasted only a moment before his face had resumed its unconcerned, even faintly amused expression. Because he knew he was untouchable by the likes of me? Even Sherlock Holmes had not been able to put a stop to the man.

Or was it merely that he knew we would find no evidence against him? Zaharoff himself would never have stood in Mrs Hudson's sitting room and pulled a trigger. If Niko was a threat, or even an inconvenience, Zaharoff would have sent someone to do it for him—someone like a large, scarred bodyguard. Feodor's immediate impulse had been to tackle me as an intruder, but he no doubt knew how to use the gun he wore. A gun that, unfortunately, I hadn't seen closely enough to see what size bullet it would fire.

And where did Mrs Hudson come in to this? She and Zaharoff were near-contemporaries who had known each other—possibly quite well—back in their wild youth. They could have met since any number of times, in Monte Carlo or elsewhere. Still, I couldn't help feeling that any actual friendship (or yes, hard as it might be to imagine, any physical attraction) had long since been buried under the weight of his sins. I could see her being forced to put up with his presence as the price of living in Monaco—but like her friend Mrs Langtry, I could also see her stifling an impulse to pull away from his presence.

Were he any less of a power here, Mrs Hudson would treat the man with the sort of polite distraction that makes even an eminent victim feel small. I'd seen her do it, often enough.

Or was I creating a pleasing story around a woman I loved, to convince myself that I really did know her true nature, deep down?

And what about the mysterious Count Vasilev of the manicured facial hair? Loyal friend of the last Czar, but also of Monaco's own Merchant of Death. Intimate of a ruling family, employer of a possible smuggler, patron of the arts, and a friend to visiting Americans—whose country he wished to make his own, because of an ill daughter.

Round and round went this cast of characters, as the train paused in Nice and Antibes and places along the way. I nearly missed Juan-les-Pins, hearing the repeated name at the last instant and hurling myself through the train's door before it jerked into motion.

Taxis waited outside. One of them took me to the Hôtel du Cap, the driver speaking over his shoulder all the time in an accent so heavy as to be incomprehensible. I made a noise of vague agreement whenever he paused, hoping to encourage his eyes to stay on the road ahead, and was grateful when we reached the hotel without mishap to ourselves or any of the bicyclists, dogs, trams, beachgoers, or wandering goats along the way. My luck held, in that I got my dress through the lobby and to the safety of my room without having run the gauntlet of astonished stares and ribald comments.

I bathed, happily putting on my own clothing—beach-suitable

garments, with no flowers, frills, or the other fillips beloved of 1910's parasolled and be-flowered ladies—and went downstairs again, stopping by the desk to let them know that I might be gaining a husband.

Then to join the denizens of La Garoupe.

CHAPTER THIRTY-FOUR

I
t was a more subdued gathering than the carefree sun-bathers of previous days. The children were down the beach with Mademoiselle Geron, while the adults, instead of sprawling about on the bamboo mats, were all sitting upright, either talking intently or staring over the little bay. Sara greeted me, Terry said I'd missed a nice evening, and Gerald handed me a full glass—which I accepted, to take the taste of Zaharoff from my tongue. The others gave me distracted smiles before continuing their talk.

They had heard about Niko, and were reacting to the brush of death against their golden lives. Not that many knew him well enough to be actively mourning. He was a charming, handsome, friend-of-friends who had been to a few parties at Villa America, but it turned out that the only member of the Murphy circle who knew him more than casually was Rafe Ainsley.

"Where is Rafe?" I wondered aloud.

"His bronze pour is tomorrow, at the Antibes foundry," Gerald replied. "He was counting on Niko to help him set things up, but ... Anyway, he's now racing around like a crazy man, trying to do it himself. I gave him the car so he could pick up the drinks and whatnot." He noticed my puzzled look, so explained. "Rafe has people coming down from Paris for it—one or two sculptor friends, an American gallery owner, a few others. They're taking tonight's Train Bleu, which means Rafe can't change the day because everyone's already setting off, and the foundry can't give him another day until next month."

That made more sense. I couldn't picture Rafe Ainsley moping around his studio, mourning a friend.

One of the women—the young film actress I'd met before—broke in eagerly. "I'd love to go, if it's an open invitation."

"You just want to watch men at work, stripped down to their vests," said a friend, also from the movies. They giggled, then looked around guiltily.

Sara disabused them of the notion. "Rafe does that sometimes, to show off, but most of them wear heavy layers of wool and leather, to guard against splashes. And yes, Rafe's pours are usually open to anyone willing to put up with the heat. Just don't wear anything you care about—with the smoke and dirt, it'll never be the same."

The thought of Rafe Ainsley resentfully doing errands up and down the Côte d'Azur gave me an idea. "Where is this foundry of his?"

"Just off the Nice road, a quarter mile or so after the *gare* in Antibes. Enough out of town so if the place burns down, it doesn't take the city with it."

"That makes sense."

"I don't think he's there until later this afternoon. He was grumbling at how long it would take him to pack up those form things. Hoping that Gerald would volunteer."

"What is that guy doing?" The voice of the actress, halfway between curious and alarmed, broke into our conversation. As one, we turned to look, and saw an aeroplane headed straight at us.

To my surprise, Terry leapt to his feet to dance about, waving his hands in the air. The plane kept on, its engine noise building. And on. Several of us were on our feet, edging to one side as the plane grew closer, louder—and at the last minute, its nose tipped sharply up, presenting its belly as it passed directly over the beach . . . leaving an explosion of oversized white feathers drifting down in its wake.

Terry and the girls raced to gather them. The three Murphy children came splashing out of the water to see what the excitement was.

Flyers, advertising the Juan-les-Pins casino.

The glum mood vanished. Nobody noticed when I slipped away.

Back at the hotel, I threw on more practical garments, scribbled a note telling Holmes I was at Villa America, and caught the tram up to the Murphy compound.

A gardener pointed me to the guest cottage across the road. In a previous life this had housed a farming family in an orange grove, but the buildings had been turned into a combination living quarters–studio by Gerald and Sara. To my good fortune, Ainsley was there, looking both hot and cross as he wrestled a bulky plaster object out of the door and towards the waiting motorcar.

I trotted over to help, lifting the lower edge of the thing to help settle it onto the backseat.

"Hullo," I said, brushing the white powder from my hands. "Mary Russell. Friend of Terry from the other day."

"Ah yes. Thanks."

"Gerald said you were doing a load of chores, so I wondered if I might lend a hand." I bent closer to the resting plaster object. It was the size and shape of a small bucket, and the smooth plaster top of it was broken by a funnel-shaped indentation and four small holes. "Is that a mould? For a sculpture?"

"Yes," he said, and walked off. Naturally, I followed.

"I've never seen bronze poured before," I confessed, putting a bit of girlish gush into my voice. "It must be really fascinating—I hope you don't mind—Sara said I could come tomorrow?"

"Plenty of room," he said.

"Ooh!" We had left the bright day to enter into what looked like old stables, and I stopped dead, eyes appropriately wide. "Look at those!"

Ainsley might only have been in Antibes a few months, but he'd been busy. There were at least a dozen finished bronze sculptures and as many in the early stages of work. He had also taken time to create a series of pieces illustrating the craft of bronze. One shelf, seven objects, following a single work from its beginning waxy sculpture to its end point—which in this case was a splendid head of Sara Murphy some eight inches high, burnished and elegant and capturing not only her surface beauty, but the gleam of humour beneath.

I walked down to the beginning of the series: Sara's head lovingly carved from a dark brown wax—although actually, I realised, there was an eighth step beside it, a plaster lump somewhat smaller than the finished head.

"Is this a sort of filler that goes underneath?" I asked.

"The core," he confirmed, but then continued, showing that a minor prompt was all he needed to begin a lecture. "The first stages differ depending on the medium of the original sculpture, but for demonstration purposes, I show a wax original. Over a core, since a bronze sculpture is rarely solid."

"Really? I didn't know that."

My ignorance pleased him. He picked up the third object in the series, a weird bit of Surrealist art showing nails driven through Sara's brown wax face and what looked like a wax octopus coming out of her scalp and base. "Sprues," he said, tapping one of the octopus legs.

"Spruce?" It did not look in the least like wood.

"A sprue is a channel. Bronze in, air out."

"And you make them out of wax because—ah! *Cire perdue.* Lost wax."

"Exactly. The wax and pins—those nails that keep the core from shifting—are inside this," he explained, patting the next object in line, an anonymous lump of plaster similar to, though smaller than, the one we had loaded into the motor. "The mould is heated to drain the wax, then the bronze is poured in to take its place. When it's cool, the mould and core are chipped away."

In the next blank lump, the funnel opening and the holes were filled to the top with dark metal. Then came Sara, freed from her plaster womb, in metal duplicating the Surrealist figurine: nails, head, and octopus-like sprues, rendered now in immortal bronze.

The penultimate shape was recognisably Sara, but in dull metal, with holes where the nails had been pulled out and rough stubs where the sprues had been sawed away.

And finally, the finished piece showing Sara for the ages: serene, intelligent, glowing with some inner joke. That one was signed, with a firm *Rafe A* at the lower edge.

"That is a beautiful piece of work," I told him.

"I was pleased with it," he admitted. It was a surprisingly humble reaction, from a man given to preening.

"I love the surface of bronze. This one has such warmth, and depth."

"Ah, well, that's an art in itself. Several arts, one might say— welding, chasing, sanding, patina. I believe in craft, wholeheartedly, but I know my limits, and I know that a good bronze is a collaborative effort. So I sent this "Sara" to Paris and had my own *patineur* work on her. He's an old madman who's breathed far too many fumes in his life, but no one does a finish like his."

This, too, was an unexpectedly generous admission, that another man might do something better than Rafe Ainsley, but there was no doubt that his Paris madman had created a surface equal to the sculpture itself. One could almost feel the warmth of Sara's skin.

The artist roused himself from his contemplation of the work. "God, I have to get on with things, there's a lot to do."

"Let me help."

Naturally, his first impulse was to turn me down. A girl, hauling heavy loads? Then he looked at my mannish clothing, practical shoes, and short hair, and I could see him reconsidering.

"I'm strong, and I can drive. No? Well, never mind. It was just a thought."

As I'd hoped, my backing away triggered his pursuit. "I admit, that would be helpful. The local man I had—well, you maybe heard. About Niko."

"I did. It's sad, he sounded like a nice fellow."

"Yes. And helpful. I was counting on him, and now . . . well, I'd hoped Gerald and the others might lend a hand, but.I suppose it sounded too much like work."

I ignored his bitterness, and said in a chipper fashion, "I won't be as good as your local chap, but what can I do?"

He led me further into the converted stables, and revealed the scope of the next day's pour: a surprising number of waiting forms, some of them the same short, anonymous plaster bucket-moulds, others taller and more closely shaped around their bases and sprues. All had funnel shapes in the top, with thick layers of wax protruding from the plaster.

I was distracted by half a dozen other, more finished pieces. These looked nothing like the Sara-head, but depicted dream-like creatures that were both human and mythic. Like men being born from a rock—or Caliban emerging from his cave. They were all rough, in design and in finish, with a sort of primitive masculinity about them, more assured and less avant-garde than his conversation had led me to believe.

I liked them, very much.

My admiration convinced him that I might be a worthy partner in his day's efforts. We finished loading the car and motored through Antibes with his precious cargo, pulling in to the yard of an ancient stone building that bore the sign *Fonderie Ferrant*— which was rather like finding an English place called *Smith's Smithy*. Inside was a surprisingly modern gas furnace alongside the tools of a Medieval alchemist, from cauldrons to crucibles.

I stifled my curiosity in favour of diligence, carrying in as many of the moulds as he did. When I had proved my worth by dropping neither plaster nor my air of eager worship, Rafe decided to trust me with his list of tasks.

I made two prompt and trouble-free deliveries: the first, of wine, drinks, and snacks; the second, of borrowed tables and chairs. Once those had been safely conveyed, I ventured a more sensitive offer. "There are still quite a few moulds at your studio. I could bring them, if you like? Otherwise, you'll still be here at midnight."

He hesitated, taking in a scrape on my hand and the wear and tear on my clothes.

"I can see how valuable those things are," I reassured him, "and I promise that if there's anything remotely heavy, I'll have the gardener help me."

"Oh, for God's sake, don't let him touch them! The man's an idiot."

"No, fine, he won't come near them. Anything heavy I'll leave for you to make a last run. Okay?"

After enduring a lot of reluctant grumbling and unnecessary instruction-giving, I got back behind the wheel and pulled on to the road.

The gardener was no idiot, and any person as skilled as he in trimming shrubs, pulling weeds, and crafting props around new trees had trustworthy hands. If I told the fellow how tired I was, and gave him a sizeable tip for doing the work on his own, it would leave me free to search Rafe Ainsley's quarters from rafters to root cellar.

An hour later, the car was packed—with considerably more attention to padding than I'd have given—and I'd seen what little Ainsley had in his desk drawers. Nothing in the way of detailed bank statements or business letters—but then, this was his temporary summer home, so no doubt he'd left his important paperwork in Paris.

I did find a large unsealed envelope he was planning to post to himself at an address in the Montmartre district. Most of the contents were personal: photographs of friends here on the Riviera, including Sara and Gerald Murphy under the fringed umbrellas of an outdoor restaurant; half a dozen small sketches of what looked to be the gears of a clock; three well-travelled letters with casual news from American friends—and a receipt from the Antibes branch of a large bank with offices in Paris, London, and New York, recording the cash deposit on the previous Monday of a little over 100,000 francs. The precise equivalent of 5,000 US dollars.

Could anyone have that much cash without being involved in something shady?

I put everything back in the envelope and returned it to where I'd found it. Guillaume the gardener was moving around in the workshop next door. The car must be nearly full: time to finish up.

I ran my hands over the high shelves and my eyes over the remaining surfaces, untidy but showing the regular attention of brooms and mops. Rafe was the sort who left plates and cups where they lay rather than carry them to the kitchen—or, God forbid, wash them himself—but also the sort who did not trust servants with things that mattered to him. With that thought, I let myself into the workshop. Guillaume was in the process of manoeuvring a form through the open doorway.

"I think I can fit everything in this load," he said in his cheerful Marseilles accent.

"You sure? I don't mind making another trip."

"If I can use the front seat?"

"Absolutely."

He gave a nod and went out, leaving me to look at the room.

Here, some degree of tidiness had made inroads. There were a few crusted plates on one of the work-benches and an overflowing ash-tray, but the floor had been clumsily swept, and some of the piles removed. Plaster dust lay on every surface—I shuddered to think of the state of Rafe's lungs—but his tools were arranged rather than abandoned, and his sketches and notes were inside a collection of filing boxes. Not that the shelves weren't laden with odds and ends: mallets and snips; various spools of wire; two shiny steel cocktail shakers like the one I'd washed in the Murphy kitchen; an entire basket of cogs, from tiny to the size of my palm; and a coffee tin containing nothing but monocles. The hotchpotch brought to mind the Duchamp-like "readymades" in the Murphy kitchen. Perhaps these belonged to one of the studio's earlier inhabitants?

The doorway went dark just as I squatted down in front of a work-bench. I turned, and gave the gardener a smile. "Dropped something."

"Shall I—"

"Oh no, thanks, I've got it."

But I hadn't. Instead, I pretended to be interested in a random scrap of paper. When the room dimmed again with Guillaume's exit, I stretched down for the small object I'd seen gleaming from an abandoned pile of sweepings, overlooked by an inexpert broom.

I wiped the dusty thing against my trouser leg, opened my palm, and looked down at one of the earrings I had last seen in Mrs Hudson's bedroom.

I felt a thump of alarm, but then my eyes—trained, after all, by Sherlock Holmes—searched out the differences, and to my relief I found that no, it was not the same. Similar, yes, in shape and material, but this stone was a lighter purple, and the filigree, a less complex pattern. It could have come from the same workshop, but it was not hers.

The room darkened again. I straightened, slipping the object into my pocket. "I'm finished here, if you—oh. Hello."

Not Guillaume: a tall, slim figure with a precisely drawn beard.

CHAPTER THIRTY-FIVE

ount Vasilev glanced around the workshop, ignoring its admittedly untidy occupant and giving no reply to my greeting.

"Are you looking for Rafe? Sorry, I'm Mary Russell, and you're Count Vasilev, I believe? I saw you at Gerald and Sara's party the other evening, though we weren't introduced."

At my accent, for which I summoned my plummiest tones, his eyes snapped onto me for a rapid reappraisal. I looked like the help, but I spoke like an English blue blood. And if I had been at the Murphys' party, where there had been a clear lack of serving girls, that made me—

"Good afternoon, Miss Russell," he said, taking a formal step forward.

"It's 'Missus,' and I won't shake your hand since mine's so dirty. I've been helping Rafe get ready for his demonstration tomorrow."

"That is most generous of you."

"Oh, the others enjoy sitting on the beach, but sometimes I like to be useful. Are you coming to Rafe's demonstration?"

"I have been invited, yes."

"I'm so looking forward to it—sounds fascinating. Have you been to one before? A 'pour,' that is?"

"I have. And found it hot and loud but as you say, fascinating."

He looked about to take his leave, so I asserted my most vivacious and chatter-filled persona, to convince him that bronze was not the only interesting thing in the room. "You prefer the final product, I see. Well, I've been helping load up the moulds that Rafe will be working from, and I have to say, who'd have thought a bunch of lumpy plaster things would end up beautiful statues like those?"

I nodded towards the work-bench collection of Caliban-figures, and nearly missed the expression on his face—surprise—as he seemed to focus on the sculptures for the first time. Had he simply not noticed them? The room was not that dim, even for someone coming in from the sun. It almost looked as if he hadn't thought of them as beautiful—but if he didn't enjoy Rafe Ainsley's work, why commission the pieces? Rafe might have been lying, or at least exaggerating, about the patronage. Or perhaps the Count's surprise came from the idea that objects of power could be judged beautiful?

More likely, the aristocrat couldn't believe that a cheerful, grubby young female would have both perceived and commented on the quality of the artist's work.

I gave him a grin, to confuse him further. "I'm absolutely parched for a cup of tea. Do you suppose Rafe has such a thing? Oh, he must—no Englishman living abroad depends on foreigners for his tea. Come, you must be thirsty, too. If nothing else we can get you a glass of water." I practically forced the Count towards the living quarters, nattering on about the hot weather and how difficult it was going to be to return to London and whether or not the Hon Terry had worked himself up yet to ask where the Count had his suits made since I knew he was wondering . . .

By this time the kettle was on and my Russian captive was settling into a chair with his glass of water, looking a bit stunned.

"Sara tells me you're thinking of moving to America? I'm half American. I've lived on both coasts—in Boston when I was tiny, and in San Francisco for a while. Do you know either of those cities?"

It took him a moment to register that the conversational ball was in his court. "Yes. That is, I have been to Boston, for a few days. A pleasant town. I have not been to California."

"So you're thinking of moving to Boston?"

"No, I don't think so."

I sat down, so as to deliver an expression of sympathy face-to-face. "Sara tells me you have a daughter who is ill. I'm very sorry about that. You're going to America to be with her, I understand."

"I—yes."

"Good. Family is everything. I lost mine, when I was young, so I can understand. Does she have good doctors, there in America?"

"She does. A woman doctor—did you know there was such a thing? She is happy, and doing as well as can be expected."

I thought his daughter's illness sounded as much psychological as physical. But then, a child who has lost every family member but one to the guns of a revolution was sure to have psychological problems, whether she had lung disease or not.

"I've known some very good women doctors. I expect you find it hard to choose between a daughter and Europe. Although I can't say I think this golden age Sara and Gerald are living in will go on much longer."

This remark triggered a reaction at last. "You are right, it will end, and soon. I have told Gerald not to bring his affairs to France, but to leave them in America, where they are safe. The War is not over. This peace will give way. The Communists will not be satisfied until they have eaten their way to the ocean. And possibly beyond."

The thoughts had made his fine features go taut against the bone: his friends, his family, his Czar, and his world, trampled into history.

The wash of cold reality silenced me. He gave me a sad and apologetic smile. "And now I have ruined your day. Mrs Russell, forgive my careless mood. Thank you for the water. I look forward to seeing you tomorrow at Ainsley's demonstration. *Au revoir*."

And he left.

I became aware that the kettle I had laid on the hob was boiling madly, so I made myself a cup of tea—yes, Rafe had all the makings to hand—and sat at the table with it, thinking about Bolsheviks and endings and dead families and how one went about building a new one.

The thought of Bolsheviks reminded me of the earring I had found on the floor, and I dug it from my pocket.

The thing was misshapen, the soft gold twisted near to flat, as if a foot had come down upon it. And yet the clasp was shut. Either it had not fallen from a visitor's ear, or, if it had, someone had found it, retrieving it by shutting the clasp—then had carelessly let it fall to the floor again.

The door-knob rattled, and I rose, casually sweeping the earring back into hiding.

"Madame, the car is finished. May I offer any further assistance?"

"Thank you, Guillaume, I'll be right there."

I returned the milk to the icebox and put my cup in the sink, and went to admire the gardener's careful workmanship. He'd done a better job of it than I would have, and I happily peeled off a number of banknotes, handing them over with my thanks. When he protested, I told him solemnly that I was hoping to buy his silence, since I'd promised Mr Ainsley I would do it all myself. Guillaume laughed, agreed to hold my secret to the death, and pocketed the money.

I locked up with the key Rafe had given me, and headed back towards the foundry.

CHAPTER THIRTY-SIX

Rafe's plaster moulds made for odd companions in the motor-car, rather like driving a nest filled with massive eggs—plus a couple of hungry fledglings, their plaster mouths raised to the sky. My companion in the front was of the type that had been built up, rather than poured into a bucket. This one was nearly five feet tall, and it had taken both of us to manoeuvre it into the front seat.

If I hadn't allowed Guillaume to do most of the heavy lifting, my arms would be dead and my back bent double. No wonder the torsos of sculptors came to resemble inverted triangles.

The sun was going down when I reached the *Fonderie Ferrant*. Light spilled through the wide double doors on the front. When he heard tyres on the forecourt, Rafe hurried out, leaning over the car door before I had turned off the engine. What he saw satisfied him, although actual praise was more than he could manage.

"You took your time."

"I didn't think you'd want me to rush things."

"You had enough blankets?"

"The gardener borrowed some from the house, just to be sure. I didn't think that big one should be without support in its middle."

Guillaume and I had propped it as tenderly as a splinted leg. Rafe could find nothing to complain about, and let me help him extricate the pieces.

The foundry was not a large building, but it had undoubtedly stood on the road for centuries—it still had a blacksmith's anvil, which showed no trace of rust though it was mounted on a log that might have been cut when the Sun King was on the throne. At some point in the building's past, there had been a fire, leaving blackened walls and a roof, considerably newer than the rest, but even these repairs had sheltered metalworkers for generations. It had the kind of brutal beauty formed by long years of harsh labour, where everything necessary was there to hand, and superfluous items had long since been discarded.

This main room was designed to give clear ground for moving tureens of liquid metal so hot that a splash would maim. Its two work-benches were mounted to the walls, as were the ironmonger's display of equipment hanging from hooks and prongs hammered between the stones. The floor, too, was of stone, with traces of pale sand in the seams, and the only thing protruding into the middle was a large, low metal trough, several feet away from the gas furnace, with that same coarse, golden sand in the bottom. Against the wall, tucked under a work-bench bristling with clamps and vices, stood a row of metal buckets, also filled with sand.

The furnace itself was in the middle of the left-hand wall. Mounted from a roof-beam was a sliding crane, to simplify the lifting of the crucibles from the furnace. Nearby stood an impressive stack of ingots and a tangle of what I now recognised as cutaway sprues, scrap for the next pour. The back corner was taken up by a masonry structure some six feet high, set with a steel door and a gas line leading to its base—the warming oven, I imagined, where the wax would be drained from Rafe's moulds. At the other end of the back wall was an opening to what looked like a hallway, narrow and unlit and doorless—unlike the next opening, which not only had a door, but a sturdy one, held shut by a big, shiny padlock.

I helped Rafe carry in the moulds. Some he arranged in the oven at the back—cold at the moment, fortunately, but his careful positioning of the forms on their heads showed that on the morrow, they would be ready for heating. The rest of the forms we lined up near the warming oven, mouths up, waiting.

"You don't melt out the wax beforehand?" I asked.

"Not usually, and I'd still need to heat the pieces. Molten bronze has a temperature around 950 degrees. If there's any moisture at all, a piece can explode."

"Ooh. Not a lot of carefree souls among metalworkers, I take it?"

"Not many with all their limbs."

I laughed, and to my surprise he grinned, his first sign of actual acceptance.

"Anything else I should be doing?" I asked.

"Do you know, I think I'm about ready." He then added, only somewhat grudgingly, "Thanks to you."

"It was interesting. I don't suppose you'll want my help tomorrow, for the actual pour?"

"No, Monsieur Ferrant insists on being there. We keep amateurs well out of range."

I hid my relief: donning thick wool and leather while the sun beat down and a blast furnace roared did not sound like pleasant entertainment. Rafe went to the forms on the floor and squatted down to check that none would tumble over during the night. While he was occupied, I wandered over to examine the boggling array of equipment hanging from the wall. It was all made of iron or steel, and resembled Medieval torture implements or modern dental tools (much the same, come to think of it, but for their size). Most were old, showed decades of hard use, and might well have been forged right here, but one shelf held a collection of smaller, newer, commercially-made pieces, including three chisels, a hammer, two pairs of dark-lensed driving goggles already pitted from sparks, and a diminutive little melting pot.

This last looked ridiculously toy-like compared to the massive stone crucibles lined up near the furnace. Curious, I reached out—

"Don't. Please." Rafe stood and walked rapidly across the room, even though I'd pulled back at his first word.

"Sorry, I just wondered . . . I was wondering how difficult it was to see through those goggles. They look a lot darker than sunglasses." The goggles lay close enough to the forbidden crucible that he might have been mistaken. He gave me a suspicious glare, then seemed to realise that overreaction might be an error, and reached up to hand me a pair of the eye protectors.

I pulled off my spectacles and held the goggles in place, peering through them at the bright doorway. "It must be hard to see details, with these on."

"We only use them for the actual pour. Even with bronze, the brightness can sear a line in your vision for hours."

I gave him back the goggles and turned away from the shelf to admire the hefty spouted crucibles, ceramic and stone. They were tapered, to rest in metal tripods. Most of the torture instruments on the wall were tongs and shanks, used to lift, aim, and pour the molten metal from the crucibles into the moulds.

No, metal casting was not a task for the careless or easily distracted.

He stood, hands on hips, to survey his domain, then nodded. "Thank you," he said. It didn't even seem to hurt him much to say it.

"You are quite welcome."

"I need to have a word with Monsieur Ferrant. You can wait in the car, if you like."

Waiting in the foundry itself was clearly not an option. I did not glance at the locked door, merely let my eyes run across the dusty, intriguing space, and strolled towards the double doors.

When I was safely outside, the sculptor's feet crossed the grit-covered floor. I heard the padlock rattle as he made sure it was locked.

When he emerged, he dragged the doors shut and worked an even larger, but far older padlock through two metal loops that I suspected had been made here. He crossed the yard, heading to the smaller wooden buildings that lay a distance away from the foundry, the padlock's key dangling from his hand. I strolled around the stone walls, idly kicking the weeds while taking in the details of windows and doors, and got back to the motor just before Rafe did. He climbed behind the wheel, barely waiting for my own door to shut, and manfully ground the gears and over-used the brakes all the way to Villa America.

Neither of us was dressed for dinner, or even drinks, on the Murphy terrace. And though looking like a stevedore did not trouble Rafe, I didn't much care to insert my sweaty, dirt-stained person among the stylishly clothed. I also thought that spending the evening at talk, drink, and dance might leave me a little the worse for wear, come morning, since I did not plan to sleep much that night.

Yes, I was looking at another evening of breaking and entering—a foundry this time, instead of a smuggler's cave.

Fonderie Ferrant was only four miles away by road. However, the tram to Antibes did not run after dark, taxis generally came equipped with nosey drivers, and going by foot would add nearly three hours to the trip. So, as I passed through the hotel grounds, I took a detour to where I had noticed a collection of bicycles—the gaudy ones intended for guests, not those used as actual transportation. Some were so shoddy, I doubted they would reach the main road, but there were a few with faded paint, solid gears, and working head-lamps. This time of year, none of them would be missed before morning.

I bathed yet again and put on some suitable clothing—dark enough to fade into the night, good enough not to instantly shout

"Burglar!" to a passing gendarme. I had a meal brought up, slept for two hours, and woke at midnight.

No sign of Holmes. What a surprise. He'd no doubt found something far more exotic than a bicycle ride followed by a foundry break-in.

CHAPTER THIRTY-SEVEN

S herlock Holmes—inhabiting his persona of Sheldon Russell, wealthy amateur musician—studied Inspector Jourdain over the half-empty glasses of wine on the brasserie table. It was early evening, and other tables had people dining, but the policeman had dismissed the idea of sharing a meal.

"So to be clear," Holmes said in French, "you are telling me that no matter what evidence comes to light, there is no possible chance that you will investigate Basil Zaha—"

"Stop! If you will insist on speaking the name, we must leave."

"Conversations are less apt to be overheard in a noisy establishment than on a quiet street, Inspector Jourdain." But the angry detective had already drained his glass and got to his feet. Holmes placed some coins on the table and followed him through a series of hot streets to the same dull little park they had met in before: a little-used space with clear lines of approach. Jourdain chose a bench shaded from the late sun and took out his cigarettes. Holmes thought about making an elaborate search for spies in the branches overhead, but relented, merely settling down with tobacco of his own.

"I would prefer you not speak that name aloud, not during the discussion of a crime such as murder," Jourdain said, his eyes watching all around, voice low.

"*Inspecteur*, there are some crimes for which even the powerful must be held responsible."

"Certainly. But taking into account my authority compared with his, I must proceed with care. Which is not helped when that wife of yours decides to step in to the midst of things and question the man!"

"She did wh—" Holmes caught back the exclamation, and hid his dismay: better to have the man assume he knew whatever it was Russell had done. He cleared his throat. "If you do not have the authority to question Zaharoff, who does?"

"In truth, it would be someone so high up I could not begin to know."

"My good man, this is all but an admission that an arms dealer has bought your country and all its laws."

He thought Jourdain was going to hit him, but the policeman clawed back his self-control, and put his anger into lighting a cigarette. After a time, the nicotine allowed him to put his thoughts together, and his words.

"Monsieur, I am Monégasque, born and bred. I have lived here all my life except for the War years, so I have no personal experience of the workings of large countries such as yours. I do know that the bigger the government, the greater the inertia. Only a large push can effect change.

"But in a place as small as Monaco, every act has a consequence. And in a country such as mine, whose economic survival requires an easy flow of people—people who vastly outnumber the permanent residents—the only way to keep from being overcome is to establish certain rock-like features, and never permit them to shift.

"When . . . an individual comes here for something other than pleasure, attention is paid. If that individual wishes to settle here, and to make investments here, then—as I understand it—certain conversations are had and certain requirements established. If, for example, an individual with a past that some consider criminal wishes to settle in Monaco, it is made clear to him that none of his former activities may be actively pursued within the borders of the Principality. He may meet with associates, even negotiate and sign contracts, but any actual goods or services would require specific approval before they would be permitted here."

"Meaning that a man could make a deal here for leaky submarines or shipments of cocaine, so long as the drugs or armaments stay out. And you, a policeman, are happy to have your hands tied that way, so long as—"

"I should consider my words, sir, before you accuse me. I have the authority to escort you out of Monaco."

"And yet your face admits that I am making no accusations that you have not made against yourself."

Jourdain glared at the burning stub between his fingers. "I am telling you that the state of equilibrium is to be considered, and that my authority is limited. Also, that I am not the world's policeman, merely that of Monaco. If you were to bring me unarguable proof of wrongdoing, I would take it to my superiors and fight to have it recognised and dealt with. But if all you have is suspicion, I am forced to consider the larger picture. The balance here is delicate. The person you are talking about is immensely powerful and immensely proud, and while he and his wife enjoy living here, he has no overpowering reason to stay. If I, or even someone who appears to have my approval, were to confront this person openly, to hound him and question him as to his whereabouts and intents, would he not take offense? What would the result be of that insult? Would he quietly remove himself to Paris—or would he wreak untold havoc along the way? Monsieur, you and I both know that this man could ruin Monaco if he wished. He could strip it and leave it a shell, to be taken over by one or the other of its neighbours. The death of Niko Cassavetes is not to be ignored, but neither is the potential ruination of my country."

"And yet you believe that your country has not sold itself to Basil Zaharoff?"

The policeman crushed his cigarette beneath his heel. "Unless you are in the possession of something more than inuendo and suspicion, you will stay away from the man. Or I shall have you arrested. Along with your lady wife." He got up and stalked away.

Holmes watched him go.

What the deuces had Russell got up to? The idea of her prodding a bear like Zaharoff in his den made him want to run for the train and drag her back to Sussex—if not Antarctica. Instead, he made himself finish his cigarette. When he'd done that, he took out a scrap of paper and pencil stub, to set about the irritating business of composing a coded telegram that would be sufficiently detailed to be useful, yet simple enough to survive the idiosyncrasies of French telegraphists.

Dear Brother Mycroft, he began.

CHAPTER THIRTY-EIGHT

When night had fallen, I pocketed my tiny but powerful electric torch and a remarkably stretchy black stocking with two convenient holes—items not generally found in the luggage of travelling bluestockings—and made my way down the servants' stairs and outside without being seen. The warm fragrant night welcomed me, the paths were dim enough that I did not have to take to the shrubbery, and I even managed to extricate a decent bicycle without causing the rest of the row to crash to the ground.

I waited until I'd left the hotel before lighting my head-lamp, then pedalled away, past the lane to Villa America and along the road that went by Antibes, narrowly escaping death only six or eight times along the way.

After the lights of Antibes were behind me, I shut off my head-lamp. However, since the moon was not even halfway full, I soon abandoned the attempt to ride and wheeled the cycle until I came to a small stone building so old it had no roof, yet so sturdy, a series of side-swipes from passing cars had resulted in tiny stone chips and large chunks of metal and glass.

I tucked the bicycle behind this relic and continued on foot until I recognised the shape of the foundry against the sky and smelled the vague miasma of heated metal. A neighbouring dog barked, then stopped. No lights shone from any of the nearby buildings.

As so often happens, the owner of *Fonderie Ferrant* had put an impressive lock on the front door, then rendered it void by leaving an open window at the back. The dog started barking again as I moved a solid-looking crate under the window, but shut up again following a man's angry shout.

Amused at the idea of the watchdog's inner grumbles, I stepped up onto the crate, pushed the window all the way open, and slithered through to the floor.

I waited, muscles braced to leap upwards again should the dog's brother come raging out of the darkness, but all was still. I turned on the torch, and saw I was in the hallway behind the warming oven. There were two rooms back here, once living quarters for the foundry's workers, but the rough mattresses now housed only mice, the clothing hooks only spider-webs. I padded through the rest of the foundry, finding neither sleeping labourers nor insomniac sculptors. Just the pale ghosts of the statues that would take shape on the morrow.

And whatever was behind that shiny padlock.

Before tackling it, however, I walked over to the shelf that had roused the protective instincts of Rafe Ainsley, to study the diminutive porcelain cup. As far as I could see, it was nothing but a small, porcelain crucible. More suitable for a clockmaker creating tiny gears, perhaps, than for a sculptor working in foot-high pieces, but since it had not even been used, it had little to tell me.

I shrugged, and stretched to put it back on the shelf—then froze, at a quick flare of light across the wall, instantly extinguished. Moments later, I heard the slow crackle of tyres on the forecourt stones just outside.

CHAPTER THIRTY-NINE

Mrs Hudson: a conversation

"Lillie, your welcome has saved my life yet again, but I think I shall go home in the morning. Things are about to become very awkward."

"Clarissa, everything will be fine! This is all nonsense—a sad accident, but nothing to do with you. We'll sort it out in a few days."

"I do not believe there was anything accidental about Niko's death, or where he was found."

"You think it has to do with those . . . *papers* of yours?"

"Oh, Lillie. If those accursed things killed the boy, I'll never forgive myself. Which is why I can't ask any more of you, my dear friend. You're already involved more than is good for you."

"Clara, don't. We've been partners of one sort or another for half a century. You're not throwing me out now."

"I am merely putting some distance between us. If things blow up on me, there's no reason for it to touch you as well."

"But the Count said—"

"I know, and everything *should* be fine. But you and I have had far too many reassurances from men to believe in them. Everything is fine—until it suddenly is not. And I've always known that it's a chance in a million."

"Well, you do have three others."

"Though if this one proves worthless, the others will as well. After all, they were my father's. What else could they be but useless?"

"If so, you're no worse off than when you started. As for Niko, you can't have it both ways. Either they're worthless, or they're worth killing over."

"Lillie, I know you're trying to be reassuring, but we both know that people will kill over nothing at all."

"Look, Niko Cassavetes was involved in shady dealings long before you showed up in Monaco. And probably before he came, if the truth be known. I'm sure he was working with loads of other shady types—so why assume his death had anything to do with you?"

"The boy died in my sitting room."

"While you were *here*. And what was he doing there, anyway? How did he get in? He could have taken advantage of your absence to break in and have a look around, with a colleague who— wait. They couldn't have found . . . *them*, could they?"

"Not in my sitting room, they wouldn't."

"They're still where you put them?"

"They were on Friday."

"Fine, then."

"But that was before Mary and Mr Holmes arrived."

"Would they have searched?"

"I am quite certain they did, though I don't know how closely. And they have no reason to know that they're looking for three bon—"

"*Sst!* We agreed the walls have ears. They are 'three *papers*.'"

"*The papers*, in *the place*—I know. Oh, Lillie, this is getting out of hand. Don't you think I ought to tell the two of them?"

"Not unless you want to let that man take control of you the rest of your days."

"They're sure to figure it out eventually."

"Why? How many times have you and I met over the years without him so much as noticing? Clarissa Hudson, you have done no wrong. You have every right to make your own decisions and arrangements. A woman who plays by men's rules is a woman who ends up in a cage."

"Or a coffin."

"Clara, we can do this. You know we can. It's merely a matter of putting on that fearless face that you did when you first walked into a crowded ballroom."

"Dear friend, I'm not feeling very fearless at present."

"I know. But you will."

The two women listened to the buzz of cicadas for a moment, then the growl of a motorcar climbing the nearby road. Clara Hudson sighed. "I am grateful for your hospitality, but I'm going home tomorrow. I want my own things around me, for however short a time. After two nights on that gaol bed, I am feeling my entire lifetime of experience."

The two laughed, a touch sadly, and took their long decades of life inside to the cool.

CHAPTER FORTY

I looked around desperately for an invisible corner, dimly aware that whoever had just driven up to the *fonderie* was taking care to go unnoticed. I was tempted by the darkness behind the blacksmith's anvil—but if they turned on the overhead lights, I would be as obvious as a beetle in a bowl.

I trotted through the room to the hallway and pushed open the door to the first workers' room, just far enough that I could slip inside if need be. But I stayed in the corridor, so I could eavesdrop on the foundry itself.

The heavy outer padlock gave a ponderous rattle. The big door creaked as one side swung open, then shut. Footsteps and low voices came—speaking English, rather than French. "I don't want to put on the main lights, they might see them from the house." It was hard to tell, with the voice pitched so low, but I thought it was Rafe Ainsley. Definitely not an American.

"You have a key?" This man's low voice seemed to have an accent. Russian?

"Yes, I had a copy made."

A torch went on, bright for a moment, before dimmed by a cupped hand.

Two sets of feet crossed the floor. I retreated as the shadows danced closer—but they had no reason to come back here, where the dust said nobody had been for years. Surely they were headed to the locked room . . . and yes, the footsteps ceased. A sound of fumbling, then, "Hold this" as the light spun about and went still again. I eased my head sideways just far enough to see the two figures standing at the padlocked door. Rafe Ainsley, his hands working the key.

And with the torch, Count Vasilev.

The lock clicked, the door opened, and closed after them. Voices started up again—but I could not make out the words.

Damnation.

If I pressed my ear up to the door and it came open, I would be caught. Was it worth the risk? Or, perhaps there was another way . . .

Back in the one-time living quarters, I aimed my shielded light at the wall. As I thought, there had originally been an opening, boarded off, rather than filled in. The old wood proved no barrier to sound—and, I noticed as I moved closer, I could even see a narrow sliver of the room beyond through the cracks.

"—not meet in the town," the Russian was saying.

"Because I don't think we want people to see us meeting any more than would seem natural, and who's going to come here, in the middle of the night?"

"You have them packed? All of them?"

"They're in the crates."

"I wish to see one, please."

"I don't know why. You know what they look like. But—hold on, let me do it."

Noises followed, remarkably similar to those Holmes and I had made in the smuggler's cave. Then: "Here—careful, it's heavy."

"Yes. And rough."

"What, you expected me to send them to the *patineur*?"

I moved my eye from one crack to another, until I found Count Vasilev. I couldn't quite see what he had in his hands until he moved, and I glimpsed a dark, dull shape a foot or so tall. His arms were braced to hold it, confirming its solidity, and his left thumb was rubbing along the base.

Then the other man's hands came into view, taking the piece and turning away with it. The rustling sounds were followed by a tapping of nails. Not a lot of nails—just enough to discourage someone from idly lifting the lid.

"You won't have any problem, when you get them?" asked the Russian.

"The first shipment arrived with no trouble at all, and I haven't heard of any with the second. So, unless the ship goes down, which it won't because we're not at war these days, it should be fine."

"You think this is a joke?"

"No, I don't think it's a bloody joke. What I do think is a joke is how you expect me to manage without your friend Niko. Unless you want to get your own hands dirty, I'm going to need another five thousand, to make up for doing it on my own."

"I will give you half that. And the other half when these are shipped."

"Fair enough, I suppose. Another week, ten days."

"Ten days? But these are ready now."

"And have to pay for another lot of shipping? It's cheaper to wait till I've cleaned and packed up the pieces I'm doing tomorrow."

"Send these now. You can send your new pieces with the next ones."

"Next ones? You mean there's more?"

"Yes."

"Where the devil are you getting the stuff?"

"That is of no importance."

"I know—none of my business. But if we're doing this again,

it'll need to be in the next month, since I have to be in New York by the middle of September. And you'll have to come up with another distraction like those fireworks, to empty out this place. Plus, I can't do it without another Niko."

"I will consider a distraction. And I may have another man. One who can be trusted."

"I liked Niko. Poor bastard. I don't suppose you know who shot him?"

"They say it was the woman Hudson."

"I know what they're saying, but she really didn't strike me as the sort. More likely it's some other criminal. I mean, if the fellow was carrying around stuff like that for you, God knows what he was doing for other people."

"It is true, Niko worked with criminals. Which is why it is better to ship this now, not wait."

"You may be right. Okay, I'll put in another layer and then write the shippers, try and have them picked up next week. Assuming I have that second money."

"Fifty thousand francs if you ship them tomorrow."

"Make it Thursday—I have to finish packing them, and I'll be too busy tomorrow. Speaking of which, can we go? I have to come in early to start the oven, and I'd like a few hours of sleep first."

The light went off in the crack. Footsteps, doors, the padlock. The men left the foundry; I heard the car start up and drive away. I waited for a time, in case they returned or Monsieur Ferrant came to investigate, but the only sound was mice in the rafters.

The shiny padlock was a simple one, and I was soon inside the locked room, looking down at six very solid wooden crates. Two were empty. The other four had their lids lightly nailed down. I prised up one of the tops.

Under the excelsior shavings was a remarkably ugly bronze lump, the shape of a large head. As modern art went, it was, as the Count had said, rough—even cruder than the Caliban pieces I had seen in Rafe's workshop. Still, there was a certain appeal in the deliberate bluntness of the thing, as if it was a matter of design rather than lack of care. Some of that crudeness might disappear in the finishing process, I thought—the octopus-leg sprues had been hacked off, leaving ugly little stubs, but the base-like pouring funnels were still in place. The dull surface still showed signs of the plaster mould, giving little hint of the bronze patina waiting beneath. I took the next one from the crate, and found it similar—no, not similar: identical, down to the marks of the carving knife in the original. So was the third, and all the rest in that layer, and the one beneath.

That, I thought, was odd. Ten identical figures, squat and unlovely, with little detail and no finish work. Did that count as art? By a man who regarded a gallery as a necessary evil?

I don't know what I expected, but it wasn't these primitive, mass-produced hunks of bronze. The conversation I had heard made it clear that Rafe and the Count were up to *something* criminal. And since it involved Niko, it was most likely smuggling, but of what—and how?

The statues were statues: no seams, plugs, or openings that I could find. They were a lot heavier than the head of Sara, but then, they were nearly twice the height, and still had the bases attached.

There could be no reason to smuggle mere lumps of bronze. I looked at the crate, built of hefty reinforced boards, and sighed.

Forty minutes later, I decided that no, there was nothing in the crates but the boards, the nails holding them together, excelsior packing, and twenty identical bronze figures.

The sculptures could, I supposed, have secret pockets within, but for what purpose? I doubted cocaine or diamonds would survive those temperatures. What was I not seeing?

The piece, though crude, did resemble some modern sculptures, most notably those of the Spaniard Picasso. I'd seen the man's studio, and privately thought his sculpting technique, like his method with oil paints, consisted of slapping and hacking at the medium for a few minutes and calling it done.

Could that resemblance be the point? Could the two be planning to sell these as Picasso originals? The Spaniard's name had become big enough to start attracting forgeries—especially if there were an ocean between the artist and the buyer. And Rafe had said these were headed for America.

Open counterfeits did not fit my impression of Rafe Ainsley, whose ego was even greater than his talent. But odd jealousies and creative revenges were as rife in the art world as they were in finance or academia, and perhaps if the goal was to undercut the value of a genuine Picasso . . .

I shook my head, and shoved statues and wood-shavings back into the crate. On my way out, I took another look at the small crucible Rafe hadn't wanted me to touch, but it was just a crucible, unused and uninformative.

I put it back, and decided that I simply didn't know enough about bronze to tell what I was looking at. Perhaps tomorrow would remedy that.

CHAPTER FORTY-ONE

I reached the hotel without mishap, stowed the bicycle with its fellows, and managed to be seen only by a sleepy desk clerk, who seemed unsurprised by the arrival of a guest at that hour.

My rooms were empty—which, while disappointing, surprised me not in the least. That they were still empty when the sun woke me was mildly unexpected, but after one glance at the clock, I had no time for speculation.

I fought my way free of the mosquito netting and dove into clothing suitable for a demonstration inside a hot, dirty foundry; then trotted up the road towards Villa America. Before I reached the Murphy house, I spotted some familiar faces in a group about to board the Antibes tram, and put on speed to join them.

I greeted Sara. She performed the introductions—in some cases, re-introductions—to the others, including some newly arrived on the Train Bleu: Luisa (a painter) and Tom (her visiting brother); Dos (a writer) and Scotty (another writer) with Zelda (Scotty's wife); and Victor (Rafe's gallery owner) and his friends Jacques and Bernadette and Louis; and the two Russian male dancers whom I never did learn to tell apart. The painter and writers all had the gleam of creativity in their eyes, at the chance to immortalise manly labour on canvas or page. The brother, wife, and dancers looked puzzled at the enthusiasm (and frankly apprehensive when they laid eyes on the foundry itself).

The last member of the party was unexpected—at least, unexpected as a person one might meet on a rumbling French tram car. "And Mary, do you know Pablo?"

"We met in Paris, a few months ago. *Ça va*, Monsieur Picasso?"

Later in his life, all the world would know Pablo Picasso, but in 1925, few Oxford academics would have heard of him. He was a small, dark man in his middle forties, with close-cropped hair, heavily tanned skin, intense dark eyes, and a Catalan accent. We had met that spring as I passed through Paris and my artist stepson, Damian Adler, dragged me to the man's studio. Picasso did not appear to remember my face, giving me a perfunctory shake of the hand as he braced himself against the shift and surge of the tram.

Not wanting to remind him of who I actually was, I figured it was safe to ask him about his work. "Are you thinking of making more bronzes yourself, Monsieur Picasso? I saw one of your bronzes in Paris, a sort of death mask of a man with a broken nose."

"My *picador*," said the Spaniard. "You think it a death mask? I suppose it could be."

I mentioned seeing the mask of Dante, and he asked if I had seen Bonaparte's, and that took us into African masks and Cubist ideas in sculpture, with a side-track into the avarice and blindness of gallery owners, then a question about the joint benefits and drawbacks of bronze kept us happily arguing all the way to Antibes' Place de la Victoire.

As we were climbing down, he stood back to let me go first—but when our faces were very close, he lowered one eyelid, perilously close to a wink, as if acknowledging a private joke. Then he turned to Sara and asked if the children were well.

The morning was still cool, in Riviera terms at least, and the foundry was little more than half a mile away, so we waved off the taxis—the same two decrepit machines that had met us the previous week—to walk through the town in changing groups of two here, three there, commenting on the flowers spilling from an upper balcony, the small boys crouched over a game of marbles, the artistic shadow cast by an abandoned piece of farm machinery. At each, the gallery owner and his pals would make some ribald joke, Dos and Scotty would study it briefly for potential inspiration, Luisa-the-painter would flip open her wire-bound pad to make furious sketches, and Picasso would stand for a moment in admiration, then return to the conversation—leaving one with the conviction that the flowers, the boys, the shadow had been etched into his visual memory forever.

The furnace was already running when we trickled in and joined the half-dozen visitors there before us. Someone greeted a rotund figure as the mayor. A glance told me which of the remaining men were Rafe's fellow sculptors and which was his pet gallery owner. The remaining figure was Count Vasilev, wearing another pale linen suit and Panama hat, looking as if he'd never met a smudge or broken a drop of sweat in his life.

Someone had strung a length of rope across the room to keep everyone clear of the work area, although with the size of the space, a dropped crucible would leave twenty people scarred for life.

I stayed near the door.

Brother Tom and the two Russian dancers took one look at the set-up and decided to walk back into town, a trio handsome enough to pull Zelda and the young actress in their wake. Sara looked after them longingly, caught me watching her, and gave me a wry smile before moving over to salute the group who had been there when we came in. Young Luisa eagerly took out her sketchbook and pencils. Scotty lit a cigarette and started talking to Dos about a bullfight. Picasso's dark eyes ate up the entire space, from the cobwebs overhead to the arrayed moulds on the floor, as he stood with his thighs against the hemp barrier.

The working side of the room held three men. One was a very tall, very muscular boy of perhaps nineteen, with an unfortunate overbite and what I diagnosed as near-terminal shyness, since he stood to one side and refused to meet the eyes of any onlooker. Next to the furnace were Rafe and an older man who had to be Monsieur Ferrant himself. They had their backs to us, conferring over some dial. Even where I was, full in the faint breeze from the wide-open doors, the waves of heat were oppressive. That close, the men must have been baking alive, especially in the woollen trousers and leather aprons they wore. They had to shout over the roar of flames, but I could not make out what they were saying.

Eventually, the grey-haired man tapped his nose at Rafe, who nodded. The older man then moved towards the equipment hanging on the wall, while Rafe turned towards his audience—and spotted Picasso. With a grin, he called to Monsieur Ferrant, urging him across the gritty stones to greet the famous artist. The old man finished shrugging on his burn-spotted leather coat and stuck out a huge hand to exchange manly greetings with the visitor. Picasso asked some technical question, but the older man made a gesture towards the furnace, a reminder that molten bronze was waiting.

Rafe turned back to the job with a cockerel swagger—and, I noticed, a singular lack of leather overcoat. He seemed more eager to impress his Spanish colleague than his American gallery owner or his Russian patron, and I was concerned that his attention might be on his audience instead of the dangerous job at hand. However, though he scorned the coat, he did pick up a pair of heavy leather gauntlets, and the moment he drew them on, his awareness of an audience fell away, and he was all focus.

There was no doubt that Monsieur Ferrant was in charge. The

big lad was some kind of apprentice, there to provide a third set of hands and eyes. But this did not make Rafe a visiting dilettante: the Englishman knew what he was doing, making no moves without preparation, never taking his eyes from the task, and even following instructions with no hesitation.

First, the masonry oven at the back was opened and the hot moulds, empty now of their wax, were transferred to the battered trough in the centre of the room. While Rafe loaded the oven with a new set of moulds, the other two worked at the trough, covering the waiting mouths with small squares of tin and pouring sand from the buckets around their bases. The gawky lad whisked off the covers, then kicked at the trough with his enormous boot, settling the sand in closer to the sides, just as Rafe shut the oven door on his next set.

What followed was a dance between three men and a lot of deadly machinery. First, clamps from the device overhead, lifting the rough, white-hot crucible free of the flames. The young man skimmed the slag off the top using a long-handled iron rod with a half-circle at its end. Casual blobs of thousand-degree metal were knocked to the floor, inches from ill-protected legs, as the chain lowered the glowing stone bucket into the embrace of one of those Medieval torture instruments. Monsieur Ferrant locked it into place. His side of this pouring contraption had two arms, allowing him to steer the crucible and control its stream.

"*Hoop,*" he called, and the clamped pot rose, moved, and hovered over the row of plaster mouths. "*Là,*" he said, and a miniature river of white-hot lava disappeared into an upraised mouth. The young man stepped forward with the skimming tool, modifying the direction of the flow to reduce splashes.

Moving down the row of forms, bronze filled one cup, then the next. The angle increased with the emptying of the crucible, until again came "*Hoop*" and the pair emptied the crucible's dregs into a shallow metal tray, then reversed the process with carrying frame and the tongs. The crucible disappeared back inside the furnace. The slabs of bronze that had been pre-heating along the top were laid gently in.

Meanwhile, the forms were cooling with amazing rapidity, going from white-yellow to dull red to barely rose. While the crucible sat in its nest of flames, slowly melting its new ingots, Rafe began to work the plaster shapes out of the trough and lay them to one side, while the young man shovelled the sand back into the buckets.

Soon, the process repeated: fresh hot moulds set amidst the sand. Open the furnace, raise the crucible, set it glowing like a miniature sun into the three-handled pouring shank, then lift. While the gaping mouths fill, the oven receives its third and final allotment. Metal cools, molten scraps are dribbled into the tray to be re-used. *Hoop. Là. Hoop. Hoop.*

The men drank long draughts of liquid—it turned out to be small beer—and resumed their gauntlets. The oven was unloaded, the sand nestled in, around these, the tallest of the pieces—but when Rafe moved to assume his handle of the pouring shanks, the older man shook his head and gestured at his assistant. The sculptor protested, but the foundry owner was adamant—and when time came to pour these, the tallest of the day's works, I could see why. Not only were the young man's arms nearly ten inches further from the ground than Rafe's, but his muscles were like iron, boosting the full crucible to chest level with an ease that made my arms ache just to watch.

Rafe didn't even need to work the long-handled skimmer, but instead stood back and watched. His attitude—frowning critically, as if to make sure they did it correctly—made me think that he'd become aware of his audience again. When the other two returned to the furnace, he absent-mindedly pulled off his right gauntlet to retrieve a handkerchief and pass it over his face. The cloth went away, the crucible was ready—but before he pulled the gauntlet back on, Ainsley made a gesture that froze me in my tracks.

He rubbed the skin high on his bare forearm, just above the edge of the leather gauntlet.

Unconscious, momentary, and without meaning—except to a person who had seen the photograph of a dead man's arm, with its lack of hair, and residual irritation on precisely that spot.

It was not a razor, preparing for a tattoo, that removed the hair from the arm of Niko Cassavetes. It had been the scorching effect of intense heat.

Not long before he died, Niko Cassavetes had donned gauntlets to help Rafe Ainsley pour bronze.

CHAPTER FORTY-TWO

The pour ended, the furnace shut down, the crucible was scraped out. I was surprised to find how quickly the liquid metal set: already, Rafe was trading his leather apron and goggles for a chisel and mallet, chipping experimentally at one of the earliest moulds filled. He took care not to rest his hand on the surface, and used the chisel handle to shift the piece around. A rough shape emerged, choked with white plaster and wrapped in the octopus-sprues, but one could see the outlines of the sculpture beneath. He then propped it up to bash enthusiastically into its centre, pausing a few times to shake out hunks of broken-up core.

When he had finished, he carried his proto-sculpture in one gauntleted hand along the rope line for the admiration of all—taking care to pull it back from any outstretching fingers. Luisa sketched furiously, with considerable attention to Rafe's tousled hair and the lines of his arms and upper torso (which left nothing to the imagination inside its wringing-wet singlet—the other two men must have been melting inside their long sleeves). Another visiting sculptor—I never did learn his name—asked a couple of technical questions about bronze alloys and the thickness of the moulds; the American art dealer squinted at the brazen face dusted with plaster; the mayor's wife giggled as the half-naked man came near; the Count nodded in appreciation, the linen of his suit as crisp as if he had just stepped out of his dressing-room. But when Rafe came to Picasso, he held the piece out as a man might display a new-born son. The Spaniard bent over it, his finger sketching a line some inches above its surface, then reached out to deliver a hearty slap on Rafe's biceps.

The younger sculptor's face opened up in happiness at the older man's gesture of approval. Grinning widely, he turned back to the scattered collection of moulds and settled his figure among them, then exchanged hearty hand-shakes with his two partners. Around me, people seized the opportunity to make for the cooler air, fanning themselves with anything to hand.

In the forecourt, under the shade of the foundry roof, two French women oversaw a celebratory meal whose parts I had transported, the tables laden with bottles of lemonade, beer, champagne, and mineral water. None of the drinks were cold, but all were cooler than we were. We drank greedily, talking about art (three of us), the weather (the British in the crowd), and speedboats (which made me wonder, why wasn't Terry here?). After several glasses of liquid, I felt considerably less light-headed, the Count looked even more phlegmatic, and the art dealer looked ready to write a cheque.

An ideal time for a spot of surreptitious interrogation, I thought—until Rafe came out and his admirers closed in.

Most of them. Looking across the gathered heads, I realised that Picasso was missing. I carried my filled glass into the foundry and saw him with the two workmen, intent on a discussion of temperatures and tools. I understood about one word in three, but if I had been Luisa, all that manliness would have sent me into a fury of sketching.

A few minutes later, the three shook hands, and Picasso came towards me, swinging his leg easily over the divider rope.

"Madame," he said in greeting.

"That was very interesting," I said.

He took the glass out of my hand and drained it in a series of swallows, then handed it back. "You are looking at the man Ainsley?" he asked, his voice low. "You and your husband?"

So yes, he had recognised me. "Only peripherally. A friend has a problem; it touches on the Murphys and their group."

"It troubles me to hear you say that. They are good people."

"I agree."

"Can I help?"

"Tell me about Rafe Ainsley. What kind of an artist is he?"

The black eyes flicked out the doorway to the refreshment table. "I have an appointment. Walk with me into Antibes? Unless you are staying for the luncheon."

I assured him I had no need for Madame Ferrant's hearty cooking, now beginning to appear.

While Picasso was saying his good-byes to Rafe and the others, I quietly left the foundry yard, waiting on the road lest our leaving together cause comment. His muscular form came striding along a few minutes later, and we walked.

"I met your wife," I told him. "I didn't realise she used to dance with the Ballets Russes."

"Some years ago, yes. Now Olga takes care of me and the boy."

"He's a bright lad," I said, unwilling to pursue the question of whether husband and child were a valid substitute for the floodlights.

"You want to know what kind of an artist is our Rafe," he said.

"His work seems skilled. A clear eye and good hands. Perhaps a little ..."

"Derivative?"

"Not as mature as he imagines," I said in agreement. "I suppose he is young."

"It's not his years that makes the problem, it is his awareness of the eyes upon him."

"Self-conscious?"

"Mannered." His word in French was "*affecté*." "Too aware of the outside of a piece, and not of its internal truth. What it looks like, not what it is."

Second-rate, I interpreted. Then I thought of the Caliban sculptures I'd seen the previous day. "He had some pieces in his workshop that were much less . . . thought-out, perhaps. Coarser, brutal almost, and though they were ugly on the surface—I don't mean ugly, merely rough—unfinished. Sorry, I don't know the proper terms. The point is, they looked as if he'd just slapped them together, but they were honest, somehow. Solid."

"I saw none of those."

"No, I think those were earlier pieces."

"Made with the hands and not the eye. That would be better. I will ask to see those."

"I wouldn't," I said hastily. The dark eyes looked at me sideways. "It's complicated."

"Having to do with the work of your husband?"

"Which often seems to be mine, as well. I take it Damian has talked about his father?"

"Once or twice. Is Ainsley committing a crime?"

"I don't know yet. Would it surprise you if he was?"

"Any man can be a criminal. Ainsley . . . hmm. I think Ainsley would not commit a clear and blatant wrongdoing. But if it was at a distance? If he could view the act as less a crime than a matter of convenience? Yes."

"You mean that if he felt he deserved a thing, he would take it?"

"It would be his."

Just as the Murphys' guest house, their terrace, their food, and the contents of their drinks cabinet were his. "Still, I'm not sure that doesn't apply to most people."

"A matter of degree, perhaps."

"So where would Rafe Ainsley draw the line?" Theft, I wondered? Murder? Did I even know where he had been the night Niko died?

But Picasso merely shook his head. "That I could not tell you. But I would ask you to do all you can to keep it away from Sara and Gerald Murphy. Gerald is an innocent, and Sara—Sara is a calm centre around which the artistic minds whirl. She brings out the best in us all."

"A remarkable person. Oh, but that's one of Rafe's pieces that you should see, his head of Sara. He's captured her essence."

"I will ask."

"And I will try to keep them out of it. Holmes and I will both try."

He thanked me, and for the rest of the way into the town, we talked about the Murphy family, and about Holmes' son in Paris.

CHAPTER FORTY-THREE

To my relief, my hotel room was no longer mine alone.

"Ah, Holmes, I was beginning to wonder if I'd need to come and bail you out, too. For assaulting an officer of the law, or at least offending him. You missed an interesting demonstration—and I saw Damian's friend Picasso. I hadn't realised that his wife was one of those who spend time on the Murphys' beach. Have you had a good day?" I tried to remember what he had been setting off to do, then noticed the ash-tray near his chair. The number of stubs suggested hours of leisurely contemplation out of the window ... but the vehemence with which the cigarettes had been smashed into it said something else entirely.

I looked at him, seeing the storm clouds on his brow, and tried for a light touch. "I take it you had another grim conversation with our friend the Inspector. Will we be turned back at the Monaco border, next time we try to get in?"

"Inspector Jourdain chose to bury his shame at being forbidden to do his job beneath a show of aggression."

"Well, I don't see any blood on your clothing, so the argument stopped short of an open brawl."

"Merely a verbal one. Which ended with a threat of arrest."

"I suppose that's to be—"

"For both of us."

"Me? Why, what have I done to offend the man?"

"Basil Zaharoff."

"Ah."

"Yes."

"Holmes, I—"

"Russell, what the blazes were you thinking? *Basil Zaharoff*? The man could swat you—"

This explained the ash-tray: not four hours of casual thought, but one hour of fury. "Holmes," I began, but he was on his feet now, in full spate.

"—like an insect and have you wiped up without anyone seeing. If you imagine—"

"Holmes, it was—"

"—that I would have an easy time finding you, or even—"

"Holmes, I—"

"—Mycroft, with all the power at his call, could bring the man—"

"Holmes, for God's sake! You think I don't know the man is hugely dangerous? You think I expected him to be there? Give me *some* credit for intelligence, please."

Say what you will about Sherlock Holmes: imperious, impatient, and patronising he could be, but when an accusation was put to him, he was also honest to his bones.

Sooner or later.

Right now, he was stung, and snatched up his tobacco to go stand at the window, back turned.

I took myself off to the bath, which also helped cool things.

Twenty minutes later, we met up and began anew.

He'd rung down for tea, which was a good sign. I walked to the tray, and poured. "What have you been doing, other than being both insulted and blamed for your wife's actions by Inspector Jourdain?"

He accepted my change of topic. "I put my head into every tattoo parlour between here and the Italian border, and found no one who would admit to a customer resembling Niko Cassavetes."

"Oh, Holmes—I'm so sorry! I just discovered this morning that it wasn't a tattoo." I explained how I'd seen Rafe Ainsley rub at his irritated arm, in precisely the same spot as the missing hair on Niko Cassavetes. "I should have remembered those gauntlets, Holmes, before sending you off on a wild-goose chase. Really sorry."

"The time was not entirely wasted. It has given me considerable insight into the mores and manners of the contemporary female. Although, Russell, if you decide to have a tattoo engraved on your skin, I beg you to give your husband prior warning."

"I promise. So, would you like me to tell you what actually happened between me and Zaharoff?"

"That would be an excellent idea."

"Well, I did telephone to Mrs Hudson, but she said she'd be too busy to see me. I couldn't see much reason to insist, so I told her I'd phone back."

"She's still with Mrs Langtry?"

"She was, although I'm not sure for how long. Then, as I was leaving the hotel room, the cleaner arrived, and I thought that perhaps local knowledge might include the whereabouts of Mr Zaharoff. I asked, and to my surprise she said that he used some rooms on the top floor of the Hermitage for meetings. I thought it might be helpful to know if the offices looked difficult to break into. I definitely was not expecting to find him there, since you said he has a house in Monaco, but the door was standing open and when I looked inside, expecting a cleaner or a secretary, it was him."

I watched Holmes closely, seeing the effort it took to keep his wrath under control. "Why did you not immediately leave?"

"Wouldn't that have appeared just a touch, I don't know. Suspicious?"

"Perhaps. But less ... suicidal than stepping inside the man's rooms."

"It took him two seconds to pull a gun on me. God knows how he'd have reacted if I'd turned and run. I know we'd like a sample bullet from his gun, but I didn't care to have it fished out of my own flesh."

I had succeeded in rendering Sherlock Holmes speechless. I grinned and dropped into a chair. "It was actually quite interesting, if you can keep yourself from exploding."

He lowered himself onto the settee, not even reaching for the distraction of tobacco.

I told him about the munitions dealer, his quick transformations from threat to joviality, then the further change to what appeared to be actual humour.

"The man's charm I should have expected—anyone who can manipulate the very highest rank of politicians and industrialists has to be able to use charm as a weapon. But I suspect that, given his reputation, it's been a very long time since anyone dared to stand up and speak honestly to Basil Zaharoff. If I'd been a man, if I'd been older, or more beautiful—if I'd even been wearing something other than that ridiculous dress—he might have felt more threatened. But there I was, in flowers and spectacles, asking him first to give Mrs Hudson an alibi and then to tell me about his ties to Niko Cassavetes. I think he found it hard to take me seriously."

He slowly shook his head. "Viyella as a means of disarmament. A weapon I can honestly say would not have occurred to me."

I didn't think the dress was made of Viyella. I also didn't think this was the time for a detour into fabrics. Instead, I gave him a detailed report on everything Zaharoff had said, and moreover, how he'd said it.

At the end, Holmes reached out to move his cigarette case around on the table, but he did not pick it up. "You were playing a dangerous game, Russell. Zaharoff is out of your league—he may well be out of my league. I trust you do not intend to make further use of his capacity for amusement?"

"I might get one more chance at him, before he tires of me and has his bodyguard throw me out." One could only hope not out of the window.

He bit back his immediate reaction, and took a moment to think. "I will admit, one chance is more than anyone else seems to have on offer. The Monaco police themselves are more concerned with protecting the man's privacy than with asking him questions."

"Is that how you heard that I'd been to see Zaharoff? Jourdain told you?"

"He did." And without my prompting, he described his conversation with the Monaco detective, the man's fury and threats, and beneath those, his air of frustration, even impotence, at the curtailment of his official powers in this, his native country.

"I'm sorry that's how you had to learn of it, Holmes. Did he happen to mention how he knew, himself?"

"Interestingly enough, he did not."

This time, we both sat and thought. Had Zaharoff sent a complaint up the Monaco chain of command? Did the police pay one of the hotel staff for information? Feodor the bodyguard?

"Is it possible," I said slowly, "that the police are watching Zaharoff, but do not want it known?"

"The police—or Inspector Jourdain, on his own? It is possible."

"Your speculation?"

"The Inspector's exaggerated show of aggression at being kept under rein is suggestive. And if he is keeping up an unofficial, unsanctioned enquiry of his own, all the more reason to be upset when someone from outside threatens to walk through it with hob-nailed boots."

"I was not walking through—"

"He could not have known of Zaharoff's unaccountable fondness for young and impertinent questioners in flowered dresses."

"Would you suggest that we consider Jourdain a potential ally? If, that is, we can find him sufficient cover to duck beneath?"

"Don't think of him as a coward," Holmes said sharply. "He loves his country, even if he does not love everything it does, or all it requires of him."

"Fair enough. But can we trust him?"

"Only so far."

Since we seemed to be past the flash-point of Basil Zaharoff and his possible, would-be protector in the Monaco police, I turned to my own day's and night's involvement with Rafe Ainsley, from fetching wine and glasses from Cannes, to packing up his plaster moulds in Antibes, then on to midnight conversations between him and the Russian Count. Eventually, I reached the morning's demonstration in the foundry and my talk with Pablo Picasso.

"He says your son is well, by the way."

He ignored that. "I should like to meet this Ainsley person."

"As it happens, the Murphys are hosting a gathering tonight," I said. "Though I can't guarantee there won't be someone who recognises you."

"A collection of Americans, in the South of France? I can't imagine we share much in the way of acquaintances."

Four hours later, we walked into the garden of Villa America.

Thirty seconds after that, I paused to let my husband greet Sara and Gerald Murphy, and found him gone.

CHAPTER FORTY-FOUR

Holmes was on the road outside of Villa America, looking at his watch.

"Holmes, what on earth—"

"As you said, the chances of meeting someone who recognised me were small, but not impossible. The ill-dressed man in the group just inside the terrace. What name do you know him by?"

"You mean Rafe Ainsley?"

"Your sculptor."

"Who is he?"

"Several people, or so it would appear. I came across him some ten years ago in Blackpool. I fear he will remember my face, since I was present during his arrest. A case of forgery."

"You're kidding. The forger in the forge?"

"Russell, I—"

"Sorry. And never mind the party, I don't need to go to—"

"No, you should stay. You may pick up something of interest."

"All right, but not for long. I'll come back to the hotel and we can have dinner."

"I won't be there." He was studying a shrub with scarlet flowers on the other side of the road.

"Oh, Holmes, not again."

"I did tell you, some days past, that I lacked the familiarity with Monaco to recognise its various soils. The same would appear true of its various characters. I require information, and need to send some telegrams, but I cannot do it from here. I shall go into Nice." He looked again at his watch.

"I'll come with you."

"No need, although after this it may be better to use the Hermitage as our base of operations rather than your rooms here. I will go back to Monte Carlo once I have replies from the cables. Probably mid-day tomorrow."

"All right. But can you give me an idea—"

"Russell, the approaching tram may be the last one before morning. I shall see you tomorrow. Just don't—" He caught himself before he could finish the sentence.

"Don't do anything you wouldn't do?" I asked sweetly. "Or were you about to order me not to do something stupid like bearding an arms dealer in his den?"

"I merely ask that you proceed with caution, Russell."

As I watched him trot off, it occurred to me that for the past few minutes, he'd avoided meeting my eye.

That meant he was trying to keep something from me. And the only things he tried to keep from me were either news that he was stepping into danger, or the fact that he was in touch with his brother.

Which suggested that the telegrams were going to London, to make use of Mycroft's connections within the government, and Holmes did not wish to open that discussion with me. I was tempted to chase him down—but in the end, gave a mental shrug and went back to the party.

Rafe had moved off, leaving Terry in his place—a Terry who

looked as if he'd been in a fist-fight. "Was that your husband?" he asked.

"It was. He remembered a prior commitment."

"Should I be offended?"

I laughed. "Terry, have you ever in your life known someone who wasn't happy to see you? But my good man, why do you look as if you'd walked into a door? And is that actually a sun-burn?"

His hand came up to prod his swollen nose, gingerly. "It sure felt like a door—who'd have thought water could be so dashed rock-like?"

"Ah—you found a boat, and tried out your new water-skis?"

"Did you meet Patrice's gent with the wall-eye?"

"I don't believe I have."

"Name of Bumpy. His racing boat's got a motor twice the size of my Runabout's—at one point we hit forty-five knots. Not with skis behind, naturally, but I did think it was going to pull my arms right out of their sockets. It's as much as I can do to pick up this glass."

"I'm glad to see you have the strength for that."

"Mary, you have to come drive us one day. You have the knack of starting off gently."

"Try changing places with the boat's owner. To illustrate precisely what's involved."

He brightened at the thought of a reciprocal dislocating of shoulders. "I'll suggest that. We're going out again—not till Friday, luckily enough. Tomorrow we have a date with Patrice's other chappie, the one with the sea-plane. Johnny—you met him, Johnny Perez. Loads of fun. Say you'll join us?"

"Terry, I'm not too keen on aeroplanes, thanks all the same."

"You don't need to come up, just come along. He's invited us for lunch after—he has the most amazing house. Got a cave for a cellar."

The final phrase caught my attention in a way that "sea-plane" had not. And although I had no particular reason to hunt down another cellar, at the same time, Mrs Hudson didn't want to see me, and Holmes was off hatching plots with his brother. If I didn't actually have to go up into the heavens, well . . .

Terry saw me give way and whooped his pleasure. Which attracted the attention of the identical Russian dancers, and one of them—either Misha or Vitya—asked for explanation. As Terry set off on an enthusiastic, if clearly baffling speech on the glories of sea-based flight, I took the opportunity to slip along the terrace before he concocted the sport of airborne skiing.

The next group included both Murphys, Rafe Ainsley, and several visitors from the demonstration—though none of the Russians. Sara moved back, by way of invitation, so I eased in to the circle beside her.

Rafe was talking about his technique, and what came after the pour. How he would do the finish work in the States, since he had to ship these off soon. Gerald was looking interested; Sara, polite but bored; the others, somewhere in between.

"It was good to see Mr Picasso this morning," I said to her, keeping my voice low so as neither to interrupt Rafe's flow, nor attract his attention.

"Such a *vital* man, isn't he? You've met him before?"

"In Paris, a few months ago."

"He hopes to spend more time in Antibes. The Grimaldi family may offer him one of their houses as a studio."

"Part of Princess Charlotte's drive to bring the arts to Monaco?"

"I suppose so."

I lowered my voice further. "I imagine Mr Ainsley has mixed feelings about *that*." She laughed, conspiratorially. "Still, his gallery owner friend looks pleased."

"They were talking just now about a one-man show in New York this winter. That's making Rafe happy."

"Combined with his Russian friend's commissions. Where is Count Vasilev, by the way? I'd have thought he'd be here."

"He has some business meeting in the morning. He sent his regrets. Mary," she said, her voice returning to a normal volume. "Have you met Mr Rosenberg?"

The evening continued, with introductions to people ranging from the gallery owner to an experimental artist working in broken vacuum tubes to the wife of the Antibes mayor. Drinks on offer ranged from astringent white wine to cloying green cocktails, with food that ran the gamut from the mundane (sliced figs, melons, and cheeses) to the peculiar (aspic salad with bits of marshmallow; sweet corn boiled and served on its cob), while everyone carried on conversations about art, politics, art, child-rearing, travel in Europe, art, fashion, the problems of finding uncrowded corners of Venice/Rome/Paris/London, art, money, wine, and art.

I don't remember making my way back to the hotel, other than my having been amidst a large and rackety group.

The next thing I knew there was a pounding on my door, far too early.

"Mary!" a voice shouted, sounding as if it had called several times before.

I replied with a jumble of syllables. This time, I perceived the voice outside as Terry's, and the words as saying, "The car leaves in half an hour." My response seemed to satisfy him—at any rate, he went away, leaving me blinking at the dawn through the windows. And it truly wasn't much after dawn. Car? Why . . . ?

Ah: Monaco. Sea-planes. Cellar lunches.

I ran the bath-tub full of cold water to shock myself into consciousness, then stuffed a bag with a disparate collection of clothing that I might need in Monaco. Would I require a costume suitable for roulette? Water-skiing? Spelunking in the pilot's wine cellar?

Eventually, I joined the other yawning residents of the hotel downstairs.

Terry, inevitably, was as cheerful as a man who'd actually had a night's sleep.

CHAPTER FORTY-FIVE

Sherlock Holmes glowered at the dark gap between a fishmonger's and a newsagent. In its recesses was a doorway. Unlike many of those he had walked by in the past twenty minutes, this one was neither stinking of urine, nor occupied by a *femme de nuit* and her client. He considered pulling out the telegram that had been waiting for him at the Hôtel du Cap that morning, but there was nothing wrong with his memory. Whether the telegraphists had inverted the numbers was another question.

He found the bell and rang it twice, listening to the jangle die away, then pulled it again, as per Mycroft's instructions. To his surprise, considering the hour, the inside bolt scraped almost immediately. The door opened, revealing a man in an old-fashioned suit.

"I am a friend of Mr Mycroft, in London," Holmes recited.

The man retreated, inviting Holmes to step through the door on to a carpet so thick, it felt like a well-maintained lawn underfoot. The door closed, the bolt slid. The air smelled of furniture polish and cigars.

"This way, sir." The clerk, or butler, ushered him through a series of quiet halls to a well-appointed office with no occupant. The room looked like a private club, with a Turkey carpet, heavy mahogany bookshelves, and several square metres of polished desk. The only thing on its mirror-finish top at present was a telephone, a boxy instrument far too modern for its setting.

The clerk settled him into the desk's leather chair, asked if he preferred tea or coffee, returned in two minutes carrying a silver tray laid with fresh coffee, and left him alone.

He did not know why Mycroft had insisted on a telephonic conversation for this. It did save on time, to use direct communication rather than telegrams, yet the process of coding telegrams was simple compared to keeping one's spoken words cryptic enough to get past the ears of the Exchange operators. Secretive telephone conversations were, in his experience, both frustrating and inadequate, generally requiring a series of cables anyway, to confirm what appeared to have been decided.

Halfway through the coffee, the instrument gave a ping. He picked up the handset and pressed it to his ear. "Holmes here."

"Hello, Sherlock. Do you hear me all right?"

So, real names were to be permitted. "Good morning, Mycroft. Yes, this is a remarkably good connection. How many exchanges is it passing through?"

"Very few. And all of them supervised by our people."

Holmes frowned at the enigmatic black shape on the polished desk. "Do you mean to tell me this call is reliably secure?"

"Completely."

"Well. That is technological advancement, indeed."

"You asked me for information about Count Yevgeny Vasilev. What has brought him to your attention?"

"I find him in a web of social and financial ties here on the French Riviera. My former—Mrs Hudson appears to have become entangled in some way, which means that we, too, are entangled. You no doubt are aware of some of the unsavoury types who are living in this area."

"You mean Basil Zaharoff."

"Mycroft, you are completely certain about this line?"

"I am."

"Very well, it's your neck. Yes, I speak of Basil Zaharoff. I don't know if he is actively involved, or if it is simply difficult to find any part of life here that does not bear his finger-prints, but I am concerned. He appears to have no part of this . . . whatever is going on here, but I have to wonder if he could be making a show of having his hands clean, while using the man Vasilev to carry on behind the scenes. Any White Russian with money, particularly one living in a small country controlled by an arms merchant, is a suspicious figure."

"Vasilev has been of interest to us for some time. This was a man with both the ear and the cheque-book of the late Czar, and there is no doubt that during the chaos of the War years, he was out of sight at several key times. Our man Reilly worked with him briefly, but when that idiotic attempt on Lenin blew up on us in the summer of 1918, Reilly came back to London and the Count went east."

"Russell is under the impression that Vasilev was in America that summer, when the Czar was killed."

"Is she? Hold on."

The line was clear enough to carry the sound of turning pages over the inevitable crackles and whines. After a minute, Mycroft came back. "Vasilev was in America, but that was earlier in the year. He has a daughter in a specialised sanitorium in Colorado. Run by and for women. Very expensive. According to our records— which are not absolutely dependable, I will admit—he was back in Russia by August of 1918."

"But the Czar was dead by then, was he not?"

"As far as we know, he and his family were killed in July. But before that, when the Germans were at the gates of Petrograd in 1915, Vasilev was one of those who oversaw the transfer of the Czar's gold reserves into Kazan. The biggest reserve in the world—

nearly five hundred tons of the stuff. Said to have filled forty rail-
road cars. Can you imagine? And we think Vasilev was also involved
in moving it a second time, when the Bolsheviks were pushing east
in October, 1918. Ultimately, about half the gold did fall to the
Communists when they took Siberia, two years later."

"And the rest?"

"Now, there's a pretty mystery for you, little brother. No one
knows. Rumours abound: secret passages under the central bank in
Omsk; buried on the grounds of an agricultural college, beneath
the bodies of the soldiers who put it there; sunk by train wreck into
Lake Baikal; fallen into the bay in Vladivostok. There's even a rumour, a fairly strong one, concerning a document with the coordi-
nates in code, locked away in a Communist vault. Two hundred
tons of Imperial gold, out there somewhere. His Majesty would
prefer it not fall into the wrong hands. If you are in any position to
ensure—Sherlock, what is that noise?"

Holmes dropped his cigarette case onto the desk. "Just me, tapping this machine. Mycroft, if Vasilev had two hundred tons of
gold, he would not be bothering with Mrs Hudson and Lillie
Langtry."

"Lillie Langtry? What does the Jersey Lily have to do with this?"

"So far as I know, nothing, apart from being old friends with
Mrs Hudson."

"Good Lord. I hadn't realised she was still alive."

"Very much so."

"Heavens. I remember seeing her in—"

"Mycroft, focus. Could Vasilev be sitting on the gold, somewhere between here and Siberia?"

"Well, someone must know where it is. Why not Vasilev?"

Why not, indeed? It would explain the White Russian's associa-
tion with Basil Zaharoff—one of the few men in the world with
the resources to retrieve that much material, then conceal it, and
finally transform it into a usable currency. For a fee, naturally.

"Are you still there, Sherlock?"

"Yes. I need to know about Vasilev—his movements, his business contacts, his property and investments. I'd also like you to confirm any of your less-certain information about his daughter. That she is in fact ill, and is in Colorado. Your friends in the American agencies ought to be able to help you."

"I shall ask."

"Then, an English sculptor who calls himself Rafe Ainsley. I encountered him a decade ago forging art in Blackpool, of all places, under the name of Ralph Ashton. His movements since then, please."

"A professional beauty, an arms merchant, a Russian Count, and a Blackpool forger. Does this cast of disparate characters actually have anything to do with one another?"

"That is what I need you to tell me. Also, several young men. A Greek named Niko Cassavetes, a Monégasque named Matteo Crovetti, and an American, Gerald Murphy. The last is the only one whose name I am relatively certain of."

"And the common denominator between them?"

"Smuggling."

"I see. Anyone else?"

"None at the moment."

"Priorities?"

"With an investigation as wide-ranging as this one at the moment, it is impossible to know which of the threads will unravel it. Although if you have anything to hand tying Zaharoff with Mediterranean smuggling operations, that could be helpful."

"I imagine you want this yesterday. Telephone to this number again in twelve hours, I will give you what I have."

"Mycroft? Russell is in the centre of this. Make it eight hours."

CHAPTER FORTY-SIX

Mrs Hudson: a conversation

The knock came at half-past eight in the morning, less than an hour after Clarissa Hudson had let herself out of her friend Lillie's house to walk through the morning streets to her Monaco home. A home missing a carpet, and with a scrubbed-out patch on the sitting room floor, but whose air smelled only of cleaning fluid and lemons. When the knock came, she put down her butter-smeared knife and walked down the hallway, opening the door to find her landlady.

"Madame Crovetti, good morning, I—"

"Gentleman on the telephone for you. We will need a line installed here, if this continues," she grumbled. "I'm not an answering service. Welcome home."

"Oh, thank you, just let me slip on my shoes."

"You'll need to hurry or I'll be late to open the shop."

"Of course. Did they say who it was?"

"A man with an accent," the messenger called over her shoulder.

Since a native Monégasque would consider nine out of ten people in the Principality to speak with an accent, that did not narrow things down very much. She followed her landlady inside, then waited for her to disappear up the stairs before picking up the earpiece.

"This is Clarissa Hudson."

"Good morning, Miss Hudson. Vasilev here. I have some excellent news for you—for us both!"

"The money?"

"It has come through."

"No! Really? Oh, Count—I did not quite believe it was real."

"It is very much real. However, my Paris associate recommended that we keep it outside of Monaco. It is difficult to remain anonymous in this place, is it not?"

"I suppose that's true. So, where is it?"

"In an office of his bank in San Remo."

"San Remo? Why not Nice?"

"San Remo is a less obvious choice. And it has so many English visitors, one more will be invisible."

"I see. Very well, when can I go?"

"We shall need to go together. For the paperwork, you understand? And why not now?"

"Sir, that is the most charming invitation I have had in many years. Train, or motor?"

"Neither. Madame, our friend Zedzed wishes to help us celebrate our partnership, and has created a small party around it. Only a few intimate friends. Those already—how do you say?—'in the know.'"

"I'm not sure that's a good idea."

"Oh, he does understand the need for discretion—so we shall use his yacht. And his champagne, which he wants me to tell you is already on ice. A leisurely cruise over to San Remo, you and I will sign the papers, then a pleasant lunch, and back to Monaco by the evening. When you step off the boat tonight, Madame, *voilà*! You will be a wealthy woman."

"Count Vasilev, I would have preferred something less . . ."

"Naturally, I understand. However, I do not think either of us would wish to affront our mutual friend, would we?"

"I suppose not."

"How about Lady de Bathe?"

"What about her?"

"She was an active part of your project, was she not? We should invite her, as well."

"She . . . no. I wouldn't call her at all active. All Lillie did was to introduce us. She knows nothing about the details, not at all."

"Your reticence is wise. And your sudden financial independence will be a grand surprise for her."

"That it will. Do you wish to send a car?"

"Perhaps you could make your way down to the harbour? We are already here, and will leave as soon as you arrive."

"All right. I'll dress and walk down, I should be there within the hour. And Count? Again, thank you."

"The pleasure, my dear lady, is all mine."

CHAPTER FORTY-SEVEN

I kept falling asleep on the train into Monaco, though my fellow passengers seemed as energetic as kittens. I parted from Terry and his pack of aeronautic enthusiasts at the Casino station, making my way to the Hermitage while the others tumbled off to the harbour. Not that I imagined Holmes would actually have returned to the hotel—and he had not—but I was able to stow my valise in the wardrobe, and drink a large pot of coffee to help prop up my eyelids.

At half past ten, I was standing with Patrice, Solange, and the others watching Terry and Johnny-the-pilot do things to the machine.

"Hello? Mrs Russell?" I turned, to find Lillie Langtry hurrying down the promenade faster than a woman in her eighth decade should.

"Good morning, Mrs—er, Lady de Bathe."

"I'm so glad I caught you—oh dear—out of breath—sorry. The hotel said I would find you down here."

"Would you like to sit—oh, perhaps not," I said, looking at the sea-bird stains on the nearby bench. Instead, I pulled her gently out of range from interested ears, while she took out a fan and waved up a breeze. "Mrs Langtry, what is it? Mrs Hudson? Is she all right?"

"Have you heard from her this morning?"

"I thought she was with you."

"She wanted to return home, and left my house before I rose this morning. Mathilde woke me at nine, since I had made an arrangement to see a friend for coffee, but just before I left, a boy arrived with a note from Clarissa. It was rather enigmatic. Which by itself is not worrying, but then as I was walking to the restaurant I saw—oh dear, I can see I'm making no sense."

The next bench had fewer white streaks on it. When we were seated, I touched her arm. "Tell me what has happened. Maybe start a little closer to the beginning."

"The beginning is a long way off, when she and I were younger than you are now—but more to the point, when Clarissa arrived in May, I began . . . helping her in the problem of income. For one thing, many years ago, she'd left a very nice diamond necklace with me, to keep safe. As soon as I knew she was coming, I arranged to sell it for her. That got her started nicely, but there was another matter that required more, shall we say, professional assistance. Something she had that required more specialised knowledge, when it came to converting it into cash."

My mind had caught briefly on the idea of Mrs Hudson with a diamond necklace sparking around her wrinkled throat—but I went after the word *cash* instead. "Something illegal?"

"No. Well, perhaps. But if it was, time has taken away all sin."

I nearly asked outright: *Does this have anything to do with the fortune that Jack Prendergast held between thumb and finger?* Holmes was going to be furious if I did not pursue the scent, but I first needed to know if Mrs Hudson was safe.

"Then what was the problem?"

"Frankly? Your husband was the problem. He has something of what they call an 'obsession' over Clarissa's behaviour. She—very sensibly, to my mind—prefers to keep her affairs as private as she can."

"His obsession is not without basis," I pointed out. "But that's an argument for a later time. What is going on?"

"The note Clarissa sent said that she will be spending the day with Sir Basil Zaharoff on his yacht, to make the final arrangements on her, er, monetary negotiations. She said he planned to hold a small celebration on board, for her and a few friends."

"I had the strong impression that she would prefer to have nothing to do with Basil Zaharoff?"

Mrs Langtry sighed. "It is . . . problematic. As you might imagine, avoiding him entirely is impossible. And as I believe you know, they were once well acquainted. He cherishes the belief that she is still as fond of him as she once seemed to be, all those years ago. When he heard she was here, he offered to support her, but she convinced him it would be inappropriate, considering that he is married." My imagination stuttered on the idea of a woman of nearly seventy and a man even older . . . but then, why should she not be . . . interested. After all, Holmes—

I cleared my throat. "And then, you sold the diamond necklace for her."

"That helped. But still, he insists on giving her little gifts, from time to time, and making introductions to people he thinks will be of help to her. The sorts of friendly gestures that to refuse would be . . . awkward."

"I see."

"But that is not the point. The problem is, I saw Sir Basil myself, not twenty minutes ago, in the Café de Paris. And yet when I had come past the harbour, I specifically noticed that his boat was missing. As you can see for yourself."

"Which one is his?"

"The big one."

I looked at the space where the gleaming yacht had previously moored. "What, the *Bella Ragazza*? That's his?"

"That's right. Oh, he doesn't own it outright, but he's leased it for the past couple of years. He and his wife use it to entertain, and they lend it to friends, sometimes. And I also understand that he finds it convenient as a place to hold certain kinds of business meetings."

So as not to be overheard by competitors or witnessed by the police, I thought. I shaded my eyes, studying the forest of masts. "Couldn't its crew simply have it out for some reason?"

"Yes—but in that case, why the note?"

"What did it say?"

"Here, I stuck it into my bag as I was going out the door."

I unfolded the page to see Mrs Hudson's dear and familiar handwriting.

29th, 9:00

Dearest Lillie, our little project is about to come to its conclusion! Sir Basil wishes to host a very small celebration, just him and the Count and perhaps Mrs Z. I told him we needn't invite you, since you know <u>nothing at all</u> about my business matters, and all you did was provide an introduction. You and I shall have our own celebration later, when I return from San Remo.

C.

San Remo was a town across the Italian border, an easy day's trip, to be home before dark. Popular with English people, for some reason.

"Perhaps she wanted to save you the discomfort of sailing with the men?"

"It's possible. But to say that I knew nothing about it? That is simply not true. I . . . well, it's not true."

I studied the words, that emphatic underscored phrase. "You think that's a hidden message?"

"I think she wanted to let me know who she's with, in case she doesn't come back."

"Surely that's a touch alarmist," I began, but she cut into my reassurances.

"My dear child, please stop thinking of Clarissa as your housekeeper! She is a woman who knows full well what a dangerous man looks like."

"Mrs Langtry, I agree that Basil Zaharoff would not be a person *I* would care to board a yacht with, but Count Vasilev? He's . . . an art collector." And a smuggler, perhaps. But also a man with a sick daughter he loved and a ridiculously fussy beard.

"Oh, for heaven's sake! Before he was friends with Basil Zaharoff, the Count was an intimate of Czar Nicholas, a person the Czar depended on to keep his business affairs out of sight. That is no task for a man with a fastidious conscience. Long before the Bolsheviks closed in, the Romanov treasure was secreted away, everything from Ottoman swords and Fabergé eggs to jewellery and plate. Unimaginable treasure, hidden and buried and scattered to the wind."

"Some of which you think Count Vasilev kept?"

"He has more funds than any White Russian I know. He would certainly have been in a position to send things into hiding. He was conveniently outside of Russia when the Bolsheviks came for the Czar. And he has been in a number of business partnerships with Sir Basil. The Count is . . . not as transparent as he seems."

The Count was also a man who uncharacteristically befriended Niko Cassavetes—a young man who lived in rooms owned by a family of smugglers. I frowned out over the harbour, and muttered to myself. "I need a closer look at those dratted sculptures."

"Pardon?"

"Nothing. How long has she been gone?"

"The boat was not in the harbour when I came by at ten minutes before ten."

I turned and looked at the large hole in the scenery. And at the white sea-plane . . . Oh, damn. "All right. I'll see what I can do."

"How can I help?"

"You can go back—no, wait. Go back to the Hermitage and leave a note for my husband telling him everything you know."

"Everything?"

"Whatever you're comfortable with. But certainly about the boat, and leave him the note she sent you. Oh—and tell him I said to have his pet policeman stop the sculptures from being picked up. He'll understand what I mean. Beyond that, I don't know. I suppose he'll find me—or at least word from me—around the harbour. Thank you, Mrs Langtry!"

I launched myself off the bench and ran. Down the promenade, dodging amblers and dogs, pounding around the harbour and up again to where I had last seen the Hon Terry.

"Stop!" I shouted with the last of my breath. "Wait, not yet!"

He saw me, rather than heard. At first, he waved merrily, then paused as he noticed the urgency of my gestures. He caught at the arm of the man who was about to board the sea-plane.

I was nearly as out of breath as Lillie Langtry had been when I finally caught up with them, causing Terry to look concerned, and the pilot to look at his watch. "Change of plans," I stammered out. "Save a life. Full of petrol?" I jabbed a finger at the sea-plane, to make it clear that my question regarded its tank.

"Don't I know you?" the man asked.

"What life?" Terry demanded.

"Mrs Hudson. Been kidnapped. In danger. Probably. No time. I'd guess they plan. On dumping her overboard, once they. Reach a current to take her body away. From the coast. How far out do you suppose they'll go?"

"Miss *Hudson?*" Terry, rightfully, sounded appalled.

I looked past him, and stuck my hand out at the pilot. "Johnny Perez, right? We met briefly, the other morning. Mary Russell. You know the *Bella Ragazza?*"

"Three decks, diesel-converted, gyrocompass-stabilised? Yes, I know it."

"I need you to head out to sea and try to find it. Her. Once you've located it, you need to circle around overhead as long as you can. That'll make it clear to the people on board that you've seen them. They won't dare do anything while you're watching."

"Even with a full tank—wait, this is idiotic. Do you know whose boat that is?"

"Yes, but I know for certain that he is not on board."

"So, who—no. I'm not getting involved with this."

"Terry?" I looked at him. He thought about it perhaps two seconds, and turned to the other man.

"I'll pay you double. If you find her, and circle until you absolutely have to come back to shore, I'll double it again."

Hard cash put a different colour on matters. Johnny shrugged, settled his hat, and prepared to climb up.

"Wait," I said, thinking hard. Those tide charts I'd amused myself with on the *Stella Maris*. The Western Mediterranean was a series of enormous slow whirlpools, mostly counter-clockwise. One of those was formed by the triangle of Riviera coastline, Corsica, and the Balaerics, and although I couldn't remember just how wide the west-bound current along the coast was, I was pretty sure that a few miles out from here, the flow grew more leisurely before circling back eastward in the direction of Corsica and Sardinia. If one wanted to dispose of an object, but did not want it to come to shore a few brief miles along the coast, one would take it some distance out to sea first. On the other hand, if the inert object was still on her feet and alert, she would surely notice that the boat was headed due south when the goal was a town to the east.

She might raise a fuss. To keep her calm, until it was too late, maybe one would choose a compromise route to San Remo? Slightly south, but still vaguely east?

God, I hoped I was right. "Head south-east, rather than due south. She was told they were going to San Remo, and her kidnapper won't want to alarm her too early."

"Are you certain?" Terry asked.

"No."

The pilot waited, but when no further discussion was forthcoming, he stepped on to the pontoon and clambered up. I expected Terry to follow, but instead he stood away.

"You go, too," I urged him.

"He can stay up longer without my weight," he said. "And anyway, you'll need me in the boat."

"What boat?" I said, just a beat too late.

He grinned. "Bumpy's speed-boat, that you're planning on stealing."

CHAPTER FORTY-EIGHT

"Mycroft?"

"Sherlock, I hope you appreciate that I have kept many men out of their beds this night for you."

"I'll pay for their coffee. What do you have for me?"

"This is all highly preliminary, since even with my people up, that does not mean the rest of the world cooperates. However, you wanted what I could lay hands on by this hour. I begin with Gerald Murphy, who is as clean as a person can be. As is his lady wife. Rafe Ainsley, on the other hand, has friends in disreputable places, but to all appearances left his own criminality behind once he achieved some success as an artist. Which as we both know, may mean either that his energies have moved there, or that he has become better at hiding his schemes."

"The temptation to easy money is rarely put aside entirely."

"As you say. Your Lady de Bathe also has ties to the demi-monde, although in a very different portion of it from the artist. But then, she has had those ties since before she took to the stage. Most of her money appears to come from past investments and her husband's allowance. Suggesting that most of her criminal acquaintances are friends rather than business associates."

"Most of them?"

"She receives gifts. None huge, and none regular, but there have been the occasional minor cheques from Basil Zaharoff."

"How minor?"

"The largest was £500, some two years ago. Pocket change, to that man."

"Still."

"As you say, and we will continue to excavate. Niko Cassavetes was an interesting type. You must know he's dead—and I see that an English woman named Hudson was taken in for questioning. Is that . . . ?"

"None other."

"Did she do it?"

"No."

"I see. Where did you come across Cassavetes?"

"Other than his lying dead on Mrs Hudson's floor, you mean? He attached himself to the community of wealthy Americans who have taken to summering in the Riviera. Gerald Murphy among others."

"Murphy isn't actually wealthy, not compared to some of the names you've given me. He and his wife are comfortable, yes, but I'd say he's living in France as much for the exchange rate as for the ambiance."

"Cassavetes, Mycroft."

"The young man didn't leave much of a footprint, as far as financial or criminal records go. Arrested twice in Greece—for housebreaking when he was fifteen, and three years later in a bar that was raided for gambling. He was let go both times as being too small fry to bother with. A few years later, just after the War, he was picked up near Marseilles when the boat he was on ran aground and the crew tried to save the cargo. Not drugs or arms, merely luxury goods—silks and the like—so they were all given a couple of weeks behind bars and let go. However, he had been getting money from somewhere—regular cash payments into a bank account in Nice."

"A man with a clear history of smuggling."

"Yes. And that may tie in with another of the names you gave me: Matteo Crovetti."

"Roommate of Niko Cassavetes, son of Mrs Hudson's landlady. Also smuggling, I assume?"

"I don't know yet; all I have is the name, which was caught by one of my people on a list of men picked up but not yet formally charged, sent from the Bahamas two days ago. I will know more when the offices open in Nassau."

"Kindly let me know if the man was moving two hundred tons of Imperial gold."

"I can't see why one would do that through Nassau, but I shall. Which brings us to Count Yevgeny Vasilev . . ."

CHAPTER FORTY-NINE

"We're borrowing this boat," I told Terry. "Not stealing." My head was deep under the boat's steering wheel—at least, I thought it was a boat. "Terry, are you sure this isn't some kind of aquatic rocket-ship?"

"She does have an aeroplane engine."

"Why am I not surprised? What about life-vests?"

"Under the bench."

"Get them out. Please."

I tried to ignore the growing crowd of onlookers, which at any minute would include a policeman. How did one short-circuit the ignition of an aeroplane motor? "Ah, here it is," I said, and the huge engine beside my head sputtered and throbbed into life.

Terry moved some levers as I crawled backwards out of the boat's innards. "You might want to cast us off," he said, sounding a bit urgent. "*Now.*"

I scrambled to obey, my fingers somewhat distracted by the rapidly approaching uniform. The rope went slack, the motor growled, and the gathered crowd began to cheer our escape.

Terry kept our speed sedate across the harbour itself, but the moment we came up with the breakwater, he shoved the engine into action and I grabbed at the rails to keep from going over-board.

The boat was designed for speed, not comfort. Hard benches, no cabin, little muffling of the engine noise, and a minimal glass screen designed less for blocking the wind than deflecting it to keep the driver from being scooped out of the boat entirely.

I was going to regret the amount of coffee I'd drunk.

Conversation was impossible. I made my way up to the front, to check that we were headed in the same general direction as the plane, then sank down out of the wind to wrestle into the kapok vest and do some calculations.

Steam-turned-diesel yachts like the *Bella Ragazza* might cruise at around sixteen knots, unless they were in a hurry. It had left the harbour roughly ninety minutes ago which, if they sailed directly, would have them dropping anchor in San Remo about now. If they were actually heading to San Remo. But if they intended to main-tain a pleasant façade until they'd got away from the bustle of coastal traffic (and yes, this was perilously near to a guess) then they would genially take their breakfast and drink their cham-pagne in the morning sun until there were no ships nearby to see their actions.

I could not help feeling that they were approaching their mo-ment of action.

Compare this progress to that of the sea-plane. I imagine it went more slowly than the average aeroplane, because of the drag of the pontoons, so . . . what? Around sixty knots?

Work into this a third variable: us. It was hard to judge our speed, but the other day, Terry had bragged of reaching 45 knots at one point. Our current speed, which felt like a hundred or more over the swells, was probably 35 or 40. Calculating speed times, the time travelled, with three separate trajectories to coordinate . . .

Terry interrupted my maths exercise with a gesture at the boat's wooden dash, the far side of which seemed to be a locker of some kind. I got it open, and found an odd assortment of equipment: ropes, two plaid travelling rugs, three pair of sun-glasses, half a dozen sun-hats, a Very pistol for shooting flares, three unopened packets of cigarettes, four chocolate bars, two bottles of mineral water, and a large pair of binoculars.

Figuring it was the last that Terry had been suggesting, I pulled them out. He nodded, so I took them over to the passenger bench, buttoning away my spectacles.

I tried to brace myself against the slap and bounce of the hull on waves. The plane couldn't be too far in front of us yet, could it? But it seemed a long time before the shape of it dashed across my view. I fought to steady the lenses, and found the wings—yes.

Thumbs-up to Terry, and an extended arm to point out the course correction.

In minutes, the white speck was beyond the reach of the powerful lenses. Which would not have mattered, except that our course correction had brought us closer to the line being followed by an Italy-bound steamer.

Terry moved the throttle up a little. A minute later, he moved it more. He was fighting to keep the wheel under control with the slaps, but the steamer was inexorable, and large. Then larger. Then looming. The throttle gauge was pressed to the end. Terry and I crouched beneath the wind, holding our breath, as if removing those tiny interferences might help us slip across the ship's bow without having to change path. The rust-speckled hull grew. Its disbelieving crew lined up along the rails. Its horn blared hugely . . .

I slapped Terry's shoulder at the same instant his arms were yanking the wheel to lay us over on our side, our prow aimed just after the worst of their turbulence.

When we hit their bow-wave, we took to the air. Terry, bless the man, was experienced enough to cut the throttle and keep the engine from surging itself to pieces—but when we came down, I was sent flying at last, tumbling to a halt against the back transom. I squawked, and tasted blood. Terry looked behind him to make sure I was still on board—but I was amazed to see him grinning like a lunatic.

I rubbed my head, checked that my glasses hadn't come to grief, and retrieved the binoculars—all while seated on the decking, since Terry kept us heading through the leaping white waves. The steamer laid on a long, disapproving blast of the horn, while her sailors trotted across the decks to look down at us on their other side. Terry raised an insouciant hand to them, breasted the other bow-waves with a shade less drama, and then set us back on to our course.

Or as near as we could figure to where our course had been.

I decided to stay where I was against the back corner, and raised the field glasses to the clear blue skies. The engine noise climbed again. After a minute, Terry turned around, raising his eyebrows in consultation. *Is this the right angle?*

All I could do was shrug. It had been hard enough to guess when our former straight line would cross that of the plane, but after a kink and a delay, all one could go by was the compass.

I scanned the blue sky. No wings, no white speck. Wait—there . . . ? No, it had only one pair of wings. And another bird there, and a cloud . . .

Some faint noise came to my assaulted ears. I pulled away from the lenses and saw Terry's mouth open in a shout. Having caught my attention, he turned to point at a spot some twenty degrees away from where I had been looking. I lifted the glasses, searched, saw it dart rapidly through my field of vision—aha.

Double wings, gleaming white, tilted, to catch the sun. The flash of it had caught Terry's eye.

Johnny Perez was circling his plane. But had he run out of petrol, or . . . ?

I held my breath. The wings held their angle, coming around, and I waited for them to flatten out for a run to shore.

No!

I snatched away the glasses and held up a thumb. Terry gave an inaudible whoop of triumph, and turned to adjust the wheel.

Closer and closer we flew. Soon, we could see the aquatic tableau, first with the lenses, then with the naked eye: two hundred feet of spectacular, three-decked yacht, flags flying from its two empty masts, smoke trailing from its single funnel, with several boats nearly as big as the one I was in hanging at the back. Its bowsprit, fitted not with sails but decorative banners, thrust proudly out over the blue sea.

A magnificent vessel, being buzzed by a large gnat. A gnat, moreover, that was not satisfied with merely circling around it, but was doing stunts. One pass was so low, the plane disappeared completely behind the yacht before climbing, straight up, higher and higher. Then high in the heavens, it seemed to stall. The white dot paused, teetered, its nose tipping and pulling it down, and it was falling, plummeting, straight down to plunge into the waves—only to catch at the last instant and skim the very tops of the waves, vanishing from us again, behind the yacht's hull. At the far side, it rose, circled around, then flipped over to perform an alarmingly wobbly pass upside-down—at which point débris exploded from the plane to flutter down across waves and boat-deck alike. White feathers: sheets of paper. As if the pilot had been hired to strafe a single boat with adverts for the Juan-les-Pins casino.

It was a perfectly brilliant series of distractions. And keeping his aerobatic routine on the far side of the yacht had allowed us to approach from the west unnoticed. Now, however, he came around again off the yacht's stern and returned, performing a series of barrel rolls that brought him what felt like inches from our own speeding boat—and, more to the point, caused his audience to cross the wide deck of the yacht, back at the aft end: there seemed to be only two.

When Mrs Hudson appeared, I thought I might weep with gratitude. She saw us, and I could tell that she knew in an instant what we were: her rescue.

The man took longer to catch on. Through the glasses I could see his precise beard bristling with irritation at this idiotic barnstormer whose antics were cutting into a neatly planned day of murder. He glanced at us, looked back up at the plane, then seemed to realise that we were heading straight at him. We were near enough now that I could see his expression through the lenses—and see his hand going to the pocket of his jacket.

"He has a gun," I shouted at Terry. "Don't get any clo—" Our deck heeled over, settling again only when we were on a path parallel to the big hull, but distant enough that only freak luck would land a bullet in us.

Plenty close enough for those on the yacht to see me. Both of Count Vasilev's hands were in view, and empty of weapons, but the nobleman radiated befuddlement as he tried to figure out what I was doing here. His head tipped, as if listening to something Mrs Hudson was saying, then he whipped around to stare at her.

He shot us another glance, then reached for her arm—but both of her hands were locked on the rail. Her spine was straight and her chin up as she spoke to him again.

I could hear it, as clearly as if I stood on the deck beside them. *If they see you drag me off, you will never be able to claim I died by accident.*

His hand dropped. He took a step away. If I'd been seeing this on a screen, its caption would have read, *The Count thinks furiously*.

After a moment, he glanced upward. I did the same, and realised that the sky was empty. Off in the distance, white wings retreated towards Monaco.

We were alone. I gave Terry a sure smile, both for his sake and for those on the *Bella Ragazza*. Perhaps our presence, and our apparent confidence, would drive the Count back to port, where he could don an affronted face. Why had we interrupted his pleasant day out on the water, how dare I interfere, how dare I accuse . . . ?

But if he simply kept sailing, what could I do? Our fuel would run out long before theirs. I had exactly no chance of manoeuvring to the side of the yacht and storming up its gangway unnoticed. At this speed, I doubted Terry could even bring us alongside.

I studied Mrs Hudson, straight-backed and implacable along the railings. Her hair, tossing in the breeze, was the only uncontrolled thing about her. She looked precisely as she had that day, being driven away from Sussex: certain, calm, indomitable. She looked ready to stand there forever.

I wished she had a fur coat on, rather than a light wrap.

A few minutes later, one of the men I had seen in the deckhouse came down to talk to his employer. The Russian gestured forcibly in our direction, his every motion bearing the caption, *The Count gives orders.* But the crewman seemed less than enthusiastic about following them. He watched us, he listened, and he did not shake his head—but neither did he snap out an obedient salute. After several minutes as the target of aristocratic fury, the sailor drew himself up with an air of delivering bad news, and spoke. I watched the pantomime through the glasses. At the end of it, the Count was cold, the sailor was apologetic, and I was somewhat reassured.

However, when the man returned to the deckhouse, the yacht changed direction, abandoning any pretense of an innocent day's outing. But the wheel was not swung very sharply, and when Terry shifted our own heading to match, the other did not attempt to run us down.

"I don't think the crew is going to actively participate in trying to kill us off," I shouted at Terry.

"Jolly good! Er, why?"

"Perhaps they don't actually work for Count Vasilev? The ship is leased to Basil Zaharoff—the captain may have decided that there is a line between allowing their employer's guest to commit a crime, and being active participants."

"Bit like hiring a taxi driver to wait while you rob a bank, isn't it?"

"Nothing to do with me, Your Honour, he just flagged me down."

"Here's to fine lines," he said, holding up an invisible glass.

The man with the beard saw the gesture, but he had regained control now. He disappeared for a moment, then returned, dragging a chair. He went off again, and this time came back carrying a small table with something shiny on it. He sat down, reached towards the shiny object, and picked out a champagne bottle.

When his glass was full, he returned the bottle to its bucket, raised the glass in our direction with a mocking salute, and sat back in his chair to drink it.

Again, I could follow his thoughts. Once night fell, what would prohibit an elderly woman from taking an accidental tumble over the side? Sooner or later, we would run out of fuel, and fall behind too far to hear the sound of cries and a splash.

In the meantime, Mrs Hudson remained at the rail, spine undaunted, chin resolute, one hand firmly grasping the shiny brass.

Stand-off. For now.

CHAPTER FIFTY

An hour later, Mrs Hudson's posture suggested that she was leaning on the rail rather than resting her hand on it. The Count was on his second bottle of champagne. The two of them spoke from time to time. I wondered what they could be saying.

The stand-off was shifting in the Count's favour.

We continued to ride the bow-wave of the *Bella Ragazza*, just beyond the accurate range of a pistol. The yacht's smoke had increased, its speed picking up, forcing us to keep pace. Between the change of speed and the shift in direction, even if Johnny Perez risked taking to the air again this close to night, he would be hard pressed to find us.

The ship seemed to have a minimal crew. There could be any number belowdecks, keeping the machinery running, but I had seen only two figures moving around in the deckhouse. And though I had to assume that any man working for Basil Zaharoff was a man who knew how to keep silent, these remained hesitant to help commit cold-blooded murder.

At least, they hadn't yet brought out a rifle.

They may have simply decided that, the Mediterranean being so heavily travelled, putting a bullet into our petrol tank to sink us would also raise a plume of smoke and attract rescue.

Until night.

Around four-thirty, Terry bent to shout in my ear. "If you want to make it back to port, we're about at the edge of how far the tank'll take us."

I met his eyes. "Terry, I'm going to leave that decision up to you."

He studied the yacht, then glanced back at the invisible shore, and stuck out his arm. "'*Courage!' he said, and pointed toward the land, 'This mounting wave will roll us shoreward soon.'*"

Having summoned Tennyson's reassurance, he put his hands back on the wheel.

Around five, I took a spell at driving the boat so Terry could stretch out his spine and shut his eyes. Half an hour later, he took over again. I stood with the wind battering at me and ate a chocolate bar, washing it down with a trickle of water. Thirty metres away, an old woman sagged more heavily against the brass rail. From time to time, she rubbed at the arthritis in her hands.

"When the sun goes down a little more," I shouted at Terry, "I think I'll send up a flare. It might attract someone's attention." It might also trigger Count Vasilev into action, but at a certain point, that was going to be unavoidable.

"How many do we have?"

"Three."

"You want to shoot one up now?"

"I'm not sure how visible they are in broad daylight."

"If someone's looking, they'll see it."

If.

The sun would go down at 8:00. Our tank would run dry alarmingly soon after that. We were resigned to spending the night adrift, but I devoutly hoped we could avoid actively sinking to the bottom of the sea. I laid my hand against his shoulder.

"Terry, you are a true hero."

He looked at me in surprise. "Good heavens, I've never had such fun. Though I'll be dashed disappointed if this ends with us simply running out of gas and watching them putt away."

We both glanced over at the ship. Mrs Hudson's bones were aching, I could tell, although I didn't think a stranger would see it. The Count was still in his chair, far enough away from her that no one could claim him a threat, near enough to reach her in seconds.

"Why doesn't your lady just hop over the rails?" Terry wondered.

"Perhaps because 'my lady' is old enough to be your grand-mother, and not a strong swimmer to begin with? Perhaps because she knows that dropping over the side could feed her straight into the propeller?"

"Mm. There is that. And I s'pose that chappie with the beard would stop her if she tried to make a great leap."

At this point, I could almost imagine Mrs Hudson climbing up on the railings and making said great leap. But I agreed, it was not likely to be permitted.

The sun touched the horizon line. Shadows stretched out for miles. I sighed, squeezed Terry's shoulder, and dropped to my knee in front of the locker, keeping my hand out of sight when I stood.

"They may react as soon as I fire this off. Don't let them run us down."

"We can dance circles around them."

"While the petrol lasts," I said grimly, then pointed the brass pistol straight up and pulled its trigger.

The spark rose, and rose—and a thousand feet over our heads, a new star come to life, floating gently on the upper winds. Count Vasilev was on his feet. A man stuck his head out of the deckhouse. Seconds later, the *Bella Ragazza*'s stack belched as the engine roar increased.

I studied the two extra shells in my hand, then put my head next to Terry's to shout, "Any idea where that thing keeps her main engine?"

He looked down at the Very gun with alarm. "That'll never go through her hull."

"You don't think so?"

"Solid teak? More likely bounce back and sink us." And then the Hon Terry said something that negated every disparaging thought I'd ever had as to his intelligence: "Though it'd make a right mess of the deckhouse."

I raised my eyes to the structure. An incendiary shell would indeed make for a considerable hazard in the close confines of the glass-fronted wheelhouse. Not that one could really aim a flare-gun. Though perhaps if one were close enough . . .

"I'll need to be right on top of them. And Terry? The Count has a pistol, and Mrs Hudson might decide to jump, so watch them both. It may blind me for a minute, so if she does go over, get close enough to pull her on board, then turn and run us as far and as fast as you can before the petrol runs out. Change direction once or twice. And no lights. Got it?"

It was a stupid, desperate plan, but when one is at the end of a rope, the only choice is to swing hard. The single thing in our favour was that the sun was in their eyes—for another five minutes.

Keeping my hands down and behind the ever-darkening shadow of my body, I fiddled to get a second shell into the flare-gun.

"I'm going to brace myself against the gunwale. When I say 'now,' duck way down and shut your eyes tight."

"Wait," he said.

"I have to do it now, before we lose the sun."

"No—hold on, there's something going on up there."

I looked up. One of the men was bent over the top-deck railing, pointing back. The Count stood, to look out over their wake. Terry and I did the same.

"What the deuces is *that?*"

CHAPTER FIFTY-ONE

Mrs Hudson: a conversation

"I thought it would be Zedzed," she told her captor once the charade had been dropped. "Who killed Niko, who wanted me on the boat. And instead, it is you."

"The advantage of moving in the shadow of a titan. No one notices a lesser figure."

"I don't suppose there was actually any money in the San Remo bank," she said. "Did you even show my bond to your banking friend in Paris? For that matter, do you even have such a friend in Paris?"

"You think I am so good an actor as that? Yes, I did what I said. To my surprise—and to his—your bond was good. The money is there. Enough to keep my daughter in comfort the rest of her life, even before my other ventures."

"Your daughter."

"She is the reason I do all this."

"Of course she is. But what if . . . what if I told you I had another bond, identical to that one?"

"I would say you are lying, to save your life."

"It is the truth."

He studied her, moved two steps closer—then stopped when her arms grasped the rails. Best that she not go overboard while in clear view of the speed-boat below. "Tell me that again."

"I have another bond, the precise duplicate of the one I gave you. It is in a safe place."

"You never said where it came from—or they?"

"My father left them to me. He found them amidst a shipwreck, when the thief whose property they were went down with all hands."

"Ridiculous."

"But true. You've seen the water stains."

"Hmm. How many are there?"

"As I say, there is another."

"And you would be willing to give it to me, if I let you go?"

"I would be willing to divide it with you, if you let me go."

"Miss Hudson, you should have said this earlier. Now? I believe that the moment you step foot on dry land, I am a dead man. Or at the very least, imprisoned."

"Count Vasilev, you are a dead man whether I survive the night or not."

Two hours later, the Count had his vicuña coat over his shoulders, one of the sailors having fetched it for him. His companion on the deck wore only her dress and a decorative wrap, tugged about by the wind.

"You look fatigued, Miss Hudson."

"As do you, Count Vasilev."

"Would you like a glass of champagne? A warmer rug for your shoulders? All you need to do is come and sit down, away from the railings."

"Thank you, I will not drink with you, and I am quite comfortable."

"Who is she? That very determined young woman who persists in following so close?"

"You mean Miss Russell? I thought you'd met her?"

"Briefly. I did not know she was such an ardent admirer of yours."

"Count Vasilev, there are many things about me you do not know. I have friends who would astound you. Some of whom will be waiting for you, at the end of this night."

"Ha! Oh, Miss Hudson, I have enjoyed your—what is the word? 'Pluck'? I have always been fond of old ladies with backbones. Like your friend Mrs Langtry. Which makes me think: she would be the ideal person to hold on to that other bond of yours. Perhaps I will have a conversation with her, when I go back to Monaco."

"You think one old woman would trust another, with that much money? My dear Count, you live in a world of dreams."

"Still, I think I shall ask."

"You do that. You, a man who lost one employee to a bullet and now a passenger to a boating accident? Monaco has a bright-eyed young inspector in its police department who is going to be interested enough in you, as it is."

The sun travelled slowly, its voyage feeling as endless as theirs. The Count got up to stand at the rails, looking down at the speed-boat that continued to echo their movements like a pilot fish its shark.

"That young woman is remarkably determined. You are sure she's not your grand-niece or something?"

"No blood relation. Though I would be honoured if she were."

An hour later, after a hushed, but clearly unsatisfactory conversation between Count and Captain, Mrs Hudson addressed her captor.

"The crew do not seem very keen on serving your needs, Count."

"They are not my men, and they fear that carrying out my orders would . . . compromise their employer."

"You don't think Zedzed is going to be angry anyway, when he finds you've killed me? Even if you don't bring his men into matters?"

"He will be angry, yes. But our friend Zedzed is a practical man. He will see that I had no choice. And if I can keep the trail from leading to his door, he will forgive my impertinence."

The sun grew low, and more chill.

"You do look very tired, Miss Hudson. I imagine you would benefit from a cup of your English tea."

"Cruelty does not become you, Count Vasilev."

"You are right. I apologise."

"In any case, I don't imagine the galley here would have milk in its cool box. I've never much cared for tea with lemon."

"The sun is nearly down, Miss Hudson. I'm afraid our afternoon draws to an end."

"Did you really have to kill the boy?"

"You mean Niko?"

"Are there other young men you've recently had murdered?"

"Not recently, no."

"Who did you have pull the trigger for you, anyway? One of Zaharoff's men?"

"Our friend Zedzed had little to do with any of this. I think he grows old and tired, and I suspect that his new wife does not approve. No, Miss Hudson, this I did myself."

"Really? You left the dinner party and raced to my house to shoot him?"

"Of course not. Your landlady might have heard. No, I arranged a meet with Niko at six o'clock, when Madame Crovetti would be at her shop, and you at Mrs Langtry's famous Friday salon. I told him earlier that I needed something from your house, and told him to find a key—which proved no trouble, since his landlady's son had kept a spare set in the rooms they share. We went in, I wrapped a throw-blanket around the gun for quiet, and when he turned around, I shot him. I left, expecting you to return home soon after. I dropped the hat I wore over the bridge, took off my coat, exchanged the bright neck-tie I had worn for one less notice-able, and I sat drinking coffee and reading the newspaper until it was time to leave for Mrs Langtry's."

"It must have been a shock to find me still there."

"Yes. Fortunately, the police did not notice how long he was dead when you called them, and they arrested you. I am not sure why they let you go again."

"Perhaps they noticed the discrepancy of the blood?"

"Perhaps. But they have no reason to suspect me. I was at Mrs Langtry's that evening."

"But why kill the poor lad? What had he done to you?"

"He helped me in ways that left me . . . vulnerable."

"But you could have offered him money to be silent—or kept him at a distance in the first place."

"Yes. I, too, thought Niko's silence could be bought. When I first met him, I was struck by how much he resembled our friend Zedzed—clever, charming, handsome, no scruples. I expected him to grow into the same man. Ruthless, yes? But in the end, Niko proved to have some troubling limitations. His affection for friends was too close to loyalty, and I could not trust that he would, as the saying goes, 'stay bought.' He knew too much about my business. He had to be removed.

"I regret having to kill him, I truly do. He was a useful man, and deserved better. But I could not take the risk, with my future in his hands. My future, and that of my daughter."

"If you imagine your daughter's needs excuse your acts, Count Vasilev, I, for one, do not forgive you."

"I would not expect your forgiveness. I would not even ask for your understanding. And yet it is true: my choices come out of my responsibilities as a father. All else is secondary."

"Tell me her name—your daughter's."

"Why do you ask?"

"If she's the reason I'm about to die, I ought at least to know her name."

"So you can curse her?"

"I think you know me better than that, Count."

"Yes. Again, my apologies. Natalia. Her name is Natalia, after an aunt my wife loved."

"Natalia Vasilev. May she live long, untouched by her father's sins."

"That is gracious of you, Miss Hudson."

"She's going to have a difficult enough time, on her own. She doesn't need my curses as well."

"But she is not on her own. I will join her, very soon."

"No, Count Vasilev. You will not leave Monaco. Of that I am certain."

"Again, that British fortitude. Even though the night is falling and the end is near. Are you sure you won't let me give you a glass of this champagne? It has gone slightly flat, but I could . . ."

He paused, turning to see one of the crew calling down from the top deck. She could not quite hear the words, but whatever they were, they had the Count on his feet, peering back into the setting sun.

She braced her numb hands, expecting trickery, but he kept his distance. "What is it?" she asked. "What are you seeing out there?"

CHAPTER FIFTY-TWO

I t looked like the last sparkles of sunlight across waves—except that the angle was all wrong for a reflection. Which could only mean . . . "Lights?"

"From more than one boat, I'd say," Terry replied.

Our heads swivelled back to the *Bella Ragazza*. A furious argument was under way. The Count pulled his gun and waved it about—first in Mrs Hudson's general direction, then after a further shouted exchange, to point at the man from the wheelhouse. The crewman's hands shot up, palms out. His left thumb jerked over his shoulder—*Not my decision, Sir, you'll have to talk to the Captain*—but whatever his words, they only infuriated the Count further. The gun shifted slightly and the end of it flashed with a warning shot, then came back to point at the man above.

Count Vasilev had his back to the captive, elderly grey-haired women being less of a threat than an uncooperative crew. The crewman started to call out—but she moved fast for an old woman, and the champagne bottle came down on the Count's skull. The gun flashed. The sailor dove for safety, a window in the wheelhouse shattered, the yacht heeled over as its Captain ducked down . . .

And yet, the Russian was not overcome. He pulled himself up on the rails and turned, a gleam at the end of his outstretched arm.

She froze, I cried out, Terry cursed—and Vasilev did not pull the trigger.

He stood, wavering, not ten feet from her rigid figure. I started to raise the flare-gun, but he was too close, the toss of the sea too uncertain . . .

Mrs Hudson spoke. He did not react—or if he did, it was only a slight shift of the head. She spoke again, her hand sketching a gesture towards the approaching lights . . . and then she turned her back to him, pressing up against the rails.

"Oh God, she's going over!" I cried—but no. Mrs Hudson stood firm, chin high, looking out over the terrible speed of the water below.

And a shot rang out.

But before the wail had cleared my throat, I saw her whirl, upright and controlled.

It was the corner of my eye that caught the motion of a fall.

The last thing I saw as the sun blinked out behind the horizon was Mrs Hudson, alone on the deck, one arm reaching out to the choppy waves below.

CHAPTER FIFTY-THREE

"So, Holmes. What made you come after us? And how did you convince Jourdain to summon his troops?"

It was hours later—it felt like days—and we had made it back to our rooms at the Hermitage. The clock on the wall claimed it was just short of three in the morning. Seven hours, I calculated with difficulty, since the Count had gone over the side of the *Bella Ragazza.*

The sparkling reflections had turned into head-lamps from no fewer than three fast boats. The first held Jourdain, Holmes, and one eager boatsman; the second was laden with five large men I would not have cared to meet down a dark alley; the third was packed with what had to be a major portion of Monaco's police department, including our constabulary guide from the other day.

The uniforms had swarmed up the yacht's gangway and taken possession. The crew of the *Bella Ragazza*—only eight men, it turned out—put on affronted faces and proclaimed their innocence. The police inspector would have kept us on board under his eye all the way back to Monaco, but faced with Holmes at his most imperious, me at my most disapproving, the Honourable Terrence Shields-McClintock at his most affably aristocratic, and an elderly British housekeeper at the end of her rope, he threw up his hands and ordered us all to report to his office no later than ten the next morning.

We'd helped Mrs Hudson descend to the speed-boat, wrapped her in the plaid travelling rug, and settled her on the bench, with water and the last chocolate bar, while one of our rescuers emptied a tin of petrol into our tank. Terry lit the running lights, started the engine, and turned our prow towards Monaco. Holmes, meanwhile, stood and glowered down at Mrs Hudson.

"What were you *thinking*?" he demanded. "That boat is owned by smugglers, under lease to the dirtiest man in Europe, and lent to a Russian Count with some highly questionable finances. What were you doing on it?"

I broke in. "Smugglers? Who are the owners?"

"Your old friends the Crovetti family. The registered owner of the *Bella Ragazza* is one Alessandro Crovetti. Who," he shot at the seated figure, "just *happens* to be your landlady's husband, father of your absent neighbour, Matteo. Both of whom, I have just learned, are currently in a Bahamanian gaol awaiting trial on a charge of smuggling rum into South Carolina. Rum which, by fascinating coincidence, they concealed in the hull of a motor yacht remarkably like the *Bella Ragazza*."

"I'm sorry to hear of the lad's troubles," Mrs Hudson told him. "Although Madame Crovetti will be pleased to hear he is safe."

"What were you up to with Count Vasilev?" Holmes snapped out, in a cold, precise voice that made absolutely no impression on his former landlady-turned-housekeeper.

"Dear me," she replied in a matter-of-fact voice. "I feel so terribly faint. Would it be possible to leave the questioning until tomorrow, in that nice policeman's office?"

"I say, old man, p'raps we should let the lady rest," the gallant Terry put in.

Holmes snorted at the idea of Mrs Hudson with the vapours, but unbending spine or no, her reaction was not entirely feigned. When I sat beside her on the speed-boat's hard bench, I could feel her faint trembling. True, it could have been simply the vibration of the motor, but if I was feeling a bit light-headed, how much more a woman almost three times my age who had stood—literally stood—under threat of death, for hours on end?

Holmes turned away in disgust and hunkered down in the lee of the tiny wind screen, lighting a cigarette and taking care to let the smoke blow in our direction. I wrapped an arm around Mrs Hudson's shoulders. Her shivers began to subside, her body growing heavier against me.

Holmes was looking elsewhere, though I was certain he was aware of our every motion. I tucked my head down to speak into her ear. "What were you saying to Count Vasilev, at the end? I thought he was going to shoot you, but whatever you said made him change his mind."

The old woman withdrew from my support, just a little. I let my arm fall away, but kept my eyes on her. She, on the other hand, was looking at Holmes.

"I told him that he had lost. I said that if he let me live, I would make certain that his daughter was well cared for, the rest of her life."

I stared at her. She gazed at Holmes, as if he had been able to hear her words.

"He believed you?"

"He could see it was a promise."

"That was generous of you."

She made a noise I knew well, a sound that suggested I might want to reconsider a particularly idiotic idea.

"Why make the promise, then? What is she to do with you?"

"She's a poor thing who does not deserve any more suffering, but she was not why I said it. Kindness can be a weapon, Mary. If one's timing is correct."

"Well, yours certainly was. And you couldn't have known that he would choose that way out."

She looked at me then, her eyes old and tired. She said nothing.

We spoke no more, as the lights of Monaco grew before us.

When Terry cut our speed to manoeuvre us in through the break-water, the silence was deafening. Holmes tied us to a set of cleats, and we walked on uncertain feet up the pavements towards town. Terry staggered away in the direction of his dancer friends' flat. Mrs Hudson prodded a sleeping taxi driver to life and gave him the address of Lillie Langtry. Holmes and I made our way up the promenade to the Hermitage, which managed to summon two heaped plates of scrambled eggs and a pot of respectable tea.

Thus, when I was fed, warmed, empty-bladdered, and scrubbed free of salt from hair to stockings, I settled into a chair across from my husband-partner. His heels were propped on the hotel's divan, his fingers tamping tobacco into the bowl of a pipe. "So, Holmes. What made you come after Terry and me? And how did you convince Jourdain to summon his troops?"

"As to the first, I learned this morning that Count Yevgeny Vasilev was closing down his holdings in the South of France and preparing to move to America. His house is for sale, and most of his possessions already on a ship bound for the coast of Texas."

"Really? Who told you that?"

He examined his pipe.

"Ah. You've been in touch with Mycroft."

"Learning that Vasilev was in the process of leaving Europe for good suggested that the killing of Niko Cassavetes had been a part of closing matters up. Which thus meant that anything else in his way needed to be swept up as well."

"But I thought we'd agreed that Niko's death was more by way of a warning shot? That Mrs Hudson would be safe so long as she kept quiet."

"If the Count planned on staying in Monaco, perhaps."

"But not when he decided to leave? Loose ends, I suppose. So you discovered that and headed back to Monaco. Where you found Mrs Langtry's note at the hotel?"

"I found Mrs Langtry herself, who very nearly picked me up and carried me down to the harbour, so urgent was she to send me on my way."

"How did you figure out where to look for us?"

"Perez reached the harbour before we left."

"But the yacht changed its heading after he'd turned back."

"And I decided that the Count would aim for open water, once the sea-plane had left. Two minutes with the local charts gave us the route that would intercept him."

"Though you then had to convince Jourdain."

"That took slightly longer than two minutes," he admitted.

"Holmes, that really doesn't explain the all-out effort. Terry and I go off in search of Mrs Hudson, and when you find out, you not only pull together a crew of your own cut-throats, but drag in Jourdain and a boatload of his own men as well. In, what—a couple of hours? I'd understand the wish to follow me, but to—"

He shot me a look of long-suffering impatience. "Russell, you do have the most disconcerting habit of stepping into the centre of things."

"I see." And I did. Sherlock Holmes had panicked, although he'd never, ever, put it that way. His fear for my welfare had him seizing the collar of Inspector Jourdain with one hand—and I'd have paid to see *that* confrontation—and rounding up a boatload of muscular Irregulars with the other, to send them all racing across the waves.

It must have been an impressive sight.

But I didn't see how the threat to Mrs Hudson was affected by Vasilev's decision to leave.

However, he was speaking again, addressing the second of my questions. "As for Jourdain, once the evidence of the drying bloodstains made Mrs Hudson a less attractive suspect, I had to offer him an alternative villain—someone other than Basil Zaharoff. And certainly a smuggling operation run by the Crovetti family is well within his authority. Even Count Vasilev would be a candidate for arrest, if his crimes could be kept separate from Zaharoff."

"You think it's possible that Zaharoff had nothing to do with it?"

"I fear there will be no evidence that Basil Zaharoff did anything but lend his boat to a friend for the day."

"So was it happenstance, that the boat was owned by smugglers? Or was Vasilev involved with the Crovettis in some fashion?"

"As you know, Russell, I mistrust apparent coincidence."

"All right, assume Vasilev was a part of it. Is that stuff we found in Niko's cave his? Or, Matteo Crovetti's cave, I should say. And I suppose the fact that Mrs Hudson may have been using that same cave ties her in somehow with whatever Vasilev was up to?"

"You cannot deny that she is in the midst of it: the cave, the Crovettis, Niko Cassavetes, Rafe Ainsley. Although I believe that what the Crovettis did for Vasilev was a separate matter from the crates of jewellery we saw in the cave."

"You do? So what was Vasilev having them smuggle?"

"Gold."

"From . . . ?"

"The Czar's gold."

"The Czar? You mean that fairy tale that pops up in the papers from time to time, about a train full of bullion that vanished into Siberia?"

"It was no fairy tale, Russell. But no, I don't believe this involves the actual Romanov bullion. If our suspect were Basil Zaharoff, who could summon a flotilla of steamers rather than one luxury yacht, perhaps, but everything about this indicates a much smaller scale. This would be but a small portion of the Czar's wealth, skimmed off the bulk. Such as would happen if, say, a trusted advisor of the Czar managed to divert a few crates of jewellery as it was being moved out of St Petersburg. Those crates might be directed into Odessa, perhaps, then across the Black Sea to Istanbul or Athens. Compact, valuable things that might be transported in the hull of a yacht owned by a family of smugglers."

"Athens," I said. "You think Niko was the middleman?"

"Niko Cassavetes had a record of working with smugglers before he came here. Let us posit that Count Vasilev either met Niko Cassavetes in Greece, and brought him to Monaco three years ago, or Niko turned up here on his own and then they met—it hardly matters. Once here, one of the men introduced the other to the Crovetti family, and set about the task of moving the gold from Athens to Monaco and from Monaco on to America."

"But you don't think this involves actual bullion."

"I imagine the records for the Imperial reserve would be considerably more detailed than the records kept for other valuables. The sorts of personal valuables snatched up as the Bolsheviks drew near. Plate, candelabras, tiaras, you name it."

"Personal valuables." I stared at my reflection in the dark window, a tiny idea gleaming through the fatigue in my brain. Gleaming like a spot of gold amongst the sweepings on a floor. "Such as Russian jewels."

"Quite likely, yes."

"Golden earrings, of exquisite craftsmanship, with superb gemstones."

"Most probably. Why?"

I slapped down my cup and went to the bedroom, rummaging through the wardrobe into which I had thrust the various garments brought from Antibes. Evening dress, clean blouse, knit mask, jumper with holes—and the dusty trousers I had worn to help Rafe Ainsley. I slid a hand deep into the pocket, felt nothing . . . then deeper, where my fingers encountered a small lump.

I held it out to Holmes.

This earring's soft gold had been flattened by a careless shoe, but one could see the quality of the work. One could imagine the shape against a long, pale neck in a crowded ballroom, while an orchestra played and snow drifted against the windows.

"I found this on the floor of Rafe Ainsley's workshop, on the Cap d'Antibes. Clasp shut, squashed and kicked into a corner."

"Russian work. Intended for melting down? Does the man work with gold—or gold leaf?"

"He works with great slabs of bronze, no gilt that I saw. Although there was an unused crucible . . . Oh."

I took the crumpled shape from Holmes' palm, my fingers clumsy with exhaustion. "Holmes, do you think Jourdain had time to contact his French colleagues and tell them to stop Rafe Ainsley's sculptures from disappearing today?"

His expression told me that it was unlikely.

"We have to go to Antibes," I told him. "Now."

Eight minutes later, we were hurtling along the Corniche Road in the hotel's car, racing the dawn.

On the outskirts of Antibes, we had the driver leave us on the road a distance from the silent foundry. I led Holmes into the yard and around the ancient stone walls, and was working to position the crate oh-so-silently beneath the still-unlatched window when I heard a door open. Alarmed, I looked over my shoulder and saw Holmes, one hand out in a gesture of invitation.

A key was in the latch. I looked at it, baffled.

"It was under that rather blatantly placed flower-pot," he said kindly.

I didn't meet his eyes, merely put down my crate and followed him inside.

CHAPTER FIFTY-FOUR

"See?" We were ankle-deep in excelsior, in the room with the shiny padlock, and I was showing Holmes one of the stowed-away pieces. "These statues are identical—at least, the ones in this crate are, I didn't go through the other three. They're heavy, even for bronze, and there seems to be something odd about the way they're put together. I'm not really sure what it is, just that they're different. I think we need to heat up the furnace."

"Can't it wait?"

"Rafe's shippers are due to pick up these crates today."

"We can stop that. Playing about in a foundry is no task for amateurs."

"I agree. But I don't feel that we should wait until everyone hears about the Count's death. Why don't you go knock up Monsieur Ferrant? I can't do it—if he looks down from his bedroom and sees a young woman, he'll just go back to bed."

He put the statue back into the crate and turned to the door.

"Offer him money," I called. "Lots of it."

In the end, it took a combination of threat—that we intended to turn on the gas anyway, because how hard could it be?—and money—enough to buy a new roof or three—to get the smith up and dressed. Even then, his stormy face made it clear that he was not going to help us, not for money or threat.

"This man, he is an artist," the man protested. "What will happen if I destroy his work? He will take me to court, my reputation will fail, none of his type will ever use my foundry again. *Non. Je n'le ferai pas.*"

"But look," I protested, "these are all identical. And we only need to melt down one of them."

"Artists—every piece is a treasure."

"Monsieur," I said desperately, "you are being used. By a smuggler. When the police discover this, it endangers more than your reputation."

He scoffed, he cursed—but when I held a statue under his nose and asked him point-blank what it was that seemed odd about its manufacture, he grabbed the thing, and went silent. He turned it over in his hands, clearly puzzled, then started excavating the remaining crates for himself.

Five bronze statues and a lot of excelsior lay on the floor by the time he stopped.

"What is it?" I demanded.

"The core," he said. "He left no way to remove it."

The amorphous lump filling the middle of the original wax figure. The plaster Rafe had so enthusiastically bashed away at, on the day of the pour. Of course.

"They do seem a lot of work to remove," I said. "Don't people sometimes leave them in? Or, I don't know. Let the middle fill with bronze?"

"Leaving the core causes the metal to decay. And why would anyone want a solid piece? He's not creating a boat's anchor."

"I'm guessing there's no way of punching through the side? Drilling, maybe?"

He glared down at the piece in his hand, then carried it through the door to the foundry.

We watched him set the figure on a work-bench, clamp it in the jaws of a vice, then reach for a chisel and mallet. A dozen powerful blows later, he dropped the tools, running a meaty thumb over the gouges he'd put in the surface.

Then his thumb noticed something else. He loosed the vice and held the thing, judging its weight. His thumb circled around on the metal.

"What do you feel?" I asked.

He pointed at a small flaw on the surface.

"Does that mean something?" I asked.

He found another one, then a third. "Core pins. That should mean the piece is hollow. But it does not feel hollow."

The man before us was as physically unlike Sherlock Holmes as two human males could be, and yet as he studied the bronze object, his face took on a look of calculation and curiosity I knew well.

I was not in the least surprised when he walked over to the big furnace, and set about getting it running. Though it did take me aback when he looked me over, head to toe, and pointed at one of the stone crucibles lined up against the wall.

"You," he said. "Can you lift that?"

Obediently, I wrapped my arms around it and lifted, stifling a grunt, then staggered around in a circle before lowering it back into place.

Wordlessly, he pointed at the leather apron and gauntlets hanging on their pegs.

Bronze has a melting point of around 950 degrees centigrade. To keep it from forming an inadvertent alloy with something inside, it would require either a great precision in the temperature, or an impervious barrier with an even higher melting point. Monsieur Ferrant, who knew his equipment like a baker knew his oven, might have managed the task of separating out the bronze without a mechanical division—but someone like Rafe Ainsley would prefer a margin of safety.

Rafe Ainsley might well choose to employ an impervious barrier. Something with a higher melting point than bronze.

Monsieur Ferrant chose a crucible with a wide mouth, positioned it in the furnace, and stood the sculpture at the edge to pre-heat it. When the heavy bowl was glowing hot, he glanced around to make sure Holmes and I were well back, then used a pair of long-handled tongs to lower the piece inside. He made a tiny adjustment to the temperature, and waited . . .

It took a long time to melt. When at last he gave me the signal, I donned all the protective garments on offer, from gaiters to apron, gauntlets to goggles. By this time, he had the crucible out of its furnace and into the frame, so I squatted awkwardly down and seized one end of the two-person pouring shank. He nodded his approval, took his own handles, then, *"Hoop"*—and I lifted, helping him carry the massive, burning weight over to the trio of ingot-trays he'd arranged on the floor.

"Là," Monsieur Ferrant said, and the rod swivelled against my gloves as he directed the molten stream into the first tray. When it was full, I shuffled to follow him towards the second tray. Halfway through this pour, the stream began to sputter, tossing around gobbets of thousand-degree metal. My hands twitched at the urge to flee—but I forced myself to stand firm.

Something was blocking the spout. Ferrant signalled a move to the third tray, waited until we were in place, then spoke to Holmes. "Bring the skimmer—that with the long handle. No, the next one—yes. Stand across from us, there. When it tilts, push the core back."

Holmes positioned the skimmer's half-circle end just inside the crucible's spout, then pushed, freeing the last of the stream to flow cleanly out. This ingot was only half filled when Ferrant let the crucible fall upright. *"Hoop"*—only this time, we stopped in the middle of the bare floor. At his next *"Là,"* he tipped, straining to turn the heavy pot nearly on its head.

Something fell onto the stones in a shower of glowing drops. It rolled, picking up grit, but he ignored it, directing me backwards, easing the crucible down onto its stand.

He shut off the furnace. The silence was deafening, but for the sounds of cooling metal.

"How long before that can be handled?" I asked.

"My wife will have made coffee," he said, by way of a reply.

He stripped off his outer garments and walked out of the big doors. More slowly, I removed the gauntlets, apron, and the rest, returning them to their pegs. The air felt remarkably cool.

Holmes and I stood eyeing the object. It was a cylinder some seven inches high and perhaps three across. Much like the cheap cocktail shakers used in the Murphy kitchen.

"You're probably aware that stainless steel has a melting point considerably higher than bronze," I said.

"Fifteen hundred ten degrees, as opposed to nine hundred fifty. Depending on the alloy, naturally."

Naturally. "It looks so harmless, doesn't it?" I asked after a time. "The hand is tempted to just pick it up."

"The hand would be seared to the bone," Holmes pointed out.

I found a stool and sat, awaiting the expert's return. Holmes took out his tobacco, and did the same.

To my surprise, the man's return included a tray with a jug of water and three steaming mugs of coffee. Monsieur Ferrant took a swallow from his, then pulled on a pair of slightly less bulky leather gloves and moved the steel cylinder over to the work-bench. He used the chisel to tap experimentally on the case, testing its thickness.

Whatever he heard satisfied him. He moved it to the vice, locked the jaws down tight, and took up the mallet and chisel again.

In moments, the steel skin was flayed back, exposing the rich colour within. Two minutes after that, Ferrant undid the clamp and overturned the contents on the bench.

The magic of pure gold washed through the old building. A fused and gleaming tangle of pieces—one could make out the remains of an earring here, a necklace there—had been relieved of their stones and pounded down hard into the stainless steel cups until the soft metal was compacted into a cylindrical ingot.

The small crucible that Rafe was so sensitive about, I thought, had been originally meant for melting down the scrap gold. But when he realised that the foundry could be used only if Monsieur Ferrant was away—off with his family and the rest of Antibes to see Niko's Bastille Day fireworks, for example—Rafe had fallen back on a purely mechanical means of inserting the gold into the steel. Portions of the outside pieces, I noticed, had melted and pooled at the bottom.

Ferrant grunted out a French curse, rustic and reverent. My eyes were fixed on the tangle of golden shapes, but my mind had set off on some rough calculations. Three-by-seven cylinder, just under 50 cubic inches—even with its relatively loose packing, there had to be nearly thirty pounds of gold on the work-bench. And at twenty American dollars per ounce—I blinked.

That lump on the work-table could be worth ten thousand dollars. With four crates, each holding twenty identical cylinders packed away in excelsior—some three-quarters of a million dollars behind that padlocked door. And two previous shipments, of how many crates, already in New York waiting for the sculptor's arrival? It might not be railway cars of Russian bullion, but there was enough to keep a man and his sickly daughter very comfortable indeed.

It took me two attempts before my voice was steady. "Er, would you like to phone Inspector Jourdain," I asked Holmes, "or should we ask Monsieur Ferrant to do so?"

CHAPTER FIFTY-FIVE

I thought Sara Murphy was the best person to hear the news first. I may have been wrong.

"Sara, I need to tell you what's been going on here, and you can decide how—and how much—to tell the others."

"Mary, how mysterious. What's up?"

"First of all, I have to admit I haven't been absolutely truthful with you. I am indeed Mary Russell, but my husband's name isn't Sheldon Russell. It's . . ." I sighed. "He's Sherlock Holmes."

"Sherlock *Holmes*?" Her sweet mouth twitched, her eyes sparkled, and she burst into laughter. "Sherlock Holmes! Oh, Mary, you're such a kidder! Sure, your husband looks like the pictures but honestly, what have you been smoking?"

I had been through this before, and as arguments go, this one was about as pointless as they come. One response was to drag out all proofs. The other was far simpler. "Oh, you're right, Sara, he's not the real one—but he and I are actually investigators, and this is what we're working on at the moment."

"You're an investigator? Ooh, how exciting!"

"Every so often," I agreed. "More often, it's drudgery during the case and some uncomfortable conversations after. Such as this one, in which I tell you that the French police have arrested your friend Rafe Ainsley for smuggling."

"Rafe? Oh, surely not. I've never even seen him use cocaine."

"Not drugs—gold."

"Gold? Why would one even smuggle that? It's not illegal, is it?"

"Various governments would not be happy to have it move across their borders. Not in the quantity we're talking about."

"Why? How much is there?"

"A lot."

"You must be wrong. Where would Rafe have got gold, for heaven's sake?"

"He was moving it for someone. Hol—my husband and I found the gold inside statues that Rafe himself poured."

"It's probably some clever Surrealist stunt. Like Duchamp entering his *pissoir* into that exhibition."

For a moment, I wondered . . . But no. "Sara, I'm sorry, but it was no stunt. Niko Cassavetes died because of it."

"Rafe could not have done *that*. He's a bit of a scoundrel, yes— and okay, I can see him smuggling to thumb his nose at the law, but he's not a rat. He wouldn't kill anyone."

"No, we think that was Count Vasilev."

"The Count? What on earth makes you think that?"

"The gold that's being smuggled once belonged to the Czar. When the Romanovs fell, Count Vasilev was in a position to divert some of it away from the Bolsheviks. We think he sent it to Greece. There he found Niko, who helped bring the gold to the Riviera. Niko also introduced the Count to a man with a boat, who could help smuggle it into America. They did one shipment during the winter, but then the man was arrested in the Bahamas, and they needed to find an alternative.

"Rafe joined you here in, what—March? April?"

"The end of March."

"Niko met him, and, as was his habit, he made himself useful.

He located a foundry for Rafe, as he located fireworks, and sketch-books and temporary nannies. But when he saw how Rafe made his sculptures, it gave him an idea. The gold could be hidden inside the bronze.

"Rafe helped him, obviously. They'd got two batches of the sculptures off, and one ready to go, but Count Vasilev wanted to close up his life here for good. And Niko was a loose end."

Her lovely face was twisted in disbelief. "You honestly believe that *Yevgeny* killed Niko? But why?"

"The Count was desperate to get to America, taking as much with him as he could. His daughter was getting better, and he wanted to join her. And as you know, he was also convinced that Europe is headed towards another War, and he could not risk getting trapped here, just as so many of his family had been trapped in Russia. Once the gold was on its way, Niko knew too much about him, so he had to be removed."

And if he could do so in a way that silenced Niko's other partner-in-crime, Mrs Hudson, so much the better. *We can aim the police at you any time,* the murderer told her. *If you open your mouth to any-one, we can do far worse.*

There was no need to tell Sara that, once Vasilev had taken pos-session of the gold in America, he might well have arranged a similar death for Rafe Ainsley. She was already sitting with her arms hugging her knees, looking too cold for a warm afternoon on the Côte d'Azur.

"I invited him into my house," she said. "I invited all of them. They ate my food, drank my wine. They played on the beach with my children."

I dropped down in front of her and took her hands, forcing her to look at me. "Sara, you and the children were always absolutely safe. Even Gerald had nothing to do with it. None of you would have come to harm. Think of this all like—like driving past a nasty accident on the road. The people are strangers, and there's others helping out already, so the best thing you can do is keep going."

After a while, she spoke, in a distracted voice. "Yesterday some workmen came to measure the beach wall, at La Garoupe. The town is going to put in a row of bathing huts."

It sounded like a non-sequitur, but I understood that it was not. Paradise had been breached. The snakes of criminality and mass tourism were moving into its edges.

"I am sorry," I told her.

"Maybe we'll take up Cole and Linda's invitation, after all. I think I'd prefer to be in Venice, for a little while."

CHAPTER FIFTY-SIX

Mrs Hudson: a conversation

"Have we managed to warm up your bones a little, Clarissa?"

"I'm much better now, Lillie. Maybe just another cup. So now, dear thing, I need to ask: how much did you tell him?"

"Who—Mr Holmes, or the policeman? Not that it matters, I didn't tell either of them much of anything. Only your young lady."

"Mary?"

"The note you sent frightened me. I could see you were trying to protect me, in case something went wrong. And when I saw Zedzed at the café when he should have been on the yacht, I went to find her, and showed her your note. I did realise it meant that Zedzed wasn't the one who was threatening you, so it had to be the Count—but I didn't go into any details with her. I simply told her that you were in danger. I did admit that I knew more about your affairs than 'nothing at all,' but I kept it in the most general of terms. I said nothing about the bonds."

"You mean the *papers*?"

"Yes, sorry. She asked me to get word to Mr Holmes, so I waited at the Hermitage, drinking endless cups of Russian tea, until he finally showed up. I told him that Mary and her young friend had gone after the Count, and that the sea-plane pilot might know which direction they'd take. He phoned to the policeman from the hotel desk—he shouted, Clarissa: who would have thought the man could lose that much control?—and threatened to drop an international incident on Prince Louis' head if the police weren't in the harbour with fast boats in ten minutes. His precise words. And I'd thought it was histrionics until I saw all those uniformed police piling into speed-boats and taking off as if the Prince himself was in danger."

"An international incident would be the least of it if anything happened to Mary. Mr Holmes does not like it when people threaten those he loves."

"To be fair, he did seem to include you in his concern."

"Yes. Although that does not change how he would react if he found out about the *papers*."

"About that. Do you think the Count actually succeeded in redeeming it?"

"He said he did. That it's in the bank in San Remo—under his name."

"Oh dear. And you have no chance of claiming it, with him gone?"

"I can't see how."

"Clarissa, I am so sorry. I should never have urged you to trust him."

"We both knew from the beginning it was a risk. That much money would tempt even an honest man. There was no way to guess that it would turn him murderous as well."

"You should have played him along. Told him about the other bon—the other papers."

"I did."

"He decided it was better to cut his losses, then."

"Hardly losses. More like deciding that ten pounds in the hand is better than twenty dangling at the end of a risk. While we were out there, waiting for the sun to go down, he told me all about it. What man can pass up a chance to explain life to the nearest woman? Whatever arrangement he had with Mr Ainsley was nearing its end, and he was absolutely terrified of the Communist threat, with Stalin coming in and the Zinoviev letter that changed last autumn's General Election. He was finished with Europe, and wanted to be with his daughter."

"But you're certain he's dead? It's not a trick?"

"There was blood on the railings. It's too far to swim to any shore. And Mary's friend and I both saw the gun go off."

"So it's over?"

"Oh, Lillie, is anything like this ever over? I suppose it's possible all the trouble will just . . . fade away. If it doesn't, I'm in for an uncomfortable time, and may end up back under the parole of Mr Holmes. I only hope I can keep you out of it."

"Do you want to leave, now? Mathilde could drive you to Nice, or maybe Cannes, and I could meet you in Paris, with the other papers once things quiet down."

"No, dear. I don't want to run. As for money, well, he's got his eyes on me now. Even if I avoid arrest, I shall have to keep my head down for a time. Yet again, I bring down catastrophe on myself. But in case I don't get the opportunity to say it in the days to come, thank you, dear friend. In spite of everything that has happened—poor Niko, my arrest, those hours on the *Bella Ragazza,* and even now the uncertainty that will not go away—the time spent with you, these past weeks, has been among the best in my life."

CHAPTER FIFTY-SEVEN

"Holmes, I cannot say our time on the Riviera has made for much of a holiday. Is crime as all-pervasive as it appears, or does it simply follow us about?"

"A mechanic's ears hear trouble in a motor long before the problem manifests," he noted.

"And a normal person would have tripped merrily through the sunshine without noticing any smuggling or murdering or depravity? I suppose you're right. But could we perhaps take a few days and—I don't know. Go explore the Roman ruins?" I knew better than to suggest lying on the sand with a book.

"You do not imagine that we are finished here?"

I stifled a sigh. "No, I suppose not. Mrs Hudson is still under threat."

"Mrs Hudson is still under suspicion."

"Of what?"

"Of having the Predergast fortune."

What was it Lillie Langtry had said? *Something she had that required more specialised knowledge, when it came to converting it into cash . . .*

I should tell him.

No, I should talk to Mrs Hudson first.

"Holmes, the only people who believed in that fortune were criminals—who thought that since *they* were always looking to commit a felony, everyone else was, too." Criminals, and chronically suspicious detectives.

"Monaco is an expensive place to retire."

"And as Mrs Langtry said, she had a diamond necklace to sell. That should keep her for a time. In any event, when Mrs Hudson sold Baker Street, she invested the money, and what has she had to spend her income on for the past twenty years?"

He was not, I thought, serious about his misgivings, merely determined to show his diligent pursual of the facts. After a few more protests, he set them aside and returned to the matter of Mrs Hudson's vulnerability, rather than her guilt.

"She ought to leave this place," he said. "If Count Vasilev felt her a threat, so might those he worked with."

"The only two still walking free are Zaharoff and possibly Madame Crovetti. And if Basil Zaharoff decides to come after her, I'm not sure it would help to hide in Patagonia. In fact, she might even be safer here, where he can see what she's doing."

"I will speak to Jourdain. He may feel that he owes me a favour."

"I have another idea."

"Russell, I forbid—I strongly prefer that you not go near Basil Zaharoff."

"The old man liked me," I pointed out, and told him what I proposed.

He disapproved. Mightily. "That 'old man' will eat you alive. If you insist on speaking with him again, you and I will go together."

"Holmes, your presence would only escalate matters. And in any event, what's he going to do? Shoot an unarmed woman in his own room? No, if I wander into the old lion's den, he won't take me seriously. At first."

He scowled, but thought about it for a time before, reluctantly, his mouth quirked. "The more fool him."

CHAPTER FIFTY-EIGHT

I had sailed away from Venice on the first day of July, I thought, as I stood between the pots of healthy flowers, waiting for the response to my knock. Today was the last day. With any luck, August would start matters afresh.

I heard footsteps approach down the hallway, and she opened the door that I had first stepped through with such trepidation, five days before.

"Mary, come in. I've just put the kettle on."

"Thank you, Mrs Hudson, I won't stay now. But perhaps I might come by, afterwards?"

"My door is open to you any time."

"Do you have them?"

She took the box from her apron pocket, but held on to it. "Are you sure about this?"

"I think so."

"That is not very encouraging."

"Well, if I fail, you'll be no worse off than you are now."

"*I* won't be—but you?"

I stretched out my hand. Reluctantly, she set the box into my palm.

This time, I had made an appointment with the monster. This time, the door was not standing open. A different large thug with a gun under his jacket opened to my knock.

I half expected this bodyguard to demand that I lift my arms to be felt all over for weapons, but apparently he'd been instructed otherwise, and merely shot me a warning scowl before letting me in.

And this time, Basil Zaharoff did not have a gun in his hand.

He did wear the same affable expression. We would see how long that lasted.

I sat in the chair across the desk from him. "Thank you for seeing me."

"Young lady, you have caught my interest in a way few people manage to do." But behind the smile, in the back of the eyes, the end of that sentence lay clear: *. . . and live.*

I could not quite control the shudder of reaction, but in hopes that motion would hide the depth of my fear and revulsion, I shifted to take the little box from my pocket. I laid it on the edge of the desk, pushing it across the polished surface with one finger.

He eyed it for a moment, then picked it up and opened it. "One of these earrings appears to be missing."

"A reminder," I told him. "Or insurance. As you prefer."

"Of?"

As I could not hide my shudder, nor could I force myself to make a blunt accusation. Instead, I shaped it into a story. "Those earrings were given to a friend of mine by one of her long-time admirers. He had received them from a colleague—let us call him Monsieur Eugene—who wished to show his appreciation for some favours my friend's admirer had done. A few introductions, some quiet arrangements. The use of a rather fine yacht. That sort of thing.

"In recent months, Monsieur Eugene recovered a quantity of valuables that had been left far away. In Athens, perhaps, although that is not where they were from originally. I imagine that Monsieur Eugene, when he looked over these retrieved valuables, judged a few of them far too pretty to be crushed and melted down. So he gave a few of the lovelier pieces to the man who had done him the favours. That man, in turn, made a gift of one pair of earrings to the woman he had long admired. I imagine he felt a certain . . . residual fondness for her, that lingered even after he married."

No sound from the old man; no motion, although I could feel the icy gaze drilling in on me.

I focused on the single earring, choosing my words with great care. "My friend's admirer is a man who wields considerable power. Were he to turn against my friend—this lady who had once captured his affections—he could make life extremely difficult for her. Even, I fear, make life somewhat shorter."

I took a breath, then raised my eyes to his.

"I wish to return that earring to my friend's admirer, as a reminder. That the lady may appear vulnerable, but in fact, she is not without friends. Friends who wish to see her happy, here in her new home. Friends who have the means to watch over her, and to ensure her welfare. Friends whose cards can be found, were you—or he—ever to require them, in the bottom of that box."

I waited to see if he would go looking, but he made no move. I nodded, but before I could rise, he began to talk, musing aloud.

"I met your friend—I met both women, come to think of it—at a ball." His hand came out to turn the box around on the glossy surface. "It was the spring of 1877, in a London house filled with dancing and diamonds, and those two girls put the rest of the beauties to shame. One wore black, the other peach-coloured silk, and between them, a man felt as if the angels had come to earth.

"Two weeks later, at a dinner party, the two introduced me to a

Swedish industrialist named Nordenfelt, who was looking to expand from railroads to guns. My life began on that night."

As I realised what he was saying, a flush of dismay rose through me—but no. English society was tiny, and had no need of one casual introduction to bring together a Swedish manufacturer with the young monster who would end up squeezing the blood of the world out of his fist. They would have met anyway. Mrs Hudson could not be held responsible for a half-century of devastation.

Still, I found that I had got to my feet. "Thank you, Sir Basil. Meeting you has been . . . educational."

He, too, rose. Then, slowly, he extended a hand over the desk. "I can in all honesty say the same about you, Mrs Russell."

I shook the monster's hand, in recognition of an agreement sealed, and left him in his room with the spectacular view. Left him to open the box and find the cards of not only Mary Russell, but of Sherlock Holmes—brother of that power behind the British government, Mycroft Holmes. Left him to make my way downstairs to the Hermitage lobby, to reassure Holmes that I'd made it out alive.

I'd done all I could to keep Mrs Hudson safe, and happy.

And if that meant she would never return home to Sussex, well, I should simply have to live with that.

In any event, Monaco was not all that distant. The Train Bleu made travel here a breeze.

CHAPTER FIFTY-NINE

That night, I dressed for the cold, from boots to knit cap. That night, I had extra batteries for the torch.

And that night, I went alone—dressed in black, as invisible as a person could be.

I had lied to my husband, in coming here. He thought I was on the Cap d'Antibes, bringing comfort to Sara Murphy. He would meet me in Nice tomorrow, to board a train for Roumania and what he persisted in claiming was a problem with vampires.

But I was not going to Antibes tonight. And I was not comforting Sara Murphy.

Despite the hour, a light burned upstairs in the Crovetti house. But then, if a woman—any woman, even if she was also a partner—had just learned that her husband and son were standing trial in a distant land, I imagined she would find sleep elusive.

I was concerned that the converted warehouse might have been left guarded, awaiting a police search of Matteo Crovetti's home, but there was no constable outside, and no light within. I pulled out the key that we had purloined and crossed the lane, letting myself in with only the faintest whisper of sound.

I stood motionless for a long minute, listening for a rustle of clothing or a stifled breath before trading the key for my shaded torch. As before, I went through the rooms to check that they were empty of people. To my interest, they showed clear signs of a thorough search, followed by the beginnings of an even more thorough cleaning job.

In clearing up after the police intrusion, Madame Crovetti had been forced to acknowledge her son's absence, at last.

The rooms where Niko Cassavetes had lived showed a more extreme transformation: his spices and pans were gone, the bed stripped to its mattress, even the tapestry-like coverings pulled down from the outer wall. All his clothing was gone.

I ran my light along the hidden door. No sign of forced entry. No indication that burly constables had carried out the crates of smugglers' booty.

But then, if Jourdain and his men had noticed the same worn trigger-spot that Holmes had seen, they wouldn't have needed a pry-bar. And they might have decided to leave a guard inside the cave, to catch whomever came to check on its contents.

Gingerly, I pressed the spot that loosed the mechanism, and eased the door open. No reaction, and no uniformed gentleman waiting to pounce. I stepped through and followed my light along the narrow passage into the cave itself.

No guard waited. The crates of smuggled goods did not appear to have been touched.

I exhaled at last, went back to close the door in case of late intruders, then turned to my task.

Where would Mrs Hudson hide something precious? She had lived around Sherlock Holmes long enough to pick up all the basic skills, as demonstrated by the brass peep-hole in her front door and the surreptitiously loosened fastenings in the back exit. She, of all people, knew the vulnerabilities of the usual hiding places—sock drawer, tea caddy, a potted aspidistra, a loose board in the bedroom floor. And the old shoes in her wardrobe showed that she had been here, stepping in that damp puddle where the planks were rotted through. Whether she had known of the smugglers' cave beforehand, or learned of it after taking up residence, she had been here. And a cave close but unattached to her own dwelling would be the natural place to hide treasure—either from a thief, or from the all-seeing eyes of Sherlock Holmes.

"Though it would help to know what I'm looking for," I muttered aloud. A drip was the only response.

It was not in the crates, since we'd have found it. In fact, anywhere too close to those illicit goods risked accidental discovery—by men she knew to be criminals. And though Mrs Hudson had delivered any number of surprises recently, I could not believe she would fall under the spell of a rogue *homme à tout faire* because of his compelling green eyes.

That meant her hidden goods would be up in the further depths of the cavern.

But first, I played my torch into the forest of stalactites, particularly those that had been broken recently enough to have sharp edges. My neck went stiff, and I fell twice, but I found no place that could hide any object larger than a thumb-nail. Which did not leave out gemstones, but it did leave out a sixty-nine-year-old woman clambering up to hide them, without so much sign as gouges from a ladder.

Along the main cavern, into the subsequent one, up the slippery footholds. I spent a long time at the odd, bottle-shaped stalagmite that grew beside the informal bench, but I could find no way of moving, shifting, or opening it. And there was little point in smashing it to pieces.

Pressing on, into the recesses, over slick chalk surfaces. Would she have managed this? Mrs Hudson was physically active for a woman of her years, but without hob-nailed boots—of which there were no traces in the chalky floor—I did not like to imagine the attempt.

I slowly traced my path back to the first cavern, inspecting every inch of what lay within arm's reach along the way. No valuable paintings on the wall, no Shakespeare folios or copies of the Magna Carta. No patched holes into which a diamond or roll of high-denomination banknotes could have been tucked.

I changed the batteries in my torch once, and those replacements were failing when I made it back to the narrow corridor entrance. I replaced them, too, and used the fresh light to search the entry, thinking that this would be the ideal place to hide ... something.

I found nothing.

I went over the hidden doorway, prodding the frame, the hinges, the trigger mechanism, knowing that an overlooked area like this—at the very threshold of a smugglers' cave—was where a truly clever person would hide a thing ...

But it was not.

I stepped out, shut the hidden door, automatically checking the floorboards for any betraying smears off my shoes. I eased my back, looking over the former quarters of Niko Cassavetes. I supposed it would make as much sense to hide something in this room as it would to use the concealed doorway. Even if Niko knew his neighbour had concealed something, would he think to search for it inside his own quarters? There was always the risk of accidental discoveries—by Niko, or Madame Crovetti, or by the room's next resident. But if Mrs Hudson had been able to solve the eternal problem of where to hide something in plain sight, then it would at least—

(*Plain sight* ...)

—mean that she could ...

Wait. I frowned, listening to the faint echo of the phrase in my mind.

Plain sight.

Edgar Allan Poe wrote a story about a purloined letter left blatantly out in the open by a man who knew that the police would focus their search on ingenious hiding places. We see what we expect, and overlook what we know to be unimportant.

How to show a man whose eyes see everything just what he expects to see? If he suspects that a person is hiding a thing, shouldn't one give him a place to search for it?

If that man expects cleverness, will stupidity be invisible?

If a person is known to be experienced, can naïveté be a bluff?

At the word *bluff,* I laughed aloud.

When is a bluff a double bluff?

I still had no idea what I was looking for—but I knew where I would find it.

CHAPTER SIXTY

A s I crossed Matteo Crovetti's half-tidy quarters next door, I was astonished to see dim light through the shutters. A glance at my watch confirmed that it was nearly sunrise.

That simplified matters. Mrs Hudson always rose early—at least, she had in Sussex. Did the same habits apply to Miss Hudson of Monaco? I gave a quick glance at the street outside before stepping out, then locked the former warehouse and eyed the neat little house next door. Was that light coming through from the morning room?

I decided I didn't care, and walked up the pristine steps to rap on her door.

Sounds confirmed that I had not woken her. I raised my face to the little brass view-hole, and spoke when her eye appeared behind the grille.

"Hello, Mrs Hudson. Sorry to disturb you so early but—" The peep-hole shut and the door opened, my resolve sagging at the sight of her comfortable figure in dressing gown and slippers. Couldn't I just . . . ?

No, I could not. "Sorry to knock so early," I said, "but there's something I need to know."

"Come in, dear, I just made tea; there's plenty for two. I'll fetch you a cup—make yourself comfortable."

The left-hand door, the one that led to the formal parlour where Niko had died, was as firmly shut as it had been when I first saw it. I wondered if she'd been in there at all since she'd returned home. But the right-hand door to the cheerful morning room stood wide open, and while she went back to the kitchen, I walked through her pleasant retreat to unlatch the shutters and throw them open to the morning.

I stood in the brightness, aware of the expression my face wore. A smile, but a complicated one: pleasure from having solved a tangled problem—and delight from having got there before Holmes—was tempered by discomfort at the upcoming confrontation and the knowledge that I was going to hurt someone I loved. There was sadness, since my triumph meant her defeat. Beyond that, there was uncertainty, from the dilemma of what to tell Holmes.

It was an expression I had seen Holmes wear, when a case came to an end that was intellectually satisfying but emotionally painful.

It was also an expression that Mrs Hudson could not miss, when she walked in with another cup and a plate of buttered toast.

Her step faltered, then continued. She poured the tea with steady hands, arranging the milk and the toast within my reach, then resumed her seat and her own cup—but she would not meet my eyes, and her face had gone suddenly old.

"What is it you want to know, Mary?"

"Mrs Hudson, I don't really *want* to know any of it. But I'm afraid I need to. So tell me: the colours in this room. Were they deliberately chosen, or was the decorating unconscious?" Her look of bewilderment was all the reply I needed. "I will take it, then, that the greys and touches of green were inadvertent?"

"Well, I did choose them," she said. "They seemed pleasantly cool. This can be a warm climate."

"I see." I laid aside my cup and walked over to the little painting on the wall, that storm-filled sky above the undulating green hillside of Beachy Head. "The colours just happen to reflect the most important item in the room."

I waited for her to laugh, to tell me that naturally, the painting was dear to her—that I had given it to her, that she treasured it . . . But she said nothing. I loved her for that, and yet I reached to take the painting from its hook, ignoring her tiny sound of protest.

"I found it in that little shop near the Eastbourne Library," I said. "The cliffs near Birling Gap. A sentimental reminder of a long-time home, given to you by someone who loves you, and whom you love. A person who knows you so well, they know that you would never, ever, hide jewellery inside a pair of stockings or banknotes in the tea caddy. No more than you would answer your door without seeing who is there, or live in a house with a barred back exit."

I carried the painting back to my chair and sat down, laying it on my knees with its brown-paper backing face up. I reached down to my boot-top for the sharp little throwing-knife I wore there, holding it poised above the paper.

"When is a cliff a bluff?" I mused. "And if a cliff, or a picture of a cliff, is used to hide something that no sensible person would hide there, does it become a double-bluff? No prudent and experienced woman would hide anything precious in her sock-drawer, in the flour canister, or at the back of a picture. Places any amateur sneak-thief knows to look.

"But what if one is dealing with the very opposite of the amateur sneak-thief? What if one fears, not a clumsy housebreaker, but a man with the very sharpest of eyes and the most devoutly suspicious of minds? A man who, moreover, has watched a woman's every move for years, who has come to respect both her wit and her accumulated skill? In that case, wouldn't a stupid act be the wisest?"

I lowered the needle-sharp point of the knife into the backing paper. Down one side, across the bottom, up the other. I folded the paper back, prised up the white card-stock below, and saw . . .

To be honest, I was not sure what I was seeing, other than it being old, and ornate, and formal.

"What is this?"

"That is what made Count Vasilev so eager to throw me from the boat—or at any rate, one very like that. There are two more underneath."

I worked the top sheet out of its frame. It resembled an amusing trifle one would find in a market stall of decorative jumble—those ornate stock certificates from long-defunct railways or coal mines that closed a generation ago. In this case, it appeared to be a bearer bond from a rural English bank, with a face value of £50,000. It had to be a joke.

So she explained.

Back in another age, the year before one Clarissa Hudson came squalling into the world, an embezzler named Jack Prendergast had enlisted the help of a career criminal to convert the better portion of a quarter-million pounds sterling into four pieces of paper. For seventy years, the pages had been lost—until this past spring, when she happened to go looking, and found them. She knew they were worthless, they had to be—and yet, various men had thought them valuable enough to kill over. So, tentatively, she had handed one of the four over to a man who was once the Czar's banker . . .

Only to discover that he also considered the piece of paper worth killing over.

She looked at the sheet in my hand—calligraphed, stamped, water-stained, and old. "I found them in the old rag dolly, the day I left Sussex. I never thought they would be worth anything. Perhaps a few francs as decorative items. Even now, I'm half convinced that the Count was lying about the money being in the bank in San Remo. Although why he'd persist with the act when it was clear he was going to kill me, I can't think."

"You told him you'd make sure his daughter was cared for."

"Monaco and France will stop his accounts, until they are satisfied that the money in them is not from crimes. But no one else knows about the San Remo monies. They could sit there forever, unless her sanitorium hears of them. And if that fails, well, Lillie will step in and care for the girl."

"Will she?"

"It was my promise. That is what friends are for."

"It's not a hospital for tuberculosis, is it?"

"No. Natalia's problems are of the mind. And heart. Her mother and brothers were murdered before her eyes, and she was . . . Well, she was broken, by the War."

Natalia Vasilev. A woman damaged by men, who might be saved by women.

After a time, my hands fitted the sheet back on top of its siblings. Tucked the cardboard behind it. Smoothed down the brown paper that curled away from its sliced edges.

"Mrs Hudson, I have to tell Holmes about this."

"I would expect no less."

I set the picture on the tea-table, face down, as cautiously as if it were a bomb. The lining paper refused to lie flat, however much my fingers smoothed it.

Slowly, I finished my thought. "I might not have to tell him right away."

She said nothing. She may have stopped breathing.

I pressed my hand against the rising paper one last time, then slid the painting across the table towards her. "I don't like keeping secrets from him. So I'd suggest you take care of this as fast as you possibly can."

"Mary, I can't ask you to do that. To lie to him. It's wrong, and he'll be very angry."

"I know. But he keeps things from me. And sometimes—well. Sometimes a woman is a wife, and sometimes she's a friend."

In any event, Mrs Hudson was probably right: her three decorative pieces of paper with the absurd sums on them would turn out to be nothing but amusements.

Besides which, Holmes and I had a task in Roumania waiting for us. After this adventure of bearer bonds and smuggled Romanov gold, a problem of vampires would be something of a relief.

Fear no more the heat o' the sun,

Nor the furious winter's rages;

Thou thy worldly task hast done,

Home art gone, and ta'en thy wages:

Golden lads and girls all must,

As chimney-sweepers, come to dust.

(SHAKESPEARE, FROM *Cymbeline*)

AUTHOR'S AFTERWORD

Portions of this Memoir, the reader will notice, describe events and conversations that took place outside of the author's point of view. Several of those chapters contain information that took months—even years—to piece together, but I found it simpler, for the sake of the narrative, to assume the guise of omniscience.

The chapters concerning Mrs Hudson's conversations with Lillie Langtry came to me in 1930 as a sheaf of poorly typed pages, heavily annotated in colloquial French with various inks but the same hand, and marred here and there by what would appear to be fallen tears. The typescript itself records a verbatim series of overheard exchanges in English. The hand-written commentary amounts to a year-long *cris de coeur*, which I imagine could only stop when the manuscript had left her hands.

These chapters, too, incorporate my later knowledge of events.

It may surprise my readers to hear that I made no effort to locate the sender. Not that it would have been difficult, but I felt there was a reason the author deserved her privacy.

Also, unlike my husband, I occasionally find myself treasuring life's small mysteries.

—MRH

EDITOR'S AFTERWORD

S ara and Gerald Murphy lived in Antibes until 1929, when
their younger son, Patrick, was diagnosed with tuberculosis. It
made an abrupt end to Gerald Murphy's brief painting career, as
he and Sara spent the next years near their son's Swiss sanatorium,
then returned to the United States in 1934 for Gerald to run Mark
Cross, the family business. Patrick fought his disease until 1937—
but his older brother, Baoth, had already died, in 1935, from a
complication due to measles.

Lillie Langtry, Lady de Bathe, died in 1929. Her faithful French
companion, Mathilde Peat, lived on in Monaco, until 1965.

The Czar's missing gold remained a mystery until 2017, when a
coded document was interpreted by a Soviet mathematician, leading searchers to an abandoned railway tunnel filled with Romanov
gold bullion. Unless that wasn't the missing gold, and it lies at the
bottom of Lake Baikal . . .

Basil Zaharoff, too, remains a mystery. Most records of his birth,
life, and history conveniently disappeared along the way, including
the extensive memoirs and papers he burned after his wife's death
in 1926. He was, however, a close friend of Sarah Bernhardt; he

did live in Monaco in the 1920s; and he did own what may have been a majority holding in the Société des Bains de Mer.

Elsa Maxwell discovered Monaco a year after the events of this Memoir. In 1926, she was brought in to help Monaco become the new Lido.

Events referred to in the story—Jack Prendergast's embezzlement and the appearance of Mrs Hudson's son—can be found in the Arthur Conan Doyle story "The Adventure of the *Gloria Scott*," and Mary Russell's earlier Memoir *The Murder of Mary Russell*, respectively.

ACKNOWLEDGMENTS

In any book like this, thanks extend in many directions and over much time.

I was grateful for the cheerful expertise of Sean M. Monaghan and Courtney Scruggs of Bronze Works in Santa Cruz, who let me get in the way during their pouring, and waste their time on endless idiotic questions. Naturally, anything wrong in this final story is my own wrongdoing, playing fast and free with the art and science of bronze casting.

Similarly, the staff of the Hôtel Hermitage in Monaco did their best with a stray American writer, ignoring her unsuitable clothing, politely responding to her questions, never reporting her for photographing odd corners and making notes of dull details, and in all, leaving her certain that the hotel would never have permitted an infamous arms dealer to take up residence on their top floor.

My editors are, as always, responsible for much that is good in the story—both Kate Miciak, who saw the book started, and Hilary Teeman, who has seen it finished. Bless you, my ladies of the sharp eyes and sensitive ears.

The rest of my team is, as always, as much family as friends. Allison Schuster, Kim Hovey, Melissa Sanford, and Carlos Beltrán from Penguin Random House are among the many who conspire to make me look better than I am. Similarly, on the other side of the Atlantic, Susie Dunlap and my other friends at Allison & Busby, UK.

Then there is my home team of Zoë Quinton and Bob Difley, who do all kinds of stuff that I'm simply useless at, while my long-time Team LRK of Alice Wright, Merrily Taylor, Erin Bright, John Bychowski, Sabrina Flynn, and Karen Buys help to keep me in line and up to date.

Thank you, everyone.

—Laurie R. King

ABOUT THE AUTHOR

LAURIE R. KING is the award-winning, bestselling author of sixteen Mary Russell mysteries, five contemporary novels featuring Kate Martinelli, and many acclaimed stand-alone novels such as *Folly, Touchstone, The Bones of Paris,* and *Lockdown.* She lives on California's Central Coast, where she is at work on her next Mary Russell mystery.

LaurieRKing.com
Facebook.com/LaurieRKing
Twitter: @LaurieRKing and @Mary_Russell

ABOUT THE TYPE

This book was set in Caslon, a typeface first designed in 1722 by William Caslon (1692–1766). Its widespread use by most English printers in the early eighteenth century soon supplanted the Dutch typefaces that had formerly prevailed. The roman is considered a "workhorse" typeface due to its pleasant, open appearance, while the italic is exceedingly decorative.